Praise for To Charm a Killer

"A magically edgy coming-of-age story, poetically penned."
—Didi Oviatt, Aggravated Momentum

"The whole narrative plays out like an HBO show waiting to be developed, combining elements of LGBTQ+ and adult storytelling into a complex character study ..."
—Anthony Avina, Readers Entertainment Magazine

"A deliciously sensuous dive into Wicca with a diverse cast of characters, a coven, and a killer on the loose."
—JP McLean, Dark Dreams Series

"There's enough steamy bisexual polyamory here to make Anne Rice swoon."
—Sionnach Wintergreen, Men of the Shadows Series

"Hawkin writes with such fluid prose that the stage upon which she places her magical tale becomes visual and near cinematic. Superb characters and a keen sense of history and mythology blend with romance in this involving galaxy of a novel. Highly recommended."
—Grady Harp, Readers Entertainment Magazine

Books by W. L. Hawkin

The Hollystone Mysteries

To Charm a Killer
To Sleep with Stones
To Render a Raven
To Kill a King
To Dance with Destiny

Lure: Jesse & Hawk
Writing with your Muse: a Guide to Creative Inspiration

To Charm a Killer

A Hollystone Mystery: Book 1

W. L. Hawkin

BLUE HAVEN PRESS

To Charm a Killer

Hollystone Mysteries (Book 1)

Copyright © 2010 W. L. Hawkin

Revised March 2018

Tattoo Edition, 2020

Issued in print and electronic format

ISBN 978-0-9950184-1-9 (paperback)

ISBN 978-0-9950184-3-3 (kindle)

ISBN 978-0-9950184-2-6 (epub)

All rights reserved. No part of this book may be used or reproduced in any manner whatsoever without written permission, except in the case of brief quotations embodied in critical articles or reviews. This is a work of fiction. Resemblances to persons living or dead are unintended and purely co-incidental.

Published by Blue Haven Press

http://bluehavenpress.com

Edited by Wendy Hawkin & V. L. Murray

Author Photo by Debbi Elliott

Original Art & Cover Design by Yassi Art & Design

For Tara,
Thank you for Ireland,
And for sharing this journey with me.

Prologue
Through the Eyes of a Killer

I came to the club that night to meet a witch named Jade but left wanting something else—something I'd never known nor wanted before.

Jade arrived at midnight, her long dark hair flying wild about her face, and I flashed the sign—the blood red pentacle etched on my forearm. It was Friday and the club was packed, but she acknowledged me, appraising me as a woman might a potential purchase. I didn't like it—no man likes teetering on the edge of rejection, whatever his agenda—but endured it. Satisfied, she moistened her scarlet lips and grinned, then shimmied wide-eyed into the fray, bedazzled—as I knew she would be—by the power of the gothic nightclub, the blazing constellations in the darkling canopy, and the musky sweat of gyrating dancers.

Squeezing in at the bar like a shiny black beetle, she ordered a shot. Bodies swayed, inhaling her pheromones. I'd chosen well on both counts. Club Pegasus, tucked into a trendy notch of Vancouver, was a voyeur's paradise. And Jade, in leather to her thighs and little else, drew their gaze. It must be primal instinct that drives humans yearning for unholy exploits, to swathe their bodies in the skins of animals.

When a server in fishnet sashayed by, I touched her arm and discretely ordered another non-alcoholic drink. Glancing back, I watched Jade swivel on the stool like a child on a carnival ride. I wondered how long she would play this game—thinking she was making me wait for her. Naïve and narcissistic, she was perfect.

Then, Michael Stryker floated by in a shadowy sea of silk and set my mind adrift. The legendary Stryker—self-christened Mandragora—was reputed to host orgies that could rival Caligula, and be tied to organized crime through his grandfather, who was the real money behind the club. Angular and tantalizing, with a libertine charm, Stryker's straight honey-blond hair was parted in the center and fell below his shoulders—a fitting frame for the hollow cheeks, painted lips, and black-lined eyes. He wore the look of a bygone era and he wore it well. When in full vampire persona, as he was tonight, he wore fangs and red contacts. Too bad he was a fraud. A man like that—

"Do you think he's hot?" A pale ginger punk interrupted my thoughts. Balancing a martini glass between his freckled fingers, he hovered over me. "*He* thinks he's the reincarnation of Lord Byron. *I* think he's an ass."

"Who gives a fuck what *you* think?"

"No need for brutality."

"Beat it," I said, and turned my back to him. I wanted no memorable moments this night, no tags, and no complications.

Sensing the punk's disappearance, I glanced back to see Stryker sweep Jade's hair to one side and flash his fake fangs across her neck. Startled by his crimson contacts, she flinched. To pacify her, he brushed her lips with the tip of his index finger, and when she acquiesced, slid it into her mouth.

Bitch. I had not spent hours chatting her up on the Wicca site only to lose her to him. I considered charging over to the bar to remind her why she had come to this club and who had given her the password. But I couldn't do that. I could, however, take advantage of this scenario.

After turning Jade to face the dance floor, Stryker pressed in close behind her—one hand curled around her neck, while the other played her belly like a cello. Discerning his discrete cue, a slave-boy appeared with a tray of cherry-red shots which Stryker, it was rumored, called blood clots and randomly laced with ecstasy. They each took one, clinked glasses, and downed the potion.

Feeling my eyes on her, she smiled coyly. "Come here," she mouthed, cocking her head. While I considered this invitation and where it might lead, Stryker led her to the heart of the throbbing room.

I was about to intervene, when an intruder wearing sweats and a ball cap appeared. Running straight for Jade, his threat reverberated over the beats. "I'll kill you, bitch."

A bouncer jumped him, but spiking on adrenaline, the man shook himself free. Then a second bouncer appeared, hooked his arm around the man's neck and squeezed. The body crumpled and hit the floor. As they dragged it out by the armpits, the crowd cheered like Romans.

Stryker crushed Jade's face into his shoulder and stroked her hair. Was she crying? Telling secrets? Apologizing? She claimed to be single and available. Was that a lie? I hated that women were liars.

Then, a sudden flash of fire from the stage illuminated *him*. The magician, in tuxedo and burgundy silk cape, hovered between two flaming torches. His raven hair, slicked back in a French braid, hung halfway down his back. Chiselled cheekbones and charcoaled eyes, his mouth was thick and perfect, his lips heart-shaped. Leaping off the stage, the magician landed in a fiery flourish and bowed to the applause. Then cruised the dance floor, laughing, and tossing flames from hand to hand as effortlessly as apples.

I knew his face. His photograph graced the glassed marquee outside the entrance. Though stunning, it had never affected me like seeing him did now, in the flesh.

I said his name. "Estrada."

He turned, and our eyes met through a sea of bodies. When he walked toward me, I spilled my drink. Tried to turn away and couldn't.

It was Stryker who broke the spell. Sliding his hand under the magician's cape, he clutched his hip and drew him in. Clinging to the vampire's arm, Jade watched the fire swirl around her, until at last, Estrada tossed it high into the air and it vanished. As the music intensified, the crowd swarmed, and amidst the sweating bodies, I lost sight of them.

Slipping out past the gate into the September street, I found the broken jock, still unconscious and slouched against the brick wall beneath the magician's marquee.

I stood staring at the image. It could have been a cover shot for GQ. Posing in a white tuxedo with tails, a burgundy orchid in the lapel, his loose hair caught the wind and flew back in a mass of waves. The deep brown irises of his kohl-edged eyes had been photoshopped to a piercing gold, and in a strange language those perfect lips uttered a private invitation.

"Estrada," I whispered. "I accept."

Nothing Is But What Is Not

Estrada took a deep breath and winked at Sensara, who stood staring at him from across the path. "It smells primal in here. Kinda turns me on."

"A dust bunny turns *you* on." With no makeup and her sleek black hair caught up in a high ponytail, she looked about sixteen, though she was a decade beyond that.

"I'm serious, Sara. This forest reeks of life, especially after the September rains. Can't you smell it?" Estrada loved the primordial odor of wet earth, imagined his beginnings in the first fecund ooze—a microscopic amoebic creature, not yet conscious of the magical transformation that would one day occur.

"*You* reek of life." She rolled her dark almond eyes and shot him a look he didn't comprehend.

They were best friends, yet Sensara put up such a front, he could rarely read her—something he considered unfair given her psychic prowess. The high priestess of Hollystone Coven, Sensara Narato's reputation was legendary in New Age circles. The police even employed her occasionally, despite her connection to Wicca—something that irked him, as he neither liked nor trusted cops.

"No, wait—" She sniffed the air like a rabbit. "It's not life, it's cinnamon."

"But cinnamon *is* life. Who can live without it? It's as essential as fire, earth, air, and water."

"Ah, of course. Cinnamon. The fifth element."

Sensing her sudden shiver, he offered his jacket. "Catch a chill when you were out last night with Bud?"

"His name is Bert."

"Right, Bert. The accountant."

The punch to his arm was so swift, Estrada lost his balance. Teetering, he caught himself before his heavy backpack dragged him down. They were on their way to celebrate the Autumn Equinox with the others, and it was loaded with squash, apples, and bottles of wine. When he righted himself and stopped laughing, he found her standing in front of him with her hands on her hips, a raging anime heroine.

"Bertram Bellows is a motivational speaker. People pay two-fifty a day to attend his workshops and he packs them in. He's not throwing fireballs around some sleazy nightclub downtown."

With pursed lips, Estrada cocked his head and considered this last insult. He was not sure what she detested more—his gig as a magician in a Vancouver goth club or his relationship with the manager. He suspected the latter.

"Have you slept with him yet?" he asked.

"That's none of your business."

"Old Bert can't be too motivating if you've been going out with him for two months and he still ain't got you naked."

"We're building a spiritual relationship."

"So are we, but I 'd get you naked in a minute, if you'd let me."

For a moment, neither of them moved, and then he winked, and she flung her latté.

"Jesus, Sara." He ripped off his scarf and wiped his face and hair. Luckily, most of it had missed his leather jacket. "If the mention of sex makes you crazy, you need a good—"

"That's not it." Another shiver. She rubbed the goose bumps on her arm. "I don't know what it is."

If only she would trust him. Unable to bear seeing her look so defeated, he knelt before her. Then, with a flick of his left wrist, he produced a perfect pink buttonhole rose. "I apologize for my crude intrusion into your private life, and I mean that Sensara."

"Yeah, yeah, Sir Lancelot." She tucked the rose behind her ear and smiled. "We should go. They'll be waiting."

Mesmerized by the forest, for a while Estrada walked in silence. There was no death in this Pacific woodland, only transformation as the dying nourished the living. Miniature ferns sprouted from crooks and hollows of disjointed upper limbs. Mushroom colonies hovered in crevasses, their thin stalks twisting like snakes as they competed for space, their rusty caps perfect circles.

Cocking his head like a raven, he flung back the long dark locks that tumbled across his eyes. "I love these shaggy tree folks." He touched the soft hairy mosses that draped in fractured folds from the decaying limbs. Hearing no objection, he rambled on. "This forest could be Fangorn. Maybe we could conjure up our own Treebeard. Befriend an Ent. Can you imagine all these trees ripping up their roots and marching off like Birnam Wood to Dunsinane, only true Canadian pines, rustling and dragging their—"

Sensara gasped and hugged her chest.

"What?" he whispered.

"Another—"

"Shiver? That's three. What is it?"

"I don't know, but I feel sick. Something's wrong."

Grounding himself, Estrada shot imaginary roots from the soles of his feet deep into the earth's crust. If there was one thing he trusted, it was Sensara's radar. "We're almost there. Come on. We'll cast the circle."

At the signal tree, they veered off a grass-flecked game trail between massive ferns. Buntzen Lake simmered below, a smoky emerald in the growing dusk. Ancient granite mountains encircled the water, their snow-tipped spires still harboring scattered traces of last winter's storms. Pine spikes jutted like slivers from the distant peaks, split only by immense mottled rock that gaped through the trees—faces of mountain spirits and Old-World giants.

When she shivered again, the energy shot through the air and up his arm like a jolt of lightning. "Jesus. I felt that."

"Something's coming, Estrada. I don't know what it is or how to stop it—but unless we do, people will die."

"Dad? What are you doing?" Maggie stepped toward her father.

John Taylor stood before the fireplace holding her mother's Waterford crystal clock in his hands. A wedding gift, it was the only treasure Shannon owned and no one touched it. Alleged to be a family heirloom—though Maggie had never seen or heard of this family—it had been carved by Irish artisans and filigreed in real gold. It possessed an unspeakable secret. The steady ticking of its precise hands contrasted with the chaotic crackling of the fire in the great stone hearth. Maggie wiped the sweat from her forehead with the back of her hand. It was an unusually warm September afternoon in southern British Columbia and the living room was as hot as hell.

"Dad," she said, slowly. "Give me the clock."

She wondered where Bastian was. He usually stayed until five on weekdays so that she, or her mother, would be home before he left. If her father had found time to light a fire, Bastian had been gone for quite some time. Perhaps he'd left before giving her dad his afternoon meds. That would explain his current state.

"Come and see the fire through the glass. Look Mags. The flames are dancing."

She was close enough now to see the second hand as it crept past each golden Roman numeral. Close enough to take it.

"You're too close to the fire, Dad." His hands were pink and shiny like giant baby paws. "Let me hold it." Her gaze travelled from the leaden crystal clock in his slick hands to the chiseled stone at his feet—stone he had lovingly laid in the time before. "Dad?" She reached for it.

"*Ahhh!*" Lurching back, he let go.

She flinched at the clink of the kitchen door behind her, and then the crash of crystal on rock crammed her ears as the clock shattered into a pile of rubble at her feet. Beneath the wild pounding of her heart, she could hear it faintly ticking, still barely alive.

"What have you done?" cried Shannon. Feeling her mother at her back, Maggie imagined her growing huge and filling the doorway, a gaping Medusa, snakes flying madly round her head.

She knelt among the shards and stared down, unable to face either of her parents. "I'm sorry," she mumbled.

"How could you, Margaret Mary? You know what that clock means to me."

She thought of her father, and why he was the way he was. "It was an accident. I was dusting, and it slipped."

"Clumsy *eejit*," Shannon said, her cloaked Irish accent escaping through her anger. "Can't you do anything right?"

Maggie bent her head to protect her throat from the piercing words. Pushing against one of the shards with her finger, she sliced the skin and watched the blood spill out on the stone in ruby beads of liquid rage. Feeling relief, she pushed and sliced again.

"Why on earth did you light a fire? It's roasting in here."

"I didn't."

"Well, who did? Bastian had to leave early, and we both know that he wouldn't start a fire and then leave."

"Bastian left early?"

"He said he'd leave you a note. Didn't you see it?"

That was a loaded question. Maggie had stayed for gymnastic practice after school instead of coming straight home as instructed. Bastian expected her home early and she assumed that he would stay until she arrived.

Maggie glanced at the fire. Her dad likely used the note for tinder.

"Why did he leave early?"

"Family emergency. Had to catch a plane. Speaking of which, your passport just arrived." She waved it in the air. "I was considering letting you go on that trip abroad. Well, forget it. That accident just cost you the price of a ticket."

"Mom, please. That's not fair." The ten-day trip to the UK and Ireland was scheduled for spring break and all her friends were going. "It's for grad, and I've never traveled anywhere."

Shannon shook her head. "Clean up this mess. I never want to see that bloody thing again."

Maggie sucked the blood from her finger, then stood and took her father's moist hand in her own, thin, wounded one.

"Sit down while I sweep this up, Dad." Leading him to his recliner, she eased him onto the worn cushions.

"It's so beautiful," he said, staring at the flames.

"Yes, it's beautiful."

She would never be free. How could she leave him to go to Europe for two weeks anyway? How could she ever leave him alone with *her*?

Estrada rolled his eyes as he and Sensara entered the clearing. "Oh, here we go." After silencing him with a backhand to the gut, she stepped in front.

Jeremy Jones was hunkered down with his back to one of the thick gray hemlocks, with a garish, and undoubtedly original, silver sequined dragon bag lodged in his lap. He'd etched a circle around himself into the dirt with the jeweled athame clutched in his left hand and was smoking a cigarette with enough intensity to power a train.

"Finally." Relief trickled off Jones in dull ripples. "Did you see that sign back there? Bears and cougars live in these woods. It's dated September 20th. That's yesterday. I could have been killed."

"Did you sing?" Estrada teased.

"Sing?"

"Yeah, you're supposed to sing or shake bells to frighten the scary forest creatures." He relished playing with Jones; found it energizing, like a wolf on a rat.

"Funny, Houdini. You weren't sitting here alone listening to branches crack. And these bloody crows! They're the size of flamingos." The birds croaked and garbled overhead, enticed by his metallic haze. He was lucky they hadn't carried him off.

"They're ravens," Sensara said, ignoring the nasty reprisal Jones shot her way. "The Indigenous People of this coast revere them."

"Yeah, I've seen the art. But did you know that cultures revere that which they most fear? Like the volcano gods?"

Sensara rolled her eyes and bit her lip. She was a woman who picked her battles.

Hearing no reply, Jones crushed his cigarette out in the dirt and stood up. "Whatever they are, they're ugly and annoying. I wish they would just go away."

Sensara cast a silencing glance at Estrada; was in no mood for shenanigans. "Pick up that butt." She hated cigarettes. Especially hated that two members of her coven smoked.

Although she was trying to keep the peace, Estrada knew that she had her own issues with Jeremy Jones. They hadn't known him long and he'd just come off, what she termed, Wicca probation. He recalled how they had discussed Jones at length one evening over a bottle of Shiraz.

Sensara believed Jeremy was a catalyst who provoked contrasting situations to trigger others into personal realizations. However painful or irritating that seemed, people like him were necessary to stimulate growth and change. According to her, the world needed people like Jeremy. She admitted her own issues of trust and tolerance escalated in his presence, but that was because she had work to do. Estrada had listened intently as Sensara revealed personal information which rarely made it past her protective shield, learning more about her that night than in five years of friendship.

He believed the world needed Shiraz more than people like Jones.

If it was up to him, the man would be gone. But it wasn't. Hollystone Coven was Sensara's creation, so she made the rules. It was a microcosm of the world, in that no one who belonged was like anyone else. The small Wiccan group was strong in its diversity. People brought unique passions and skills, along with idiosyncrasies and conflict.

When she finally wound down that night, Estrada confessed. "I know it will stunt my spiritual growth, but I want to smack him just once." She laughed and shook her head. She thought he was joking, but he meant it. It was his respect for her that stopped him. That, and his admiration for the self-made entrepreneur. He knew what it was like to create something from nothing, and Jones was an exceptional designer. Specializing in medieval clothing and ritual tools, he'd made a fortune through Regalia, his online shop, designing costumes and paraphernalia for film and theatre companies around the world. He'd even created two of the costumes Estrada wore when he performed his magic act at Club

Pegasus. Jones frequented the club and liked to point that out to people.

Estrada broke the awkward silence. "You do recall we are a coven of nature-revering witches, intent on saving the planet in its entirety? Not just the cute and cuddly creatures." He produced an apple from his pocket, in the conventional way, and took a bite. "That's why we choose these remote natural locales for our ceremonies."

Jeremy rolled his eyes and mouthed the syllables, *blah blah blah*.

Estrada continued, encouraged by the man's irritation. "Our aim is to connect with the forest creatures in a positive way. Especially the elementals."

As they were all aware, Estrada dreamt of seeing faeries. He believed in their existence, had read a great deal about them, and tried several methods to see them. One woman named Dora Van Gelder wrote of opening the pituitary gland to enable a different kind of seeing. Situated in the center of the forehead, it was known in many cultures as the third eye. According to Van Gelder, this third eye could sense the subtle vibrations of faeries and make them visible.

It hadn't worked. Nor had countless hallucinogens, or sleeping in the woods under the full moon, or doing both simultaneously—though perhaps that accounted for his passionate earthy connection.

"Oh, I know, Merlin. If the faeries appear, I'll send them your way."

"Keep your faeries, Jones. I do fine on my own."

"Yeah. Well, so do I." Jones lifted his robe and tucked the butt into the pocket of his jeans. "And I did feel something watching me. I'm not crazy. Just a city kid that feels, you know, vulnerable, way out here."

"Maybe you're right," Sensara said, as another shiver spun through her body. Most of them were city kids and wild places like Buntzen Lake were well out of their comfort zone.

"Oh great. The priestess has confirmed my fears."

"Blesséd Mabon!" Daphne stormed into the glade, followed by Dylan and Sylvia. All three were loaded down with supplies.

"Blesséd Mabon," they echoed.

Dropping her backpack, Daphne crossed her arms over her chest to curb the jagged ginger waves that emanated from her upper body. "Have you heard? Another woman disappeared in Vancouver. Raine called just as we were leaving."

Estrada hoped to calm her down. "Women disappear all the time, for all kinds of reasons."

"This is the third this year," Sylvia said. They'd obviously been discussing the news as they walked. "The first disappeared just before Yule last December. The second, just before Beltane at the end of April. Now, here's the third, gone just before Mabon. It's perplexing." As she struck a match to light her cigarette, anxiety spread like silt over the glade.

Sensara lit a bundle of dried sage. After smudging herself, she walked among them, fanning and offering the aromatic herb, cleansing the negative energy with the comfort of familiarity.

"I hope the police do a better job than they did with the Downtown Eastside women," Daphne said. Her girlfriend, Raine, had loved a woman who disappeared and turned up later on the list. The mention of that horrific tragedy sickened them all. "It happened right over there." She gestured east, toward the degraded pig farm where the DNA, and other horrific evidence of several missing women had been appropriated by forensic experts. Convicted on six counts of second-degree murder, another twenty never made it to the courtroom and hovered in the air like vengeful ghosts. No one uttered his name. It was too fresh and too close, mere minutes away through the clouds.

"Jesus," Jeremy said. "Way to wreck the mood."

"That happened years ago, Daphne," Sensara said. "Things have changed with all the publicity, the trial, and the missing women's task force."

"Besides," Jeremy said, "those women were whores and drug addicts."

Estrada snarled, and Sensara clutched his arm.

"They were women." Daphne's eyes blazed.

"Yes," Sylvia said, "and *these* women are witches."

Peace, the Charm's Wound Up

Maggie stepped off the porch just as Father Grace pulled up in his black SUV. Shiny and luxurious with tinted windows, it was the kind of vehicle police used to chase down thugs in the movies, and ironically, local gangsters drove in shootouts. She smiled and waved, then went to meet him.

"Taking Remy for a hike?" Maggie's black Labrador retriever circled the priest, wagging and grinning.

"Yep. He needs exercise and I need a thesis. My *Macbeth* essay is due on Monday and I have to get an A." She hoped to get back in her mother's good graces. "Any ideas?"

"Can't help you there. Shakespeare's tragedies are too dark for me." He shrugged ingenuously. "All that blood and violence. It's not good for the soul."

Shoving her slashed hands self-consciously in her jacket pockets, she nodded.

Father Grace was the only priest under thirty Maggie had ever met and that alone made him special. Moreover, he played rugby, worked out at the gym, and took the teens on camping trips over the summer holidays. Since his recent arrival at St. Mary's, women of all ages were congregating at Mass, desperate for a sip of his charm along with their communion wine.

"I think *Macbeth* is cool. The play I mean, not the man." She twisted escaped tendrils from her ponytail. The priest's eyes were bright green—not mossy like her own—and matched the emerald cross he wore on a gold chain around his neck. "Why are you here now? Did she—?"

"Yes. Your mother called and asked me to sit with John for a while."

Maggie was glad that Father Grace had taken on a caregiver role. Her dad seemed as charmed by the priest as the rest of the world.

"Bastian had to leave early, and I don't think my dad got his afternoon meds." She hung her head, still shamefully aware of her error. "He's had them now, of course. Did she tell you what happened?" When she glanced up her breath caught in her throat.

Father Grace leaned casually against the truck. Wearing a black button-down shirt and blue jeans, with his wavy hair shining like chestnuts, he looked like an actor. Except for the white collar. No, even with the white collar. Glancing at his lips, she noticed the shadow of a moustache and grinned nervously. It was too much to imagine kissing him when he stood only a step away.

"She did." The priest narrowed his eyes. "Was it really you who dropped the clock?"

Maggie shook her head. "You know how it is."

"No, but I'd like to. Maybe one of these days, we can go somewhere alone and talk. You can tell me how you feel about this . . . and other things." His voice, suddenly low and breathy sent a shiver through her belly. "The full confession."

Was he flirting? He was a priest! Still. Priests were just men, weren't they?

"Sure. Why not?"

"I look forward to it, Maggie. It's important to have people in your life you can trust." He sighed, as if there had been a time when he had not, and she felt a sudden urge to comfort him.

"I trust you, Father."

"Good. Your friend Macbeth trusted the wrong people and ended up with his head on a stick."

Guilt. It was a complex thing, especially considering Maggie's personal situation. If a man was not responsible for his actions, was he still guilty of the crime? People must be held accountable. Without accountability, the world would be in a constant state of anarchy; however, sometimes there were complications—temporary insanity, demonic possession—and what if a man was under a spell?

As Maggie hiked the trail to Buntzen Lake, one line from *Macbeth* resounded in her mind. She uttered it aloud. "Peace, the charm's wound up."

Remy loped to her side and she tossed him a treat.

"Thrice to thine, and thrice to mine, and thrice again, to make up nine." Chanting, she danced to the right, and left, and back again. She savored the freedom of her forest. "That's how the witches wind up their spell," she explained to the lab. "They do it just before they greet Macbeth."

Obviously, the witches cast a spell on him; and if a man was under a spell, how could he be considered sane? Maggie reflected on this as Remy bounded toward the off-leash dog beach. It was Friday evening, so only a few folks were still there playing with their dogs. She dumped her books on a picnic bench and tossed his ball into the water. Skidding back, he dropped it at her feet. She threw it again and wiped her slobbery hand on her jeans.

Despite her parents, Maggie knew she was fortunate to live in this place. Their home perched between two bodies of water close enough to walk between—Buntzen Lake and the Pacific Ocean. Sometimes the inlet was rank with decaying sea creatures and slick fetid muck that could suck down small children and gumboots; while other times, the water flowed deep, charged by the invisible force of the tides. Bordered by beaches, boardwalks, and parks, it attracted boaters and paddlers, along with salmon-chasing harbor seals and bald eagles.

Shadowed by the Coast Mountains and groves of giant red cedars, their yard was shaded, yet brilliant with blossoming rhododendrons, planted by Shannon in one of her gardening frenzies years before. Anchored by the log house that John had built for them with his own hands, the Taylor family lived in tenuous tranquility at the end of Hawk's Claw Lane. Their lives were so well constructed that Maggie had told only two people—who absolutely required an explanation at the time—that her father suffered from a severe head injury and required medication and constant monitoring to keep up the façade.

She had told no one that she was the cause of the injury. Once uttered, the truth was irrevocable and could unleash forces over which she had no control. Forces that could change her life forever.

As she watched a float plane climb over the mountains, she thought again of escape. She was a fraud. Her life a fake, from which she was desperate to flee. Yet, she could not. Such was her penance. Like Macbeth, Maggie was trapped in guilt, sunk in so far, she could go neither back, nor forward. Perhaps erasing Macbeth's guilt could lessen her own.

She decided that Macbeth was not guilty of his murderous actions because he was under the witches' spell. It was their fault, not his, and that meant the theme had something to do with the evil power of witchcraft.

Scanning the footnotes, she searched for evidence. Shakespeare wrote the play in 1603, for King James VI of Scotland, who had recently been crowned King James I of England. The King had been victimized by a coven of witches in 1590. The North Berwick Coven was charged with having raised a tempest to destroy the fleet that escorted him back to Scotland with Queen Anne, his young Danish bride. The source said that over two hundred witches gathered in an old haunted church at Anchor Green on All Hallows Eve to consult the devil. Whether it was true or not, that was the story revealed under torture. The women named names, were tried, and swiftly executed.

Imagine belonging to a coven that would attempt such a thing. What power. What audacity.

Apparently, King James attended witch trials and wrote a text entitled *Daemonologie*, in which he argued that a witch should be severely punished for being in league with Satan. Witches obviously scared the hell out of him.

She wondered if Father Grace knew any of this. He was a priest, and hadn't the Catholic Church administered the witch craze—trials, torture, burnings, and all? Of course, that was four hundred years ago, in a very different time. Still.

Shakespeare wrote *Macbeth* for his patron, King James, to illustrate the political ramifications of witchcraft. To charm a king was reprehensible, but to kill a king was treason—punishable by nothing less than a gruesome death.

According to the footnotes, the Weird Sisters, like the Three Fates in Classical Mythology, had the power to affect human destiny. As diviners, they could foretell the future, command nature, and conjure storms—just as the North Berwick coven had allegedly done to King James. They could shapeshift, and did, appearing and disappearing in view of both Macbeth and Banquo. Possessing a supernatural power, no human could resist, the Weird Sisters transformed a brave soldier into a ruthless killer. Obviously, the play affirmed and justified the king's support of the witch burnings.

Sighing, Maggie closed the book. Everyone was gone from the beach and Remy was digging a massive hole in the sand. Looking skyward, she realized how much time had passed. Icy leaden clouds caught in the cracks of mountain peaks, drew the darkness inward, and pierced to the bone. She slipped off the picnic bench and was zipping up her jacket when she heard music. *Bagpipes? The music of Macbeth? Here? In the forest above Buntzen Lake?*

Remy stopped digging and sprang from the hole. Hackles rigid, he pivoted to face the forested mountain at their backs. A shiver struck Maggie as her dog bolted. In his haste, he leapt off a stump, cleared the chain link fence, and vanished into the trees. Chasing after him, she hit the top bar with both hands, vaulted over the fence and raced into the forest. "Remy!"

Estrada smiled as he watched Dylan drop a gourd, dust it off and hand it to Sylvia, who placed it on the altar. It was his first Mabon ceremony and he was nervous, his innocence enviable.

Perhaps because he couldn't ever remember feeling innocent himself, Estrada was drawn to the shy kid with the *Trainspotting* accent. Over the summer, they'd gone hiking and shared stories. Both he and Dylan had been fatherless boys, whose crossing of miles and cultures had led to discoveries about the complexity of the world and themselves.

Dylan was obsessed with stone lore. His grandfather introduced him to megaliths in Scotland when he was ten and sent there by his sluttish mother (his adjective). He carried their photographs in his wallet like they were his family. Magnificent stones carved with cup and ring marks. Some set in circles five thousand years ago, the work of prehistoric artisans. Dylan's grandfather lived near a place called Kilmartin Glen—a cemetery rife with the spirits of ancient clansmen and their kin. It was there that the medieval grave slabs and burial cists first spoke to him. Estrada asked him what they said.

"It's hard to explain. Sometimes it's just feelings and images. Other times I hear voices."

Estrada had heard of stone mages and believed he had much to learn from the boy who devoted his life to communing with stones.

When it was time to begin, they stood and admired the altar against the backdrop of the misty forest. Draped with a dazzling saffron scarf courtesy of Jones, yellow candles burned to signify the sun that would dissipate in the coming months. A cornucopia of freshly harvested produce—hazel nuts and pinecones, crazy knobby gourds, striped squashes, Indian corn, fat apples, and juicy grapes collected from the local farmers' market—was strewn about the altar. Incense smoked on the brazier and spread into the dusky sky. After the ceremony, all would be donated to the local food bank. That was the coven's way of giving back to the community.

They took their positions and Sensara cast the circle to claim their sacred space. Three times, she walked clockwise around the outside while pointing her crystal-tipped wand and chanting:

> *"I conjure this circle as sacred space.*
> *I conjure containment within this place.*
> *Thrice do I conjure the Sacred Divine.*
> *Powerful goodness and mystery mine.*
> *From East to West and from South to North,*
> *I cast this circle and call Magic forth."*

After returning to her place at the altar, Sensara said, "We will now call the spirits of the four directions into our circle."

Having acted as her high priest for three years, Estrada understood it was a position of trust which legitimized him in the eyes of the coven. Though he was known as a player around town, mostly because of his liaison with Michael Stryker, he had never crossed boundaries within the sanctity of the coven. Not that it had ever come up. Jones frequented the club, but the others respected his right to privacy, as he respected theirs.

For this ceremony, each of them had created an invocation to call in the spirit of the direction they represented.

Dr. Sylvia Black, a professor of Celtic mythology, stood in the East, the place of intellect. She placed her glass jar with its flaming yellow candle on the ground, then stood facing out and drew an invoking pentacle with her athame as she spoke. *"Powers of the East, of wind and air, of thought and breath, I invite you into this sacred circle. Aid and protect us with light and love."*

Jones followed. Swirling his bright orange cape, he mimicked the fire he invoked. "Powers of the South. Force, passion, and heat enliven our spirits with power and magic. Hail Fire Spirits of the South!" His candle exploded in a flash of smoke and fire. He'd obviously sprinkled a pinch of magician's flash powder on the flame again.

Estrada rolled his eyes and wanted to smack him. He hated the way Jones used parlor tricks like pyrotechnics and reamed him out regularly for cheapening the rituals with dramatic bullshit. "Harry Potter," he muttered. But Jones ignored him, too caught up in his own spectacle to notice. A subtle act of revenge for this afternoon's mockery? Perhaps. After the stench cleared, the ritual continued.

Dylan was to call the Spirits of the West. His violet candle glittered in a cobalt-blue jar. Estrada watched the kid's hand tremble as he set the candle down on the ground and the earth lit up in its circumference. As Dylan etched the invoking pentacle with his willow wand, its silvery threads conjoined like sparklers. Estrada felt his anxiety and sent him a visual wave of peace. Flowing across his sapphire robe in lilac shimmers, a sense of calm enveloped him, and the invoking words flowed from his lips.

"Powers of the West, please hear my refrain.
Powers of water, of ocean, of rain.
Powers of dreamtime, of pleasure and pain.
Join in this circle and with us remain."

Dylan glanced at Sylvia and caught her subtle smile. He'd obviously sweated to create a quatrain of rhyming iambic pentameter that conveyed the essence of his element. A witch took time and pleasure in creating ritual pieces, especially words, as they held such power.

At last, it was Daphne's turn. She was the quintessential earth goddess, so it was fitting she would invoke the Powers of the North using her brown candle. A landscaper by trade, her hands were dry and etched with dirt from long hours spent digging and planting, tending and beautifying the gardens of the planet.

"I call the Ancient Earth Powers. Spirits of fertility and all creation. Spirits of mountains, valleys, and plains, of rich soil, cracked rock, and desert sands. Be with us in this time of equal day and night. I welcome you into our Circle of Light."

Sensara nodded. "Our circle is cast. We are between the worlds."

Like ancients, they settled cross-legged on the ground. Language and symbols transported them to places unreachable in the mundane world. That was what drew Estrada to Wicca and kept him enthralled. That, and the power they created.

"Tonight, we celebrate the Sabbat of Mabon," Sensara said. "The Autumn Equinox. This is the second of only two days in the year when light and dark is in perfect balance. Tonight also, we celebrate the second harvest of all the food that grows in our fertile land. We have all brought produce from the local market and are grateful to live in a place where we can grow so much to nourish us body, mind, and spirit. Mabon is a time of thanksgiving.

"We will begin with a silent meditation. You may invite the gods and goddesses of your choice into the circle. You may ask for blessings, help, or guidance from the appropriate powers, whatever you feel is needed at this moment.

"A few cautions before we begin. Be careful what you ask for and pay attention to your words. Remember the Wiccan Rede. Do no harm. And, the Law of Three. Whatever you cast out will return threefold. Blesséd Be."

When Sensara roused them, she was distracted, off-center in the gray mist which was rapidly descending on the darkling wood. The others didn't notice, but Estrada caught the subtle twitch in her eyelid, and the glassy stare that meant she was looking beyond them into waters only she could navigate. Perhaps, she was still feeling ill, or perhaps she had seen something disturbing in her reverie. She may even have caught sight of something just outside the circle; or worse still, something within. He observed warily, as she called on Dylan to play some music.

As he adjusted his bagpipes, Dylan's anxiety faded. "I wrote this tune for my grandfather, Dermot Dylan McBride." Estrada was baffled by the kid's ability to manage the complexities of the ancient instrument. A magician was adept at sleight of hand, but Dylan's fingers danced with real magic. "I am named for him and inherited his passion for the pipes. Granddad can play a tune on a whiskey bottle. I can't do that yet."

The boy was humble. He traveled the world with the university pipe band. Estrada had recently watched him perform at the Highland Games and razzed him about his tartan kilt, knee socks, and the furry rodent that bounced between his legs.

"Granddad's a kitchen player, born in Tarbert. That's a fishing port in Argyll, on the southwest coast of Scotland. He's seventy-seven years old, but you wouldn't know it. He's white-haired, weathered and tough, a Presbyterian, but we can't hold that against him. He was there for me when I needed him. So, this tune is for you, Granddad. I can see you now, standing on your front lawn, staring out over the harbor at Loch Fyne."

The drone began rich and low in the belly of the pipes, then swelled as the music flowed into a realm of its own—a pagan terrain of lilting trills that emerged from some past blood memory. The spirits of Dylan's ancestors swirled around them like gray ghosts in the trees, as the pipes conjured memories of ancient rebels charging into battle; as well as modern heroes revered in ceremony and planted in the earth to that same gut-wrenching sound.

Daphne cried. Jeremy looked overwrought, but then, judging by his ginger hair, he likely had Celtic ancestors of his own. Really, it didn't matter where people came from, Dylan's music could catch the human heart and wring it inside out. He finished the tune and put his pipes away as they all sat stunned in the wake of his magic.

Estrada flinched as something brushed against his thigh, but then Sensara called out, "Time to dance. Time to raise the power. Time to make the magic happen." And jumping up, they prepared to dance.

"We all come from the goddess and to her we shall return, like a drop of rain flowing to the ocean," she chanted, then grasping Estrada's right hand, she pushed him off in the rhythm of the Grande Allemande.

He greeted Daphne with his left hand and began the counter chant. "Corn and grain, corn and grain, all that falls shall rise again. Hoof and horn, hoof and horn, all that dies shall be reborn."

They danced around the circle, singing the contrary chants, feeling the energy build with the sound of their voices and the rhythm of their footfalls. Panting and touching, swimming in the musical breath, they built to a climax and then fell, laughing in the dizzying vortex of their creation.

"We have raised the power in the sanctity of our circle," shouted Sensara. "Libations and blessings for all."

This was Estrada's cue to join her at the altar. The others stood pensively as Sensara held a silver chalice in both hands and he filled it with red wine. The rich aroma of sunburnt grapes and spices filtered through the twilight. After setting down the bottle, he picked up a medieval dagger encased in a black sheath and tipped in silver. Holding it in his right hand, he unsheathed the six-inch blade and held it aloft to salute the moon.

"As the chalice is to the goddess," Sensara said.

"So the blade is to the god," he said, plunging it into the cup.

"United the god and goddess create blessings for the Earth and for all," they chanted together. Sensara leaned forward to meet him in a swift sacred kiss, as was customary, but as their lips touched above the chalice and the blade, Estrada grew aroused. Sensations magnified. Sparks exploded from his skin. Blood tingling, pupils dilating, his flesh hardened, and he stood electrified—the Horned God.

As Sensara held the cup to his lips, he sipped and stared into her coppery eyes. Part of him shouted, *this is wrong*. While the other laughed, enthralled. *You are the god and she is the goddess.* It was all he could do not to pull her to the ground. He waited for her to speak, but she turned her back to him and passed the cup to Daphne. Standing rigid, wanting, like a wolf poised to spring with every ounce of blood pulsing in just one place, he glimpsed the too obvious protrusion beneath his black cloak.

Daphne mumbled something about ecstasy and Dionysus being in the circle and passed the chalice to Dylan.

Estrada crossed his arms over his chest in a feeble attempt to control the pounding of the blood and the shuddering desire that would not dissipate. Skin tingling, the vibration careened through his palms, rushing up and down his body in dazzling waves. He watched Sensara remove the lid from the dish that contained the corn cakes. If she felt like this and could still maintain control, she was something other than human. Dylan passed the chalice to Jones, but before he could speak, Estrada caught Sensara by the shoulders and spun her around.

Grasping her cool cheeks in the palms of his blistering hands, he brushed his lips against hers. Lowering his heavy lids, he screamed his desire, *I want you. I want you now.*

Arching her back, she opened her mouth and caught his invading tongue with equal passion. He felt her fingers crawl up his back beneath his cape. Grinding her belly against him, she caught and held him with her thighs, and they danced to the beat of some brooding blood rhythm.

"Hey! Get a room," yelled Jones.

Estrada ignored the sniggering, the delicious scent of her urging him on. As his passion deepened, he loosened her dark silky hair and drank the wine from her tongue. Her spine arched like a cobra as he backed her up against the golden altar and laid her down, covering her body with his own. Pausing for what seemed an eternity he stared into her eyes and sang of his love. Then, running his hand up her leg beneath her gown, he pushed aside the flimsy fabric that barred his way, clutched, and growled. She gasped, then moaned. Catching her bottom lip with his teeth, he reached inside his robe—"

"Remy!"

The urgent cry caught his attention, as in the periphery a great black shadow careened across the circle, straight at them.

"Rem-ing-ton!" A girl appeared chasing something. A dog—a big black dog that was wolfing down their cakes. Grasping it by the collar, she dragged it from the circle and dashed into the woods.

Then Dylan bolted.

In the after-second, Sensara shoved Estrada off with a vicious thrust. Careening over a log, he fell on his back with a thud that knocked the wind clean out of his lungs.

"You can't break the circle!" she shouted after Dylan.

"She's been watching us," he yelled back. "She's scared."

Estrada lay on the forest floor and fought for just one breath.

Thrice to Thine & Thrice to Mine

Maggie raced through the forest, leaping mossy logs and boggy spots, flying with the force of the encounter. Witches! There were witches, right here in her forest at Buntzen Lake. Suddenly, the amazement Macbeth had felt became very clear and very real, and these witches hadn't even melted before her eyes. But they had made out.

That man in the black cape with the long black curls and Egyptian eyes— He could be a rock star. She couldn't shake the image of him bending that white-robed woman over the altar—had never seen anything like it, or like the others in their brilliant cloaks—like movie stars only a million times better because you could smell them, and they smelled like earth and exotic spices and sweet September smoke, and she had almost touched them… and the dancing and the music and the *sex*. If Remy hadn't run into the center of it all, they would have done it right there on the altar.

No one at school would ever believe this.

One of them was chasing her now. She could hear him tramping through the bush behind her, breaking branches and panting like a tired dog. Why was he chasing her? What would they do to her for what she'd seen? Hurt her? *Hex* her? Irrevocably change her in some wicked way?

Yet in all this trepidation, Maggie felt something brilliant, something she had never felt before and therefore couldn't name. All she knew was she wanted this feeling to go on, wanted to be like them, to dance and sing, wanted to make love in the forest with a beautiful man who had nothing on his mind but her—a man who would spin her, and bend her body like a willow branch, and paint her lips with cinnamon.

She could hear the slow ragged breaths of her pursuer. If she kept running, he would lose sight of her. Once safely inside, with the door to her prison barred, the memory of this experience would fade. But, if she let him catch her, maybe she could become a witch—learn to wind up charms, raise vengeful storms or perfect sunny days, appear and disappear at will.

She chanted the charm from Macbeth aloud. "Thrice to thine, and thrice to mine, and thrice again to make up nine." Could she learn to foretell the future, even *change* the future? If witches could harm people, surely, they could heal people too. *My father?*

Maggie stopped and raised her arms to the sky. *What should I do?*

Blood pounded through her heart in answer. Words spun like ancient chants and threaded through her brain. The trees danced in the wind, and as she smelled their twilight sap, she realized she was alive with the earth; more alive than she had ever been.

She whistled sharply for Remy. The dog turned and raced toward her, bear bells jangling. Might as well show her pursuer exactly where she was. She waited until he was a few paces away, and then ambled on.

At the top of the hill, the terrain leveled out and the path merged with the short dead-end lane. Father Grace's truck was gone. That was a relief. How would she ever explain to the young Catholic priest that she had allowed a witch boy to follow her home?

She ran up the front steps of the veranda into the kitchen and searched for signs of her parents. Her mother was in her bedroom watching television with the door shut. Her parents had always had separate rooms, something that made her wonder how she'd ever been conceived. But once, she suspected, there must have been love between them. Love in the time before. Leaning against the wall, Maggie twirled her hair, and tried to slow her pounding heart.

Her dad was not in the house. Perhaps Father Grace had taken him out on one of his jaunts. It was important not to isolate someone with a brain injury, he said, knowing that Shannon had kept John locked away for years, like Edward had imprisoned poor mad Mrs. Rochester. Maggie could not understand how someone with Shannon's skill as a nurse made such a dreadful wife and mother. Lately, the priest had been taking John out more often and for longer periods of time—for gelato at the Italian place, or for country drives, or for hot chocolate at the café. With any luck, they would be gone a long while.

Confident she would not be caught, Maggie slipped back outside. She sat on the top step and stared at the bushes beside the driveway, where she knew the boy was hiding. His shiny cobalt cloak was visible through the leaves.

When he didn't venture out, she said, "Hey!"

"Oh, hey," he echoed. Emerging with a casual wave, he sauntered by the driveway.

"Thirsty?"

"Parched." His cheeks were stained red, his short brown hair curly with sweat. He pulled a white handkerchief from his pocket, unfolded it, and swiped it across his forehead.

She stood and gestured to the steps. "Have a seat. I'll be right back."

After returning with two blue bottles, she handed him one, and sat down beside him on the step.

He cracked the cap and took a swig that half-emptied the bottle, then tipped it in her direction. "Cheers."

"Matches your cloak." She ran her fingers over the fabric. It was embroidered in spiraling Celtic knots of silver thread. Elfish. "This is beautiful. Where did you get it?"

"Uh, Jeremy made it."

"Jeremy?"

"Jeremy Jones, the lad in orange." She wondered if he always squinted and twitched when he spoke or if she just made him nervous.

"Cool."

"Jeremy's a good, uh—"

"Costume designer?"

"Aye, he has an online shop. It's dead brilliant."

"What about the man in black? Who is he? What does he do?"

"Estrada." He blushed, embarrassed by what she'd witnessed. "He's a magician."

"I'll say. He's amazing."

"He doesn't... He doesn't usually act like that." He dabbed his face again with the cloth. "That's what I wanted to explain to you."

"Oh." He was more intriguing by the minute. She was used to Shannon slipping into mad Irish, but this guy sounded like a nervous Paolo Nutini.

"See, what you saw there, uh, that wasn't, uh, that wasn't normal, like."

"There's a normal?"

"Aye, sure. We're all just people. Like my friend, Dr. Black teaches at the university on the mountain. And Sensara, our high priestess ... She's a massage therapist. And Daphne's a landscaper."

"And what are you?"

"Ach, I'm just a student at the university."

"You're not from around here, are you?"

"No. I was born in Nova Scotia." Catching her inquisitive look, he explained. "I went to Scotland to live with my granddad when I was ten."

"Right. You're the piper."

"Aye. My name is Dylan McBride." With a nod, he offered his hand and she grasped it. "So, you heard the tune? Is that what brought you to us?"

"Yeah. My dog went crazy and took off. When I caught up to him, he was just standing there watching you. I guess after a while he smelled the cakes." She giggled. "I couldn't believe it. I mean, I've lived here all my life and never heard bagpipes or seen anything like that in the park."

Dylan grimaced, obviously embarrassed by what she'd witnessed.

"Are you studying music at university?" she asked.

"No. Archaeology."

"That's cool." When he grinned, she couldn't help but giggle again. He was cute, nerdy, and painfully shy. "And you're all witches."

"Wiccan."

"Isn't that the same thing?"

"Not really. It's—"

"So, how do you get to be—" Maggie stopped speaking at the familiar sound of Father Grace's SUV. "You gotta go."

"Where? Where should I—?" Stammering, he scrambled down the steps.

"Hurry. He's coming."

"Which way?" His voice trembled.

"Pretend you're a hiker. Walk down to the end of the lane." She gestured. "Turn right and follow the road. You'll end up back in the parking lot."

"Right." He took a step, then stopped and stared at her. "Can I ask your name?"

"It's Maggie."

"Maggie." He repeated it softly as if committing it to memory.

She waved her hand to hurry him up, as the voices in the side drive grew louder. Thank God, her father was slow.

He glanced at the lettering by the front door. "Maggie Taylor."

"Yes. Now go!"

"Would you mind if I called you? On the phone?"

"Jesus. No," she said. Any second now Father Grace would appear on the porch. Dylan looked dejected. Didn't understand. "No, I wouldn't mind. Call me. Now, go."

Estrada watched the priestess slip her fingers through her shimmering black hair—hair he had fondled seconds before and still ached to touch.

"Wow! Now what?" asked Jones, who loved the drama.

"Whoever we invited into the circle needs to leave, and then we close the portal," Sensara said.

"Damage control?" quipped Jones, with too much cheek.

"Sounds good to me," Daphne said.

"Close your eyes and visualize whoever you invited in, thank them, and ask them to depart." She glared at Estrada. "Especially Dionysus."

"Hey, it wasn't just me." Still reeling with the feel of her flesh, Estrada had lost all interest in words and incantations.

"I know." Sensara was trying to regain control. "Would you please just take Dylan's place?"

As he ambled off, she addressed them all. "Each of you should use the banishing pentagram while thanking the powers of your point. Sylvia, you start."

Poor Sylvia was ashen over Dylan's disappearance; still she followed Sensara's instructions. Jones followed, and then Estrada, and finally Daphne. Each was brief and specific, focusing less on ceremony than on getting the job done. Then, from the altar, Sensara took a jar containing a black candle.

Beginning in the East, she walked slowly widdershins around the circle three times. On her final round she stopped, picked up Sylvia's yellow candle and blew it out, then chanted the familiar closing lines. "Fire seal this circle. Let it seep into the ground. Spirits shall return, and all shall be as it was found."

Continuing her journey, she snuffed out each candle while asking its element to seal the circle. Estrada watched mesmerized as she revolved around them like a lithe ballerina in her white gossamer gown. He had never seen her like this before. Radiant violet rays stretched far beyond her body while golden light burst from the crown of her head.

In all the years they'd been working together, he'd never seen her as a woman, only as a friend, a kind of kid sister. He'd teased her and played with her, and now all he wanted to do was throw her to the ground and make love to her. It was wickedly wrong, yet both delighted and unnerved him.

At last, Sensara returned to the altar. "Our circle is sealed underground. Merry meet, and merry part, and merry meet again."

"Merry meet, and merry part, and merry meet again." They echoed the reply, but an air of vexing uncertainty shifted through each of them in the mounting dusk that was not merry in the least.

As they packed up, Sylvia fretted. "What should we do about Dylan?"

"It's a dark moon tonight and the light's almost gone. Let's pack up our things and get out of these woods," Daphne said. "We can wait for him in the parking lot."

"Will he know to go there? What if he gets lost? I have a bad feeling—"

"Dylan's a big boy," Jones said. "He'll turn up."

Loathing his callousness, Estrada repressed the urge to throttle him.

"We can call Search and Rescue if he doesn't appear within the hour," Daphne said. "I'm sure he will though. He's probably just trying to calm that girl down."

"I'll take his bagpipes," Sylvia said.

"He'll be fine," Estrada said, as much to allay his own fears as hers. Somehow, he felt responsible, and it bothered him that Sensara refused to make eye contact.

As the downcast group staggered back through the woods, silence swelled around them like the lichen encasing the trees. Gasping, he hunched forward as if he'd taken a fist to the gut. He knew it for what it was—had felt it before. Fear. It smashed into his solar plexus, stole his power, and left him staggering, wounded, and helpless. And with it came awareness. No matter what Sensara said, all would not be as it was. Things would never be the same again.

Indeed. By the time they reached the parking lot, things were decidedly worse.

"Look, what happened during the circle was my fault," Sensara said. They were loitering beside the cars, waiting for Dylan. "My intuition must be off. I should never have suggested an open invocation. I apologize."

Estrada wondered why she would say such a thing. She was a gifted psychic and her voices never lied. If they advised her to hold an open circle and invite in whatever was needed, then it—no matter how odd or frightening—was necessary. Walking on the edge of uncertainty energizes some people, but he knew it would drain her. Having always relied on her inner guidance to deliver the truth, self-doubt would be paralyzing. If she couldn't trust her intuition, she couldn't trust herself to do readings, to lead the coven, to do anything.

"We're a coven. That means we're all in this together," Daphne said. "You shouldn't take on the responsibility for something going awry, Sensara. It might not have been that at all."

"I agree," Sylvia said. "When we perform rituals it's our responsibility as a group to make sure we don't do something that results in harm to anyone or anything. If we inadvertently created a situation, it's up to us to determine what occurred and why."

"And fix it," Daphne added.

Sylvia nodded.

"Nothing bad happened," Jeremy said. "Sensara and Estrada made out, a dog ate the cakes, and Dylan took off after some girl."

"Shut up," Sensara said. "Save your insecure bullshit for your boyfriends!"

A communal shudder reverberated through the group. She had never exploded, and the realization of her recklessness sent the blood rushing to her cheeks.

"Whoa, sister. Where did that come from?" Jones smirked. "Looks like we know whose button got pushed tonight."

"*Fuck off.*" Glaring through slanted eyes, Sensara slithered back a step.

For a moment, Estrada wished for storybook power, the kind that could transform a jerk into a frog, but then, distracted by this new Sensara, he let it go.

"That's enough." Daphne was the rock among them and the only one to whom even Jones would acquiesce.

"A black dog is an evil omen to be running through a sacred circle," Sylvia said.

"Oh, come on. A black dog?" Jones sniggered. "Hey, maybe it was Sirius Black?" Sensara's outburst had no effect on his infantile mind. "At least we know he's one of the good guys."

Ignoring Jones, Estrada stole a glance at Sensara. His toes twitched. Then the tingling surged up the inside of his legs. Was she feeling it too? Is that why she refused to meet his gaze? He remembered touching her cheek, the taste of her breath in his mouth. Raising his musky fingers to his lips he inhaled her scent.

God, he wanted her. But why? Was it love, or some kind of magic? It could be a charm that revealed and amplified their true feelings for each other, making the concealed obvious. The only thing he knew for certain was that if he ventured anywhere close to her, anywhere his aura would brush even slightly against hers, he would be sucked down like a leaf in a vortex.

Sylvia was lecturing. "The black dog is one form of the *pooka*, a Celtic solitary faerie that can shapeshift. It can be a real nightmare according to the legends."

"A *pooka*? Are you serious? That was no faerie. That was a Labrador retriever." Jeremy laughed.

"That remains to be seen," Sylvia said.

"Honestly. Can nothing ever happen without it being some big friggin' phenomenon?" Jeremy rolled his eyes.

"Well, Jeremy, it might not be a big friggin' phenomenon," Sensara said. "But if it is, I hope it goes after *you* first."

"Sensara!" Sylvia's eyes widened. "You are our high priestess. Can you please exert some control?"

Sensara shrugged. "I'm sorry, everyone. I don't know what's come over me. I apologize Jeremy. You're right. If people will share, I think we should talk about what entities we called into the circle, and why. Maybe we can determine what's happened. What do you all think?"

"True confessions," teased Jones.

"Enough." This time it was Sylvia. "Do not exacerbate the situation."

"We're not here to judge anyone, but I really don't know what else to do," Sensara confessed. "Who wants to go first?"

"I will," Sylvia said. "I invoked the Celtic fertility god, Cernunnos. I am beginning a new book about Celtic shamanism and asked for help with its creation."

"Thank you. As for myself, I invoked Aphrodite. I thought a visit from the love goddess would benefit us all."

Jeremy sniggered.

"That remains to be seen," Estrada said.

Sensara cast him a wicked look.

"Hey, I'm just—"

"What about you, Jeremy?" she asked, cutting off Estrada in mid-sentence.

"Oh relax, people. I'm just trying to lighten things up. I invoked Demeter and Dionysus. You know me. I'm always looking for the same things—cash and a date."

They all turned to Estrada, who had hoisted himself to the roof of the car and sat wrapped in his cape like a drowsing raven. Really, it was to cover the erection that would not recede and which he hoped would not require medical intervention.

"Dionysus," he said. Mabon is his sabbat. I thought we could use a visit from our lord of frivolity."

"All right, then. We don't know who or what Dylan conjured, but we've got love, fertility, prosperity, and amusement. I suppose that accounts for some of it," Sensara said, eyeing Estrada venomously.

Why was she so angry? She had fully opened her body to him.

"But what about the girl? Why did she appear?" Sensara asked.

"It must have been me."

Heads turned. They had forgotten Daphne. She sat slouched against a cement curb behind the car. As she rose, a gray balloon of sadness enveloped her.

"What do you mean, Daphne?" asked Sylvia.

"I just kept thinking about those witches, the ones that disappeared. They're just like us. You didn't see Raine when she lost her friend. They'd been like sisters since they were kids. And I kept wondering, what if one of us disappeared? What would we do? Would we just say, oh well, women disappear all the time?"

Estrada pulled his hood up over his head.

"No, of course not," Sensara said.

"Well, it is one of us. The woman was a witch," Daphne said.

"You're right," Sylvia said. "Too often people do nothing until it touches them directly. But, what did you do?"

"I summoned Hecate. It seemed appropriate to invite the goddess of justice."

"Hmmm, that's interesting." Sylvia wrinkled her brow. "Because Hecate roams at night, she's associated with dogs."

"Oh please. Let sleeping dogs lie," Jones muttered.

Sylvia squinted down her nose at him. "And wolves."

"Anything else?" Sensara asked.

"The Morrigan," Daphne said, and bit her bottom lip. "I know. The Celtic goddess of war was probably too much." She shook her head. "And I did something else."

They all stared, wondering what that could mean.

"What did you do?" Sensara whispered.

"I cast a charm. It felt right at the time, but now, with the way you two were acting and the girl running into the middle of it all . . . I'm afraid I might have conjured something beyond our control."

"What kind of charm?"

"Well, when women disappear, they rarely return alive, right? So, my thought was to catch this man before he could do any more harm."

"So you—?"

"I charmed the killer."

A palpable silence settled around the witches, who, knowing the risks of spell-casting, pondered the depth and intensity of a spell such as this; a spell that could radiate unfathomable ripples before reaching its intended mark.

To charm a killer exposed them all to peril.

Finally, after several moments the silence was shattered by Sensara's incredulity. "What have we done?"

And Sylvia's panic. "Where the hell is Dylan?"

"Who was that, Maggie?" Father Grace rounded the corner of the wooden porch, another darkling shadow in the drowsing dusk.

Maggie didn't like his tone and ignored the intrusion. She was desperate to remain in her reverie where the words of *Macbeth* mingled with the images of the witches she'd just encountered. Perched on the top step, she wondered what effect opening this new Wiccan doorway would have on her old boring life. There were kids at school . . . kids who wore long black trench coats, had blackened lips and eyes and tattooed pentagrams; whose pale skin attested to long nights and sequestered days. They claimed to be into Wicca, and they were just kids like her. Weren't they? Did they have powers, perform spells, chant and dance in the woods, have sex on altars? She shivered with the first stirrings of rebellious power. What could her mother do if she discarded her Catholic upbringing and embraced Wicca? Surely by the time a girl was eighteen she had the right to choose her own religion.

"Maggie," repeated Father Grace.

"Hmmm?" She took a deep breath and sighed.

"Who was that you were talking to?" The casual disparity in his tone was possessive, jealous even.

"Just a hiker." Noting his suspicion, she continued with a cursory explanation. "He got lost in the trails and ended up here. It happens sometimes. I told him how to get back to the park." It was a glimmer of truth in an otherwise murky story.

"And gave him a drink?" He gestured to the half-empty blue bottles on the steps. He wasn't going to give up. What was this? The Inquisition?

"Well, that's the Christian thing to do, isn't it, Father?" Her sarcasm left him looking puzzled, so she softened her tone. "Look. He was lost and thirsty. What's the big deal anyway? I'm nearly old enough to vote."

He sat down next to her on the step. "I know that. But I worry about you."

"Why?"

"Because you're a young woman and you spend all your time either studying or looking after your father. You take life too seriously."

"Too seriously?"

"It's not normal. You've got to get out and play sometimes."

"I do gymnastics," she said, but sensed there was something else on his mind.

"You're often here alone in this house. It's a dead-end street right next to a massive forest. I don't want to scare you, but this could be a setting for a horror movie."

In all the years she'd lived at the end of Hawk's Claw Lane, the thought of being frightened in her own home had never crossed her mind.

"Think about it. Your mom often works double shifts at the hospital, and we both know that John would be no help if something happened. I mean, you just never know who or what might come out of those woods." He gestured to the dark trees beside the house.

Until today, she would have argued that point, but now?

"Well, I have no choice. Bastian just works for us a few days a week. He doesn't live here. Someone has to keep an eye on my dad."

"I know." He rested his hand on her shoulder. "And, I know you feel obligated." She could tell he was choosing his words with care. "But you deserve a life too. You didn't come on any of the camping trips this summer. I wish you had." She quivered slightly under his touch. "I'm here for you, Maggie. I understand, and I care." He squeezed her shoulder gently to show that he really meant it.

Maggie wondered what in his life had given him an understanding of her situation. Whatever it was, she was intrigued by this new intimacy, and turning, gazed into his bright green eyes. His soft lips, mere inches away, were moist and begging to be kissed. *Oh God.* This was just too weird. She wished he would stop touching her and wished he would not. Where the edge of his thumb rested against the bare flesh of her neck, the tingling nerves sent shivers spiraling down her belly.

"I know what it's like to feel obligated to a parent," he said, shaking her back to reality.

Did he know how guilty she felt? Did he know that she was to blame for John's pathetic life? Had Shannon told him? She thought of the confessional and what secrets he must hold.

They were so close, so intimate. She noticed the trace of a scar along his cheekbone and then another—a tiny cross just below the hairline. Her finger stirred in a reflexive desire to touch it and know its story.

"I was hoping you could join us for a fall drive. The Fraser Valley is beautiful now, and your dad's just like a little kid on a car trip. We could go out to the old bridge at Yale and stop for lunch somewhere along the way. Perhaps, one Saturday when the weather's fair. Would you like that?"

If we went alone, she thought. "Oh, sure, Father. If I don't have homework. Gotta keep those marks up, you know." She meant it—was determined to get a scholarship from a solid university. It was her only way out of this prison.

"I look forward to it." As he rose, he leaned on her shoulder, and when he took his hand away, she wished he hadn't. "How did you make out with *Macbeth*? Did you find a thesis worthy of an A?"

She stood and leaned against the column, then tilted her head and admired his silhouette. She'd never really noticed his height before, or the curve of his biceps beneath his black shirt. He seemed edged in gold, as angelic and formidable as his namesake, Gabriel.

"I think so. I'm arguing that the witches created the tragedy. Macbeth was just a victim of their charm."

"You defend him?"

"Well, yes." She remembered how perfectly the paper had come together in her mind just hours before. "The Weird Sisters were incredibly powerful. The man couldn't help himself."

"They cast their spell on you too."

"Well, you have to admit they turned a loyal soldier into a killer."

"Soldiers *are* trained killers."

"True. Macbeth was from a Celtic warrior culture and killed his enemies, but the witches made him kill his king and his friends."

"The Celts were barbarous pagans. They didn't need witches to charm them into killing."

Dylan is a Celt. Smiling, she glanced at the forest. "Do you think witches really have that kind of power?"

"Perhaps once, gleaned from the devil. Shakespeare wrote his plays hundreds of years ago, before the pagan problem was dealt with."

"Right." *Pagan problem.* "Father, did you study the persecution of witches when you were in the seminary? I mean, I heard that the Catholic Church murdered millions of people. What do they say about that?"

"It was the Protestant Church that spurred that campaign. It's exaggerated and irrelevant. Ancient history."

"I don't mean to be cheeky Father, but isn't the Bible ancient history?" A tiny nerve in his cheek beat furiously, then his cheeks reddened, and she realized she'd crossed some invisible boundary.

"The Church did what was necessary and it's not up to you or me to judge. They brought reason and sanity to a world fraught with superstition and evil. Someone had to take control, didn't they? If not, the whole world would have gone to the devil." He stroked the emerald cross that hung around his neck and then kissed it. "Though it may seem harsh, it was done in Christ's name for the good of humanity. For you and me. Never doubt the Church, Maggie, and never doubt your faith."

"I'm sorry Father. I was just curious—"

"No harm done," he said, cutting her off. "I confess I'm defensive. We Catholics are always being accused of something heinous."

Heinous. Yes. Murdering witches was heinous, and yet when perpetrated by the Church—regardless of what church—it seemed it was necessary for the good of humanity.

She remembered the priestess in white, bent backward over the altar by the stunning man in black. If they had been alive then, would they have been among the innocents who were tortured and burned? And Dylan? And, if *she* had been alive then, would a man as devout as Father Grace have shaved her head, tortured her, and set her ablaze for the good of humanity?

Fair Is Foul & Foul Is Fair

With his hair caught back in a bun, wearing faded blue jeans and a moss-green leather jacket that matched his eyes, Michael Stryker looked deceptively normal. When he left his alter-ego, Mandragora, behind at Club Pegasus, Michael looked like the boy next-door—only much sexier. Estrada adored the dichotomy between sweet and raunchy that Michael wore so well. After an ecstasy-fueled orgy, he often offered tea and cookies. The thought made Estrada smile.

"Is the divine Sensara still giving intuitive readings?" Michael said, rubbing his smooth chin.

"I suppose so." It struck Estrada as an odd question. Michael and Sensara were his two best friends, yet they disliked each other. Sensara blamed Michael for what she considered Estrada's indecent behavior, and Michael just thought the priestess was a prude. After blowing on his cinnamon latté, Estrada took a careful sip and wiped his lip, all without taking his eyes off his friend.

"God, that intense Latin stare is titillating. You're sexy even when haggard."

Estrada rubbed his eyes. He hadn't slept and was well aware of the black circles that grazed his cheekbones.

When he made no reply, Michael persisted. "I noticed you were a little off your game last night. Couldn't quite get the rabbit out of the hat. What happened, compadre? Did your woodsy dance get a tad too rough?"

"Something like that. I thought you didn't believe in psychics."

"I just wondered if your lady could assist me with something."

Estrada exhaled deeply. *His lady.* He'd never thought of Sensara like that, but now . . .

"Was that a sigh?"

"I'm just tired."

"If you insist. You know if you're in trouble you can always talk to me. Sometimes it's good to have an objective view."

"If I knew someone objective." Estrada took another sip. "But we were discussing *you*."

Michael extracted one of his hand-rolled, gold-banded cigarettes from the gunmetal case. After careful examination, he lit it and blew the smoke over his left shoulder.

Estrada willingly sat outside at the Creel Café, so that Michael could smoke his imported James Bond cigarettes, even on days like this when Vancouver was shrouded in rampant mist. As Michael continued to smoke in silence, Estrada grew anxious. Had Daphne's rippling charm somehow touched his friend? "So, why do you need a psychic?"

Michael crushed out the cigarette and lowered his voice. "There are several people standing beneath the awning of the bookstore across the street."

Naturally, Estrada raised his head.

Michael gasped, "Don't look!"

"Sorry."

"Now, without seeming to, if that's possible, check out the man in the brown raincoat and fedora."

Estrada glanced over Michael's left shoulder and then quickly back at his friend. "Looks out of place for the casual Kits crowd."

"He does, doesn't he?" Michael lit another cigarette. "I've seen him frequently the last couple of days—skulking around the club, outside my home, now here." He exhaled dramatically. "I believe that man is stalking me."

"Why would he—?"

"I don't know. That's what I thought your lady might assist me with."

"Cop?"

"Possibly. They were at Pegasus this morning, asking about a young woman who disappeared."

"A witch?"

Michael rubbed his chin. "Perhaps. She called herself Jade. Is that a witchy name?"

"Could be."

"She was at the club last Friday night, and no one has seen her since."

His memory suddenly jogged, Estrada remembered the dark-haired woman who had enchanted his friend. "Wasn't that—?"

Two cops appeared at that moment, as if on cue, and flanked Michael—one a uniformed officer, the other a graying detective. They flashed their badges. "Michael Stryker?"

"In *this* incarnation."

"Would you come with us? We have a few questions, if you don't mind." It was astounding how polite the cops were to the Stryker family.

Michael took one last drag of his cigarette and crushed it out. "I'm supposed to meet Nigel at the club around six. Go for me? Be sure to tell him about . . ." He gestured with his eyes to the far side of the street.

Estrada turned, but the man in the brown fedora had vanished.

On Saturday afternoon, Maggie Taylor borrowed *Malleus Maleficarum* from the local library and studied the Church's judicial rules and procedures regarding the extraction of a witch's confession by means of torture. Brutal and dehumanizing, a captive woman would say whatever was necessary to end it. A multitude of horrific devices were invented for just this purpose.

Preferred method of execution: burning. Sometimes she was hung or garroted first. Sometimes, she was burned alive.

The Hammer of the Witches, written in 1486, by two Catholic judges from Germany, legitimized the mass murder of women. They were blamed for everything bad that had ever befallen men, including impotence. This, the judges termed "removal of the male member." Maggie smiled at the obvious euphemism. Along with bat wings and lizard tongues, witches, it seemed, had a penchant for the penis.

Disappearing witches and stalkers in brown fedoras. This was not a conversation Estrada was looking forward to, especially not with Nigel Stryker. An entrepreneur, who fashioned dreams and despised bullshit, he was the only man in Estrada's world whom he truly admired. Nigel Stryker had learned to use the power of manifestation long before New Age prosperity gurus like Bertram Bellows laid claim to it.

A well-preserved Englishman in his mid-sixties, Nigel worked with a personal trainer and had the strength and stamina to prove it. He was rich in every possible way, and not because he hoarded, but because he believed in generosity and flow. To illustrate this, when Michael turned twenty-one, Nigel financed Club Pegasus for his grandson. It was the gothic nightclub Michael had always dreamed of. While still retaining legal ownership, Nigel allowed Michael to manage the nightclub as he desired. Within reason. Nigel ensured his police contacts turned a blind eye to the drugs and everything else that went on there, as long as Michael kept it subtle. Of course, subtlety was an ongoing challenge for Michael, whose alter ego, Mandragora, was anything but, especially when it came to sex and drugs.

When Estrada entered the club at 5:50 that evening, Nigel was sitting at a table dressed in an expensive gray tweed suit. And sitting next to him, with a rather smug look on his face, was the man in the brown fedora.

"Mr. Stryker, sir, it's good to see you."

"Always a pleasure Sandolino and please, call me Nigel."

Estrada shook the extended hand.

"But where's Michael? I have someone here he must meet."

The man in the brown fedora took it off and ran a hand through his short spiky brown hair. A younger healthier version of Michael with the same high cheekbones, sharp angular features and dimpled chin, the man was clearly related.

"I can see that you're as shocked as I was," Nigel said. "Sandolino Estrada, may I introduce my other grandson. Clive is Michael's younger brother."

Estrada nodded and shook the extended hand. "Hey man."

"Clive Stryker." The slight snarl of his upper lip—an action Michael played with on occasion—evoked a prickling of Estrada's flesh. A hungry young lion sprang from those malevolent hazel eyes. Estrada couldn't help but compare the two brothers. As nefarious as Michael attempted to be, his angelic heart revealed his goodness; whereas this man exuded something of a Machiavellian charm, and rather crudely at that.

"I didn't know Michael had a brother. You sound so—"

"British?" Clive fondled a hefty signet ring on the little finger of his left hand. Was it nerves or some ring of power that amplified his arrogance? Smirking, Estrada tried to read the silver letters, but his view was obscured.

"Clive grew up in London. My grandsons haven't seen or heard from each other since they were infants. Remarkable, isn't it? But tell me, where *is* Michael?"

"I need to talk to you alone, Mr. Stryker."

"Nigel, please. You know you're family, Sandolino."

Clive's flash of haughty disdain did not go unnoticed by his ever-astute grandfather. "Get yourself a drink and explore the club," he instructed.

Clive pushed back his chair and sauntered off.

Nigel turned to Estrada and lowered his voice. "Now, tell me. What's going on?"

"The cops picked him up for questioning this afternoon. It may have something to do with a girl who came here last Friday night and disappeared."

"Sarah Jamieson. I'm aware of that situation. But, how is Michael involved?"

"Well, he . . ." Estrada paused, wondering how much to reveal. "He met her that night. She told him her name was Jade. He spent some time with her."

"You mean he took her to bed. I'm sure she was consenting. Nothing illegal in that."

Estrada shrugged. Bedding young women was one pleasure both grandfather and grandson shared, though thankfully not together. "It makes him the last person to see her, in their books."

"I'm sure nothing will come of it. Michael's a good boy. He'd do nothing to jeopardize our family or the club."

Estrada's cell phone rang, and he excused himself to glance at the screen. "It's him, sir."

"May I?"

He handed the phone to Nigel. Out of the corner of his eye, Estrada saw Clive studying them from the bar. Michael's words echoed in his mind. *I believe that man is stalking me.* What was little brother's game?

Nigel ended the call and handed the phone back to Estrada. "Michael is being detained. Apparently, the police have a witness who saw him carry Miss Jamieson out of his flat early Saturday morning. I'm sending our lawyer."

On Sunday morning, Maggie Taylor stuck her finger down her throat and vomited up her cereal. She did not want to go to church.

The next morning, she skipped math class and went down to the creek with Damien Morrison. Flooded with fall rain, the water gushed over the rocks and sang in her head. Yellow leaves twirled in the wind and fell by Damien's curly black hair, as he sprawled in the grass, his head resting on the root of a giant cedar. He had smooth brown skin and eyes like an Egyptian.

"I can't believe you're doing this." Damien's voice was low and husky. She knew he'd been attracted to her for months but had never approached her because she was one of the good girls.

"Do you want me to stop?" Glancing up, she ran her fingers across his taut brown belly. "From this angle, you don't look like you want me to stop."

"No. Please, don't stop. I'm so close."

The warning bell rang as Maggie stood and fluffed her hair. It was not quite what she'd imagined; still, she felt a rush of power knowing that she could control the length and intensity of a boy's bliss. Perhaps she would begin her own collection.

Damien lit a cigarette. "You've changed, Maggie Taylor."

She smiled coyly. "Give me a drag of that." The tobacco sent a dizzying rush to her brain. Settling down in the leaves, she continued to inhale this intoxicating new drug, while he lit another. "Listen Damien. If you tell anybody, this will never happen again."

He leaned over and kissed her. "Hey baby, my lips are sealed. I'm glad yours aren't."

The man swallowed his disdain; had never been to any place so blatantly gay before. Yet here he was, sitting with crossed legs at a fireside table in one of the trendiest pubs on Rainbow Row. It stank of chic cologne and trepidation, most of which wafted from the sweaty flesh of Jeremy Jones, the red-haired punk across the table. They'd been flirting on the Wiccan website for days—since Jones mentioned he knew Estrada. Jones used the name Jem online, but the man knew exactly who he was—one of the Hollystone witches.

"I'm intrigued. What do you do?" asked Jones.

"I'd rather not say. My dates usually bolt when they discover my profession." Already on their third round of cocktails, Jones was slurring his words; while he, having tipped the waiter to make his discretely virgin, was sober.

"Oh, come on," Jones said. "I promise I won't leave. Trust me."

"Trust you?" The man enjoyed the squirming. "Fine, but if you run out on me it's your loss." Leaning back, he uncrossed his legs and gazed down at the bulge beneath his belt. "I've been told I have much to offer."

"*Oh my God.*" Jones sighed dramatically. "I don't care who you are or what you do."

"You're a little crazy, Jem."

"And you're hot." Jones downed his martini, then reached across the table and grasped the man's hand. "Your fingers are perfect, so long and elegant. I can just imagine—" His eyes were glazing over. Perhaps he'd been drinking before their date to bolster his courage. "Oh, but you've hurt yourself."

"Minor burn. I love to barbecue. It stimulates my biological urges."

"Oh. You're paleo."

The man smiled. The caveman diet was one of the latest fads. "I sure hope you're not a vegan or one of those animal rights freaks."

"No, I eat meat. As long as it's, you know, organic."

"I can tell you look after yourself."

Jones beamed, then kissed the man's hand.

Struggling with repulsion, the man swallowed. "This coven you mentioned sounds fascinating. Any chance I can come to one of your gatherings?"

"Maybe." Jones leaned across the table and lowered his voice. "There's this new girl who wants to join. She's just a kid really, but Dylan's crushing on her."

"Oh yeah?"

"Yeah. I don't know if she'll get in. Estrada's for anything that makes Dylan happy"—he rolled his eyes—"but Sensara's playing the hard-ass, as usual, and she's the boss. The bitch put me on probation for a year, if you can believe that."

"Really? What do you people do? Go out in the woods and dance naked under the full moon?"

"Sometimes."

The man grinned, then leaned in and brushed Jones's cheek with his own. "Tell me about this Estrada. You mentioned him before."

"Now, there's a man who thinks he's all that."

"And is he?"

Jones scoffed and pulled back. "I wouldn't know." He signalled the waiter for another martini. "He's attractive in that bad boy sort of way. I'll give him that. This week, he's off playing Houdini on a cruise. Have you ever been to Pegasus, the goth club downtown?"

The man squinted curiously from beneath his tweed cap and leaned back. His disguise had worked. Jones hadn't recognized him from their brief encounter at the club—the night he'd gone to meet Jade.

"Estrada performs his magic show there every weekend when he's in town. We could go—"

"It must be a decent act if he's there all the time."

"Well, he's thick with the manager, if you get my meaning."

"Man or woman?"

"Michael Stryker."

Of course. The man remembered watching Stryker that night, the way he'd slipped his hand under the magician's cape and drawn him in. "So, Estrada's like us."

"He's like us *and* them. You should have seen him making out with Sensara at our last ceremony at Buntzen Lake. He nearly screwed her on the altar." Turning up one corner of his lip, Jones rolled his eyes.

"If you can't stand them, why are you in the coven?"

"Because they're friggin' great at what they do," Jones said.

"You mean they really cast spells and all that?"

"You bet. When they raise the power, shit happens. How do you think I got to be so successful?"

"Not because of magic?"

Jones nodded.

The man considered the implications of this. Just how powerful was this magician? The thought of danger made him somehow even more appealing. "Buntzen Lake? That's out east of here, isn't it?"

"Yeah. That girl, Maggie, the one who wants to join? She lives there. It's wild country. There are bears and cougars and God knows what else." As Jones shivered, the man pulled free his hand, leaned back, and crossed both arms over his chest.

A waiter appeared, smiled, and set another martini in front of Jones.

Rising from his chair, the man yelled in the waiter's face. "Did you think I didn't see that? I can't believe you're flirting with him right in front of me. Can't you tell we're on a date?"

"But, I didn't—" The waiter backed up, holding the tray to shield himself from the assault.

"He didn't—" Jones echoed.

The man ripped off his leather jacket and threw it over the back of the chair. Then, he turned on the waiter. "Let's go, *fucker*." He hit the waiter's shoulder with the heel of his hand. "Outside. Now."

"No. No. Please don't—" Jones struggled to his feet and grabbed the waiter's arm.

"Oh, how sweet. You don't want me to hurt your boyfriend. That's why you chose this place, isn't it?" Before Jones could say anything more, the man grabbed his jacket and turned to the waiter. "You can have him." Even as he shoved wide the door, he could hear Jones's pitiful denial. He didn't care. He didn't care about anyone but Estrada.

This bitch, Sensara, was the one to watch. *He nearly screwed her on the altar?* And Maggie? What would *she* offer the magician to get her in? The man bit his lip. The way to him was through *them*.

He couldn't get Estrada out of his mind. He must have him. He *would* have him. Whatever it took.

One week passed with no word from Dylan. Maggie worried and fretted, then googled a love spell from the Internet. Friday night at midnight, when she was sure her parents were asleep, she took a small red Christmas taper and etched the words "*Dylan come to me*" three times into the wax. Then she lit the candle. She visualized Dylan knocking on the front door, then gazed into the flame until the candle melted into a small red puddle of her intentions. When it had cooled sufficiently, she carefully scraped up the remains, wrapped them in a piece of red cloth, and tied it with a small red ribbon. Fearing her mother might discover it on one of her snooping expeditions, she stuck it in a corner of her purse, and waited.

She heard the sound of Dylan's footfalls as he sprinted up the porch steps on Sunday afternoon. Having just emerged from the shower, she stood wrapped in towels at the top of the stairs, in a state of momentary panic. Shannon was at work, but John was in the kitchen.

As she slipped into jeans and a soft black sweater, she thought about the spell. The witch had suggested a white candle for purity, but she had chosen a red candle hoping it would heat things up. Now she wondered if that had been a mistake. What if all Dylan wanted was sex? Could she control him like she controled Damien?

She listened to the exchange from the top of the stairs where she stood brushing her damp hair.

"Who are you and what do you want?" John said, as he opened the front door. Jehovah's Witnesses frequently suffered the same fate and returned undaunted. She wondered if Dylan had that kind of resolve.

"My name is Dylan McBride. I'm here to see Maggie."

"How old are you?"

She was surprised by John's lucidity.

"Nineteen, sir."

"Too old."

When she heard the door slam, she dropped the hairbrush, and thundered down the steps two at a time.

Dylan thumped on the door. "Maggie! Are you there?"

"Look out, Dad! You're being ridiculous!" She shoved him out of the way and opened the door.

Red-faced and grinning, Dylan stood holding the biggest bouquet of pink roses she'd ever seen. "Maggie. I had to see you."

"Well, come in." Maggie turned to her father. "Everything's fine, Dad. Go watch *Longmire*." It was his current favorite. When she turned back, she was pleasant and in control again.

"These are for you." He thrust the roses toward her.

She smiled. "Thank you. They're beautiful. Shall I put them in water?"

"Aye, sure." After handing her the bouquet, he wiped his sweaty hands on his khakis. "They're pink on purpose. I'll explain later." He nodded toward her father.

"Please don't mind my dad. He's just old-fashioned and sometimes forgets that a religious man must also be a gracious and hospitable host. Isn't that right, Dad?" There was no response, but she knew that he'd picked up her tone, even if he didn't understand her words. As they walked into the kitchen, she heard him shuffle into the front room.

"No one has ever brought me flowers." It was true. Bringing a girl flowers was as outdated as Dylan.

"Do you like the pink?"

Maggie nodded. "It's pretty."

"Like you." He looked away, embarrassed by what he'd said. "The color is symbolic." He glanced back and lowered his voice. "You see, yellow denotes jealousy and unfaithfulness, so that's no good. And white denotes purity and virginity—not that I don't think of you as pure, but I was hoping for something not entirely pure, if you catch my meaning—and red just seemed too much, you know. A little too fiery when we don't know each other yet. Ah, I'm spillin' over. I just can't help myself—"

Maggie stared at him in disbelief. Was this babbling because of the spell or was this just Dylan?

"Pink, you see. Pink seemed just right because it signifies a fusion of purity and love."

"Wow, that's amazing, Dylan." She'd have to record that spell in her journal. "Would you like a cup of tea?" She fluffed up the roses.

"I'd love a cup of tea. It's weird how you remind me of my great-grannie."

"Really?" she said, with a hint of venom in her breath. "How's that?" Being compared to someone's great-grandmother was at the farthest end of her compliment spectrum, though he didn't seem to notice.

"Well, there's the physical resemblance. She had the same fiery auburn hair, peachy skin and green eyes, and then there's just a way you have about you. She passed on before I came to live in Tarbert, but Granddad said the kettle was always whistling on the hearth."

"So, was your great-grandmother a witch?"

"Heavens no. She was a Presbyterian, the same as my gran."

"Well, Dylan. I'm not like your great-grandmother at all then, because I've become a witch." It came out in a rush—partly because she was offended at being compared to some ancient woman, but mostly because the spell had made him vulnerable and obsessed. If there was ever a time to push him, it was now.

"Oh, I hope it wasn't because—"

"And I want you to get me into your coven."

"But Maggie, it's not that simple. It's up to Sensara. She's our high priestess, so she decides who comes and goes."

"Well, talk to her. Recommend me."

"I'll do what I can, but there are things you should know. Like, it takes a year and a day of learning and practicing before you can be initiated. That's our tradition."

"Dylan." Taking his hand, she raised it to her lips. "If you care about me, you'll convince Sensara to let me in. You do want me, don't you?"

She kissed his fingertips with soft full lips and for the first time since he entered the house at the end of Hawk's Claw Lane, Dylan McBride was speechless.

"You look decrepit, man," Estrada said. It was late Thursday afternoon at the Creel Café in Kitsilano and the place was packed with the university crowd. When a perky barista appeared with their order, he turned and smiled. Like Sensara, she had a soft Asian charm he found most appealing. Another day, he would have slipped her his card.

"My life has been bloody hideous lately," Michael said. He was prone to bouts of melancholy which Estrada frequently ignored. "While you've been off charming the cruise crowd, I've been locked away with the local constabulary." He rubbed his temples. "You should have taken me with you."

"It was only two weeks, down the coast to L.A. and back. Trust me, you would have hated it. Besides, who'd look after the club?" Grasping his coffee, Estrada paused. "Inside or out?"

"Out, if you don't mind. My need for tobacco has escalated."

Settling into a corner table under the awning, Michael immediately took out his cigarettes and lit up. "Life's just so desolate when you're not here." He exhaled and took a sip of his espresso. "You know, the police told me that I fit the profile of an organized serial killer."

"As opposed to one who is *unorganized*?"

"You know what they say. I'm 'mad, bad, and dangerous.'"

"I'm intrigued, Lord Byron. How do you fit this profile?"

"Well, there's a checklist: intelligent male—don't laugh, the police affirmed this—aged twenty to thirty, has a social life, holds down a good job, and indulges in sexual fantasies."

Estrada scoffed. "That describes most males in Vancouver, particularly patrons of Pegasus."

"I know, and I told them, 'It's not fantasy if you *do* it.'"

"That *does* make it reality."

"Exactly. I think the bastards are persecuting me because of the fangs." Raising his upper lip in a snarl, he exposed a very long canine tooth. Estrada thought of Clive and how much fun it would be to scare the hell out of him one night. "It's medieval. Soon they'll be chasing me down Robson with torches and pitchforks."

"If you could only be a good boy and live in this century."

"We are who we are."

"Perhaps they're aware of your sideline." Nicknamed The E-vamp by his clients, Michael dealt in erotigens of the highest quality and randomly shared them with the patrons of Pegasus. He trusted his sources so well; he offered a money back guarantee. No one had ever complained.

"Oh yes. Drugs were mentioned. *Someone*—and I have a damn good idea who—told them that I drugged the girl at the club. And later, *someone* saw me carry her out of my flat, dump her in my car, and drive off." He took a sip of his coffee. "Of course, that's just bullshit. I said, 'If *someone* is hanging around my flat at four in the morning, watching my comings and goings, perhaps I should be the one pressing charges.'"

"Indeed. So, you suspect Clive?"

"Yes, I fear my dastardly younger brother is intent on framing me. I get that he wants the club. It's a great club. But why now?"

"Good question. Nigel said you hadn't seen or heard from him in years."

"That's true. Nigel's been airing the family skeletons since Clive's arrival. Before that, neither of my grandparents said much about our past. Care to hear the sordid story?"

Estrada nodded and leaned back in his chair.

"My parents were killed in a car crash. I was two-and-a-half and Clive was still an infant. Nigel filed papers to adopt us both, but the Twyfford-Farringtons—that's my mother's family—disputed it.

"Of course, I can understand why. They'd just lost their daughter and Nigel had plans to immigrate to Canada with both their grandsons. Still. When the legal dust settled, we were split apart. I came here with the Strykers and Clive stayed in London with the Twyffs. I really don't know him at all."

"Families," Estrada said, thinking of his own severed relationships.

"What I don't understand is what the little shit is doing here now. It's not like he's destitute. According to Nigel, the Twyfford-Farringtons are a wealthy and influential family." He sipped the last of his coffee and put down the cup. "Apparently, Clive's a doctor—studied medicine at Cambridge." He took a drag from his cigarette and blew a smoke ring. "You know that Byron went to Cambridge."

Estrada ignored the aside. "Maybe the club means more to him than money."

The server came by and Michael ordered another double espresso. "I think she winced. Do I really look that bad?"

"Not for a dead guy."

Michael shrugged. "We need to find that girl. Even if she's dead. I know that sounds morbid, but a good investigator could prove my innocence. All they've got now are profiles and lies."

"No suspects besides you?"

"Worried?" Michael smirked and smoothed his loose hair with pale thin hands. "Nigel's contact says that Jade—I realize her real name is Sarah Jamieson, but she will always be Jade to me—Jade has a jealous ex-boyfriend who's been stalking her."

"Really. Did you get a name?"

"Clayton Cole. And get this. He's a computer nerd, a webmaster for some Wicca site."

"He could have monitored her chats, known where she was going, who she was talking to."

Michael shrugged. Computers were not part of his archaic world.

"So, Cole may have been following her that night."

"Oh, he most definitely was. Do you remember that maniac who burst into the club? The guy in sweats? That was Cole. The poor girl was most distressed."

"Oh yeah. The boys threw him out, didn't they?"

Michael nodded. "I think *he's* the prime suspect."

"Maybe so. Do you think that Clayton Cole could be the witness who saw you put Jade into your car?"

"You mean considering that I *didn't* put Jade in my car?" Pausing, Michael bit his lip. "But why would her ex frame *me*?"

"Why not? Let's suppose, Cole followed you two back to your place and waited outside. When she emerged, he confronted her, and things escalated. You'd be the perfect fall guy. Then there's the revenge motive. She chose you over him that night." Estrada took a sip of his mocha latté. "I mean, this is all just speculation, but there are at least two men who could have been hanging around outside your flat that night."

"Clayton Cole and brother Clive."

Estrada nodded. "So, what *did* happen? I mean, I know you partied, but did she call a cab or anything before she left?"

Michael shook his head. "No clue. I passed out. And I feel horribly guilty because of it. That's probably what the cops see in me." Michael sighed. "The woman was a goddess. I should have insisted she spend the night, or at least made sure she got home safely considering how exquisite she was. Jade was so good to me. I can't get her out of my mind."

Estrada smiled as he watched Michael close his eyes and conjure his dream woman.

"Violet eyes, long glistening neck. I do adore a long neck. A snake tat crawling down her ass, nipples like rubies, a pierced belly button. Oh, and the pièce de résistance . . . a diamond-studded—"

"Ah, the woman with amethyst eyes. I remember her now."

"'She walks in beauty like the night, of cloudless climes and starry skies.'"

"I'm amazed how enchanted you are. I don't think I've ever heard you quote Byron after one night with one woman."

Both men and women clamored for invitations to Michael's orgies. Estrada indulged when he had an appetite. Both men were hedonists who found nothing immoral in their lifestyle, though there were times it came back to bite them.

"Yes, I was enamored of the lady. I suppose I still am."

"Maybe she's just skipped town for a few weeks."

"Perhaps. You know, she's quite like your own little darling." As another tray of drinks arrived, Michael stifled a yawn. "God, this espresso is just not working for me. I'll get a bloody bullet at the club. That'll help me shoot through."

"Yes, those can wake the dead."

Michael stretched. "She's been frequenting the club the last couple of weeks."

"Who?"

"The Divine Sensara. It's rather odd come to think of it. I've seen more of her than I have of you lately. Hasn't she mentioned it?"

Estrada shook his head. "We haven't been speaking the past few weeks. We had a falling out and then I left town."

"I suspected as much. Pity. She's quite the exotic creature."

"No, man. It can't be Sensara. She came to the club with me once and called it decadent debauchery. She was not thrilled."

"Well, she is now. Quite thrilled."

"Really?" Estrada's eyes narrowed. "Is she coming alone?"

"Yes, but she's not leaving alone."

"Sensara wouldn't do that. It must be some woman who resembles her."

"Ah, yes. Her *Doppelgänger*." Michael lit a cigarette and blew the smoke over his shoulder. "So, you don't mind if I indulge? Do you suppose a psychic would know—"

"Don't."

"You always said there was nothing we couldn't share."

"That's true but—" He couldn't explain.

There was no way that Sensara would party at the goth bar. It just wasn't her style. It had been three weeks since the ill-timed spectacle at Buntzen Lake, and still she wouldn't speak to him. He wondered if she read his emails or just deleted them. He couldn't understand why she had erected those bloody shields. She had wanted him as much as he wanted her. Spell or no spell. He saw it in her eyes and felt it in her kiss. And it wasn't just sex. So, what was the problem? If she was embarrassed by the inappropriateness of the setting, she should have forgiven him by now. They were best friends, had been for years, and he wanted her back.

But there was more than friendship at stake. If Sensara really was frequenting Club Pegasus, she could be in grave danger, given this new threat of a killer lurking in their midst.

"We need to figure this out before anyone else gets hurt. I mean, if Cole grabbed Jade, that's one thing. That's personal. And if your brother saw Cole grab Jade, and decided to frame you, that's personal. But, if there really is a serial killer hanging around Pegasus who's preying on witches, then a lot of innocent people are in danger."

"Like Sensara."

"Yes."

"Let us vacate then, compadre. I'm desperate to depart this mundane world." Leaning over the table, Michael opened a mirrored compact and popped in his red contacts.

"What's the word for the gatekeeper?"

"Styx. Are you ready to wade in the water?"

Daggers in Mens' Smiles

Maggie hated the dark. As long as she could remember, she'd always hated the dark. She still kept a nightlight burning despite her mother's scolding that fear was not a viable reason to waste electricity. Yet, here she was in the blackest pitch, without even a faint glow of moonlight or streetlight. It was as cold and dank and dusty as the Capulet crypt.

Standing with her back firmly wedged against a cold stone wall, she pressed a damp palm over her nose and mouth to shield, what could only be, particles of the dead from being ingested. Beyond the silent ringing in her ears, she searched for sounds in the dark, but could hear nothing save the fierce beating of her own heart. And then, something. Breathing. Not her own.

Startled by the touch of a hand on her shoulder, her first thought was of Father Grace and the strange familiarity of him. Then, she turned her head and saw the most delicious almond eyes—eyes that glowed in the dark, eyes edged in Egyptian kohl, black eyes so brilliant, they illuminated the long tan nose, slightly bumpy where it had been broken. One curling lock of black hair fell casually across his brow. Uneven stubble covered the strong square jaw. And those lips, thick and heart-shaped.

Estrada.

Her hand dropped from her face and she exhaled loudly.

He raised his hand to cup her cheek. *Easy love. You're safe.* He had not spoken, yet she heard his thoughts, mind to mind in the silence. Her face melted into the warmth of his palm like a honeyed candle, and as she leaned against him, she felt for the first time in her life that the darkness was nothing to fear. He was her light and she would love him forever.

Rising through the veils of consciousness, she fought to keep Estrada in her bed. His warm thumb caressing her cheek; his lithe body stirring against her own, pressing, desiring, but never entering. His beautiful eyes searching her soul. His lips a mere breath away. With all her power, Maggie resisted the inevitable wakefulness that lurked beyond, and then in the final moments, as those sensations became thoughts, she surrendered. The dream was over. Maggie was alone in her ordinary bed in her ordinary world.

Grabbing her journal from the nightstand, she scribbled what she could remember. But words could not capture his beauty. So, she sketched—his luminous eyes in the darkness, the bumpy nose, stubbly jaw, the lips she longed to kiss. Estrada was hers now, captured forever in her imagination. She could conjure him whenever she desired, and she desired him now. Closing her eyes, she kissed the soft curved side of her fist, and remembered.

Startled from her reverie by a metallic crash, Maggie flinched, then jumped from her bed and raced downstairs, praying she would not meet with another shattered clock.

"Bastian." She was relieved to see his familiar face in the kitchen. His pale complexion and blond spiky hair created a stark contrast to the dark man of her dream. Wearing a turquoise shirt that matched his eyes and pale jeans, he suddenly reminded her of a blue-eyed Justin Bieber. She stifled a laugh. "I haven't seen you in ages."

"Yeah, we've been missing each other." He smiled awkwardly and turned away, embarrassment flushing his face. She wondered if her erotic fantasy was visible. "I'm sorry if I woke you," he mumbled to the two pieces of disassembled frying pan he clutched in his hands.

Gazing down she noticed her nipples popping from her tight baby T. Her baggy pants hung way below her navel. It was obviously too much for poor shy Bastian. Strange how she considered him a brother without even realizing it. Probably, it was because he was always coming and going from her home, and they shared the experience of caring for her father.

"Have you got a girlfriend, Bastian?" It was a random question and he stood momentarily stunned, opened his mouth, but did not speak. "I don't mean to pry, it's just . . . I've seen you here for years, but I feel like I don't know anything about you."

Shaking his head, he continued to concentrate on the frying pan. Then he coughed awkwardly and cleared his throat. "Have you got a screwdriver? I can fix this."

She opened a drawer and rummaged around. "I didn't know you were a handy man too." Casually, she hiked her plaid pants up to her waist. "Here you go." As she crossed her arms over her breasts, she felt her taut nipples and her mind drifted back to Estrada. She smiled furtively, knowing it was a crush. There was no way she could ever compete with his sort of women. Still, it left her feeling hot and sexy to think such things. Guys were fun to play with. She'd have to be careful with this one, though. Without Bastian Stone, the Taylor family couldn't manage a week. In the three years since he'd been coming to care for John, he'd become an integral part of their lives.

"When I pulled it out of the cupboard it fell apart," he said as he worked.

"If it wasn't for you, this whole place would fall apart."

One corner of his lip turned up in a grin. "After I fix this, I'm frying a big pan of hash browns for John's breakfast. Would you like some?"

"Yes, please. Hash browns are my favorite any time of day."

"I know," he said, placing the pan on the stove. "How come you're home today?"

"Pro-D."

The crunching of rubber on gravel startled them both. Glancing together out the kitchen window, they watched Father Grace slam the door of his SUV. Remy, who'd been sleeping under the kitchen table, scampered toward the door.

"Why is *he* here?" asked Bastian. "He knows that I work with John weekdays."

"Don't you like him?" asked Maggie, surprised that anyone could dislike the priest.

Bastian just clenched his jaw and shrugged.

When the doorbell chimed, Maggie walked into the hall. "You can't go like that," Bastian said, coming up behind her. Turning, she cocked her head curiously. "I mean . . . he's your priest. Why don't you go change? I'll see what he wants."

"Okay." But she climbed just far enough up the stairs to be out of sight, yet still able to hear. If Bastian had a problem with Father Grace, Maggie wanted to know what it was.

She heard the familiar sound of the front door opening, the scurrying sounds of Remy's paws on the wood floor, and then the priest's voice. "Oh, Stone."

His terse tone, so unlike anything she'd heard before, caught her by surprise.

"Where's Maggie?"

"Maggie?"

"Yes. Is she here?"

There was a silence. Bastian did not reply.

"She's probably still sleeping," suggested Father Grace. There was another rather long pause. "Well, aren't you going to invite me in?"

"Kind of like inviting a vampire in."

"What's that supposed to mean?"

"I know what you—"

"Listen, Stone, you better watch your mouth. I can get you axed from this menial blue-collar job."

Bastian snorted. "My collar may be blue, but at least I don't hide behind it."

"What are you implying?"

Bastian said nothing in response; at least, nothing she could hear.

"My business here has nothing to do with you. Now move."

Bastian was blocking the doorway. Maggie could imagine him, standing like a sentry and shooting evil looks at Father Grace. But why?

"Shouldn't you be changing a diaper or something? You're here to babysit John. So, go. Do your job."

"I don't take orders from—"

There was a sudden thump, followed by scuffling, and then another thump. Galloping down the stairs two at a time, Maggie arrived just in time to see Father Grace's fist connect with Bastian's face. Having seen no one hit before, she was not prepared for the adrenaline that coursed through her body.

Bastian reeled backwards, then caught his balance and shot forward. Blood spurted from his nose. He seized the priest around the throat with both hands and squeezed. Both tall and equally matched in strength, the two men grappled like angry bears.

"Bastian!" she cried, concerned for the young man she loved like a brother.

His gaze flickered toward her, and in that second, Father Grace brought up a knee and caught him squarely in the groin. Bastian crashed to his knees.

"That's better," sneered the priest. "Back where you belong—kneeling at my feet."

"You bastard," Bastian said, wiping the blood from his nose.

"Father! Get out," shouted Maggie. "How could you—?"

"He tried to kill me."

"You hit him. I saw you." Stunned by the lie, Maggie clutched Bastian's shoulder, and glared at the priest. *"Get the fuck out of here!"*

"I've never heard you talk like this, Maggie." Turning, he shook his fist at Bastian, who huddled on the ground. "I'll get you for this Stone. You just wait."

"I'll wait," Bastian mumbled. And when he raised his face, Maggie saw such misery, it broke her heart.

Narrowing her eyes at the vile priest, she cast her threat. "If you ever hurt Bastian again, I'll kill you my *fucking* self."

"Remind me again why we're calling on Clayton Cole?" asked Michael, as he shut the door of the BMW roadster with a soft thud. An older model, the 2001 convertible was one of Nigel's hand-me-downs. Michael had christened her Crimson because she was blood red inside and out and told everyone he'd chosen this shade as it helped to cloak any evidence of his nocturnal activities.

"Subterfuge," Estrada said. "If Cole is the webmaster for a Wiccan website, he has access to information about everyone who uses it—names, addresses, propensities."

"Really?"

"Yes, and if he's a stalker, undoubtedly he monitors conversations."

"How do you know these things? You haven't gone all cybersex on me, have you? The flesh is so much more—"

"No, I haven't. But I do like to keep up."

Michael had parked a block from Cole's apartment building and the two men strolled along the leaf-strewn sidewalk in jeans and leather jackets. It was a misty Saturday, and Estrada felt they blended quite well with the busy residents of the East Van neighborhood. He was feeling cocky. Cruising in Crimson had that effect on him.

"Technology is so mundane," Michael said.

"Yet useful."

"If you say so."

"Listen, if Jade was chatting with someone online and Cole knew about it, that could be why he followed her to the club. He might also know who she chatted with, and who she hooked up with that night."

"Wouldn't the police tap him for that?" Michael asked.

"Probably. But considering you're their number one suspect, wouldn't you like to know what they know? I mean, it's possible that Jade was a random grab—wrong place, wrong time—but it's more probable that she knew her assailant."

Michael paused, extracted a cigarette, and lit it with a flick of his monogrammed lighter. "What if he attacks me?" he asked, releasing a stream of blue smoke into the air. "I mean, the last time the man saw me, I was nuzzling his ex, and my boys threw him out of the club. Moreover, if he's innocent, he probably thinks I'm guilty."

"Relax amigo. I'll protect you. I know fighting's not your forte."

"Wonderful," Michael said sarcastically. "I know what an experienced street fighter you are."

"Actually—"

"Hey, is that Cole?" Indeed. Clayton Cole had emerged from the lobby of the building and was striding toward them at a brisk pace, a laptop case slung over his left shoulder. "What should we do?"

As if in answer to Michael's plea, Cole raised his eyes from the sidewalk in front of him and caught sight of the two men. A panicked look crossed his face, then he turned and sprinted in the opposite direction.

"Run."

Surprised by Estrada's command, Michael dashed mechanically after Cole. The chase was brief. Within seconds, Cole disappeared down an alley and vanished.

"Thank God." Michael collapsed on a bench at the nearest bus stop. Holding his chest, he coughed so hard tears wet his face.

"You're scaring me," Estrada said.

Michael rolled his eyes and burst into another bout of coughing.

"Really, man, should I call 911?"

He shook his head as the cough subsided.

"Don't you order that tobacco because James Bond smoked it?"

Michael nodded and mouthed the word, "Turkish."

"I never understood how Bond could smoke two or three packs a day and still catch the bad guys."

"Fiction," was the feeble response, followed by another short rasping breath. Then, after reaching inside his jacket pocket, Michael extracted an invisible gun and pointed it at his friend.

Estrada laughed and sat down beside him on the bench. "Sorry man, but you'll never be Bond no matter how many of those cigarettes you smoke, and you'll need a real gun if you plan to stop anyone."

Michael sighed, as the spasm ended. "But why run? Guilt?"

"Not necessarily. There are two of us."

"True."

"And perhaps he's heard about you." Michael was a joy to tease. It was a quality Estrada adored about his friend.

"Heard what?"

"That you're connected to the mob? Or that you're a vampire?"

"Don't be absurd. It's daytime."

"Ah, but it's also overcast, and we do live in the Pacific Northwest. Apparently, this is one of the more preferred territories for those of your species."

Michael furled his brow.

"I'm amazed you don't know that. If you're going to play vampire, you really should keep up with popular culture," Estrada said.

"What are you talking about?"

"Well, for one thing, vampires only sparkle now in the sunlight. Their skin dazzles like white marble. In some circles, the whole solar incineration thing is passé."

"Where did you hear this?"

"My twelve-year-old vampire-obsessed neighbor. You know, the one who wants to meet you."

Michael scoffed. "That's ridiculous."

"It's true. And they're much faster than you are, and healthier."

"How can a vampire be healthy? That implies— Wait. They *are* still dead, aren't they?"

"Still dead and still drinking blood, although the good ones are vegetarians."

"Don't be absurd."

"The vegetarians only drink animal blood."

"That's just ludicrous." Reaching inside his jacket pocket, Michael clutched his cigarette case.

"Oh, don't, man. They'll be hauling you off in an ambulance, and I don't want to be the one breaking that news to Nigel."

Michael rolled his eyes.

"I'm serious, man, you can't keep smoking like you do and remain unscathed. No one can."

"Fine," Michael said slipping his cigarette case back into his pocket. "Though I don't see how my pathetic life matters one iota in the grand scheme of things."

"Oh, don't get all broody now. What would Nigel do without you? Who would manage the club? And what about all your fans?"

Michael shrugged.

"What would I do without you?"

"Well, it seems we accomplished nothing in this escapade, except to intimidate the one man who might have provided us with some useful information."

"I don't know. I think we may have proven something else. Look over your shoulder," Estrada said.

Turning casually, Michael stiffened, gasped, and coughed again. "Clive. You little wanker." He fought to catch his breath. "Stay right there. I want a *fucking* word."

When Shannon dropped the bag of groceries on the kitchen floor, Maggie heard the eggs crack. Her mother's amazement made her smile.

"What on earth have you done to yourself?"

"Isn't it awesome?"

"Awesome? Hair poker straight and black as the ace of spades? *Holy God.*" Shannon held the kitchen counter as if her knees were buckling. "And those nails."

Maggie held out her hands proudly. "Banshee Black."

"Who on earth did this to you?"

"My friend, Alicia. She's in the hairdressing program, so it was free. I love it."

"It's grotesque."

"Yeah." Using the kitchen window as a mirror, Maggie admired her violet lips. The shade was intense and far more sensual than black. Her smoky eyes, thickly lined in kohl, mirrored Estrada's. Contrasted with the white face powder, the effect was startling. She most definitely would not remind Dylan of his great-grandmother now.

"And those clothes—"

"Thrift store."

Remy's nose was scrambling the broken eggs, but Shannon didn't notice. Standing, trembling, with a wide-mouthed stare on her face, she continued to shake her head. She surveyed the jagged side-slit dress, the ripped black leggings, skinny leather boots and tight leather jacket. And then she spied the silver pentacle that dangled between her daughter's breasts like the devil's mark. Her hands flew wild across her chest as she crossed herself. "Jesus, Mary, and Joseph! Are you pierced and tattooed as well?"

Maggie shook her head. Perhaps she'd gone too far too soon.

"You'll not set one foot out of this house looking like that!"

"Witch," said her dad, lunging into the kitchen. "Call Father—"

"Father Grace punched Bastian in the face." Maggie spoke slowly and emphatically so both her parents would understand. "He's a jerk."

"Stop her before she gets in trouble like—"

"John. Hush now. I'll handle this." Grasping his upper arm, Shannon ushered him into the living room.

When she returned, she stared directly into Maggie's eyes—it was her way of detecting deceit. Fortunately, Maggie was used to it and could outstare her mother, lie or not. "Tell me about this business with Bastian and Father Grace."

"When Bastian comes to work on Monday—if he comes—check out his face. I was here. I saw it. And Father Grace kneed him in the balls. Priest or not, he's violent. You're not really going to leave Dad alone with him now?"

"He must have been provoked. He wouldn't just—"

"But he did, Shannon. *Christ,* you never listen to me."

"Ah, my head hurts. I can't think. And don't be calling me Shannon. I'm your mother." She turned to the sink, filled a glass with water and swallowed two pain pills. "Now, go to your room and wash that paint off your face."

Ignoring her directive, Maggie opened the refrigerator and poured herself a glass of chocolate milk.

Shannon counted out John's evening pills, then walked into the living room. "It's time for your meds," she said, then stood and waited while he swallowed the lot. "I'll make you a cup of tea. I need one myself."

Returning to the kitchen, she noticed Maggie. "I told you to go—"

"I want to know what Dad meant."

"He meant nothing. The poor man doesn't know what he's saying ninety percent of the time."

"No. Somebody got in trouble. Who? What kind of trouble?"

"Let it be, Margaret Mary. We've enough to deal with in the present without dredging up the past."

"So, it's true. Someone got in trouble. Tell me. If you don't, I'll ferret it out of Dad. You know I will."

"You leave your father alone. You've done enough to him already."

Pushing the one button she knew could devastate her daughter, Shannon invoked the whole tragedy yet again—John's fall from the roof twelve years ago. His broken bloody head. Silent vigils in the hospital where he laid comatose for weeks, wrapped in bandages, pale, shrunken and alien. And then, at last, consciousness, and unending years of convalescence, doctors, homecare workers, and guilt. Guilt piled on top of guilt. Maggie's guilt. For it had all been Maggie's fault and Shannon knew it and never let her forget it. In one moment, Maggie's world had careened from innocence to tragedy.

A horse had wandered into the yard—a beautiful white horse—and Maggie, only five at the time, was thrilled at the chance of seeing up close, the animals she worshipped from afar. Crawling beneath the creature, she hugged its front legs and tickled its chest, talking and laughing as it nuzzled her hair with its velvety lips, breathing hot horse breath against her eyelashes in big horse kisses.

John, who was on the roof cleaning the eaves trough, saw her and panicked. When he bolted upright, he lost his balance and tumbled over the shingled incline. He hit his head on the ledge and again on a tree, then landed in the rock garden for the final assault. Skull fractured in several places; the impact damaged his brain. Maggie would never get the image of his broken blood-soaked head out of her own.

The doctors said he was fortunate. He could have broken his neck and been left paralyzed. He could have died. When he finally regained consciousness, the doctors warned Shannon that a traumatic brain injury was complicated, and he would be safer in an institution. She refused. They said he would probably never recover. He hadn't. Nor had they.

"I hate you." Maggie said, waking from her reverie. "I *will* find out what you're hiding, and when I do, I'll leave here and never return."

"What did Sensara say?" Estrada had to shout over the tangled throng of ink, flesh, leather, and sweat that was Club Pegasus. The music, just before closing, escalated to such an orgiastic pitch, it obscured mortal language. In the blistering darkness, lips were judged on potential. Flesh sought flesh in a sea of pulsating preverbal libido, often uniting in a shattering climax without ever having left the dance floor. Estrada admired the primeval freedom of it all. Usually. Tonight was different.

"She said, and I quote, 'I've almost scraped the taste of burnt cinnamon off my tongue.'"

Estrada bashed the top of the metal railing with his fist.

"She laughed at this too." Michael pointed to the black patch that covered his left eye.

Estrada rolled his eyes. Clive had won some boxing title at Cambridge and unmasked that secret gem on Michael's face. The only gain made from the brotherly confrontation was that Nigel had banned the little weasel from the club for the weekend. Though inadequate, it was something. Michael felt the outcome was entirely positive. His pirate's badge, and the shiner it hid, only added another dangerous element to his sinister persona and he was getting more than his usual share of attention.

Staring through his one red contact, Michael stroked his fang with his little finger. "Forget her, compadre. She's much too weird."

Ironic, but true. In just a few weeks, Sensara had become the woman she detested, the woman she'd judged repulsive on countless occasions, the woman she'd vowed never to become. What intrigued Estrada was why. What had happened? Was she enchanted? Or could a kiss from him really turn a woman inside out?

After sucking back another double tequila, Estrada wiped his mouth with the back of his hand. "I need to know why."

"Sorry compadre. I can't help you there. I could, however, conjure up something to allay the pain."

With a subtle signal, a slave boy emerged from the shadows, a white fragment tied loosely around his narrow hips. Michael kept several of them on payroll to keep patrons intoxicated and amused, whatever that involved. They were all of age and took Ancient Greek names. Dion offered them his wares on a thin silver tray.

"No thanks, man. I'm not in the mood." Waved off, Dion vanished.

"Watch the blood clots then. I was feeling rather generous earlier."

"Why the fuck would you do that?" The thought of Sensara ingesting even a sip of Michael's ecstatic blend was terrifying. "Are you out of your mind?"

"Not yet, but I feel it unraveling." Reaching across the table, Michael ran his fingers through Estrada's long wild hair. "Relax. You know it's not for the plebeians."

But how could that be ensured in a place like this?

"My, that's a wicked look," Michael said. "Feel like blazing?"

"No."

"Suit yourself."

"She's not up to this," he yelled to Michael's back. Scanning the crowd, he sought Sensara out. Then found her romancing some guy dressed in a hooded chain-link shirt, long black tunic, and cape. Estrada scowled. He knew that game only too well—errant knight needs love. Why did beautiful women always fall for the lonely brooding bad boy?

Words were exchanged, and then the man stood and followed Sensara toward the center floor. Above them, Circe weaved on the stage, the three singers' curves visible through pale diaphanous gowns. Crooning a sultry blues number, the harmonic trio funneled their ardent voices into a slow deep throb.

Damn her. Licking the salt from the rim of his glass, Estrada downed another double tequila and bit the bitter lime.

Bending together and bruising flesh amidst the glistening horde, Sensara and the knight danced. Surely, she knew he was watching, knew what it was doing to him. Mesmerized, he couldn't take his eyes off her. Like a great black thundercloud, Estrada's anger exploded around him, threatening to block out everything but its own existence. He realized that he must control it. Rage rendered him impotent and this man could be a killer.

Closing his eyes to shut out the scene below, he focused on slowing his breath. The invading tequila enhanced his imagination, and he visualized cutting through the darkness with a crystal sword that left only white light in its wake. Something had happened that night at Buntzen Lake. Sensara was not herself. She was under a spell, possibly even possessed. Every impulse told him so. He needed to get inside her head, the way she could get inside his.

She'd taught him a technique once, and they'd practiced it repeatedly at Stanley Park. She laughed at each of his failed attempts to read her mind, so he kept trying, if only to amuse her, and after a while he prevailed. She would visualize a birthday cake blazing in candles and he'd see it too, or a tall ship in full sail on the ocean, and they'd share a euphoric moment.

The trick was to clear the mind of all negative emotion—a formidable, but not impossible, task—and then focus only on the thoughts projected by the other. The more they laughed, the lighter his vibration became and the more they connected. When for an instant he could feel everything she was feeling and clearly see each image in her mind, he panicked, and the connection severed.

Now Estrada determined to rekindle that state and engage long enough to understand what was happening to her. Uplifted with the memory, his vibration lightened. Closing his eyes, he merged his mind with hers, sharing images and sensations, rather than words.

The stranger was tall, so tall she could barely reach his armpits. His hands felt cool against her hot bare skin, his rippling pecs hard against her cheek. Her fingers crawled beneath his cloak as she explored him, stroked his tight thighs and ass, and then reaching behind, she pulled him hard against her weaving belly.

Motherfucker. Jealousy claimed the magician and he opened his eyes. She wasn't thinking about *him* at all. She was into this guy.

The stranger stared up at him, noting his interest, and calling him out.

I'll fucking kill you, Estrada shot back. Slamming his right fist into his left palm, he shook it at the man. *Let's go.* As they locked eyes, Estrada searched for the mind behind the Herculean body. But, in his present state, he could make no connection. The only thing he knew was that this knight was all about power and control. Some women hunted men like that, craving cold disconnected sex—no names, no ties, just a time out from the constant stress of running the show. But, surely not Sensara?

Suddenly, she spun around. Had she seen something? Felt something? Did she sense his fears, or have fears of her own? He watched her slink through the crowd, watched as a slave boy maneuvered by clutching a tray of blood clots, watched with horror as Sensara took a vial of the spiked juice in each hand and downed them before the boy could stop her.

Estrada glared at Michael, who'd just returned and was tripping in his own psychedelic world. He had no choice. He couldn't leave her now. This bastard was likely the witch killer.

He flew down the stairs and touched her shoulder. "Sara, we need to talk." Flashing his biggest, most soulful eyes, he begged.

Recognizing him, she glowered. "*Fuck off*, Estrada."

"Sensara, you're in danger." He grasped her arm.

"Let me go, or I'll scream."

"What's wrong with you? Look at you." He continued to hold her arm as she struggled against his grip. "What are you wearing?" She'd always mocked the sexy corsets and bustiers women wore to the club, yet she was poured into a black snakeskin corset. It was unlaced to expose her breasts and barely covered her ass. She had tiny blonde braids threaded through her wild black hair, glittery lids, false eyelashes, and leopard boots that rode halfway up her thighs. "What's happened to you?"

"How dare you judge me? You and the E-vamp are the fucking rock stars of this show."

"Listen to me, Sensara. This place is dangerous and you're not yourself. Please come with me." Pleading was all he could do. "The blood clots—"

"Don't you get it? I'm tired of being myself. I want to lose myself. Isn't that the whole point of this place?" She sighed and softened. "Isn't that why you come here?"

He folded her inside his cape, nuzzled his face into her neck and inhaled her sweet scent. She was still a goddess, even in her wretchedness . . . especially in her wretchedness. As memories enveloped him, he took her face in his hands and fought back the urge to kiss her again as he had that night in the forest.

"Sara, I love the old you. And I miss you."

"I miss you too," she said.

"Then come with me. Don't be angry at me." Holding her face in his hand, he rubbed his cheek against hers and breathed in her ear. "I'm sorry I kissed you like that at the lake. I didn't mean it—"

"No, you never mean anything do you, Estrada? You just play games." The muscles in her jaw tensed beneath his fingers as she clenched her teeth. "Just leave me *the fuck* alone."

Wrenching away, she edged her way back across the floor into the arms of the waiting knight, who cocked one eyebrow to Estrada in icy triumph and slid his hand up her thigh.

Pretending to choke him with both hands, Estrada sent the threat careening across the room.

With a smirk, the bastard bit her neck.

Still, Estrada couldn't leave her alone. Not with him, and not with Michael's special chemical blend percolating in her veins. He knew exactly what she'd experience in a matter of minutes, had swallowed his own share of blood clots over the years. Worse still, she'd been drinking alcohol and the combination would make her sick. Dangerously sick. So, he leaned against the wall and watched. And as Sensara's world kaleidoscoped into a graphic novel, so did his. Dancers' thoughts burst from their bodies, rising into the fog in fluorescent shapes, giant bubbles flashing and fading into the ethers. Laughing, she rubbed against them in a rush of love.

Estrada understood a neon high, relished the charade of omnipotence, the feeling of infallibility, as the drug coursed through the brain, fucking with the pleasure centers. Simulated euphoria. Soon she'd want nothing but sex, as the world morphed into a sensational sea of love. And it wouldn't matter where she was or who she was with. He had to move fast. The knight was leading her away.

Stumbling out through the gate, wobbling madly on her stiletto heels, Sensara clung to his arm, raving as visions capered through her mind. The image of Lady Macbeth making thick her blood for the murderous calamity of the coming night, pierced Estrada's psyche and shivering, he padded after them.

The alley behind Pegasus was typical of those in the inner city. Used mainly by delivery vans that supplied local businesses, it ran only one way—the opposite direction to which they were walking—its narrowness constricted by the overflowing garbage bins, painted in gang tags that lined both sides. How the garbage trucks ever made it past the bins and illegally parked vans was a mystery and explained why they were constantly in a state of excess. Why the knight had chosen this alley, rather than the street as his escape route, concerned Estrada, and he loped along in the shadow of the bins, watching and waiting for the right moment to attack.

Halfway down the alley Sensara doubled over and clutched her stomach. Then, collapsing to her hands and knees, she retched. As the knight leaned over to grasp her shoulders, Estrada sprung from the shadows, launching himself through the air with a roundhouse kick. The force of the attack propelled the two men several feet down the alley. While the bastard was stunned by the assault, Estrada kicked again, catching his jaw with the heel of a boot. The knight flew backwards, hit the brick wall and gasped. Grasping him by the throat with one hand, Estrada punched again and again.

Distracted by Sensara's cry, he let loose his grip, and swung around. Another man had appeared. He'd bound her in a straitjacket with her hands tied across her chest. He held a syringe at her neck.

Estrada's yowl pierced the night, and then the world went black.

Restless Ecstasy

Clive Stryker jumped sideways to avoid being hit by the white panel van as it careened out of the alley. After shaking off the shock of what he'd just witnessed, he pulled out his mobile and punched in 911. Running toward the unconscious man, he listened for the voice of the dispatcher.

"Hello. Hell—" Clive gasped as both his arms were seized and wrenched behind his back.

Ejected from his fist, his mobile skidded across the pavement, hit the brick wall, and died. He knew his assailants. The Sentries—a security team who patrolled Pegasus. He tried to explain but a succession of rapid jabs to the face and gut silenced his attempts.

Now, slumped in a pile of garbage, more pissed than he'd been in a long while, he hoped they wouldn't drag him away and beat the crap out of him again, before he could tell someone of consequence what he'd seen. Sirens and red flashing lights alerted him to the arrival of the police. Perhaps they'd listen, perhaps not. He had, after all, been apprehended in an alley outside a club he'd been banned from, while standing over an inert body.

"Fancy meeting you here." For all his literary imaginings, Michael was a cliché.

"Listen. I tried to tell these thugs. Your mate and his woman have been abducted."

"My mate?"

"Yes. The magician." An eye roll revealed his feelings of disgust. "I was trying to help *this* man," he explained, gesturing to the unconscious knight, "when they ambushed me." Feeling a trickle of blood, Clive wiped his nose.

Michael smirked. "Go on brother. Regale me with your tale."

If the two boys had not been separated as infants, they'd likely have killed each other before now. Though physically similar, they were oceans apart. Clive knew he was a threat to Michael and enjoyed antagonizing him but did not want to be blamed for something he didn't do—especially something as serious as manslaughter. Watching the paramedics lift the victim's body onto the stretcher made him nervous.

"Believe me, Michael. There was a man—a man that resembled— Well, for lack of a better comparison ... Jesus Christ."

"Jesus Christ."

"Yes. Long brown hair, full beard. He even wore the long white robe."

"Well, praise the Lord."

Michael's perpetual smirk infuriated Clive, who took a deep breath to steady himself. "Do you want to know what happened, or not?"

"Go on. I'm intrigued."

"This bearded character bound the woman in a straitjacket. Then he aimed a syringe at her carotid artery—"

"Jesus Christ bound Sensara in a straitjacket?"

Clive nodded. "Yes. Your mate, Estrada, was throttling this man here, and winning I might add, until he turned to look at her. That's when his opponent brained him with a brick."

"Really Clive, you should be a writer, not a doctor."

"I thought you cared about him."

Michael produced his fags and lit up. "Then what?"

"Then *this* man attacked Jesus Christ—I think he was trying to rescue the woman. And that's how he ended up with the syringe in *his* neck."

"That will be simple to prove."

"I know that, moron. I'm a doctor."

"So, why didn't you intervene, doc?"

"Would *you* have?"

"I wasn't standing here watching and taking notes."

"It happened like *that*." Clive snapped his fingers. "Anyway, Jesus threw the woman into the van, tied Estrada in a straitjacket, and shoved him in too."

"It takes more than a few seconds to tie a man in a straitjacket. You could have done something."

"I didn't want to get involved."

"Now, that I *do* believe. But the rest of it? Jesus Christ, straitjackets, and syringes? It's absurd."

"Stranger than fiction, yeah?"

"I'll tell you what I think, Clive. I think you're a psycho who abducts women. You tried to abduct Sensara, only Estrada and this guy, who we saw romancing her earlier, intervened. Then you, Dr. Stryker, stuck him with a syringe to sedate him—"

"Then where are they now? Sensara and Estrada—where are they now?"

"Probably off fucking, which is where I'd like to be. Estrada's been trying to get with her for weeks. Saving her life gave him an edge, so he took it."

"Michael—" Clive was tired, bruised, and exasperated.

"It's Mandragora." As his brother curled his upper lip to expose a fang, Clive noticed that his pupils were far too dilated for any darkened alley.

"You're wasted."

"Not enough to fuck with," Michael said, crushing out his cigarette with his boot. "You're fortunate, though, little brother. E opens my heart." He motioned to the Sentries "Without it, I'd have given you to the boys without a second thought." Leaning in, he grasped Clive's cheeks and kissed him full on the lips.

Clive backed up against the wall and spat. "*You* are one sick son-of-a-bitch."

"Pure brotherly love, Clive. You're not my type." Several seconds of silent glaring ensued. "But I do think, you could be a junior Jack the Ripper."

"Please, Michael. Call Nigel. Let me talk to *him*."

"I think that you must talk to *them*," Michael said, pointing to several policemen milling around the alley. "Officers, meet my baby brother, Clive Crispin Stryker. He claims to be a witness. You'll love his story."

The throbbing pain in the center of Estrada's skull brought the tequila rushing back up his throat. Grimacing, he spat the bitter fluid as far away from his body as possible. Perhaps he'd puked already. The sour stench of vomit permeated the air. Blindfolded and bound, he fought through pain for fragments—A white van. A bearded man dressed like Jesus Christ. Sensara dangling in a straitjacket.

He prayed she was here beside him in the darkness; that way at least, he had a chance of saving her life. Blood clots on top of all that liquor? He knew better than to do that, but she was naïve. Too new to know, too stubborn to care. And for that she could die, maybe even choke on her own poisoned puke if she was, like him, bound face up.

He had to focus. Get his bearings. Find her. Save her.

Lying on his back, wedged up against something cold, hard, and metallic, Estrada felt a vibration beneath him, heard a motor. The white van was on the move and he was trussed up in a straitjacket, wrists crossed over his belly, just as Sensara had been. That was an advantage. It was harder to escape if your hands were tied behind your back.

He used a black leather straitjacket in his nightclub act. Having perfected Harry Houdini's escape routine, he'd tweaked it for his particular audience. Bound and hanging by the ankles a few feet above the stage, he played victim to Michael's sadistic teasing. At the last moment, before anything violent or overtly sexual occurred, he would rip free of his bonds and send the straitjacket flying into the audience to a raucous blend of jeers and applause. He'd already begun his technical trickery; gauging the tightness of the jacket, its cinches and gaps, and the secret places he could maneuver his muscles and bones to free his hands.

Over the hum of the motor, he could hear nothing save the echo of Sensara's pathetic cry resounding in his brain. More fragmented images floated through the darkness. The face of that bastard who'd taken her down the alley. A hypodermic. Surely, Christ hadn't stuck that in her neck. If he had, she could be dying. Dead even.

How long had they been moving? The van was cruising at a fast, even clip, not stopping and starting as it would be if they were driving in the city. Sadly, Estrada realized, they were on the freeway. But going where? And why? He assumed Sensara was there, since she'd been tied in the same type of straitjacket just before he was slugged.

And there were two of them—that had been a shock—and both in costume. Christ and a medieval knight. One must be driving, the other riding shotgun. He must stay conscious and alert for her. Must find her in the darkness and let her know she wasn't alone.

What motivation could they possibly have for abducting witches? And why the costumes? Was the ruse somehow symbolic? Were they religious freaks? Or after money? Working alone or for someone else? An organization, perhaps? The word *Inquisition* flashed through his brain.

But there was no time for this madness now. He had to stop this delirium, control his thoughts. Willing his body to relax, he consciously slowed his breath, observed and counted each inhale and exhale, concentrated on nothing but now. No past, no future. There was only this moment and this task—to become so calm and centered, he could speak to the woman he loved in the dark silence of his mind. If they were as aligned as he hoped, she would hear him, despite the drugs, and respond. By the time he had counted twenty slow breaths, his mind had stilled, his heartbeat subdued.

Sensara can you hear me?

In the darkness, he heard retching. Dry heaves.

"She's sick," he said impulsively. Waiting, he heard no sound in the darkness save Sensara's heartrending snivel. "She drank too much alcohol and took ecstasy, some really potent shit. It's a lethal combination. She could die."

Though there was no response from his abductors, he felt heartened that no one had hit him or told him to shut up. Somewhere he'd heard that humanizing yourself to a kidnapper increased your chances of survival.

"Listen. If you're after witches, I'm a witch. My name is Estrada and I'm the High Priest of Hollystone Coven. Sensara is really sick. She needs to go to a hospital. Please let her go and take me. Do whatever you want to me. Torture me. Burn me at the stake. I won't resist. But I beg you, please let her go."

After several minutes, the driver of the van veered off the highway, made a wide turn, and cruised slowly down a bumpy stretch of pavement. The vehicle stopped. Estrada heard the driver's door open, then gasped as the side door slid wide and a cold fresh breeze slapped his face. He heard the sound of a body—her body—being pulled across the floor. *Stay alive, Sensara. Please.*

"Thank you," Estrada said. "And you have my word. I will submit to anything—whatever you want."

Cool damp fingers stroked his cheek. Then the door slid shut, and Estrada was engulfed in the dark metal tomb, once again.

"I don't know why *you're* so pissed, Clive. If you hadn't been skulking around the back alley—" Michael leaned back in his chair, jacked one foot up on the table and lit a cigarette. He sipped his coffee, then blew a significant smoke ring across the dance floor and glanced at the time on his cell: 5:08 a.m. Irritated by his little brother's pouty-lipped silence, he snarled. A three-hour police interrogation was nothing compared to the harassment he'd experienced of late. "I don't see how this righteous indignation is justifiable in the least. You arrive from London unbeknownst to anyone. You stalk me, and then scream victim when the cops want to know what you're up to."

"Tosser," Clive spat.

"Such eloquence, and from a Cambridge man."

"If I hadn't been skulking, you'd know nothing about Estrada's disappearance."

"Don't speak his name. Don't even *think* his name—"

Nigel ended his phone call and slammed his palm against the table. "That's enough now, boys." He'd just been speaking with

Mowbray, the cop he kept on payroll. Michael straightened in his chair and waited.

"Sensara is safe and en route to hospital. She was discovered in the parking lot of a convenience store in the valley." Nigel glanced at Clive. "Bound in a straitjacket. She's quite ill."

"And?"

"No word on Sandolino. I'm sorry, Michael."

"Damn."

"Why leave her and take him?" Clive asked. "Even if she's ill, it makes no sense if his motive is murder."

"Murder is never a motive," Nigel said.

"Where *is* he?" Michael fumbled with his gunmetal case, took out another cigarette, and tapped the end of it against the table.

"You haven't even finished the one you're smoking," Clive said. "Have you any idea what cigarettes do—?"

"Any idea what my boys can do?"

"Something else." Nigel cleared his throat. "The man who left the club with Sensara and ended up drugged in our back alley is a police officer."

"The knight? The one Estrada attacked?" Once past his disbelief, Michael grinned.

"Apparently the officer was off duty and just looking for recreation."

"Oh, is that what they call it here?" Clive stood and stretched. "Wait, that's brilliant. There's a copper to corroborate my statement."

"Possibly. The officer was injected with a very strong opiate. He's still intoxicated."

"What does this psycho want?" Michael mused.

"A man dressed like Jesus Christ who abducts witches? Obviously, he's some sort of religious freak," Clive said.

"Oh, yes. There's one other thing, Michael. They gave Sensara a toxicology screen. Besides the alcohol, she had a very high dose of MDMA in her system. They're wondering where she would get that much ecstasy."

Michael hung his head, refusing to meet Nigel's eyes.

"Combined with the alcohol, she was so loaded, she could have died. You do know what that means?"

Michael nodded. "I'm sorry, granddad. I'll take responsibility for any fallout from this." He tilted his head slightly to catch Clive's reaction in the periphery. It was gleeful, as Michael expected, and really pissed him off. What kind of doctor was more concerned with his brother's ruin than a woman's life?

Love is a powerful motivator. It will rouse a man to action more emphatically than any other emotion. Estrada pondered this as he lay trussed up in a straitjacket he could easily remove, wondering what he'd promised to do for love. But perhaps there was another way out. A way to keep his promise and still survive.

He needed to know where he was, where they were going, and why. Recollecting that night at Buntzen Lake, Daphne's comment filtered through his subconscious. *I invoked a charm so the killer would be caught.* Estrada didn't want to believe that his love for Sensara was conjured, but if it was—if they were enmeshed in Daphne's charm—playing out his role was crucial.

When the van stopped, and silence replaced the hum of the engine, Estrada heard the man sniff and clear his throat, then the door opened and shut. Perhaps they'd reached their destination. Having been deprived of sight for so long by the blindfold, his other senses were keen, his mind ripe with visions. He focused. Listened. Could hear other car doors slam, muted voices, the crush of rubber on pavement, the man's footsteps as he walked away. This was a public place—perhaps a restaurant or gas station. Beyond these noises were natural sounds. Leaves rustled by wind. The light patter of raindrops on glass. The garbled chatter of ravens.

He'd read of shapeshifters—shamans who could take the form of other creatures. If it was possible to merge with Sensara's mind, could he connect with a raven? Use the bird's form as a kind of avatar to determine his whereabouts? Listening intently, he imagined the raven, the intelligent flicker of black eyes, sleek head dampened from rain, a taloned foot holding down prey, a sharp hooked beak ripping through flesh.

The scent of death deepened, and he gagged. Several ravens were ingesting the innards of a rabbit, and he realized that *he* was among them. He hopped back from the carcass, dipped his beak in a nearby puddle and swallowed to rid his mouth of the carrion taste. Then, cocking his head from side to side, he ruffled his inky feathers and stretched his wings.

Another raven, sensing the shift, swaggered toward him, ears erect, and flashed the whites of its eyes in a macho display of power.

Estrada flew into the air and landed on the hood of the van. Staring through the front window he saw two empty seats, though only one door had closed. Was his abductor traveling alone?

Swiveling his head, he stared through blackbird eyes at the man who strolled toward the shop at the 24-hour Chevron. It was the man who resembled Christ, and like Christ, he'd shown compassion to Sensara and touched his cheek with tenderness. Could such a man really be a killer? Having taken off his robe, he now looked like any other traveler in blue jeans and jacket, long brown hair blowing freely in the damp morning wind.

Perhaps, it was the other man he had to fear—the cold one who led Sensara from Pegasus and knocked him unconscious. What had become of *him*? Did they intend to rendezvous or did the other man only lend muscle to the abduction? Gazing back through the window, he remembered that his trussed-up body lay just beyond the seats. No matter how kind the man seemed to be, Estrada was still a captive.

Overwhelmed by a sudden desire for freedom and assured that the man posed no immediate threat, he took off and flew into the sky.

The land below was a tangle of evergreens, severed by dark rock canyons and black serpentine rivers. Huddled against the bank of a river, that could only be the flat, silty Fraser, the town twinkled like an earthbound constellation. So close to the freeway, it must be Hope. The town acted like the hub of an unbalanced wagon wheel.

If his captor continued following the Trans-Canada Highway, they'd travel north through the Coast Mountains toward Cache

Creek and the hinterland beyond. Nothing much there but Indigenous land and abandoned gold mines. If he turned northeast onto Highway 5, they'd climb steadily, and he could end up virtually stranded in the barren lands surrounding the Coquihalla Highway. Well-intentioned friends had kidnapped him several summers ago and driven to the Merritt Mountain Music Fest via this corridor. There was nothing between Hope and Merritt but seventy miles of mountains, riverbeds, and steep canyon gorges. This time of year, the summit could be capped in snow. Finally, if he turned southeast, they'd follow the meandering Crowsnest Highway through Manning Park. All three routes had limited traffic on this October night. Too late for campers, too early for skiers.

Perching in a hemlock, Estrada watched the man leave the store carrying two bags of groceries. He was nothing special, an average guy in his late twenties, though his features were masked by a beard and the low-slung ball cap that shaded his eyes. One thing was clear. He planned to shack up somewhere for a while.

Abandoning his raven guise, Estrada returned to his body, astounded at how easily he'd mastered this new trick.

As they drove, he heard the river on his right. After speeding along for, perhaps, an hour, the vehicle veered off the highway onto a gravel road. The van bounced slowly over potholes, until at last, the driver braked and shut off the ignition. For a moment, silence. Then, the driver's door opened and slammed shut.

When the side door slid open, heavy morning air, laden with the stench of river silt, whipped across his face. Breathing deeply, Estrada filled his lungs. Fingers brushed his face below the blindfold, and then he was yanked out.

When his feet touched the ground, he took another deep breath. The air smelled fresh and green. They must be somewhere in the country north of Hope. When the man grasped his arm and pulled him forward, Estrada stumbled, his legs stiff from hours of confinement. Steadied by his captor, he shuffled along.

I could run right now. Rip off this straitjacket and run like a wolf into the trees. But no, I gave my word. If I break it, what kind of man am I? And what vengeance will follow? This man could come after every witch in the coven, everyone I love.

Metal jangled, hinges creaked, and then there were new smells—mold, dust and decay. The odors of abandonment. Once inside, he stood waiting while the man shut and barred the cabin door. He heard the screech of a stove opening. Wood was tossed inside, and a match struck. The scent of smoke provided strange comfort. Then Estrada was spun around, and the man's mouth was so close he could feel warm breath against his neck. The salty scent of beef jerky made his empty stomach growl.

"Take it off." The voice was dry and distorted. Unrecognizable.

The man wanted a show. Was he from the club? Had he seen his act before? Was this the reason for the straitjacket?

Twisting, Estrada dropped his shoulders and rearranged his bones and muscles, flexing and relaxing in the dance of escape, exaggerating his movements as he did onstage. After unleashing the knotted strap between his legs, he caught the bottom of the straitjacket with his freed hands and prepared for the final flourish. But when he tried to yank it over his head it caught in his hair. Reaching back to entangle it, he realized that his hair had been pulled back and twisted into a tight bun at the nape of his neck. The blindfold, still firmly in place, was tied directly above it.

Finally, free of the straitjacket, he stretched and reveled in the rush of blood through his veins. Then palms touched his chest and he was walked slowly backwards until his calves caught a soft edge. Grasping the shoulders of his leather jacket, the man slid it off.

Bound by his promise, Estrada didn't fight or resist. Even when the man began unbuttoning his shirt. He caught the scent of nervous sweat. Perhaps, his captor was not as confident as he appeared. Clammy hands touched his flesh beneath the silk. Fingers stroked his naked shoulders, and then, it too slipped away. Feeling space between them, Estrada felt certain he was being appraised. Then fingers unclasped his trousers and he heard the slow chink of his zipper. As they fell around his ankles, the cool air pricked his naked flesh and he grew aroused. Pressing one palm against his breast, the man ran his fingers along his neck and chest, and then down his belly, stopping just shy of his genitals. Grasping his shoulders, the man pushed him down. Perched on the edge of the bed, Estrada waited, as boots, trousers, and socks were peeled off.

For a moment nothing happened, and Estrada breathed in the pause, feeling how good it was to be alive and free of constraints. He complied, even when the man wrapped a rope around each wrist and bound him hand and foot to the bedposts. When something cold and metallic touched his thigh and his scant underwear were sliced off, a slight gasp escaped his lips.

Like so many men and women into bondage who came to Pegasus, he wondered if this man was only after power. Yet, he did not seem like a sadist and Estrada had run across many of them over the years, given Michael's reputation in the community. This man was different—gentle, reverent even.

I don't fear him. And I can't call this rape. Coercion perhaps, but not rape. Rapists derived their power from forcing their victims and Estrada had not only given consent, he was aroused by the game. There was something about this man that intrigued him. Thrilled him. Still, he was confused. If all his captor wanted was sex, why not approach him at the club? Did he fear rejection? And why such an elaborate ruse? Why disguises? Straitjackets and drugs? Why kidnap Sensara and then release her? Was it all just meant to heighten the experience?

"What do you want from me?" he breathed.

In answer, his captor threw a blanket over his naked body, curled up beside him, and laid his cheek against his chest. Within minutes, his captor's breathing deepened into a slow relaxed rhythm and, weary from the whole ordeal, Estrada closed his eyes and joined the man in sleep.

When Estrada awoke, his captor was spreading a balm over his dry lips. He was still blindfolded and bound but the cabin was warm, the blanket gone. A familiar scent brought comfort.

"Cinnamon." A tiny hard candy was wedged between his lips. As the hot spice caught his tongue, he remembered red valentine hearts from a time long past, as well as Sensara's recent comment. His friends knew about his passion for cinnamon, but how did this man? Had he been stalking him? "Tastes good, but it's hot. Could I have some water?" He felt the man rise, and then a plastic bottle was pushed between his lips. Tilting his head back, Estrada drank.

After removing the bottle, the man straddled his pelvis, and with the touch of a blind painter, explored his body. He too was naked. Though the dalliance grew slowly, the damp weight wedged against Estrada's groin left no doubt what was desired. And Estrada had no qualms with that, was aroused himself. Gentle fingertips stroked the smooth skin of his cheekbones below the blindfold, then drifted along each ridge and hollow of his ears, his neck, his throat, and finally across his stubbled chin, to his lips.

Estrada opened his mouth and kissed the fingertips, explored with his tongue, the smooth rippled flesh and manicured nails. Leaning forward, the man grasped his cheeks and replaced his fingers with his own cinnamon tongue. The kissing went on and on, fading to flickering brush strokes and then growing in intensity as the two men rode the same ragged breath.

Drifting down his body the exploration continued and Estrada grew harder, fueled by the man's skillful passion—until he could think of nothing but the quick heat, the soft tongue and mouth against his skin, the fingers everywhere, tantalizing, stroking, probing to their own distinct rhythm, as the man's growls merged with his own.

It was as if this man, this *lover*, was inside his mind giving him exactly what he wanted, moment by moment—the teasing relentless, as always in control, the man would bring him to the edge, and then pull away completely, leaving Estrada shivering, pushing against the ropes that bound him and begging for release. When at his pleading, the man began to drain him, Estrada met him stroke for stroke, needing to give everything his earnest lover could take. He couldn't help himself.

Finally, assuming he was too satiated to consider escape, the man untied the ropes that bound Estrada's wrists and ankles and in a surprising gesture of trust, collapsed on the bed beside him. Time passed as Estrada basked in the afterglow.

Then, he sat up and rubbed his wrists. Reaching back, Estrada unbound his hair and ruffled it with his fingers. It felt good to be naked and unfettered. Falling forward, the thick curls brushed the flesh below his nipples, and they grew rigid. He flicked one with his fingernail and felt the spark as a wave of fire ignited in his belly. Turning, he hovered on his knees. He wanted to take his lover where he'd been and beyond. Possess him. Still blindfolded, yet sensing the man beneath him, Estrada caught the soft open mouth with his.

Groaning suddenly like an angry bear, the man thrust his palms against Estrada's chest and shoved him with such force he flew backwards against the wall.

Estrada gasped. "What the fuck?"

Reaching up to rip off the blindfold—wanting to know, needing to know—he was stopped by a vice-like grip and a sharp jab in the arm. As the vile fluid surged through his veins, he felt as if he were falling through a cascade of stars into a deep black hole.

Estrada awoke in the gravel beside the highway. Somewhere. Nowhere. Rain was falling in torrents. Sprawled on his back, head cradled in his hands, he felt the cold drops pelt his face. Poets said that rain could cleanse a man's soul. He needed to believe that. His was dirty. Not because he'd been with a man, but because of the man he'd been with. The violence that followed sex negated any tenderness that came before. The man was mad, unpredictable, and more than capable of murder.

He laid there so long a puddle formed around the edge of his body. Images tormented him as he recalled the events of the previous night. Sensara's bizarre behavior at Pegasus. The scuffle in the back alley. The killer's keen perception.

Was it physical? Chemical? Or something else? Another facet of the spell? A lover conjured from his fantasies? *God*. The memory of the man's touch aroused him still. But that was insane. He couldn't go on thinking like this. He had to find Sensara. She was sick. What if he hadn't persuaded the man to let her go? What would he have done to her? What had he done to Jade?

"Good God, Estrada." Michael's arrival in Crimson brought no relief.

The top step of a ghost shop along the highway afforded some protection from the storm, but not from his disparaging thoughts. Hunched over, face buried in his hands, Estrada shuddered and sighed as his friend hunkered down beside him.

"What did he do to you?" Michael whispered.

The question, asked with such tender pity, provoked tears. Estrada had never realized how much he hated being alone and this night, rife with demons and self-abuse, had pushed him over the edge.

Glancing up, Estrada saw another man in the passenger seat of the car. If it had only been the two of them, he would have told all in great detail, just puked it up like so much poison. There was nothing he couldn't share with Michael. But, for some bizarre reason, he'd responded to Estrada's summons with his younger brother in tow—the same brother who'd been stalking him and blackened his eye only days before. The bruise still lurked beneath his pirate patch.

Michael touched his shoulder and winced. "Ah, your jacket's ruined. The leather's soaked."

Estrada swiped a hand across his tear-streaked face, erasing his weakness from Clive's prying eyes.

"You look like hell. Sorry compadre, but—"

"Keep it up. You're saying all the right things."

Michael smiled pitifully and reached inside the car. "Here's a blanket. Take off your wet clothes and wrap up before you get sick."

"You just don't want me to wreck the interior." When he peeled off his leather jacket, the charcoal calfskin, once soft as butter, felt hard and heavy. "You're right. It's ruined." He saw a garbage can beside the steps and decided to put the jacket out of its misery. Sensara would be glad to see it gone—at least the old Sensara. A supporter of animal rights, she was a natural hemp girl all the way. Checking his inside pockets, he pulled out his cell phone from the right and his wallet from the left.

"Anything missing?" Michael asked.

Estrada checked quickly and shook his head.

"Why didn't he take your phone or credit cards?"

"The man's no thief." Though he rarely put anything in the outside pockets, he checked them. When he pulled his hand out of the right pocket, his fingers were stained red.

"What's that? Blood?"

Estrada smelled his fingers and snorted. "Cinnamon."

"Cinnamon?"

"You know those valentine hearts?"

"God, how long has that been there?"

Estrada shrugged, stuck his fingers in the pocket and extracted the tiny red heart. The man had left him a memento. "I used to love these." Grimacing, he flicked it into the brush.

As he walked toward the garbage can, Estrada wondered how the man had known about his fondness for cinnamon. He must know him. If he'd only seen his face. He thought of the hundreds of people who frequented the club. Fans often sent gifts and notes backstage—propositions, love letters, sometimes threats. He lifted the lid and shoved the leather jacket inside the metal can.

"You can't do that!"

Estrada froze, momentarily stunned by this new authoritative voice. *Clive.*

"It's evidence. The police need it." Clive thrust a plastic bag out the window of the car. "Put it in here."

Ignoring the proffered bag, Estrada rammed the lid down on the can. "Why is *he* here." It wasn't a question so much as an accusation.

"We called a truce. Leave it. Please." Michael shrugged and took the bag. "Come on. Take the rest of your wet things off and put them in here. I'll have you home in no time."

Estrada shook his head. "I need to see Sensara. Where is she?"

"She's safe. She's in the hospital—"

"Take me there." He took the blanket and wrapped it around his shoulders.

"But, you're all—"

"Please, man. I have to see her."

"You should go directly to the police," Clive interjected. "You're a piece of evidence. That man's a crim—"

Estrada opened the car door and jerked him out. Shoving Clive against the wet metal, he held his jacket in his fists and braced his torso so tightly, he could feel the skinny kid's belt buckle through his wet shirt. "Mind your own fucking business or the next body the police find will be yours."

Clive averted his gaze like a kicked dog.

"What? You're not going to box me in the eye?"

"Come on, compadre. I'll take you to her." Michael grinned slyly, then opened the driver's door, slipped inside, and revved the engine.

"Crimson's a two-seater. Looks like you're hitching, kid." With a violent shove, Estrada sent Clive reeling several feet into the parking lot, his rage easing his despair. After climbing into the car, he shut and locked the door. "Drive amigo."

Sensara's loose hair fell like black silken threads against the bleached bed sheets. Like Snow White she slumbered, beautifully poisoned, while her dwarfish coven huddled outside the door awaiting word of her awakening. Estrada savored the stolen moment, while the drama of the past few weeks hovered just beyond him like a bad dream. Leaning over, he inhaled the fruit of her perfectly glossed lips, thinking how Snow White, once awakened by the prince's kiss, lived happily ever after. He paused, basking, gathering courage, while she inhaled deeply and sighed, her eyelids riffling in drowsy dream.

As his lovesick lips brushed hers, Estrada closed his eyes, feeling her warm lips thicken, quivering in response, opening, allowing, wanting. He gazed down. Had his princely kiss awakened her or was she merely dreaming?

"Am I dreaming?" she asked, startling him with her uncanny ability to read his thoughts even in her sleep. Her brown eyes flickered with a smile and then she grimaced. "Oh Lord. I'll never drink again as long as I live. I feel like death."

"You look as enchanting as a princess in a faerie-tale."

Smiling, she touched his cheek. "Storyman. I've missed you."

"You're not mad at me anymore?" Whatever insanity possessed her during the last few weeks appeared to have abated.

"How can I be mad? You saved my life." He cocked his head like a raven, and she answered his question, her voice softening conspiratorially. "I heard you in the van. I know what you did."

Brow furling, he pulled up a chair and perched alongside the bed. "What do you mean?"

"You offered yourself in exchange for me. You said, 'I'll do anything you want.' I heard you." She took his hands in hers and ran her fingers over each knuckle. "I hope the price was not too great. Did he hurt you? What did he do to you? How did you get away?"

"Too many questions for now."

They stared into each other's eyes, and then she said, "Yes."

"Yes?"

"You want to know if you can kiss me again. The answer is yes."

Leaning forward he caught her lips with his. He liked the soft caress of her tongue in his mouth, the feel of her warm sleepy hands in his hair. She was sweet and gentle and nothing like the man.

"You're right," she whispered, stroking his hair. "There's plenty of time for talking later. I know you're cold and tired, but will you lie beside me for a while?"

"I'd love to, but you knew that, didn't you?" Kicking off his boots, he crawled beneath the soft blue hospital blanket. She turned to face him, ran her fingers through his curls and buried her lips in the flesh of his neck.

Estrada shivered when he remembered her gifts. Could she sense the last face buried there? Why hadn't he gone home first, showered and changed and washed away all traces of *him*? Clive was right. He was a piece of fucking evidence, his flesh stained with the man's DNA. Tainted. Desecrated. Sensara would never understand. She must never know.

To distract her, Estrada caught her chin with his fingertips and kissed her hard and deep, resurrecting the night at Buntzen Lake when it all began.

Aroused, her pupils dilated, and she slid her leg over his, squeezing in hard against him.

Why did she want him now? Was it love or gratitude, or did Ecstasy still surge through her veins?

"You're my hero. My very own knight." She kissed him tenderly. "Now I know you'd do anything for me."

Yes, I would. But would you still want me if you knew what I did? And, how much I liked it? How I crave him still?

Hecate

Maggie barely had her ear to the phone before Dylan spoke. "Christ! Something awful's happened to Estrada and Sensara."

"What? What happened?"

"I can't tell you."

"Listen Dylan. You can't announce that something bad happened and then not tell me what it is. That's not fair." She heard a quick intake of breath. He was gauging his words, wondering what to say and how to say it.

"It's bad. Really bad. It's changed everything. The meeting with Sylvia tomorrow—"

"Yeah?"

"It's off."

"No!"

Bad was an understatement. This could ruin her life. Dr. Sylvia Black was a celebrity professor who'd published several books on Celtic spirituality and was a key player in Hollystone Coven. Her main area of expertise, a collection of Welsh tales called *The Mabinogion,* was hard slogging especially on top of all her other homework, but Maggie had ripped through the ancient stories to make a positive impression. Dylan had assured her that if she could convince Dr. Black of her sincerity, she'd get her foot in the coven door. She remembered the woman, standing regally in golden robes that night in the woods. With her burgundy hair upswept from her pale face, she had the aura of an ancient Celtic queen, and the power.

Samhain—Dylan pronounced it *saw-ween*—was only two weeks away and she was desperate. Now, the plan to meet Dr. Black—a plan Maggie had manipulated so meticulously—was off. No, she couldn't allow that to happen.

"Dylan. I will never speak to you again if you don't tell me what's going on." She was betting on the power of her love spell to make things right.

"*Christ,* Maggie. All I can say is, there's a man abducting witches. He's dangerous. Right? So, lie low and wait."

"But what happened to Estrada?" She needed more than this vague threat of danger. Had he been abducted by the man? Was he hurt?

"I can't tell you. And Maggie—?"

"What?"

"Be discreet. Don't be talking about us or advertising the craft in any way. Understand?"

Gazing down, Maggie realized she was clutching the pentacle so tightly, blood was leaching from the old wounds in her hands, wounds she never quite left alone long enough to heal. Releasing the pentacle, she stared at the blood trails on her new black dress. "Yeah, I heard you. No advertising."

"Look, I gotta go. I'll call you later."

"Dylan!"

The line went dead.

"I'm shocked The Divine Sensara let you come up for air, compadre. How did you escape her sticky web?" Michael asked. They were backstage preparing for the biggest selling show of the year. It was Halloween Friday, and every freak in town was gathered outside Club Pegasus, inhaling, injecting, and wallowing in whatever magical potion might bring them closer to the edge—an accelerated escape from their vanilla worlds. Thankfully Sensara was not there. Since the incident, she'd sworn never to venture inside the club again.

Estrada rolled his eyes. "You're jealous, man." Michael had never liked Sensara, and now that she and Estrada were involved in something beyond friendship, his dislike had blossomed.

"Perhaps, but not of you. You're just so bewitching my sultry Mestizo. Everyone loves you." With a strange melancholy smile, Michael leaned across the table and pinched his cheek.

Flinching at Michael's touch, Estrada knocked over a coffee cup. No matter what he did, he couldn't forget the man or the thrill he'd felt that night in the cabin.

"*Jesus*, Es—"

"Sorry, man. I'm just edgy." Leaning across the table, he squeezed Michael's fist. Truthfully, his relationship with Michael was complex, intense, and more real than any he'd ever experienced, including the one he was enmeshed in with Sensara. The threat of not having it, the sheer thrill and freedom and potency of it, unnerved him.

Not that Sensara would ever break up their friendship. It was the other stuff. He'd never told her about his liaison with Michael, but anyone who saw the two men together knew they were intimate. Still, they made no demands on each other. They had sex with whoever they chose, whenever they chose—sometimes together, sometimes apart. Sex was just sex. And although Michael might taunt him or claim to be jealous, he'd never expect Estrada to choose him over her, or anyone else.

Sensara, on the other hand, demanded fidelity. Estrada was willing to try, though he felt judged and confined. He remembered her words and also her tone. *Sex is never just sex, Estrada. Intimacy binds us to each other in complex ways. Even if it's just a kiss.*

If that were true, why did he always feel so free before?

"I just . . . I miss *this*." Estrada gestured between them. "I never want to lose this."

"Don't worry about *us*, compadre." Michael sauntered over to the bar, examined a forty-dollar bottle of Merlot and popped the cork. After pouring two glasses, he handed one to Estrada, then guzzled the other himself. He refilled it to the brim and settled himself into the corner of a beaten leather couch. "Come, sit and talk to me. Honeymoon over already?"

Estrada drained the glass and pursed his lips as he poured another. Leaning back, he glanced at Michael and laughed.

"What?"

"Do you have any idea how ridiculous you look in that skeleton suit?" Dressed in a skin-tight black leotard painted in neon skeletal bones, Michael couldn't wait to play his role as Mandragora, the demon executioner.

Michael sucked in his belly and stared down at the significant bulge in the spandex. "I think it's quite enhancing."

"Yeah, you'll be getting offers to do gay porn."

"Getting?"

"God, I've missed you."

"And I you. Now stop fucking around and tell me what's really bothering you. If it's Sensara and the whole monogamy thing, I can have you cheating in no time."

"It's not Sensara. It's *him*. He's here. I can feel him."

"Who? The killer?"

"We don't know that he's a killer."

"Yes, well. I wasn't going to tell you until after the show, but since you're already about as fucked as you can possibly be . . ." Michael picked up the bottle of wine. "Drink up." Estrada swallowed the wine in one gulp and Michael refilled both their glasses. "Nigel heard from Mowbray today, you know, his man on the force. Apparently, after your abduction, the Mounties searched the area north of Hope."

"And . . . ?"

"And something turned up yesterday. Some . . . remains." He took a drag on his cigarette and exhaled. "Jade."

Estrada choked, then clasped his chest and doubled over.

"I know, compadre. It's ghastly."

"They're sure it's her?"

"They found a ring—a silver toe ring engraved with a pentacle. I saw it myself the night we—"

"What did he . . . ? How did she . . . ?"

"Burned. They're testing to see if she was . . . I can't even imagine what it would be like to be—"

"Burned alive?" Estrada couldn't breathe, couldn't swallow. His throat felt filled with ashes.

"They found gasoline stains. They think she may have been lying on the bed at the time the fire started. That part of the cabin—"

"Whose cabin?"

Michael shrugged. "Abandoned."

"Jesus Christ. He took me to a cabin too. He *is* a serial killer. I had sex with a serial killer."

"He forced you."

Estrada sat dumbstruck, remembering those fingers touching his skin, in his mouth, wet sensations in the darkness, and the man's lips against his flesh. How good it felt, how much he didn't want it to end, how he craved it still. Just thinking about it made him hard. "*Intimacy binds us to each other in complex ways.*" It was too much to think he could be bound to a serial killer. Is that why he knew the man was in the club? Why he could feel him? Why did Sensara have to say that?

And then, the realization struck him. "He would have burned Sensara."

"Probably. It seems you really *did* save her life. I, on the other hand—"

"How could you know? How could either of us know?"

Michael downed another glass of wine and ran his finger around the rim of the glass. "So, if this madman burns witches, and you're a witch, why didn't he burn you?"

"He did burn me, amigo. He's burning me still."

Even if everyone in the crowd hadn't been in costume, Estrada wouldn't have been able to identify the killer—at least by sight. Blinded by stage lights, he could discern nothing but shadows and scattered fluorescence under the black lights. Still, he was sure the man was there, so sure he'd tweaked the act, hoping to flush him out with a little of his own fire fetish.

When the curtains opened, a guillotine stood centerstage—a replica Sixteenth Century Scottish Maiden. Built of wood, the blade was greased to gleam in the spotlight. Michael appeared, his effulgent bones dazzling in the darkened room. Like their medieval ancestors, people shouted, lusting for blood. "Bring out the prisoner! Bring out the prisoner!"

Estrada was escorted onstage by two barefoot women in white unlaced corsets and gauzy skirts. His hands were tied behind his back. Resplendent in a black tux with tails, the women fawned over him. Forcing him to his knees, Michael sent the crowd into hysterics with his sexual antics. Then he locked the magician's head in the wooden circlet with his dark hair hanging in one long braid down the side of his face. Brandishing a knife, he cut the rope that bound his hands and bolted him in the stocks.

Estrada stared up at the skeletal face. "Mercy, brother. I am innocent."

One of the women screamed hysterically, while the other set a white willow basket on the floor beneath his head. Pausing theatrically, Michael brought the crowd to silence. Then, in a flourish of metallic scrapes and human screams, he released the blade.

Cleanly severed, Estrada's head fell into the basket. Plucking the bloody head up by the braid, Michael swung it while the crowd yelled feverishly. Then the lights cut to black. All that could be seen for a moment was Michael's bones shimmering in the darkness as he swung the severed head. And then— Total darkness. Murmurs in the crowd, a few unrehearsed screams, and the spotlight hit centerstage.

Estrada stood in front of the guillotine. Clasping his bloody neck, he feigned reattaching his head to his body. Michael, who had removed his skull mask and donned his vampire cape, watched hungrily. Head successfully reattached, Estrada raised his arms in triumph and as the crowd cheered, he danced in the applause.

Then Michael attacked from behind. Grasping Estrada by the shoulders, he sank his fangs into the bloody neck. Women screamed. At first, the magician leaned back into the vampire's arms and rolled his eyes euphorically, and then he broke free.

Producing first one fireball, and then another, from the palms of his hands, he threatened the vampire. Michael backed off, and then attacked again. Estrada hurled the fire balls at his chest and his cape burst into flame. Falling to the floor, the vampire writhed in agony. Grasping fire in each hand, Estrada leapt from the stage, danced through the crowd, and right out the door.

Once outside, he waited alone in the alley. He'd felt the man's presence in that crowd and was sure he'd come.

Perched awkwardly on a stool at the University Café, Maggie fretted about the impression she'd make on Dr. Black. The meeting was finally happening. Several times her hand reached mechanically for her hair, only to find it gone. She'd pinned it up to appear older and more sophisticated for the professor and now had nothing to twirl.

She glanced again at her watch and noticed how dark it was at only 4:45 p.m. The time had fallen back that week and she was now "out of joint" as Macbeth would say. Sure, there was that extra hour of sleep, but she couldn't walk Remy down to the beach through the week unless she skipped her last class.

Her latté slipped and soaked one of the black silk gloves she'd worn to hide her scarred palms. "*Damn*," she whispered, ripped them off and stashed them in her bag.

She'd been waiting all week to meet Dr. Black—could barely focus at school. Now it was Saturday, and Samhain was just seven days away. Dylan had finally revealed, after much prodding, that Estrada and Sensara had been abducted by a lunatic. Both had recovered. He'd assured her that he'd spoken with Sensara. She could join them for this Sabbat, so today's meeting was just a formality. Still, she was trembling. What if Dr. Black didn't like her? Or something else happened?

She lifted her long black sleeve and glanced at the stinging tattoo on her left inner forearm just below the elbow. It hurt like hell, but she hadn't flinched. An exquisite Celtic war horse, it reared up on its hind legs and kicked out with its front. The body was solid black, the mane and tail, a rippling white and black ribbon of Celtic knots. It had amber eyes and nostrils that flared like an angry dragon.

Maggie had always loved horses, except for that brief time when she'd blamed the horse for her father's fall. All summer, they whinnied through her open window and sometimes she could even hear the heavy sighs and soft nickering that proclaimed their innocence. By winter, she'd exonerated them. Shannon had not loved horses. She hated them and refused to allow Maggie to ride, even though her friend's parents owned the stable next door and it would be free. Shannon blamed the horse almost as much as she blamed her daughter for John's current state.

"Maggie? I almost didn't recognize you."

Startled, she pulled down her sleeve at the sound of Dylan's voice. "Oh, you like?"

His nervous smile was enough to show his distaste. As they settled in, he leaned over. "I told you, no advertising."

"It's just a style," she said, feeling suddenly self-conscious. The two of them looked deceptively normal.

"Dr. Black. I'm very pleased to meet you." Feeling as if she were meeting royalty, she fought the impulse to curtsey.

"I'm pleased to meet you too, Maggie. Dylan tells me that you've been reading and are ready for some experiential learning."

"Yes, it's all I've been able to think about." She spoke quietly, aware of others nearby and the need for discretion among witches.

"Sensara has given me permission to formally invite you to Samhain."

Maggie's heart flipped as she vigorously nodded her assent.

"I want to talk to you about our plans so you're not shocked or uncomfortable by what occurs." After asking the server to bring a pot of tea, she continued. "Before each ceremony we meet and prepare. Now, as Dylan has told you, this is a dangerous time, so we'll be doing everything we can to raise power."

"Sounds intense."

She smiled. "Indeed. The forecast is clear, the moon will be full, and we'll be gathering in the woods where we met before. It's quite near your home, I understand."

"Yes."

"Dylan tells me that you know the Buntzen Lake area quite well."

Maggie nodded. "I've been playing there all my life."

"Sensara wondered if you know of a private place where three paths converge."

Maggie thought a minute. "There's a place near the creek where the paths meet from three directions, yes."

"Ah, near water. Even better," Dr. Black said.

"Good," Dylan said. He was no poker player and Maggie could see his discomfort. Still, she didn't care. He had no right to tell her how to dress.

"We often wear robes but this ceremony we'll be skyclad."

"Naked."

"Yes, it will enable us to experience nature in a very personal way and heighten the intensity. Are you comfortable with that?"

"Of course."

Maggie glanced at Dylan and saw the blood spring to his pale cheeks. She turned to him and shook her head. "You're so transparent."

"Right then," the professor said. "Can you lead us to this place from the car park? We're meeting around seven."

Imagine. They're asking me to help them.

"They lock the gates at eight, so perhaps you should park along my lane. We could meet just inside the forest. That way no one will see you. I can lead you through the trails from there even in the dark."

"Perfect. Dylan will tell you what to bring." Standing abruptly, she offered her hand. "It was lovely to meet you, Maggie."

She replied to Dr. Black's formality with her own, but inside she was bursting.

Naked under the full moon with witches on Halloween!

When Estrada slipped Sensara's cape from her shoulders, her naked body shimmered like polished ivory in the moonlight. In any other venue, her sheer splendor would have slain him, but there in the silvery forest, he felt only awe. This was where the sacred lay waste to the profane and true rapture prevailed.

The six of them stood around her like stark sentinels and watched as she tiptoed into the glacial stream. When she laid down amidst the smooth rocks, the frigid current washed over her body and her dark hair streamed about her face. As moonlight brushed her breasts, he imagined Anuket, goddess of the upper Nile, bathing beneath the waterfall.

Tonight, Sensara would draw down the moon and, with it, the goddess Hecate, who would use her as a channel to impart knowledge to the coven.

Maggie stood beside Dylan, wrapped in an emerald-green cape that made her eyes seem like oceans. Elated that Sensara had given her permission to attend, she'd found the perfect place and led them through the trails. Estrada was pleased for Dylan, glad that he'd found a girl who seemed to be a kindred spirit. For this reason, he'd championed her cause and persuaded Sensara to allow her to join them. He just hoped his friend wouldn't get hurt. Maggie was young, and young eager girls could set a guy spinning like nothing else.

Still, she'd provided this rare place where three paths converged in a Y that symbolized the liminal border between worlds. Hecate was the guardian of boundaries. Wild lands, graveyards, and crossroads—places where the unholy were buried—were sacred to her and Samhain was her night.

In ancient times, it was said that people left sacrifices on crossroads for Hecate to consume. So tonight, the witches of Hollystone would leave an offering. In some legends, she wore a saffron cloak and one golden sandal. She was the blood-drinking Queen of the Underworld, and as the veils lowered and spirits passed between the worlds, they would appeal to her for help.

The coven had already cast a large circle that encompassed the crossroads, the stream, and a section of sand large enough for the bonfire that crackled and hissed in the darkling solitude of the pines. Earth, fire, water, and air conjoined within its borders. Each point in the six-pointed star they would form with their bodies had been marked with colored candles set in glass jars. Together, they formed the Seal of Solomon, a mystical symbol with bisecting triangles that portrayed the harmony of the four elements—fire as the upward triangle, water as the downward, and air and earth in the center at the bases. Mystics and wizards of old believed that to meditate upon the seal was to bring the power of transformation to the beholder.

As Sensara rose, Estrada grasped her hand and helped her from the stream to the altar. Sylvia then slipped off her robe and entered. Each of them would purify their body, mind, and spirit in the rushing water, and then stand skyclad throughout the ritual. To withstand the cold showed control over their bodies and spirits—to mark the Sabbat naked showed their commitment to freedom and the natural ways. Daphne went next, and then Jeremy.

As Dylan stood and walked to his point on the seal, Maggie slipped off her robe and entered the stream. The first painful sensation that flashed through her body was followed by numbness. She feared her body would betray her with shivering and chattering teeth, but when she concentrated on a place deep within, she could immerse her body in the icy stream as calmly as if it were a tepid bath. Proud of her young athletic body, she emerged from the water feeling like Nefertiti—eyes lined in kohl, black hair wet and dripping down her back like kelp.

Estrada was last to slip into the stream. Observing his curves and shadows, Maggie understood why the Greeks had sculpted their warriors naked, emphasizing the musculature, the genitals, and the exquisitely formed physique. He was a god. She shuddered at the sheer beauty of him. To love a man like that and have him love you back, surely that was the ultimate dream come true. Although she knew this was to be a spiritual experience, she couldn't help but imagine making love to him—would give anything to have him be her first.

Entranced, she watched the crystal water swirl around his body and then gasped as he emerged, a sleek and sinewy black wolf, whose long straight legs moved with grace. Even his face had changed—nose elongated, large almond eyes glistening like obsidian. His countenance seemed edged in gold, while his sleek black hair slicked back from the smoky hollows of his cheeks.

Scanning the circle to see if anyone else had noticed his transformation, Maggie saw love emanating from Sensara, saw him absorb and return the love as glittering bonds like sunbeams connected the two of them.

Envy erupted, and she fought to suppress it, but couldn't take her eyes off the sleek black wolf that was Estrada. She'd read about shamans who could shapeshift into animals. Was he one of them?

She thought of the Animalia Tarot cards Damien brought to school to impress her. Everyone was allied to a particular animal, reflected the animal's qualities and could use its adaptations for personal power. Sensara's slanted hypnotic eyes and lithe body reminded Maggie of a cobra, especially the way she moved, and Daphne was like a grizzly bear, solid and comforting, with her dark skin and thick spiky mahogany hair.

Closing her eyes, Maggie heard the distant thunder of hooves beating the earth, then felt the presence of something ancient and powerful akin to her own soul—the horse. Glancing down at the image of the Celtic war horse on her arm, she broke out in a shiver of goose bumps. All her life, she'd drawn horses to her. Was it because the horse was her ally, her power animal?

Marking this as the moment when she understood this was no game, her breath caught. These were not just empty rituals like Father Grace performed when he poured the wine and doled it out in shots; reciting in Latin that this was the blood of Christ—*In nomine Patris et Filii et Spiritus Sancti*—as if the empty syllables of a dead language could have any real power.

People had the power to truly transform reality, could bend and shape energy with their minds. People made the magic, and that was why religious zealots had hunted witches and murdered them, and perhaps, why this crazy man pursued them even now.

Estrada came then, his back tattooed in black angel's wings, and stood before Sensara. Daphne reminded them all to ground as Sensara was doing. Maggie breathed deeply, relieved that she had read about visualization and practiced. Closing her eyes, she shot roots from the soles of her feet through the forest floor and deep into the earth. Cosmic energy swirled from the stars through the crown of her head, down through her chakras, arms, legs, and feet, and finally into the earth. If a hurricane struck at that moment, she felt she could survive, as solid and rooted as an ancient oak.

Estrada picked up a basket from the altar, then came around to each of them and offered their bolines. These were the small white-handled knives they used to carve symbols in candles, or cut herbs or fruit, whatever was needed for the ritual. This night each person had cleansed and disinfected their tools and they would use them for a special purpose. Sensara had brought one as a gift for Maggie because she didn't have one of her own and had found them this place.

On his second round, Estrada brought a clay chalice which contained a few drops of liquid honey. One by one, each person used their boline to cut the flesh of one palm, then squeezed a few drops of blood into the chalice.

Maggie chose a new place in her palm—a place she'd never cut before. She didn't want to mix the scars of her past with the thrill of the present. After this night her life would never be the same.

When each had added their blood sacrifice, Estrada knelt in front of Sensara, dug a small pit and placed the chalice inside. This was their offering to Hecate.

On their way through the forest trails that night, Dr. Black had lectured her about Hecate. It was important, she said, to understand the symbology, not just perform the rituals. Fascinated by the professor, Maggie vowed to learn everything she could about mythology.

Favored by Zeus, Hecate was given dominion over Heaven, Earth, and the Underworld, along with the ability to grant wishes to humans. Those who died unnatural deaths clung to her. Canines could see these unsettled spirits and howled as she passed in the night with her disembodied entourage. It was said, she could be summoned at a crossroads because that was the place those who died unnatural deaths were often buried unsanctified by the Church. Hecate's compassion for humans who suffered injustice extended to revenge. Known by many epithets, Queen of the Night, Goddess of the Underworld, or Goddess of the Witches, she was often summoned with offerings of cakes, blood, or meat.

Dylan told her that the coven often mixed elements of several ancient tales to create specific rituals. The gift of honeyed blood offered this night came from a Greek epic called *The Argonautica*. In the story, Hecate's priestess, Medea, tells her lover Jason to placate the Goddess with an offering of honey and sheep's blood while she bathes in a stream of flowing water at midnight.

Although the stories were ancient and the elements timeless, the crossroads, blood, and honey were all very real, and Maggie's immersion in the stream brought her into immediate focus with the present. This was the magic.

Estrada picked up his wand from the altar and touched the middle of Sensara's forehead where the third eye for spiritual seeing was said to be. As he began the chant of invocation, the others echoed each line in an array of tones that merged into one resonating thought—to draw down the ancient goddess through their high priestess.

> *"Great Goddess Hecate,*
> *Who guards all boundaries and secret sites*
> *We conjure you this hallowed night.*
> *Grace us with your presence here*
> *In this wild place where the elements collide.*
> *Share with us your profound knowledge*
> *For we are much in need.*
> *Great Goddess Hecate,*
> *Descend into the body of this thy priestess*
> *Who offers her eyes, her lips, and all her cells and senses*
> *In the name of truth and goodness."*

As he spoke, Estrada used his wand to draw a pentagram across Sensara's body. Maggie watched the traces of light that burst from the quartz crystal, seeing clearly the five-pointed star. Raising her arms to the moon, Sensara shuddered and her shimmering aura expanded in the firelight. Stardust swirled about her head and shoulders.

"What is your desire?" Her voice emerged as thick as the bloodied honey buried in the dirt.

"Knowledge." Estrada paused. "Remedy."

"A panacea? Tell me what ails you."

"A man seeks to harm us."

"You invoked the man, as you invoked me."

"Yes. But can we stop him? Catch him?" The passion burst from him like tears. "Can we undo what we have done?"

"The charm is astir. As momentum builds, ripples multiply."

"Please," he pleaded.

She shook her head. *"I cannot halt what has begun. But know this:*

> *As one of you has spun the charm,*
> *Now none of you are safe from harm.*
> *One who all felt they could trust,*
> *Breeds deception cloaked in lust.*
> *One will gain their heart's desire,*
> *While yet another pays with fire.*
> *Before the dark of winter night,*
> *Four souls pass over into light.*
> *Once begun it cannot end,*
> *But circles round as circles bend."*

In the silence that followed, Maggie felt as if she'd been struck by lightning. Every molecule in every cell was fully charged, the energy spiraling through her body. Had she touched tinder in that moment, it would have ignited.

Sensara's arms dropped as her knees buckled. Estrada caught her as she plunged her hands into the earth.

Maggie glanced around the circle at the others, noting the looks of bewilderment and confusion on their faces. She didn't know these people very well, but the portent was alarming. Suddenly Maggie realized that in the vibrating rush of adrenaline, she'd stopped breathing.

She watched Sensara rise, naked, dripping, and intensely majestic, even as she stood before the fire shivering. Estrada wrapped her in a blanket. He then thanked Hecate and closed the circle. As he blew out the last candle, Maggie realized that nothing in her life had prepared her for the thrill that descended on her body like the sticky feet of a hundred-thousand spiders.

Night's Black Agents

Maggie could scarcely contain herself as she and Dylan trudged back through the trails. While everyone else was solemnly mortified by Hecate's prophecy, she was euphoric.

"That was the coolest thing I've ever seen," she said, when they were finally alone.

"Cool?" Dylan caught her shoulder and spun her around. "Did you not hear what she said?"

"I heard. But, come on, Dylan. Wasn't that the most fantastic thing you've ever seen in your life?" Maggie danced on her toes. "Or, maybe you're used to seeing a god or spirit or whatever that was talk through a human."

"Maggie, this is no role-playing game."

Sniggering, she rolled her eyes, then clapped her hand over her mouth in a fake gasp. Though almost twenty, Dylan acted like he was forty. He needed to loosen up.

"I knew you weren't ready. That's why I didn't want you to come until you'd had the proper training. Perhaps, matured."

She laughed outright then, unable to suppress her glee.

"It's not funny!" Dylan shouted with frustration. "I saw the way you looked at him. It was bloody embarrassing."

"Who? Estrada? Oh, come on Dylan. The man is a god. Who wouldn't want to have sex with him?"

"You want to have sex with him? Christ! All this time I thought you were innocent, but you're as sluttish as—"

She slapped his mouth shut, so hard her palm stung. "No one calls me a slut."

Dylan touched his face, streaked red by her fingers. "He's my mate. I thought . . . Ach, forget it." He turned to leave, then stopped and glanced back. "Did you not hear the part about paying with fire? And people dying? Do you think magic comes cheap?"

"Don't patronize me." Maggie stamped her foot.

"Like a child throwing a tantrum."

"Listen, if all you're going to do is ridicule me, you might as well leave with them." Sticking out her chin in defiance, she pointed down the street where the cars were pulling away.

"Right," he said, and stormed after them.

"No. Wait!" she cried, with outstretched arms. "Dylan! Please. I don't want you to leave. Just please don't judge me. I have enough people judging me." Her mother was at the top of that list.

He turned slowly and scratched his head, then stood and stared as if waiting for an explanation.

Sucking back the urge to scream, Maggie realized that she needed to act penitent even if she didn't feel penitent. Anything was better than being left alone with all of these feelings. "Don't you see?" she said, finally with feigned innocence. "I'm just blown away."

"I see. I just want *you* to see." He followed her up the front porch steps and leaned against the cedar column with his arms crossed over his chest. Muscles taut, a tiny nerve twitched in his strong square jaw. Dylan was handsome. Not a boy like Damien, but a man with the quiet strength of a mountain. If only he could learn to bend. But then rocks don't bend. They chip and break and wear away and mostly last forever.

They stood awkwardly, watching the taillights disappear around the corner. When, at last, he raised his eyes to hers, they were glassy. Was he crying? Had she made him cry?

"Look. I'm not supposed to talk about Jade, but you need to hear this. Maybe then you'll appreciate the peril—"

"Peril?"

"For Christ's sake, Maggie, this is no reality show. The bastard burns women—"

"Good evening," said Father Grace, his surreptitious approach unnerving. "Out trick or treating? A little old for that, aren't you?"

"What are *you* doing here?" Maggie asked, the memory of Bastian's bloody face still fresh in her mind. She'd eluded him the past three weeks. But now he'd cornered her by foisting himself into the middle of something that was none of his business. Dylan had just said something—something about burning women, and she wanted him to explain.

"We need to talk," Father Grace said. "I know you're angry and you've been avoiding me."

"Avoiding the priest?" Dylan whispered. "How could you, Maggie?"

"It was easy, believe me." The priest had snuffed out her magical evening like a candle.

"Have we met?" he said, turning to Dylan.

Holding tightly to his crossed arms, Dylan shook his head once. "Uh, no."

"Perhaps you should introduce me to your friend," the priest said.

Lips tight, Maggie refused to speak.

"Come on, Maggie. You can't stay mad at me forever. People have disagreements—sometimes they even lose it and slap each other."

Following his gaze, she eyed the fading imprints of her fingers on Dylan's cheek. She shrugged and rolled her eyes. "This is Father Grace. He's the priest at my parents' church."

The man was either observant or he'd been spying on them. She hoped it was not the latter, but she couldn't be sure. She tried to replay their conversation in her head, knowing how far voices carried on a still night in the country. Now that she thought about it, she was almost certain he hadn't come out of the house but had simply appeared from the shadows. Had he been there all along? Hiding? Watching and listening?

"The collar gives it away," Dylan quipped.

"And you are?"

"Dylan McBride," he said, and reluctantly shook the outstretched hand. The tall, muscular priest was a good head taller, and as he pumped Dylan's arm, the veins in his neck stood out.

"McBride. That means, follower of St. Bride. I wrote a paper once on Bride, or Brigit, which is her other name. She's the patron saint of Ireland."

"Aye, she is. St. Brigit founded thirty convents in Ireland. Her flame burned in Kildare until her nuns were raped and driven out in the Twelfth century." Dylan cleared his throat and spit sideways into the shrubs. "I've written papers too."

Sensing the same adversarial energy, she'd seen the priest invoke in Bastian, goose bumps erupted along Maggie's arms. She knew he could get physical and dreaded an altercation Dylan had no chance of winning. Her sudden shiver did not go unnoticed.

"Out with wet hair on a cold night like this, Maggie?" Father Grace asked, turning his attention to her. "You'll catch your death."

"Oh," she stammered, touching her neck where the damp ends lay. He'd not seen her black hair before, her pale face, or wine dark lips. What must he be thinking? "There were some kids hiding with a hose down in the trailer park. The little brats sprayed us."

"Halloween pranks." With a slight cough he cleared his throat. "It amazes me that in the midst of the fall rains, God should provide such a clear sky on Halloween night. Even a full moon. It's almost spooky. Of course, really it's the Eve of All Saint's Day."

Dylan remained stoic, rooted to the floor.

"Did you need something else, Father?"

"Just to invite you in. Your dad and I are drinking tea by the fire. Why don't you and Dylan join us? It's warm. You can dry your hair."

"Maybe later."

"Of course. I interrupted your conversation. Please, do forgive me, Maggie, for this and the other. If you give me a chance, I'll explain. I don't want bad blood between us."

His apology brought her old guilt springing to the surface. "Sure, Father."

Once he'd closed the door, Dylan turned on Maggie. "I don't really feel like having tea with your dad, who hates me, and the bloody priest, who seems to have more than a fatherly interest in you."

"Relax. He's just fishing. I don't think he heard anything and right now my family needs him."

"The man gives me the willies."

"You're probably still creeped out because of the *prophecy*," she said in a spooky tone, hoping to lighten his mood.

"You shouldn't mock it, Maggie. No good will come of it. You heard what she said. Someone's betrayed us."

"You think it's me." She hadn't thought of it before, but it suddenly made sense. That was why Dylan was acting so strangely.

"I didn't say that."

"But you considered it. You must have. Of the seven people in that circle tonight, I'm the one you know the least. I'm the one who appeared just when all this crap started to happen."

"Crap?" he said mystified. "It's not crap. And you're wrong. I don't think that at all. I just want you to understand the gravity of the situation."

"I get it. But, Dylan, it's just so exciting!"

"Exciting? Deception, fighting, witches getting abducted and burned. You find that exciting? Ach, I have to go."

As he turned to leave, Maggie caught his shoulder and stared into his eyes. "It *is* exciting, Dylan." She brushed her lips against his and felt an immediate response against her belly. "You feel it too. I know you do." Kissing him, soft and slow, her tongue teased the edge of his lips. "I've wanted to do that all night. Estrada wasn't the only naked man in the forest."

Dylan's eyelids fluttered and he opened his mouth to speak, but she covered it with her own, parting her lips to lure his inquisitive tongue. Wrapping her arms around his back, she drew him in.

"I worry for you," he whispered, touching his forehead to hers.

Sweet and protective, Dylan was more of a man than any of the boys at school and she could feel how much he wanted her. Their lips touched again and as the kisses grew, moist and swirling as the stream, she danced him slowly backwards, moving her hips rhythmically against his, carrying him along, until he stood braced against the porch wall. She moaned softly as his fingers slid down her neck, and then louder as his thumb caught the edge of her rigid nipple.

"Christ, Maggie." Quivering, he bent his head to kiss her neck.

"I want you," she said, kissing the edge of his ear. "Let's go back into the woods. I want you, Dylan. I want you inside me."

His ragged breath warmed her ear. "But Maggie—"

"I suppose that's why they call it necking," Father Grace said.

Dylan pushed himself away as the blood rushed to his face, scorching his cheeks scarlet.

"Don't be embarrassed. They say the full moon has this effect on young people."

"You're young, Father. Does it ever affect you?" Maggie said sarcastically. His sudden rude intrusion had spoiled everything. He had no right to interfere.

"Perhaps it's time you said goodnight to Dylan."

"No. This is *my* house and you're not my father."

"Later." Dylan stumbled down the front steps, a string of incomprehensible Gaelic curses tumbling from his swollen mouth.

"Dylan, wait," she whined, as she watched him walk away.

"Let him go, Maggie. He'll get over it once the blood recedes. Boys always do. And we need to talk."

She rolled her eyes and sneered. The priest was determined to spoil her evening.

"I owe you an apology, two in fact. The first for this. I *am* sorry for interrupting at such an inopportune moment, but one day you'll thank me for it."

"Yeah I know. I'm supposed to save myself until I'm married."

"Not necessarily. But you should save yourself for a man you love, who also loves you. Not just give it up to some horny boy because you're feeling juicy."

"Father!"

"Well? Is it love or lust? Can you look me in the eye and tell me you'd marry Dylan McBride, bear his children, and love him forever?"

Maggie sighed. She couldn't imagine loving anyone forever.

"I thought not. Now Maggie, we've let this fester too long. I really want to explain what happened the last time I saw you."

"With Bastian?"

"Yes, with Bastian." For several seconds they stared at each other and she stood, hands on hips, waiting. "What you witnessed was unconscionable. There's no rational excuse for my behavior, and I know what you must think of me. But Bastian and I have history."

"What kind of history?"

"A rather complex history, and I'm sure our perceptions of it differ greatly. But that doesn't matter now." He was fidgeting—nervous in a way she'd never seen before. "Maggie, what I'm trying to say is—"

"Yes?"

"This collar doesn't make me immune to feelings. Underneath, I'm still a man, and I feel what any man feels."

"You're not supposed to."

"I know. But I'm confessing to you, and only to you, that I do." She watched his cheek pulse and wondered where this was going.

"Father, I—"

"Please Maggie. Let me say this. Because I'm forbidden to express myself like a man, sometimes it comes out in other ways—ways it shouldn't—especially when it involves a pretty girl. One that I care about. One that I've fallen in love with."

"What?"

"Seeing Dylan touch you like that . . ."

"Father?"

"Please don't call me that. Not now." He made a wide gesture with his arms as if to encompass the moon. "You're in my head, Maggie. I can't stop thinking about you." With one finger, he gently stroked her damp hair. "And this . . . This is so exotic. You've beguiled me, Maggie. I can't blame him for wanting to touch you like that. I want to touch you myself."

"But you're a priest." Was he really in love with her? Flattered, she cocked her head and exposed her neck. He was a sexy man and to hear him disclose a desire for something she too fantasized was alluring. His green eyes, shimmering and flecked with gold, were mesmerizing. Still feeling tricksy from the ritual, the excitement she'd felt earlier rippled through her belly.

"I know. I took vows, and I meant them. And I try to live by them, but—" His voice, low and thick with emotion, seemed to catch in his throat. "I am also a man." Taking her hand, he lowered it until her palm touched the length of his hard cock through his jeans. "Do you feel what you do to me?"

It was huge, and she stood stunned, knowing she should pull away or slap him, do something to stop this, but she couldn't move.

Taking her paralysis as a sign of consent, he drifted closer, so close she could smell the scent of smoke on his skin. "You witch. How can I resist you when you look like this and smell like this?" He inhaled deeply, his nose nuzzling her hair, and then moving closer still, he backed her up against the wall and wedged her there. "You've put a spell on me. Bewitched me with your charms, just like you did that boy."

"No," she said, pushing against him with both hands. Jerked suddenly to action by his intimate knowledge. Was he guessing, or did he know about her candle spell? About the coven? Had he read her diary? Searched her room? It would be easy enough to do when he was alone here with her father. "Stop it."

"You lit the fire, Maggie. Feel the heat." Grasping her from behind with both hands, he thrust hard against her pelvis.

"Stop it! You're hurting me." She squirmed and shoved but couldn't break free.

"It only hurts for a moment and then it's bliss. Just like you dreamed about with your magician. You want him inside you. And you want Dylan inside you. And you want me."

She shook her head pathetically. "No."

"Yes, you do. I know you do. I can smell it on you." Her struggling only aroused him more. Pinning her against the wall, he forced his knee between her legs, set his mouth on hers, and shoved in his tongue. She choked and thrust her head back, could feel his hand beneath her dress pushing aside her panties, his fingers searching, finding.

A sudden movement above his head caught her eye and she glanced up. A chair hovered in the air—then came crashing down on his head. The priest crumpled at her feet and she stood looking into the angry eyes of her father.

"Dad?" She gasped and covered her mouth with her hands.

"He's a bad priest."

"Oh God. You saved me." She looked at Grace groaning at her feet. "What about him? What should we do with him?"

But the full moon had caught her father's attention and he was no longer listening. "I can see the man, Mags. The man in the moon."

"You're the man, Dad. Come inside. I'll call Dylan. He'll know what to do. That's if he's still talking to me."

But he wasn't. At least, he wasn't answering his cell phone. She was on her own. She remembered the priest warning her about spending so much time alone in this house beside the forest. How ironic.

After locking all the doors and checking to see that his SUV was gone, Maggie went up to her room and changed into her gray sweats. He'd know better than to try that again. He probably went home to hide, fearing she might tell. She pulled her hood up over her head and slumped on the bed.

Father Grace had nearly raped her—would have, if her dad hadn't stopped him. And as much as she was all for a woman's right to tease a man and then refuse him, a critical voice nattered inside her head. *You flirted with him and you asked for it.* And, it was true. For a moment, she had wanted him. But not like that. He had no right to do *that*.

What was happening to her? A year ago, no one noticed her. Now Damien was all over her, and Dylan, and Father Grace, and they all wanted sex. Even Bastian got all embarrassed around her. Was it only her new style or had something else changed? Maggie had to admit, she was tired of playing the coy virgin. Perhaps what her girlfriends said was true—when a girl wants sex, she gives off a scent males find irresistible. Is that what he meant? Could he really smell it on her? *Yuk.*

Quick high-pitched yips filtered up the stairs. Remy was asleep and dreaming beside her dad's bed. Those two seemed to be the only males she could trust lately. He whined sharply, chasing something in his dream, something that was just out of reach. She knew how he felt. Something was bothering her too, something about the priest. Sure, it was creepy that he lost control and almost raped her, but she could almost understand it. Forbidden sex and all that. And, she hadn't pulled her hand away. She rubbed her scarred palm, could still feel how hard and thick it felt, like a tree branch—

Gagging, she ran for the toilet and puked. After rinsing her mouth and brushing her teeth again, she returned to her bed and pulled the quilt up around her shoulders. She wished Shannon was home. Even if she didn't believe her, she still had to tell someone. If she held it all inside, she'd go mad. Who could she call? None of her friends. It was almost two in the morning.

At last, Maggie picked up her diary from the bedside table and ran her hand over the leather cover. Had he read her private thoughts? Searched her room? Rifled through her drawers? Touched other things? Her clothing? Her underwear? The possibility he'd been there revolted her as much as his hands on her body. She picked up a pen and wrote:

October 31
After our Samhain ceremony, Gabriel Grace—I can't ever call him Father again—almost raped me on the front porch of our house. My dad hit him over the head with a chair and knocked him out. My own amazing dad rescued me. I think there's something really wrong with Grace. It was like he was waiting outside for me tonight and he knew things he shouldn't—like about me being a witch and the love spell I worked on Dylan. He even knew about my dreams. I think he's been spying on me, reading this diary, maybe even stalking me. I think he could be dangerous. And when I think back to how crazy he got when I asked him about witch burnings—I don't know, but I'm scared. It will never be the same between us. I mean, how could it be? If my dad hadn't hit him—

Suddenly exhausted, Maggie slipped her diary between the sheets and closed her eyes. She envisioned Estrada as she'd seen him earlier—an exotic wolfish creature shining in the moonlight, glimmering rivulets streaming down his sculpted body. It was crazy but imagining him always made her feel safe.

Distracted by a sound, her eyelids fluttered open. Hovering above her was a shadowy image. A man. A ninja mask concealed his face. Even his eyes—the one feature that might humanize him—were hidden behind dark glasses. She opened her mouth to scream, but only a slight gasp emerged before a sharp point pierced her upper arm.

"Play it again." Estrada leaned further forward on the couch, as if proximity might solve this crisis.

Dylan pushed the button on his cell phone and turned up the volume. They all focused on Estrada's face as he listened to the message for the third time in as many minutes.

Estrada felt the tiny muscles below his cheekbones tense. Taking a steaming mug of coffee from the tray Daphne was passing around, he set it on the table in front of him.

"Sorry. I couldn't find the cinnamon," she said.

Waving her off, Estrada pushed the button again himself. Maggie had made the call from a pay phone to Dylan's cell—it was obviously the only number she knew—and although it was *her* voice, she was clearly reciting a message from the killer that contained instructions for Estrada.

"This one's on you, magician. With all your power and all your skill, can you find her in time? You have forty-eight hours—ample time for a man with your talents. Come alone. No cops. No gangsters. No witches or wannabe vampires. Just you and me, the way it should be. What will you trade for her?"

Sylvia was the first to comment. "Religious fanatic?"

"Who else would kidnap a witch just before a Sabbat and then burn her?" Daphne said.

"It's that bloody priest. I know it is." Dylan was frantic.

"How does he know so much about you, Estrada?" Sensara asked. "And what does he mean, 'Just you and me, the way it should be?'"

Having missed the first two airings, she was now standing behind him. They'd gathered at his Commercial Drive flat after Dylan had called in a panic, wracked with guilt. He'd left Maggie alone with a demented priest, who, he was convinced, had kidnapped her.

Estrada turned, took Sensara's hand and kissed it, but ignored her question. "Why are you so sure it's this Father Grace?" he said to Dylan.

"Because he was there last night leering at her. He doesn't act like a priest, and I've known my share of them. The son-of-a-bitch is a fraud."

"Perhaps, but that doesn't make him a killer." Estrada thought of asking for a physical description but realized the only way *he* could identify the man was by *feel*. Even with raven eyes, he saw no discernible features. Really, everything he knew of the man he'd garnered from his imagination.

Dylan talked on, oblivious to his friend's remark. "He must have grabbed her after I left. There was no one there to stop him."

"What about her parents?" Sylvia said.

"Her mom works shifts and her dad isn't well."

"Do you think they know?"

"That she's missing? If they don't, they'll discover it soon enough."

"We need to talk to them." Sylvia patted him on the shoulder. "You mustn't blame yourself, Dylan."

"We really should go out there and see them," Daphne said.

"No, not yet. They'll call the police and I need time." Estrada's emphatic plea set off a chain reaction.

Tears appeared in Dylan's eyes. "I left her there. She called to me and I walked away and left her there with him. I was so damn mad I didn't pick up her call. *Christ!* I didn't even listen to the message until this morning. God knows what he did to her last night."

There was an audible silence as they all pondered his words.

"You're not going to do what he says, are you?" Sensara's eyes narrowed.

Estrada cocked his head, incredulous. "Of course I am. He's got Maggie."

"So, what *will* you trade for her?" she asked, her face a maze of suspicion. "What did you trade for *me*?"

"Tricks," he said, looking her straight in the eye. "The man likes tricks."

"The man likes *you*." Daphne spoke plainly.

Estrada's narrowing eyes cast a bitter glare. He was trying to defuse the situation, not inflame it.

"Well, come on. He's obviously after you, Estrada. Maggie's just bait."

"Why's he after you?" Sensara asked. "And why did he take *you* that night when he already had me? Was I just bait too?"

"Sara, please..."

There was no way he could tell her what happened in that cabin. Not now. Not ever. He'd kept it hidden far too long. She'd consider it dishonest and even if she forgave his impropriety, she'd never understand it. *You had sex with the man who'd just tied me in a straitjacket, kidnapped me, and then tossed me out in a parking lot? A man, who is likely a serial killer?*

He didn't understand it himself.

Daphne spread a map out on the kitchen table. "I think we should use the pendulum and try to scry his location. If we know where he is, we can come at him from two or three angles, maybe bind him somehow."

"Who do you think we are? The friggin' FBI?" Jeremy had been huddling quietly on a corner cushion and Estrada had forgotten he was there.

"On the contrary," Sylvia said. "That's a brilliant idea." Ignoring Jones' sullen stare, she joined Daphne at the table. "Sensara, your divining powers surpass any of ours. Why don't you give it a whirl?" Grinning at her own pun, she offered the pendulum.

Sensara sat and hunched over the map, her elbows firmly planted on the table. Holding the silver chain between her right thumb and index finger, she watched the faceted crystal sway. Then closing her eyes, she focused her energy while the rise and fall of her breath echoed like ocean waves in the small flat. "Spirits, I call on you to aid me in my work. Show me you are present with an affirmative answer."

The crystal began to move in circles, spinning like a horizontal disc, growing wider and faster with each rotation. When the gyrations seemed almost level with the underside of her wrist, she said, "Thank you. Now Spirits, show me a negative answer." In mid-swing the crystal veered off its circular cycle and swung straight back and forth across the map, slashing the air with a force so strong, it nearly flew from her grip. "Excellent. Thank you. Now

Spirits, there is a man holding an innocent girl prisoner. We need to find this girl and this man. Can you show us where they are?"

Sensara seemed to be the only one breathing as the others crowded in, waiting and watching. The pendulum, which had been moving rapidly in a straight line, slowly decelerated and came to a complete stop over the map. They waited as it continued to hang limp and still.

"What's it doing?" Dylan whispered.

"Nothing. It's not working." Sensara caught the crystal in her left hand and plunked it down on the map. "It's Estrada the man wants." She turned to him. "You try."

He looked anxiously at the pendulum as she stretched out on the rug. He did not want to pick it up. Not now.

"I'll see if I can discover anything else." Breathing deeply, she cupped both palms over her eyes.

What would she discover in her meditation? Sensara needed no crystal ball. She worked with guides who whispered in her ear and envisioned images no one else could see. Some things she just knew, as if her mind was open to the secrets of the cosmos. When she was clear, anything was possible. Just last year, she'd found a missing child and returned him to his grateful parents. Unfortunately, the waters were muddy when it came to him and that skewed things considerably— something he was counting on. With the taste of the killer still fresh on his lips, his shame welled up, silencing him. He couldn't bear her to see—especially now in front of them all—what he'd kept secret these past few weeks.

Finally, crossing her hands over her heart, she gazed up at them with tears in her eyes.

"What is it? What did you see?" asked Daphne.

"A dark-haired woman lying face up on a bed . . . and then a puff of smoke, a flame, and the whole bed blazing."

Estrada stood and held his breath.

"Oh Lord!" Daphne covered her face with her hands.

"She doesn't know it, doesn't feel it. She's not conscious when—"

"Maggie? Is it Maggie?" Dylan's horrified whisper turned Estrada's stomach.

"No. I don't know this woman." Sensara rose from the floor.

"Bloody hypodermics." Reaching out, Estrada clasped her hand. Convinced she'd seen nothing of his liaison with the killer, he relaxed and pulled them both down on the couch. Wrapping his arm around her shoulder, he watched her eyes close. He, too, was exhausted and wished all of this would end.

"We've *got* to find her. Estrada, will you please try the pendulum?" Dylan asked, wide-eyed.

How could he say no? He moved to the table, sat and held the pendulum in his fingers, then dangled it over the map. The man seemed drawn to the Fraser Valley, so he started in Vancouver and followed the route they'd driven that night in the van. It was also the area where the police had discovered Jade's remains. At Hope, the crystal swung in swift wide circles. He moved it slowly around, hoping the crystal would drop in some particular spot, but it just continued swirling.

Estrada stood. "He's here somewhere. I'm going to go find him."

"I'm coming with you," Dylan said.

"No, not you. It's not that I don't think you're capable. You're just too close to this. I need someone disconnected. I need Michael."

"He said no wannabe vampires," Jones said.

"You haven't heard? Michael's no wannabe anymore. If I were you, Jones, I wouldn't go out at night."

"Wait." Sensara opened her eyes and looked around the room. "I saw something just now. An image. Clasped hands. Someone here knows this man, has been close enough to touch him."

Estrada held his breath.

"Was one of them manicured?" Jones asked in a low voice.

They all stared.

"Why?" asked Sensara.

Jones shook his head. "I met this guy a few weeks ago."

"Where?"

"Online. We chatted—"

"Wait—was it wiccacharm.com?" Estrada asked.

Jones nodded.

"*Christ!* Jade's ex is the webmaster for that site. We figure that's how he knew she was at Pegasus that night."

"Jade?" Jones said.

"The last woman to disappear."

"Finish your story, Jeremy," Sensara said, "and don't leave anything out."

Jones shrugged. "We met for a few drinks."

"What does he look like?" Estrada asked. Finally, an eyewitness.

"Gorgeous. Tall and built like a—"

"Hair? Eyes?" Sensara rolled her eyes.

"Oh. Dark brown eyes. I didn't see his hair. He was wearing a tweed cap."

Estrada rose and paced around the small room. "So, what did you tell this guy? Did you talk about us? About the coven?"

"Look. I'm sorry. He was interested and asked about joining. I may have mentioned Maggie—"

"*Maggie?*" Incredulous, Dylan too was on his feet.

"I just said that she wanted to join and that you and Estrada were all for it."

"So, you mentioned me too," Dylan said.

"I don't see how anything I said—"

"Really?" It was Sylvia's turn. Incensed, she began a condemnation of Jones. "Do you really not see a connection, Jeremy? You talk about us to a stranger. You mention Maggie and Dylan and Estrada, and suddenly Maggie's missing, and Dylan gets a message on his cell phone that Estrada is to come and ransom her. How do you not see a connection?"

"One who all felt they could trust—" Daphne whispered.

"Breeds deception cloaked in lust," Sylvia said.

Jones stood speechless in the center of them all.

"Are you going to see him again?" asked Sensara.

Jeremy shook his head.

"And you didn't think to mention this before?" asked Estrada.

Jeremy looked suddenly shrunken.

"What's our first rule, Jeremy?" Sensara's composure sent shivers up Estrada's spine.

"What happens in the coven stays in the coven."

"That's correct. Did you share coven business with a stranger?"

"Why is it always me? *Christ,* the guy probably hangs out at Pegasus. For all we know, Estrada and the E-vamp had sex with him at one of their orgies."

"*Motherfucker.*" Estrada's fist connected with Jones' face and sent him crashing into the wall.

"Jesus. You broke my nose, you friggin' maniac."

Hoisting him by the shirt, Estrada raised his fist and punched his bloody face again. Jones' head flew back and hit the wall.

"Stop it," Sensara said.

Enraged, he glared at her.

"Let him go, Estrada. Now."

Growling, he shook Jones by the shirt, then released his grip and flung him down the wall.

Edging between them, Sensara pushed Estrada away with her rigid back. "Jeremy, I'm sorry that Estrada hit you like that. You obviously pushed a button. But you broke our rules and caused us harm. I have no alternative but to banish you from Hollystone Coven and forbid you to divulge anything about us to anyone ever again."

Estrada stood behind her rubbing his bruised fist. "I hope you got that Jones because next time she might not be around to save you."

All Causes Shall Give Way

The scarlet streaks rimming Dylan's swollen eyes skyrocketed Estrada's guilt to a whole new level. There was no denying he was responsible for the nightmare that continued to unfold.

"I just can't believe it," Dylan said. "We stood right here on this porch last night. Maggie kissed me. *Christ.* She wanted to . . ." He glanced away. "Tell me something Estrada, why does this lunatic think you can find him in less than forty-eight hours?"

"I don't know, Dylan, but I'll get her back. I promise." He glanced at Sensara, who huddled beside Sylvia, and thought back to that day in the woods when she'd had her first premonition. *I don't know what it is, or how to stop it, but unless we do, people are going to die.* He could not allow another innocent girl to be burned to death because of some psychopath's obsession with him. But, could he stop it? Could he find her in time? Hecate's prophesy haunted him. *Four souls pass over into light.* Jade was dead. If Maggie died too, he'd never forgive himself.

When the door opened, they were confronted by an equally anxious young man, whose cropped blond hair stood on end, as if he'd run his fingers through it a million times. The mottled shadow of a bruise marred his startlingly blue eyes. Like a tropical sea in sunlight, they were an intense turquoise, an unnatural shade Estrada had never seen before; and for a moment, he stood speechless, taking him in. Bleached baggy jeans and beaded moccasins. Though pale and lean, muscles rippled beneath his simple white T-shirt. Estrada's gaze traveled back to his eyes—unsettled eyes that surveyed him apprehensively.

"Good afternoon. I'm Dr. Sylvia Black. This is Dylan McBride, Sensara Narato, and Sandolino Estrada. We would like to have a word with Mr. and Mrs. Taylor if that's possible. It's regarding their daughter, Maggie."

The man nodded and shut the door, leaving them to wait in the drizzling November chill. Estrada drew the collar of his black raincoat up around his neck, hugged Sensara in close and kissed her lightly on the forehead. He'd spent most of last night convincing her of his love. They were both exhausted but, for the moment, she was pacified.

"I think they were real," she said.

"What?"

"I don't think he was wearing contacts."

Cocking his head, he eyed her curiously. "Sorry. I guess it's from growing up in Mexico. You've been to my flat. Anything turquoise catches my eye and kind of draws me in."

"Anything pretty and shiny you mean. You're such a raven." She said it jokingly, but he caught the muted edge of sarcasm and realized that she did not trust him and likely never would.

The door opened, and the young blue-eyed man beckoned them in, just as Mrs. Taylor came bouncing down the stairs. A small fair-skinned fireball of a woman, her auburn ponytail bounced behind her. From what Estrada had seen of Maggie, he assumed she resembled her father.

"Holy Mary, Mother of God." Wiping her damp eyes with her fist, she held up a book. "You're him."

"Him?" Both Dylan and Estrada asked the same question, but it was obvious from the way she peered at Estrada, that *he* was the man in question. Dylan, vaguely chagrined, hung his head for a moment, and then regained his composure.

"Him, yes. The man whose face she sketched in her diary. The man from her dream. Estrada, is it? Tell me. Do you know where my daughter is?" The hand that held the book trembled.

"I don't know what you mean, Mrs. Taylor, and I don't know exactly where Maggie is, but I'm going to do my best to find her."

"You and the police."

"Police?" repeated Dylan.

"I'm forgetting my manners. Come and sit." She ushered them into a cozy wood-paneled living room. The young man stood beside her like a sentinel. When at last they were settled, she launched into an anxious conversation.

"My daughter's missing. Why wouldn't I call the police?" She eyed them warily. "I know she was with you people last night at your ceremony. She's written about it. I also know she came back here afterward, and our priest tried to rape her on the front steps of our home." She gasped then and crossed herself. "Can you believe it? Our own priest tried to rape our daughter on the front steps of our home. My husband, bless his heart, saved her."

"That bastard!" Dylan's anger quickly morphed into guilt. "This is my fault. I didn't trust him, and I left her alone with him—"

"It's not your fault. Father Grace was our *priest*. Maggie trusted him. We all trusted him. Now, I fear he's taken her off somewhere to finish what he started."

They stood, momentarily stunned.

Sylvia was the first to speak. "We don't know that, but we do know that Maggie sounded sleepy, but fine, when she called Dylan's cell phone at three a.m. She left a message. Would you like to hear it?"

"I would." When Mrs. Taylor shuddered, she almost lost her balance. The young man grasped her arm and helped her to a chair, then vanished into the kitchen. "Thank you, Bastian," she murmured. Turning to Sylvia, she nodded her head. "Play it, please." As Dylan played the message, they all watched her brows furrow in confusion. "I don't understand. Magician? What does he mean?"

"He's playing a game. He wants me to find him," Estrada said. "I'm a magician, you see. I work at a club downtown, and I think this man frequents it. He seems to be captivated by magic." He didn't want to bring the image of burning witches into the conversation, if he could avoid it.

"He's captivated by Estrada to be more precise," Sensara said. He glanced at her quizzically. "She needs to know the truth." Turning back to Mrs. Taylor, she continued. "It's not a bad thing. It will probably help Estrada find him."

"Forty-eight hours," she said, looking at the kitchen clock. "Seven have passed already. The police need this."

"Give me a chance first," Estrada said. "If we bring the police in now, we'll lose control. I have a better chance of finding him than they do. Please, let me try."

Mrs. Taylor laid the open book on the table. "Maggie's in love with you."

After recovering from the bluntness of that statement, all eyes stared at the page where Maggie had sketched Estrada's face.

"She's not in love with me. It's magic that Maggie loves." He glanced at Dylan, who sat looking dejected in a corner of the room. "It happens sometimes, especially to young girls."

"That's true," Sylvia said. "Maggie was determined to come to our ceremony, not because of Estrada, but to experience her own power. You'd know her best, but she appears to be a strong and capable young woman. That will help her through this ordeal."

"You're the university professor, aren't you? The one she writes about."

"I suppose."

"Yet you're involved in this Wicca stuff?"

"Wicca is our religion. It's not all that different from Catholicism really. It's a reverent religion and certainly nothing to fear."

"I didn't fear Catholics until today," she said, and rubbed her eyes. "I still believe in God though, and if He sent you, then I'll have to trust you, won't I?"

"You *can* trust us, Mrs. Taylor."

"Call me Shannon."

The young man brought a steaming cup of tea and set it down on the table in front of her. "Thank you, Bastian. I don't know what I'd do without you." He nodded and slipped from the room.

"Do you mind if we borrow this?" asked Estrada, pointing to the diary. "There might be something useful—"

Nodding, she took a quick breath. "It's embarrassing. I didn't realize Maggie was growing up so fast."

He picked it up and flipped to the last page where she'd written about the priest. After reading it silently, he walked over and handed it to Dylan.

"This Gabriel Grace, what do you know about him?" he asked Shannon.

"Just that he's the priest at St. Mary's. He arrived less than a year ago. I don't know anything about his past. I just trusted him. Why wouldn't I?" She buried her head in her hands, and then exclaimed angrily, "It just makes me sick. He's here often helping my husband. John suffers from a traumatic head injury, you see, and Father Grace works with him. He said that he wanted to understand mental disorders so he could help people. He volunteers at Creekside."

"Creekside?"

"It's a local psychiatric facility."

"He works at a psych hospital? Where patients stay and they dispense drugs, that sort of thing?" Estrada thought of straitjackets. Hypodermics. Drugs.

She nodded. "Yes, of course."

He glanced at Sensara, unsure of how much to share.

"We've heard of a man that abducts women by injecting them with a sedative," she said. "If Grace works at a psych hospital, he could have access to—"

"Holy God! That's how he got her out without a sound. Remy here, knows him well and wouldn't bark." Hearing his name, the lab poked his head out from under the table. "The devil probably had a key cut. How many times have I left him alone in this house with my husband and daughter?" She drifted off, trying to come to terms with the magnitude of it all. "Ah, it makes me want to scream!"

"Whatever drug he's using—" Estrada stopped mid-sentence, caught by the abrupt revelation that if he'd gone to the hospital and been tested, he'd probably know what drug. He'd been slathered in the man's DNA. He stood and began to pace.

"He injected a police officer with the drug and the man recovered," Sensara said. Was she covering for him or just trying to put the woman at ease? "We'll do everything we can to find Maggie. I know it's impossible but try not to worry."

"You seem like good people," Mrs. Taylor said. "Do you really think you can manage this without police?"

"Yes," Estrada said. They had called it on, when they spun that charm and they would have to end it. But he sought his own absolution.

Sensara eyed him quizzically, then stepped close beside him. "You're hiding something from me," she whispered.

"We all hide things," Mrs. Taylor said. "Secrets. At first it seems a small thing, the right thing to do, but then, before you know it, it's grown into something unspeakable."

They looked to each other, each in their own bewildered worlds.

"I feel like I can trust you. I don't know why, but I do."

"Trust your feelings," Sensara said.

"If you find Maggie—*when* you find Maggie—unless you know for certain that Grace is dead. I mean, you see his pitiful body laid out on the ground. I wonder ... Could you take her someplace safe? I'll pay, of course. It's just that we don't have family here. I have to work, and I can't leave John. I don't know what else to do. Could you do that? Just until things get sorted?"

"Aye," Dylan said. It was the first word he'd spoken since they entered the house. "We'll find Maggie and get her someplace safe."

"You're a Scot."

"And you're Irish, if I'm not mistaken."

"Right so. Born and raised in the West counties." She shook her head forlornly. "But that was a long time ago."

"Does Maggie have family in Ireland?" asked Dylan.

"Another long story, too long for today."

"I think I know what Dylan's getting at," Sylvia said. "You want Maggie to be somewhere safe. Well, if she has family in Ireland ... I know it's far away, but I have a close friend in Galway who'd take excellent care of her until this man is apprehended."

Mrs. Taylor shrugged wistfully. "Ireland." She sipped her tea and stared dreamily at the teapot for a moment. "Do any of you believe in destiny?"

Dylan drifted to the window drawn by the muted clunk of car doors. "It's the police."

"*Damn*," Estrada said. "Please Mrs. Taylor. Tell them about the priest. Maybe they can find out more about him. But, don't mention us or the message. Give me a chance—"

"*Ah Jesus*. What if—"

"Please. They'll want to interrogate us, and it will waste valuable time. It's just after ten now. Give me until midnight? Twelve hours. If we've made no progress by then, you can tell them everything."

"Midnight it is, and Estrada, you better be as good as Maggie claims you are in her diary. I'm counting on you."

"Jesus, man. What happened to you?" Less than an hour later, Estrada stood in a hospital room, surveying the battered body of his best friend. He could literally feel his blood boil as it rushed to the surface, scorching his taut skin with swift pink streaks.

Michael was laid out in the bed. His right forearm was in a cast, his left hand bruised and swollen, but that was not the worst of it.

"Ambush," he mumbled through a swollen lip. The universe was stacking up against Estrada and his plan to catch this psychopath. Though Michael never claimed to be innocent—and for the record, neither did he—his friend did not deserve this.

A diagonal welt stretched across his face from the top of his left temple to the right side of his chin—the obvious signature of a blunt weapon. It had nearly taken out his eye. One brutal swing had found its mark before he could throw up his arms and shield his face from the ensuing blows. Another huge bruise rose on his forehead—it looked like he'd been kicked. This was no random act of violence. Whoever inflicted this intended to disfigure Michael. Whether because of jealousy or revenge, such cold-hearted violence was never impersonal.

"Who? Who did this to you?"

"Cole," he said.

"Clayton Cole? Jade's ex?" Estrada reflected on the obvious cause of Cole's anger. This assault could have been avoided had they connected with the man that day. It was a mistake on his part not to have tried again. Another mistake. "Did you see him, man?"

"If you want to know—" Clive, who'd been sitting quietly in the corner of the small room on a pale vinyl chair, spoke up suddenly, paused for a second to gauge Estrada's reaction, and then continued. "Michael was beaten unconscious. He doesn't remember what the man looked like. But just before it happened, a man called claiming to have information regarding the woman's murder."

"A man?" Estrada's gaze settled on the kid. A maze of thin narrow angles with an unusually long sharp beak, Clive reminded him of a sandpiper—a passably pretty shore bird that scavenged the beaches and tidal flats on long skinny legs. Daphne was always pointing them out when they hiked across the boardwalk at low tide. Deprived of his brother's designer looks, the kid was a disparate replica. Where Michael had high cheekbones and finely sculpted shadows, Clive looked simply starved. There was something unsettling about him that Estrada loathed—something that Michael had apparently found a way around, as was the nature of family. But he could not.

"Yes, I took the call myself."

"How convenient. What exactly did this man say?"

Clive shrugged off the snide. "Something like, tell the vampire, if he wants to meet Sarah Jamieson's killer, he should step out back."

"He called her Sarah Jamieson, not Jade?"

"He was her boyfriend."

"Did he *say* he was her boyfriend?" Clive glared at him. "So, no. Then what happened?"

"Michael went straight away. When he turned the corner into the alley, Cole was lying in wait with a crowbar."

"You didn't go with him?"

"He told me to stay in the club."

"And that was enough to stop you? What, brothers don't have each other's backs in England?"

"We're more inclined to respect each other's wishes."

Estrada ran his hand irritably through his hair and pulled at the tangles with his long fingers. "How do you know it was Cole? It could have been anyone."

"You mean . . . Did *I* lure my brother into an ambush?"

Estrada's narrow-eyed stare spoke volumes.

Clive shrugged. "Michael believes it was Cole. Ask him." He sniffed belligerently. "And I'll tell you this: I have no reason to hurt him."

"You'd better not be lying, little brother."

Estrada stared at Michael, who shrugged from his own personal hell. Lowering his voice, he pleaded with his friend. "Are you absolutely sure it was Cole? It was dark, you'd probably had several drinks, some tokes. You couldn't have seen much before he smashed you in the face." Michael squeezed his eyes shut. "You're not sure, are you?"

"You sound like the ruddy coppers."

Clive Stryker was an unnecessary obstacle in an already complex situation. He needed to disappear.

"When you accuse someone of assault and battery—which is clearly what this is—you better be fucking sure." Things could come back on people in myriad ways. He knew that from experience. With a loud sigh, Estrada settled on the edge of Michael's bed. "I suppose if the cops told Cole what happened to Jade. If she was *my* girlfriend—"

"He shinks itz me," Michael said through clenched teeth.

Estrada squeezed his shoulder. "I know you'd never hurt anyone and maybe he does too. Maybe he just needed somebody to vent on, you know? We all need that sometimes."

One corner of his upper lip curled as he flashed a quick glance at Clive, and then focusing on Michael, he sighed again, and touched the one perfect cheekbone with his finger. "You're a good man and you have an exquisite face. Even now, amigo, you're more beautiful than Dorian Gray ever was. And I promise you, I will avenge you."

Visibly relaxing under his friend's touch, Michael's eyes shone.

"We all know you didn't kill Jade." He thought a moment. "And neither did Clayton Cole."

"Hmmm?" Despite the plethora of painkillers coursing through his bloodstream, Michael was trying to keep up.

"There's this girl named Maggie Taylor. She came to our ceremony last night. Later, she was abducted by the same guy who grabbed Sensara and me. If Cole was outside Pegasus beating on you, he couldn't have been kidnapping her at the same time."

Michael blinked his eyes. He was fading.

"The problem is, I needed you, amigo. I needed you to help me rescue her, and now there's no way you can—"

"I can." Across the room, Clive stood poised in a boxer's stance.

Estrada rolled his eyes in a look merging doubt and suspicion and then laughed out loud.

"Look, I'm smart and I'm a doctor; if someone gets hurt. And, I can handle myself in a fight. What more do you need?"

It was true. Clive Stryker was a wiry little prick who could pack a punch, but—

"Someone I can trust," Estrada said.

"Well, I will just have to do because Michael is clearly out of commission. I know you don't like me but I don't like you either, so that makes us even. What's critical is finding this girl, yeah?"

"I can't work with someone I don't trust." Estrada looked back to his friend for assurance, but he'd fallen asleep. Reaching over, he laid his palm lightly along Michael's forehead. "You're going to come out of here as clean as Keith Richards and twice as popular."

"Listen Estrada. You trust Michael and Michael trusts me."

"Your point?"

"If Michael trusts me, so can you."

"It doesn't work like that." He turned to leave. Then he stopped and stared Clive down for almost a minute. Finally, satisfied that the kid could take it without flinching, he said, "I suppose I could use backup and I might need you to drive. You *can* drive a stick."

"Of course."

"And you realize that the steering wheel is on the left side of the car?" Clive held up his middle finger in response. "You can come under three conditions. One, you don't ask questions. Two, you don't get out of the car. And three, if you fuck with me, in any way, I'll put you in the hospital."

Clive rolled his eyes. "That's not a condition."

"The kind of condition you'll be in when I finish with you, it won't matter."

Cruising down the freeway in the red convertible with Estrada at the wheel, Clive felt almost as if he were Michael. It was something he'd wanted all his life. Michael, the infamous older brother, had been chosen by the magnanimous Nigel Stryker, and been handed everything he ever wanted including freedom, while *he* had been cloistered by the parsimonious bastard his mother died trying to escape. Life was not fair. But it *was* looking up.

Leaning back, he jacked his elbow up on the plush leather seat and smirked. His plan to take over that ridiculous brothel, they called a nightclub, was working. As much as he hated Nigel for spawning the father he despised, he'd almost convinced him that Michael was running a drug cartel out of the club. That he had no proof mattered very little. Clive knew Nigel had spies working the club now and Michael was under close scrutiny.

This latest business—getting beaten in the back alley—just gave credence to his case. Michael, as caught up as he was in acting out his inane vampire fantasies, was playing right into his plan. And the magician's involvement with a serial killer was a gift from the gods. Clive couldn't wait to see how this next scenario would play out.

"Have you been in contact with the kidnapper?" he asked.

"No questions, remember?"

"I was just wondering how you know where to go. I assume the man designated a meeting place?"

"You'll know when we get there."

"What does he want anyway? Money?"

Estrada jammed on the brakes. The tires slid on the greasy pavement as the car shimmied from side to side. He swung it into the right lane, and then veered off onto the gravel shoulder.

Clive braced himself against the dashboard, exhaling in a frightful rush. "Are you trying to kill us?" he said, as the car finally stopped.

"You don't have a very long memory for a doctor." Estrada sat calmly with his hands on the wheel and stared out the front window as the windshield wipers jerked steadily back and forth. "Get out."

Clive, his temper triggered by the memory of the last time this asshole had left him hell and gone from the city, reached into the pocket of his trench coat and pulled out a derringer.

"I am *not* getting out and *you* are going to answer my questions."

Estrada glanced at the tiny pistol and sniggered. "Like that's real."

"Oh, it's real," Clive said, cocking the .38 special, "and loaded." He pointed the short steel barrel at Estrada's abdomen. "I won't kill you, but at this range, a lead bullet in the gut hurts like hell, and I know exactly where to place it. Believe me. I've dug them out of young thugs in London."

"What is it that you want, little brother?"

"Stop patronizing me with that *little brother* shite for starters. I've had quite enough of your disrespect."

"Is that it? You're gonna shoot me for that?"

"If need be." Clive sniffed. "Now, tell me what's going on."

"Put the gun away."

"No. And you know what? Get out of the car. I'll drive."

He watched as Estrada opened the door and stepped out onto the gravel shoulder. Still holding the gun, but shading it with his left hand, Clive did likewise. Vehicles zoomed by on the freeway, oblivious to the armed carjacking. The two men passed each other in front of the red car and climbed back in. Estrada clipped on his seatbelt and gazed straight ahead.

Feeling elated with his sudden power, Clive smirked at his new sidekick. "Right. Now. What's our destination?"

"I don't see how it matters. You're not even from around here."

"That's insignificant."

"You little shit. You're working with the cops, aren't you? What are you going to do? Pull out a cell phone and call them while you hold me at gunpoint?"

"I told you. I just want to know what's going on."

"The man said no cops. If the cops show, you'll get this girl killed."

"I'm not working with the cops."

Estrada slammed his fist against the dash. "I knew this was a mistake. Look, we're running out of time. Can we just get back on the *fucking* highway?"

Clive took his time ruminating just to piss Estrada off.

"I'm serious, man. It's already two. By five, we'll have lost the light and if he's in the woods . . . Just drive. Please."

Clive sat and stared out the front window, as the magician had done moments before.

Estrada huffed. "Fine. I don't know who he is or even where he is. He sent a message telling me that I had forty-eight hours to find him, and I only have until midnight tonight before the police become involved. He doesn't want money. I don't know what he wants. I used a pendulum to scry his approximate location. It's somewhere near the Old Alexandra Bridge just north of Yale. We just keep cruising up this highway until we get there. I'm going to negotiate with him and get Maggie back. Now you know everything."

"Right," Clive said. He turned the key in the ignition and the vehicle purred. He didn't understand what *scry* meant, but at least he had the magician's attention. "Right. Now we're on even ground." After putting the safety on the derringer, he slid it, barrel down, into the front of his belt.

"You better hope that safety works, little brother, or your wee weapon might leave you without one."

Stones Have Been Known to Move

Drawn toward the killer by some unfathomable force, Estrada took his first steps across the Old Alexandra Bridge with trepidation. He couldn't help but look down through the open u-shaped steel decking that stretched like rusty metal waves beneath his boots. Resting a leather-gloved hand on the orange railing, he stared, mesmerized by the roiling green-brown river. Beneath him, the Fraser River, rife with sediment and autumn rain, funneled through a canyon of colossal gray rocks into spiraling white-capped eddies. It was deep, cold, and forbidding.

He closed his eyes against the unexpected vertigo and inhaled deeply. With the exhale came a knowing. Once, in a past life, he'd been cast into water like this with his wrists and ankles bound by chains. His body grew numb even as his lungs burned. Then, surrender followed terror, as death ushered his weightless spirit from a watery darkness into light.

Fretfully, he opened his eyes. A hundred yards distant, a decorative circle was embedded in the cement arch high above his head. He made this his focus. There was no turning back. No room for uncertainty or fear. The pendulum had brought him here, and his gut told him that the man who held Maggie captive was somewhere on the other side of this gorge. It was his destiny to see this through.

Once across the bridge, he examined an old cement wall painted in graffiti. Was it too much to ask that he'd left a message among the jumble of words and tags? Seeing nothing significant, he pulled the hood of his long black trench coat tighter against the rain and surveyed the area. A few men were fishing upstream. The killer wouldn't venture near them. He'd lurk somewhere on the outskirts like a lone coyote.

Estrada was not, as the madman assumed, some sorcerer with omniscient power. He was simply a man besotted by magic, who performed illusions with the passion another man might play the cello or compete in triathlons or sail. He believed in the spirit's power to inform the mind through dreams, intuition, and tools like the pendulum. He could spin spells and visualize energy, but he was no psychic like Sensara.

Squatting by an old hemlock tree, he checked his cell phone. It was after three—less than two hours of daylight left. Closing his eyes, he asked for help. He knew he was too close to this, too involved to be objective. Still he had no choice. Around him were sounds—rushing water and the hum of transport trucks on the nearby highway. Acknowledging them and letting them pass, he focused on his breath.

When it came, it was no searing vision, just an insistent voice that urged him to stand and walk. He chose a trail to the left that followed the river's edge. It was likely where the old road ran years before. He raced down it, but not far along it ended abruptly, severed by a high waterfall. *Damn.* There was no time for error.

Retracing his steps, he noticed a break in the bush. A trail, littered with broken branches, rose straight up into the forested mountain. Something told him, this was the way.

Using both hands, he began to climb the steep hump. His long coat protected him from the rain but tripped him up mercilessly. He slipped and grasped a tree root, then used the gnarly roots to hoist himself up. Skirting moss-strewn boulders and deadfalls of hemlock and Douglas fir, he climbed steadily upwards, ever mindful of the slick ground beneath his boots.

At last, he came upon the old track and followed it across an open gorge, praying that it was out of use and no train would come. Despite his recent vision, he knew that he would jump into the river rather than be crushed by a train. Some things men had no power over, like their will to survive.

Safely on the other side, he continued to climb. He edged his way up the mountain diagonally, using his hands to balance against the pale gray rocks. Finally, as he paused on a ledge to catch his breath, he glimpsed an inviting clearing against the side of a rock wall. Venturing closer, he realized the glade was paved in granite slabs that prevented tree growth, though moss and lichen shrouded several boulders.

Near the rock wall, an overhang offered protection from the rain, so he squatted again and waited for inspiration. Time was running out. Perhaps he should have involved the police. Who was he to take on a killer? But cops. He'd hated them since—

A branch cracked breaking his thought. Peering sideways, he spied the man, leaning casually against the rock wall some ten paces away. With keen eyes, Estrada surveyed the body he knew only by touch—brown hair beneath a sopping ball cap, a green rain poncho, blue jeans, hiking boots. He carried no obvious weapon, but anything could be hidden under that ugly plastic poncho.

The man nodded, then sauntered toward him. "I'll need to search you." His voice was raspy and low. Unrecognizable. "You won't mind though, will you? Undo your coat."

"So, you're sociable this time."

While patting him down, the man's hands tightened on his inner thighs and lingered. Estrada tensed under the focused squeeze of his fingers.

"I said to come alone. You don't listen very well."

So, he'd seen them arrive in the crimson car and felt betrayed. He had no right. This was no relationship.

"Where's Maggie?"

"You broke the deal. We're going someplace where your puppy can't find us. Move."

Estrada sauntered ahead, skirting trees and fallen rocks, turning where instructed, and all the while, trying to remember landmarks. After twenty minutes, he realized they were heading directly toward a steep mountain.

"Through there." The man pointed to a cleft in the rocks.

Estrada maneuvered his slim body sideways, through an impossibly narrow rift that seemed to cut its way upwards through the center of the mass. When his right hand brushed against the man's fingers, he jerked reflexively, hit hard stone with his knee and yelped.

"Keep going," the man barked, hurt by his too-obvious repulsion.

Winded from the climb, Estrada breathed heavily. As the cleft opened wider, the rain poured down. At this altitude, he realized with chagrin, as night drew on, it could easily turn to snow. How bizarre it seemed, that only the night before last, he'd been submerged in a rushing stream under the clear silver light of the full moon feeling the power of the gods surge through his soul. If only they'd help him now. He sent a silent prayer, then paused, confused, seeing nothing but a vertical mass of rock and a few straggly trees.

"Through there," the man repeated and nodded toward the trees. Finally, he pulled back the stunted pines and shoved Estrada down and through a small cleft in the rock.

Motionless in the pitch, Estrada listened. All he could hear was the ringing of his ears in the tomblike silence. Then, the rattle of wooden matches. A minute flare appeared, and he smelled the stench of sulfur. As the flame grew, fire illuminated the man's face. He was wearing a crudely applied rubber mask. He could be anyone. Visible fissures around the lip lines and green eyes enhanced the distortion.

The man squatted, picked up a torch from the ground and lit it. Just as the flame reached his fingertips, he flicked the match aside. "Keep walking."

"Is Maggie here?"

"I'm impressed by your concern."

"She's just a kid."

The floor rose slightly as they stepped through the shadows and followed a curving passage. Estrada tripped and swung into the wall. "If I have to go first, at least let me hold the torch."

"So you can turn around and punch me?"

"If I wanted to punch you, you'd be on the ground. I came here for Maggie."

"Did you?"

"Yes, and until she's safe—"

"Relax, magician. We're nearly there."

Indeed, a few steps later, Estrada turned a corner into an oddly-shaped cave. Strewn with dried fragrant grasses, it offered comfort after the long climb in the rain. The man jammed the torch into a crack near the wall, then picked up a fresh one, lit it, and planted it in another corner. Satisfied with the state of his den, he pulled off his wet poncho and hung it over a rock. After sliding off his small backpack, he perched on a bench-shaped boulder and took out a canteen. A small gold crucifix, set with green stones, fell from his collar.

Estrada eyed the cross. Emeralds. Expensive. Perhaps Dylan was right, and this *was* Grace. Observing his interest, the man tucked it beneath his sweater.

"What is this place?" Estrada asked, sensing ambient energy in the cave. He wondered how the man knew about this hidden grotto. Perhaps, he'd lived nearby as a boy or had a father who was an avid outdoorsman, as he appeared to be. He wished *his* father had taken him exploring in places like this, where the graffiti might be thousands of years old and the spirits of the ancient ones still lingered.

"Indian cave? Gold mine? I knew you'd like it. You're a romantic and—"

"Where's Maggie?" Estrada interrupted, his eyes narrowing. This sordid attraction tormented him.

"Your fear makes you tense, magician. I'm a good masseuse. Better than your priestess."

"How do you know—?"

The man laughed, amused by his reaction.

"I'd rather you kept your hands off me. I came here for Maggie, not you."

"You keep saying that. Why don't I believe you?"

"Look, if this is your idea of a date, I'm not impressed or interested." The man scratched at the corner of his eye where a drip of glue clung to the mask like a static teardrop. "That can't be comfortable. Why don't you take it off and show me who you really are?"

"Who I *really* am? We all wear masks of one kind or another. Even you, pretty boy."

The flaming torches cast intense heat into the small confined space. Accepting that he was stranded in conversation, Estrada took off his dripping coat, spread it over a boulder and sat on the stone floor. Lifting his leg, he wedged one foot against the edge of a rock. He hated that *pretty boy* shit. He'd been judged by it all his life. He wiped the rain from his face, then wrung out his wet hair and tied it in a knot.

"I suppose you have me all figured out," he said.

"I know you're into me, despite your denial. I can feel it. Hell, I can almost see it," the man said.

Estrada could see it too. Faint trails of light connected them—bonds of intimacy. He wondered if the man had some innate ability similar to his own for visualizing energy.

"The last time we—"

"Don't make it more than it was. I gave my word to let you do—"

"You loved what I did. Admit it. I'm the best lover you ever had. Better than your Michael Stryker. You want me right now."

"No." Estrada swallowed to moisten his dry throat. He had to stop this banter. Everything the man said was true. Their connection was more potent than anything he'd ever felt in his life, and as lovers go . . . *Christ*. If he didn't maintain control, he'd lose himself, and this time there'd be no coming back. He was beguiled—as charmed as the killer. "No. That was before . . . Before I realized that you burn women. How could I ever—?"

"There are many ways to burn women. You and your friend burn women frequently and indiscriminately."

"*And* he's a philosopher," Estrada said, rolling his eyes.

"It's true. You choose only the beautiful people for your soirées and reject all others without a thought. You glorify violence and death. That Halloween performance was obscene."

"Sorry I offended you." So, he *had* been there.

Ignoring the sarcasm, the man continued. "You feed unsuspecting women drugs that alter their senses and morals, and you transform innocent girls into whores—girls like Maggie. Did you even notice how she changed to seduce you?"

Maggie had changed her appearance, but Estrada assumed it was because she was delving into goth, not because of him.

"Did you ever consider that the women you select for your parties, might be daughters, sisters, or mothers with children waiting for them at home? No magician, you are selfish and capricious."

"Enough. I get your—"

"You use and discard. Just as you are about to do to me."

Estrada felt a chill sweep the backs of his arms.

"The only difference between us, is that you burn women recklessly and I burn them with reason," the man said.

"To save their souls, I presume." A moral psychopath? The man was more complex than Estrada imagined. "If I'm such a monster, why do you—"

"Want you? Aye, there's the rub. As you well know, a man cannot always control his desire. The soul seeks its counterpart."

"You think I'm your soulmate?" Estrada snorted. "If I'm anything, I'm your Nemesis."

"Here to mete out justice? Great Mythic Hero Saves Innocent Girl from Evil Beast? Be honest. There's more on your mind than that. You can't stop thinking about me. You wonder why you're so drawn to me, even now. It tantalizes you. It makes you crazy. It makes you *weak*."

"Listen. Because of you, at least one girl is dead. My friend is in the hospital because her ex thinks he killed her, and you've abducted Maggie Taylor. So yes, I am here to save the innocent girl from the evil beast. And, despite this bizarre attraction, I don't want to be your boyfriend."

"But you long to be my lover."

"Listen. I don't know what condition Maggie's in, but I imagine she's scared out of her mind. You offered a trade. I accepted. Can we just get on with it?"

"Fine. What will you trade?"

"What do you want?"

"Hmmm..."

Estrada shook his head. "Not sex. Something else."

"Your freedom, perhaps? Would you stay in her place? Ah, but sex would undoubtedly arise." The man stroked his chin. "I know. How about your life? Are you willing to trade your life for hers?"

"If I make *that* trade, how can I be sure you'll release Maggie unharmed?" Clasping his hands behind his head, Estrada leaned back against the rock and mused.

Daphne's spell must had morphed into some kind of sexual enchantment. Maggie had morphed into a sexy goth. He thought of Sensara, the unusual way she'd acted for those few weeks—frequenting Pegasus, changing her behavior, the way she dressed—and how she'd suddenly changed back. He must be bewitched himself. *And* the man. Both of them were enthralled in some Bacchic charm that amplified feelings, created potent pheromones, and compounded desire. *Should I give in to it, or resist? Which action will facilitate Maggie's release and stop this man from killing other witches?*

"You'd have to trust me, magician."

"Trust you? I don't think so." Estrada shook his head and sighed.

"You seem to like magic. I could teach you a trick."

"That would only spoil it for me. Let's see. What do you have to trade? Ah, I know. Your hair."

"My hair?"

"Yes, I like you with your hair off your face, the way it is now."

Estrada remembered how the man had bound his hair in a bun that night. "Why do you want my hair?"

"I don't want your hair, magician. I want your power."

Estrada considered this. He had not cut his hair since becoming a magician. Seven years. Soaking wet, it touched the bottom of his rib cage and encased his solar plexus like a protective shield. He loved his hair. It was his brand.

The man smiled, already delighting in his power. "Did you know executioners shaved the heads of witches before they burned them?"

"Are you planning to burn me?"

The man ignored the question. "They claimed to be searching for the Devil's mark, but really they shaved their heads to shame them. Witches were instruments of Satan that led men into sin."

He spoke like a priest. Estrada thought again of Grace, the priest who'd assaulted Maggie. He'd read that women accused of witchcraft were sometimes sexually assaulted while being held captive. Jade had been burned on a bed. What had this lunatic done to her before lighting the cabin on fire?

"How many men and women have you led into sin, magician?"

"Please, just tell me where Maggie is. Then you can do whatever you want with me."

"Oh, don't tempt me." Agitated, the man stood. "I love you, Estrada. Don't you see that? Can't you feel it? I love you so much it breaks my heart to refuse you anything."

"You *love* me? You murder Jade. You grab me and Sensara. You play sex games with me, then shove me away, and dump me on the highway. Then you kidnap Maggie to get me back? All because you love me?"

"Narcissistic fool. Do you think it's all about you?"

"Explain it to me then, because I don't—"

"And Maggie is far from innocent. She needs to learn—"

"Did you rape her?" Estrada tensed.

"Did I rape you?"

"I didn't fight you. Answer my question."

"I don't have to," the man said.

"Fine, you win. I submit. Take my hair and let Maggie go."

"Deal." The man sat down on the stone bench across from Estrada and held out his hand. "Give me your cell phone."

"Why?"

"Maggie's not here, but I'll type the directions in a text to . . . ?"

"Dylan." At last, he was getting somewhere.

"When our deal's done, you can press send. Agreed?"

"Agreed." Estrada reached into his coat pocket and pulled out the phone. Dylan, Sensara, and Sylvia were sitting in a restaurant just off the highway, awaiting instructions. Once they knew Maggie's location they could go and get her.

The man typed the text and flashed it before Estrada's eyes, so he could see the words that signified her release. Carefully, he set the phone down on the bench.

Estrada rubbed his skull, feeling the odd bumps and dents of life. His mood had lightened. He hadn't had a buzz cut since he was a kid, but if sacrificing his hair could save Maggie's life, he'd do it gladly. Once she was safely out of the country, he'd come back and finish this.

The man extracted a pair of shears from his pack.

"You came prepared," Estrada said.

"Perhaps I'm psychic too."

Estrada didn't laugh but focused on his quivering gut as his captor gathered his hair in his hands and hacked through it with the shears. When he finished, he waved it in the air. "Head feel lighter?"

Estrada closed his eyes. "You're not really going to shave my head, are you?"

The man chuckled. "Has a razor ever touched your head?"

"*Jesus.* Not with a razor."

"Relax." He reached into his bag and produced a battery-powered shaver.

"You knew it would come to this."

"I know you." Tilting Estrada's head, he ran his fingers softly up his neck, across his jaw, and over his lips, then touched them to his own lips. "Because I love you."

"If you really loved me, you wouldn't do this."

"You're wrong about that." He ran his palm over Estrada's scalp. "Your hair's still damp."

He took a small towel from his bag and dried his hair. The man's touch was a crazy comfort. "You like this. I'm glad."

"Just get on with it," Estrada said, coming to his senses.

He closed his eyes and cringed as the man turned on the shaver and began to buzz his head from the base of his skull to his forehead. Hair fell like leaves around him. When at last the buzzing stopped, silence crammed the cave. Estrada shook his head and felt nothing but a rush of air.

"How do you feel?"

"Strong and free. Now give me the fucking phone."

The man stood in front of Estrada and ran both hands over his skull. "I do love you. That's why I had to shave your head. It was the only way to save your life." When he leaned down and kissed him on the mouth, the force of it rushed through Estrada's body like an electric wave as memories of that night in the cabin surged through his senses.

Estrada jerked away. "Don't—"

"Here." The man tossed him the phone, his voice dismal. He wanted more than power and submission. He wanted love.

Estrada read the text:

FOLLOW GAME TRAIL 2 MILES EAST FROM SADDLE ROCK TUNNEL

He pressed send.

"And I would walk five hundred miles." The sound of The Proclaimers erupted from directly outside the cave, startling both men, who looked to each other in astonishment. Then, Estrada grabbed his coat and dashed toward the opening.

Behind him, rocks came crashing down in a clattering chaos of dust and debris. As the cave convulsed, he heard the man cry out. Halfway through the opening, Estrada stopped. Should he go back and save him? Then a boulder rolled from the inside, seemingly by the hand of Gaia herself, sealed the cavity.

Estrada squeezed through the tunnel and emerged on the other side. Dylan stood there clutching his cell, and despite everything, Estrada laughed. Wearing a green and blue plaid kilt, black leather knee boots, and navy windbreaker, Dylan's cheeks glowed like ripe apples. He sniffed and nodded. The two men embraced, and then sized each other up, their eyes a maze of questions.

"How did you—?"

"I followed you," Dylan said. "Thought you might need a hand."

"Where's Clive?"

"No idea. The car's parked by the trail entrance. But I didn't see him."

"So, where is he?"

Dylan shrugged.

"Did you do that?" Estrada pointed to the cave. He knew the kid could communicate with rocks. Could he also command them?

Dylan smiled proudly. "What's this now?" he asked, and gestured to his friend's shaved head. "Your scalp's as white as my arse."

Estrada rolled his eyes. "Did you hear—?"

"I arrived just now and didn't hear a thing, but if you ever need to talk."

Estrada turned toward the cave and started heaving rocks away.

"Ach, don't fret about him," Dylan said.

"I have to be sure. He knows this terrain. If there's another passage out of that chamber—"

"Let the police deal with him. If he does get out, the first thing he'll do is go after Maggie. Don't you think we should get there first?"

"Yeah, you're right." Estrada sighed. "You know Dylan, one day you're going to have to show me that rock trick."

Maggie awoke in darkness. The acrid scent of smoldering wood teased her nostrils. Lurching forward to catch a sneeze, she realized she was bound and lying on her back. Overwhelmed by the urgent impulse to escape, she panicked. Writhing and screaming, throat aching, head throbbing, the skin on her wrists and ankles scorching against the ropes, she spasmed; until finally, exhausted and defeated, with one great sigh, she caved.

Was he here, watching, taking pleasure in her pain?

If she could just open her eyes. But a blindfold held them so tightly shut it was causing her head to burst.

Memories surfaced. This was not the first time she'd awakened. Each time, he'd wrenched down her sweatpants and rammed a needle into her thigh. Was he here now? Watching and waiting? A syringe in hand? His thumb on the plunger? Poised and ready to fill her with his venom?

Niggling at her mind was something Dylan mentioned that night, something about witches getting abducted and burned, and with that memory came another—a memory of Father Grace, so close she could smell the wood smoke on his skin and his thick tongue choking her and his cock like a slab of driftwood against her belly, the kind they piled high for tinder. Gagging, she turned her head and spat out the bitter bile that filled her mouth.

The smoky stench conjured images from historical films of burning Catholics and burning witches, and she thought how ironic it was that Protestants burned Catholics, and Catholics burned Protestants, and they all burned witches. It was all just madness—madness to torture and kill another human because of beliefs, and if she laid there any longer tied to that musty bed wondering what was to become of her and why, she'd go mad herself.

The scream escaped from somewhere deep in her chest, acutely high-pitched like something from a horror movie, and though it hurt her parched throat, she let it pour forth, knowing it was either scream or go mad.

"Christ. She's wailing like a banshee," Dylan yelled.

Estrada dropped the dirt bike on its side and watched the kid race toward the cabin. He wanted to give him this moment with Maggie, wanted her to see Dylan as the hero who saved her from the monster.

They'd waited out the storm in a local motel and left in the dark, anticipating the dawn that now unfurled like a ghostly shadow over the eastern mountains. The proprietor, who knew the area, had accepted their fabricated story—a friend had broken his ankle hiking. Eager to help, he'd drawn them a rough map and even lent them his bike.

Sylvia and Sensara had lost the argument to call in the RCMP to help with the search for Maggie. Though Estrada had spoken with Nigel and suggested that the cops search the cave near the bridge. "We're this close," Estrada insisted, "and if she's really that far from the highway, he can't get to her until morning either." Still, he couldn't sleep and laid awake for hours tormented by doubts about Clive, who was grating him like a sharp pebble in a tight boot.

The kid had disappeared in Crimson before they'd made it back to the car park. Estrada had a hunch that he was as dangerous as the killer; in fact, more than once he'd suspected Clive of being the killer. Wasn't he always hovering just around the edges? He had full access to the club which gave him opportunity, and he had a motive for mayhem. Obviously jealous of everything Michael possessed, including his relationship with Estrada, it was only natural that he would seek that too. Moreover, he considered whether Clive's biological similarity to his older brother could enhance his sexual attractiveness—perhaps create a kind of encoded desire that might lure Estrada to him like a bee to pollen. It was a ridiculous theory because he had nothing but repulsion for the man, still, who knew what crafted a man's particular cravings?

Driving down the highway, he'd looked for flashes of the crimson car, half expecting to see it concealed behind some stand of trees. Even now, he wondered if he was about to find Clive hiding behind the locked door. The cabin was right where he'd said it would be—two miles up the trail from Saddle Rock. Still, it bothered him that the man had given Maggie up so easily. Estrada knew he was engaged in some bizarre game he couldn't quit because he was not in control.

Is this a trap? Another ruse? he wondered. If it was, Dylan might need help.

"Bloody door's locked." Dylan played the handle, shaking it viciously, as if the charged anger of his vibration might jar its release. "Why's she screaming like that?"

"Is he in there?" Estrada ran to the window, spied the vague outline of Maggie, stretched and bound to the bed—just as he had been—picked up a rock and smashed in the dirty glass. There was no sign of the man. With the shattering, the screaming stopped, and a sense of disquieting calm permeated the thick air.

Forming a stirrup with his fingers, he swung Dylan up and through the broken window, whistling as he saw that the kid dressed true to his heritage. "Had I known ye'd a bare arse beneath your kilt, Scotty, I'd have let ye drive the motorbike and cuddled up behind ye," Estrada teased, in an appalling Scottish accent.

"You'll ne'er get near my arse 'cept in your dreams," Dylan replied. Turning, he gave him the finger and they both laughed. Two days of pent-up pressure escaping. They'd found her alive.

As Dylan leaned over the bed, Estrada surveyed the room. Careful not to disturb evidence, he opened the door of the small wood stove. The fire had burnt low. The man had not been here for hours, probably since before their meeting yesterday. There was nothing in the room but the blankets on the bed and the ropes he'd used to bind her—nothing he could see, at any rate. The forensics team would surely find something.

"I'm here, Maggie. I've got you," Dylan said, gently sweeping off her blindfold.

"Dylan," she said, blinking, "I'm so sorry." In shivering waves, she cried.

"You've nothing to be sorry for. You've done nothing wrong." He sat on the edge of the bed and watched her as Estrada cut the ropes with his knife.

"But how? How did you—"

"Find you? It's rather complicated," Dylan said.

"That's an understatement," mumbled Estrada.

"For now, let's just get away from here."

Maggie swung her feet to the floor, leaned forward, and rubbed her cramped arms and legs. "I have to pee. Come with me."

Dylan's face reddened.

"Oh, *go* with her. Man up. Then take her back on the bike."

"You're not waiting for *him* to show up?"

"The bike seats two. Drop Maggie at the motel and come back for me," Estrada said. "She needs to go to the hospital. Sensara and Sylvia can take her." He wouldn't make that mistake again. He turned to Maggie, who sat half-paralyzed gazing at the floor. "Did he hurt you?"

Maggie raised her head as if seeing him for the first time, and her jaw dropped. "Oh my God! What did you do?"

"Not I." Estrada ran a hand over his naked scalp.

"I love it!" Maggie said, a smile brightening her face.

Well, that was one for and one against. Sensara's reaction to his shaved head had not been quite so complimentary.

"Can I touch it?" she asked.

"I thought you had to pee," Dylan droned.

Estrada nodded. Maggie stood and ran her hand over his head. It was good to see her relax and smile.

"Did he hurt you?" he asked again.

"He's been jabbing needles into me. I think every time I woke up, he—"

Dylan interrupted. "Estrada means, did he . . . ?"

She shook her head wildly. "Oh. No. I don't think so."

If it was the priest, why didn't he finish what he started on the porch? Perhaps Maggie didn't remember. She had been drugged. Then again, she was still dressed in her sweats, wearing slippers even. Estrada remembered being covered with a blanket that night in the cabin. The man was a considerate killer.

"That's good," Dylan said.

Good on two counts, thought Estrada. *Good for the girl—no one should ever have to experience rape—and good for Dylan, who wouldn't feel obliged to avenge that crime on top of this.*

Standing in the open doorway, backlit by the gray morning, Maggie leaned wearily against the kid. Dylan was too pure for this game. Even now, he eased his arm around her shoulder, and tucked her into his chest with gentility.

"He wanted to, though. He almost raped me the other night. My dad hit him with a chair!"

She was sure it was Grace.

"I've been thinking about it," she said. "Maybe he's a split personality—like one part of him is the good priest and the other is evil, you know? Like when he feels sexually attracted to a girl, he has to get rid of her, because he knows it's wrong. So he abducts her and—"

"Burns her." *What had the man said? "I burn them with reason?"* Even that didn't explain the bizarre attraction between the two of them or why he'd shaved his head. *"I had to shave your head—it was the only way to save your life." What did that mean? And why the talk of love?*

Estrada jumped at the sound of The Proclaimers. "You gotta change that ring tone, man."

Dylan answered his phone. "Hello. Aye, we're with her now. We were just about to call you. I'll put her on." He handed the phone to Maggie. "It's your mum."

"Hey mom . . . Yeah, I'm okay . . . What?" She let out an incredulous gasp, paused, and then sniffed back her tears. "Jesus. Is he . . .?" A fist to her temple, she stared rigidly at the floor. "Okay, I'm coming now."

They stared at her, waiting and wondering.

"It's my dad. He's in the hospital."

"What happened?" Dylan asked.

"He fell down the basement steps last night. He might . . ." Maggie scraped at the ragged skin on her palms. "She said to hurry."

Your Spirits Shine Through You

Maggie's gaze shifted from the tranquil face of her father to the anxious face of her mother and back again. She imagined that John Taylor had been an attractive man at one time and could understand why Shannon had fallen in love with him. Many years as an invalid had dulled his eyes, jaundiced his skin, plumped his belly, and eroded his hairline, but he was still fine-boned and handsome for a man of forty. His long delicate hands, resting on the blanket with their perfect fingernails, looked as if they'd been carved of wax. The manicure was Bastian's doing, of course. He always kept John as clean as a baby.

Shannon touched Maggie's shoulder. "We need to talk."

"Now?" she whispered. It seemed to Maggie, that she and Shannon were like two strangers who waited for the same bus every morning, but were so caught up in their own worlds, neither noticed the other.

"Now. Come on," urged her mother with a jerk of her small freckled head. "He's on the monitor. If anything happens, they'll come running."

Shannon marched with quiet purpose in her tiny white trainers. At home in this place of managed pain, accustomed to the smells of disinfected body and quiet discomfort, the awkwardness of visitors, and the too soon familiarity of fretful patients.

Maggie trailed behind her through the long pale corridors and wondered what was coming next. She'd already endured a pelvic exam. The police wanted blood and swabs. Wanted to concoct their own story because they didn't believe hers. Convinced she'd been sexually assaulted, they thought she was denying it out of fear or embarrassment. She read it in their faces.

"In here," Shannon said over her shoulder. She pushed open the heavy door to the chapel and ushered Maggie inside. The cool, dark, empty chamber emitted a welcoming sense of comfort. Just two fake candles flickered on the altar beneath the plain Christ-less cross. Maggie was glad. She could stand no more sorrowful sad-eyed crucifixes with their tortured saviors or anything vaguely reminiscent of the Catholic Church. She perched on the edge of a metal folding chair and watched her mother genuflect and cross herself. Then Shannon seated herself across from Maggie and looked her straight in the eye.

"I've been a bad mother," she said, and, for a moment, Maggie felt disturbingly like a priest.

"Ah, don't, Mom."

"Let me finish. It's hard enough to confess after all these years. If you interrupt me, I might not get it out."

Leaning back against the cold metal chair, Maggie bit her lip and watched the blinking candles.

"I've been a bad mother, but not because I don't love you. I *do* love you. You know that, don't you?"

"I know."

"I've been bad because I've been lying all these years, to you, and to myself. I convinced myself it was for your own good, but that wasn't so. I was lying to cover my shame." She pulled a balled-up tissue from her sleeve and dabbed her nose. Then she took a deep breath and sighed.

"I'm just going to say it." She took another deep breath. "John, the man who's lying in that bed, is *not* your real father."

"What?"

Her mother held up her hand. "Listen now," she chided, then lowered her voice lest someone overhear her terrible secret. "I got pregnant when I was your age and the boy . . . Well, it didn't work out."

"You're the one Dad meant. The one who got in trouble."

"Strange the things that man remembers. I had to leave Ireland. I came here to Canada and had you. Then I met John, and he loved you right from the get-go, and he married me. We moved here, and he built our house, and everything was grand, until—"

"Until he fell."

Her mother nodded. "After that . . . Well, nothing was ever the same again. I just couldn't—"

"It's okay." Maggie placed her hand on her mother's. Girls got pregnant. It happened all the time. Some kept their babies. Some didn't. It could have been worse. She might never have been born.

"It's not okay. I lied about your father, and that's the whopper, but there are other lies too." She blew her nose again. "All these years, you've wanted a big family with grandparents and uncles and aunts and cousins. You've hated that you had only us two. Well, the truth is, you've got a family just like that in Ireland. I don't know exactly where they all are now, but they're good people and they love you."

When Shannon paused, Maggie found she was holding her breath, poised to hear the words that might change her life forever. And then Shannon said them. "I want you to go there and find them."

"Find them? In Ireland?"

"Aye. Now, I've made up my mind. This crazy fool has not been caught and until he is, you're not safe."

"But—"

"Maggie, I've got to look after John and—"

"I can't leave Dad like this. What if—?"

"Listen now. Your dad, above all else, loves you and wants you to be safe. He spent the last two days wandering around that bloody house looking for you."

"That's how he fell, isn't it?"

Her mother sobbed. "Yes. I fell asleep on the couch. It was late, and I was just so tired. He was supposed to be asleep in his room." Tears dripped down her cheeks. "I heard a noise and got up. The basement door was open, and there he was, lying at the foot of the stairs."

"Ah, Mom, I'm sorry." She tried to imagine what it would be like to find her dad's broken body at the bottom of the basement steps.

"It's not your fault," Shannon said. "None of it was *ever* your fault. John broke his hip through the fall, but he's also had a stroke."

"*Jesus.*"

"So, you have to go to Ireland and find my parents and stay safe, at least until this madman's caught."

"But Mom—"

"Maggie, I can't worry about you *and* John. It's too much. Please. Just do as I ask this one time without an argument."

"What about my passport?"

"I've got it."

"But you said—"

"Forget what I said. Did you really think that I cared more for that old clock than I cared for you, my own daughter? I was just upset. My eldest brother, Eamonn, sent me that clock just after I left, with a note that said, 'one day the time will come for you to come home.' And when it broke . . ."

"You thought you'd never get home." Maggie cried then, caught up in the maelstrom of a million conflicting feelings. Finally, they hugged, both women needing the firmness of flesh to absorb their emotions.

"Now." Shannon opened her purse and took out a large manila envelope. "Here's your passport and ticket. Your flight leaves tomorrow at noon."

"Tomorrow? Are you crazy? I can't just get on a plane and fly to Ireland tomorrow. I've never traveled anywhere. I don't know what to do or where to go. I'll get lost."

"You'll be fine. Professor Black has a friend in Galway."

"Professor Black? You've been talking to—"

"Aye. She came to the house with the others when you disappeared. She's a lovely woman. I took to her straight away. In fact, *she* suggested it. Her friend will meet you in Shannon and look after you, so you won't be alone. I've written it all down here." She handed Maggie the envelope. "I've put cash in too, but you must change it into euros, and I've—"

"Mom. Stop. It's too much."

"Too much? Why Maggie, it's barely enough."

"Our house looks so sad," Maggie said, as Dr. Black parked her new hybrid in the driveway. "My dad built it with his bare hands. It's not one of those kits you buy in pieces and assemble like a puzzle. It's real. He designed it, drew it, and then measured, stripped, cut, and lifted every one of these logs."

The photo albums were stored away in a bottom cupboard, but she'd seen the pictures of the house in all its stages from conception to finish. Seventeen years ago, this corner of Hawk's Claw Lane was part of the vast pine forest that flanked the back and side yards. Seventeen years ago, John Taylor had been a robust young father—her father, no matter what her mother said.

"I'm so sorry, dear," Dr. Black said. "This must be incredibly hard for you. Try to remain positive. Perhaps, picture your father standing on the porch the way he was when—"

Maggie shuddered, and Dylan poked the professor in the shoulder, silencing her. "Dead brilliant," he whispered. The last time John had stood on that porch, he'd saved her from the priest. It had been an amazing feat for a man in his condition and could quite possibly be the last memory she would keep of him.

"Come on." Dylan opened the car door and took her hand. As she stepped out, Daphne pulled her pickup truck in behind them and flashed the lights. Maggie smiled and waved. The coven had volunteered to set up a protective circle and spend the last night with her before her journey. It made her feel as if she was one of them—initiated or not. Whether they felt responsible for the events that had transformed her life really didn't matter. What mattered was that they were now her friends.

Remy greeted her at the door, his tail drumming against the wooden railings in a familiar rhythm. "Ah Remy, I missed you." The beat quickened.

"Has he been alone all day?" Daphne asked, as she petted the vibrating black lab.

"No. He was with the neighbors. My mom asked them to bring him home, so I could see him before— Oh my God. What's she thinking? I can't go to Ireland. I can't leave my dog. Who'll look after him? We can't just expect the neighbors to—"

"Relax," Estrada said. "He'll be perfectly fine and waiting for you when you come home." He stood at the counter unpacking a bag full of Thai food.

"What do you know about dogs? Do you even like dogs?" This sarcasm from Sensara.

"Of course I do. Who doesn't like dogs?" Grabbing a handful of bone-shaped biscuits from the glass canister on the counter, he knelt down. "Come here, buddy." Remy ran immediately to Estrada and crunched down the cookies. "See. He likes me," he said, patting the top of the dog's head.

"He likes cookies. Not bald Mexicans." Sensara smiled coyly.

Maggie's mouth dropped. He was wearing a black toque and looked incredibly handsome. Obviously, the priestess didn't like his shaved head. Nevertheless, her teasing worked.

Estrada grabbed her from behind, hooked his arm around her waist and scooped up her long black hair. "Dylan, find me a razor. The priestess wants her head shaved. She's goin' Sinead."

"I am not." Sensara pulled away and whacked him, then yanked him back and kissed him as if there was no one else in the room.

"Shall I light a fire?" asked Dylan.

"There appears to be one going already," Daphne said.

"Aye. It's heating up in here." Dylan's cheeks had taken on their usual pink tinge.

"There's kindling and wood beside the fireplace." Maggie couldn't bear to see his embarrassment.

As Dylan dashed from the room, Dr. Black popped the cork on a bottle of red wine. "You know, Maggie. You don't have to worry about Remy. He's a special kind of dog."

"What do you mean?" Maggie asked, as she spooned steaming red shrimp curry on top of pineapple rice. She hadn't realized how hungry she was until she smelled the food.

"Well, it was Remy who brought you to us in the beginning, wasn't it? He obviously has a role in all of this."

"Yeah. He freaked when he heard Dylan's bagpipes. It sounded so creepy coming out of the trees over the lake like that. Weirder still, I was reading *Macbeth* and thinking about witches and suddenly there you were."

"What are these, so withered, and so wild in their attire, that look not like th'inhabitants o' th' earth and yet are on it?" Estrada drawled in a terrible English accent.

Maggie blinked. "How do you remember quotes like that?"

He shrugged. "I read."

"Our high priest has literary leanings," Sensara said. "It's one of his many secrets."

"I thought we looked resplendent that night," Dr. Black said, ignoring Sensara's dig. She dabbed the corners of her lips with a paper napkin.

Remy, who was wandering around the table following the scent of food, dropped his head in Daphne's lap. "You know, Maggie, I could take care of Remy for a while. At least until your dad gets out of the hospital. That way your mom wouldn't have to worry about him. He could come to work with me. I'm outside all the time. I'd like it. I think he would too."

"Really?"

"Absolutely," she said, as she scratched Remy's ears. "I love dogs. You wouldn't mind staying with me, would you, boy?"

"That would be great."

"It's settled then," Daphne said. "As long as your mom agrees. We could take him along when we drop you off at the airport."

"At four in the morning."

"Don't fret. I fly back and forth to Scotland all the time." Reaching over, Dylan rubbed her back. The warmth of his hand felt so good she leaned into him and settled her head against his shoulder. "A bit boring is all. Ten hours to London. Be sure to bring along a good book."

For several moments they ate in silence. Then Estrada lifted Sensara's hand to his lips and kissed it.

"Perhaps, we should retire to the living room," Sylvia suggested.

"Not yet. I have a small parting gift for Maggie." Daphne reached into her pocket and pulled out a white linen cloth. "Here you go."

Inside was a beautiful crystal mounted in silver knots and dangling from a silver chain. "A pendulum," Maggie said, a little in awe of the tool.

"Have you ever used one?"

"No. I've just read about them."

"Well, I'll show you then. You want it to capture your energy, so hold it in your hand for several seconds."

Maggie was sure she could feel faint throbbing from the moment it touched her palm.

"Now, balance your elbow on the table and hold the tip of the chain very still in your right hand. Perfect. Let the crystal fall straight down and hold your left palm open below it."

Maggie opened her hand and then closed it, embarrassed by the scars on her palms.

"Don't worry. Crystals can do many amazing things, including healing."

Maggie looked at Daphne with her spiky hair and cheerful smile and thought how incredible it was that she'd made friends with these witches, who were just the most wonderful kind and caring people in the whole world. She opened her hand.

"Now ask the pendulum to show you what an affirmative answer looks like. You can ask aloud or in your head."

Maggie asked silently, and the crystal swung in a great circle around and around.

"Fabulous. You're a natural. Now ask it to show you a negative answer."

The crystal stopped midair and then moved rapidly straight back and forth.

"You have the gift," Daphne said.

"You do," Sensara said. "It took me a long time to get my pendulum to respond with that kind of animation. You can use it to answer yes or no questions, but also to find things. Like places on a map or lost articles. Estrada used it to find you."

"You did?"

He winked.

So, that's how he knew where she was. "Could it find lost grandparents?"

"Perhaps. But these tools work along with destiny, so if they don't appear directly, don't blame the pendulum," Sensara said. "The universe might have something else in store for you, another lesson on the journey."

Maggie nodded.

"I have a little something for you too." Taking a small blue vial from her bag, Sensara handed it to Maggie.

"Frankincense."

"Yes, it's good for many things—grief, anxiety, depression, fear, loneliness. But most of all, it's known for bringing peace and joy."

"Huh," Maggie said. *Frankincense was one of the three gifts the wise men brought the Christ child*, she remembered. She opened the bottle and inhaled. "It smells weird."

"My gift's a little weird too," Dr. Black said.

"Oh?"

"My gift is a friend—your guardian in Ireland. Primrose is the woman I trust most in the world. I can think of no one I would rather entrust my daughter to than her."

"Thank you. But this is too much. I hope you didn't all get me gifts."

"I've never seen a girl yet who didn't like getting gifts." Estrada was just finishing his second helping of pineapple rice and shrimp curry. "My gift is really for me."

"*Qué sorpresa*," mocked Sensara. What a surprise.

"Ah, I love it when you speak my language," he said messing up her hair. She punched him as he rose from the table and walked toward Maggie. He rubbed his hands slowly together, then reached behind her ear and produced a small paperback book. "Yeats is one of my favorite poets, but this is all about Irish faeries. I expect you to find me at least one while you're there."

She read the cover as she accepted the lovingly battered book. "*The Celtic Twilight* by W.B. Yeats. Oh, I love his poems too."

"I love his faeries," Estrada said. "They're nothing like Queen Mab and those twittering fireflies Shakespeare wrote about. Irish faeries are much like us, only better because they can do *real* magic. They're ghostly gods who live in a kind of parallel world of music and dancing and feasting and *lovemaking*." His voice grew husky as he moved behind Sensara and rubbed her neck. "Your mission, Maggie Taylor, is to find faeries, and when you do, you must take me to meet them."

"Estrada's been trying to see faeries for years," Sensara said.

"Then finding faeries is my quest. Faeries and grandparents. I wonder which will be easier," Maggie mused.

Once everyone had eaten their fill, they cleaned up together, and then wandered drowsily into the living room with another bottle of wine. Daphne lit candles, while Estrada plunked down in the corner of the sectional and pulled Sensara onto his lap.

She pulled off his toque and flung it across the room. "I suppose I'll just have to get used to it," she said, running her hands over his head. "It *does* feel like velvet."

He pulled her close and kissed her.

Maggie tried not to look, as no one else paid them any attention. She wondered if they were always this amorous. She was jealous and knew it. If only Dylan could be more affectionate and less shy.

As the others settled back into the soft floral cushions, Maggie sat on the rug in front of the fire and petted Remy. She'd never been away from him and hoped he'd understand.

Startled by the sudden chime of the doorbell, she hopped up and crossed the room with the black dog at her heels, while Dylan hovered behind her in the doorway.

"Bastian," she said, as she opened the door. "I was hoping to see you before I left. Come in." She closed the door behind him. "We've just eaten, but would you like a glass of wine?"

"Oh, no thanks," he said, his gaze shifting quickly from Maggie to her champions in the other room. "I'll come back later. You've got company."

"No, it's fine. I'll introduce you."

"We met last week," he whispered. "And I'm coming down with a sore throat."

"That doesn't matter. Come and join us anyway." She clasped his hand. "These people are healers. And you know you're like a brother to me."

"I feel the same. Like you're my sister, I mean. But I'd just like to speak to you privately for a minute, if that's okay."

"Sure. Come into the kitchen. It's where we always meet anyway." She dragged him through the door with such intensity he tripped over Remy, who was circling his feet. The dog yipped, and Bastian nearly fell.

"Jeez Remy. Are you okay?" The lab answered by sitting perfectly at his feet.

"He doesn't sit like that for me," Maggie said.

"He's just after this." He pulled a wrapped steak bone out of his jacket pocket, ripped off the plastic and slipped it into the dog's gentle mouth. Turning to the sink, he washed his hands while he continued talking. "Your mom mentioned that you're going to Ireland. I was hoping we could exchange emails, so we could keep in touch."

"Yeah, for sure." She scribbled on a piece of paper and set it on the counter. "Hey, I just thought of something. With my dad in the hospital, are you going to be okay? Financially, I mean? Do you have other work?"

Bastian shrugged. "I'll survive."

As he slowly dried his hands with the towel, Maggie got the feeling he hadn't finished what he'd come for. "Is everything okay, Bastian?"

"That's typical. You're worried about me while you're the one who's got some lunatic after you." He picked up the scrap of paper and tucked it in his pocket. "That bloody priest. That day he punched me I should have finished him. He didn't hurt you, did he?"

"Not really. He just tied me up and kept me drugged for a while. I had a rather long sleep."

He ran both hands through his short hair and clasped them on his head. "Jesus! The next time I see him, I'll finish him."

"Bastian. Don't." She shook her head. "You're scaring me."

"Alright, Maggie?" She turned at the sound of Dylan's voice, then saw the look that passed between the two men and shivered. Like a pair of angry guard dogs, she hoped they wouldn't end up devouring each other in their frenzy to protect her.

As he pushed past Dylan, Bastian elbowed him in the ribs.

"Hey, watch it." The front door slammed, and Dylan came to her. "What was that all about?"

"I'm not sure. I think he's upset about my dad. Bastian's like one of the family, so whatever happens to us, happens to him too."

Glad to finally be alone with Dylan, she wrapped her arms around his neck, cuddled against his shoulder, and closed her eyes. *Carpe diem.* Hours tied down in a cabin wondering if she would live or die, her father's poor prognosis, and her mother's startling confession—everything she'd experienced in the last few days—had convinced her that seizing the moment was the only thing to do. While stroking the back of his neck, she tilted his head forward and kissed him on the lips. Easily aroused, Dylan opened his mouth and kissed her back, perhaps feeling the same urge to gather rosebuds.

"I have something for you," he said, when the long kiss ended. "I didn't want to give it to you in front of everyone." He reached into his pants pocket and pulled out a small jeweler's box.

"Oh! What is it?" She slipped off the pink bow and opened it. Inside was a necklace with a stone heart.

"It's rose quartz. They say the stone opens your heart to love." He blushed.

"Thank you, Dylan. It's beautiful." She hugged him, and then kissed him again. "I love kissing you. Stay with me tonight. I don't want to sleep alone. I want to sleep with you."

"But your mother—"

"Even if she comes home, she won't notice. Besides, she was young once. She knows what it's like.

"No, I don't think so," Dylan said, pulling away.

"I thought you cared about me."

"I do care about you, but—"

"But what? Jeez Dylan, what's wrong with you?"

"What's wrong with *me*?"

"I've never met a boy who would turn down sex."

He sneered. "What kind of boys have you been meeting?"

Wrapping her arms around him, Maggie drew him in. "I just really want to be with you, and this is my last night here for who knows how long." She kissed his neck. "I thought you wanted me."

"Look, Maggie. When I have sex with a girl, it will be because I know we both love each other, not because one of us, or both of us, are scared or horny or under some kind of spell."

"Spell! What? Has everybody read my diary?" Feeling suddenly exposed, Maggie pushed away from him.

Dylan shrugged. "Well, yes. Your mother was worried. She thought it might help us find you."

"Jesus, Dylan. I conjured that spell weeks ago. Things have changed since then. Now we really care about each other."

"Do we, Maggie? I know I care for you. I'm just not so sure it's me you love."

"Oh, I get it. You still think I'm in love with *him*," she said, gesturing to Estrada in the other room.

"To tell you the truth, I'm not sure you've ever been in love with anyone." Stepping away, he leaned against the counter, hands on his hips. "And like I said, I don't want to have sex until I'm sure the girl I love, loves me back."

"You sound like *him*."

"Who?"

"Father Grace."

"I sound like the priest who tried to rape you?" His face burned scarlet.

"That's exactly what he said to me that night on the porch."

"Why? Did you want to be with him too? Is that why he tried to rape you?"

She raised her hand to slap him again, as she had that night, but was caught by the truth in his words. She *had* wanted to be with the priest. "How can you even think a thing like that?"

"Because I've been watching you, Maggie. When I first met you, I thought you were different. I thought you were—" He paused searching for words in his anger. "I don't know . . . Innocent? But you've changed." He stamped out of the room and left her standing alone in the kitchen with her mouth open and her heart beating so fast she thought it might burst.

"But I'm still a virgin," she said, as the front door slammed for the second time that night. Dylan left her feeling more alone than she'd ever felt in her life—even with a coven of witches in the next room.

As the bus trundled along, Maggie perseverated, first on Dr. Black's instructions, and then on the whole situation. *Primrose will meet you by the copper fountain in Eyre Square.* They were running late—a full hour and twenty minutes late. What if this Primrose had given up and gone home? What if she couldn't find Eyre Square or the copper fountain, or the bus broke down, or they hit one of the wandering sheep? Maggie's stomach growled. She took a deep breath and tried to calm her anxiety by focusing on the myriad lights that twinkled in the darkening fields.

The crazy old bus driver, who tackled the two-hour route from Shannon Airport to Galway City, came within inches of scraping everything he passed. The roads were half as wide while everyone drove twice as fast, and on the wrong side of the road. Several people who boarded along the route were regulars who said, "Afternoon Malachy" to the driver. He winked and nodded in return, then said, "God Bless" to each passenger who disembarked. Maggie remembered reading in Yeats' *Celtic Twilight* that saying, 'God Bless' to someone would keep the faeries at bay. This seemed ironic coming from a man who appeared more fey than human.

As another branch scratched the window beside her head, Maggie caught herself asking for God's blessing. It poured forth as a prayer that, despite her recent angst with churchy things like wayward priests, gave her comfort. She prayed to arrive safely and for help in finding this new mysterious family. She prayed Gabriel Grace would be caught, that she could return home, and that Dylan would no longer despise her. Finally, she prayed for her father, lying unconscious in a hospital bed, and her mother sitting by his side. Would he ever wake up? And if he did, would it only mean more pain for him, more loss of his faculties, and more worry for her mother? Would it be better for him, for them all, if he—

The bus driver blasted the radio suddenly, wrenching her from her thought. She glanced up to find him staring directly at her through the rear-view mirror with the queerest expression on his face. Could he read her mind? Maggie shivered. She'd taken the seat directly behind him—needing to feel connected to someone in this strange land—so could see his reflection clearly. His skin was as weathered as tree bark, and he winked oddly and frequently—cocking his head to the right and closing his right eye, while the other half of his face twitched upwards. This tick or wink squeezed the leathery skin of his right cheek into one small puffy pouch that resembled a walnut shell.

In between these episodes, he jabbered along with the DJ on the local radio station, who spoke entirely in Irish, and played what could only be the traditional music her mother mentioned. Accordions and fiddles and flutes flew through fluid melodies and rhythms that made her want to both dance and cry simultaneously. Taking Shannon's crumpled letter from her pocket, she read it yet again.

My father's name is Padraig (that's pronounced Poe-rig) Vallely, but everyone calls him Paddy Vale. He plays the fiddle and is a well-known trad player. My folks move around, but if you ask any of the trad musicians in any of the pubs, they'll know where to find him.

Paddy Vallely, the traveling fiddler, a leprechaun bus driver, and a father in Ireland. A real father who may or may not know she exists. A father her mother had neglected to name. Like all good Catholic girls, Shannon bore the sin of pregnancy alone. Maggie sighed. If Remy hadn't run off into the forest chasing Dylan's bagpipes. If she hadn't wanted so much to be part of the coven. If she hadn't flirted with a crazy priest. A thousand *ifs* led to this moment, this crossing of an ocean of lives.

Seeing a turnoff for Thoor Ballylee, the medieval Norman castle once owned by William Butler Yeats, Maggie was struck by an epiphany: she really was in Ireland, the land of *The Celtic Twilight*, of poets and priests, of faeries and famine. Hadn't she just read several of Yeats' poems in literature class? Now she was whizzing past places where the man had lived and loved. Was her life nothing but a bizarre series of coincidences?

"Turning and turning in the widening gyre, things fall apart; the center cannot hold," Yeats prophesied in "The Second Coming," and now the frantic spiraling of his gyre had brought her to this place, in this moment. There was nothing to do but breathe and allow fate to unfold.

She tucked her mother's letter back in her bag and grasped Estrada's gift. Opening the book, she reread what he'd written on the front cover: *Like Yeats, I long to see faeries. If this book helps you find them, remember, I want to meet them too. Bendiciónes, Estrada.*

"Here now. I'll take that." Primrose grasped the handle of Maggie's suitcase and wheeled it off across the damp square. In skinny knee-high boots of patterned lime and burgundy leather, with pointed toes and tipsy heels, her feet barely touched the sidewalk. Tucked inside were apricot tights and over top flew a gauzy gold-flecked skirt that shimmered as she danced along the cobbled street. Except for the tight burgundy leather jacket and orange crocheted cap she wore on her head, Primrose could have been a ballerina.

In her dark gothic garb, Maggie felt suddenly stodgy and drab. Desperately jet-lagged, she followed in the witch's wake, grateful to dash along, stretch her cramped legs, and breathe in the fresh sea air after twenty hours of oxygen-deprived travel.

"I've an errand to run, but we'll get ya settled first."

"Where?" yelled Maggie, looking in all directions as they careened along a narrow street flanked by vibrant two-story shops and pubs. Thank God, it was closed to cars. She was having enough trouble avoiding the pedestrians.

"My flat of course. My mate's a lad name of Kieran. He's a chef and—" Maggie's stomach growled loudly causing Primrose to stop so abruptly Maggie crashed into her own suitcase. "Ah, you're starved," Primrose said, and turned toward a quaint pub painted azure blue. The double wooden door had stained glass windows and was trimmed in scarlet. Above it, a red sign said: THE QUAYS.

"The Keys," Primrose said, correcting Maggie, who'd never uttered a sound.

Did everyone in Ireland have access to her private thoughts? First the bus driver and now this fey witch? Still, it was both curious and exciting and she wondered what *these* keys might unlock. Yeats wrote that red was the color of magic. Maggie took a deep breath.

Stepping through the threshold of THE QUAYS was like plunging back through time. The pub was enormous and packed with people, all laughing and talking and drinking. It was nothing like she imagined—three floors joined by carved wooden staircases, gothic arches, and stained-glass windows, even thick church pews. And over the enormous bar hung the steering wheel of a wooden sailing ship. Maggie, who'd never been farther than Vancouver, stood momentarily stunned.

"They went to France, packed up a Seventeenth century church, and rebuilt it here," explained Primrose. "Well, go on then. Have a wander."

Trying to look casual, Maggie strolled through the pub admiring the beauty of the old wood against the spotlights, the shining glasses, and barrels of ale. The tall slanted pipes of a huge organ dominated the center stage, and between the second and third floors, a naked man carved from wood and etched in spirals, crawled up the wall.

"It's amazing," she said, when she returned to Primrose. "From the outside, you'd never believe it looks like this in here."

"Well, you can't tell a book by its cover. Isn't that the cliché?"

Primrose whisked off her cap as they settled into one of the wooden snugs and Maggie was startled to see that her shaved head was tattooed in colorful swirling symbols. Seeing her fascination, Primrose bowed forward to reveal the heart of the design—an intricately patterned mandala etched on the top of her skull. Three violet trees with intertwining roots formed the center, while their branches connected in a circular knot. Between the trees were coiled spirals in emerald green. Another circle of knots wrapped around the first and split near the base of her skull into two trails that merged at the top of her spine.

"That's amazing. Does it go all the way down your back?"

"Aye and ends in a serpent's tail. St. Patrick did not rid Éireann of all the snakes. A few of us survived."

Feeling a new kinship with the strange cryptic witch, Maggie pulled up the sleeve of her black shirt and displayed her rearing Celtic pony.

"Ah, Maggie, that's grand."

"All right, girls?" asked a friendly server.

"Just jet-lagged," replied Maggie. "I've been traveling—"

Primrose giggled. "She's only asking what you'd like."

"Oh. Is there a menu?" Maggie asked feeling her face flush. The waitress passed one over and chatted with Primrose while she scanned it. "I'll have vegetable soup and brown bread." She'd decided, during the long plane ride over the ocean, to become the kind of witch who did not eat animals.

"Excellent choice," Primrose said. "And I'll have your strawberry cheesecake with extra cream. Cheers."

The woman smiled and nodded, then went on her way.

"Your granddad's a fiddler, Syl tells me."

"That's right. His name is Paddy Vallely."

"Well, this is as good a place as any to start our search then. Tell me, how old are you?"

"Almost eighteen."

"Just when's your birthday?"

"First of February. Why?" Primrose raised her eyebrows. "Oh, this is a pub," Maggie said, suddenly realizing the problem. "She didn't card me. Will they kick me out?"

"Not yet, Cinderella. Not until nine. And you'll see your share of pubs after I've secured the proper documentation."

As Maggie watched Primrose speak in her quick clipped way, the slender woman's huge anime eyes changed from gray to blue to aqua, settling at last in a shade quite like green grapes. Maggie rubbed her eyes. Jet lag? But no. Like a chameleon, Primrose was taking on the emerald green hue of her tattoo. Then it wasn't just her eyes, but also her fingernails, which had grown as long and tapered as willow leaves.

Wild Imaginings

Maggie heard Primrose speak but didn't take in the words. Squinting, she stared at the fey witch.

"A name and photo," Primrose repeated. "For your ID."

"Oh. Right," Maggie said, rubbing her eyes. She'd just stumbled out of bed to use the bathroom. Glancing at the clock on the stove she was startled to see six o'clock. Barefoot and wrapped in a long emerald robe, Primrose was whisking around the kitchen, chopping fruit for a smoothie. Did the woman never sleep? They'd stayed up half the night eating their way through a tub of double-churned maple walnut ice cream while Maggie told her tale.

"So, what name will you be using then? You can keep your legal name if you're attached to it, or you can make up a whole new identity. It's really up to yourself like."

"Can't I get in trouble for using a fake ID?"

"Depends who knows it's fake."

"Look, I don't want to get into any more trouble."

"Ah stop. You get kidnapped and almost raped by a maniacal priest and you're afraid to use a fake ID for a worthy cause?" She shook her head as if she couldn't understand Maggie's trepidation. "You do want to find your granddad?"

"Yeah."

"Who's a trad player?"

"Yeah."

"Well, the only way you'll get into the pub at night is if you're eighteen. Now, a session doesn't get going until at least ten and wee seventeen-year-olds are expected to vacate by nine. That's the law here and folks obey it. You could pretend to be eighteen and you might get away with it, but if they asked to see your ID, which a good barman will, you'll be out on the street. No music. No granddad. So, you see, this is the most efficient means to an end."

As she talked, Primrose poured two cups of black tea from a pottery teapot and set out a pitcher of milk and a bowl of brown sugar. "Think of it so: you're only stretching the truth by a few months and in the end, you'll have your family."

"Oh fine. But if the police catch me, you better be there to bail me out. I don't know anyone else in this country." The thought was disconcerting.

"Ah, the Gardai won't bother you. It's just a precaution really—something to flash the barman to ease his worries."

Maggie didn't want to disrespect John Taylor, but she wanted a new name to go with her new self—even though, she didn't really know who that was yet. "I like the sound of my grandfather's last name. Vallely."

"Aye. It's a real old Irish name and it suits you. So, Maggie Vallely then?"

"Not Maggie. I want a name that means something—maybe a Wiccan name or a Celtic name. What does your name mean?"

"It's a flower."

"But it must mean something?"

"A rose by any other name would smell as sweet. Didn't I hear that somewhere?"

"Shakespeare. Juliet says it."

"Right so. Well, the sooner you give me a name and photo, the sooner we can find your family. Ireland's changed some since your ma's time—influx of blow-ins. It may not be as easy as she thinks."

"I have my school photo." Maggie reached for her bag. "What name do you think I should use?"

"Can't help you there. A name's personal, especially if you're looking to use it for power. I will tell you this: traditional witches don't write their names on their ID. They don't even speak them aloud outside the coven." Maggie looked downcast. "Still, if that's what you're after, you should know that a name like that only comes in a dream or a flash of knowing." She stood and picked up her mug, then rinsed it and tipped it upside down in the rack. "I've errands to run. Perhaps you should consider what sort of witch you really are, inside like. Ask the spirits and listen for an answer."

"You think they'll talk to me?"

Primrose smiled. "You've got to know it's you, not just say it's you. Do you get my meaning?"

"I do." Maggie sipped her tea and glanced at Primrose, who'd grabbed her bag, doffed her robe, and was halfway out the door wrapped in a deep purple shawl. "Wait! Are the shops open? How are you running errands at six a.m.?"

"Who said it was six a.m.?"

Estrada pulled his Harley into the driveway and stopped.

"Wow." Sensara wrenched off her helmet. "Is this really where Michael Stryker lives?" With its wraparound porch, railed balconies, and slanted roofs, the Vancouver mansion had a distinctly Gothic feel. "This must be worth millions. How can he afford this?"

Estrada winked. "It belongs to his grandfather." He pointed to a turreted tower shadowed by tall evergreens. "Michael lives there."

"Doesn't granddad mind having a pleasure palace upstairs?"

"Turns a blind eye to his grandson's happiness, I suppose." He didn't intend to tell her that Nigel had an attic room in Michael's suite he sometimes used for his own pleasure when his wife traveled abroad. She'd despise the man before she'd even met him.

"Happiness. Now there's a euphemism."

Estrada fought to ignore Sensara's gibes about their lifestyle. It seemed the only way through her jealousy. It had become a constant irritation and made him wonder if she'd repressed a desire for him all the time they'd been friends. Sometimes a spell only amplifies or reveals that which is hidden.

"Thanks again for offering to give Michael a healing," he said.

"I know what he means to you. I also know he had this coming. Karma is the inescapable dealer of justice."

"Be nice, Sensara. Use your power for good."

"Have I ever done otherwise?"

"This way," he said, grasping her hand. "Michael has a private entrance."

"Of course he does." She halted in front of the heavy oak door. The top half framed a stained-glass window, a Gothic masterpiece of black swords and blood-red teardrops edged in gold. "The man certainly has a fixation."

Estrada grinned and thought, *you don't know the half of it*. He snatched a key from behind a low loose brick. "Ah good. Sometimes he remembers to leave it and sometimes he doesn't." The door groaned open. As they ascended, the old oak stairs creaked beneath their feet.

"No sneaking in here at night."

He felt Sensara's mood suddenly darken. Since they'd been spending copious hours together their connection had tightened. He could pick up the slightest shifts and wondered if she shared that same ability. She hadn't mentioned their abduction since that night in the hospital.

"What's the matter?" he asked.

"It just struck me that this was the last staircase she ever descended."

"Jade?"

Sensara nodded. "Her killer was likely waiting just outside; maybe on the street or in the shadows. Maybe even right where we came in."

"I'm glad you believe Michael's innocent. As much as you despise his lifestyle, you know there's no one with a greater heart."

"I know you believe that, and you seem to know him well. Perhaps, a little too well."

Her final words bit, but he turned away and ignored them. Relieved to finally have her back, as his friend and now his lover, he hoped nothing else would go awry. Sensara was not the same woman he once knew; at least, he didn't know her in the same way. Still he felt judged and confined. If only she would allow him his freedom. He wouldn't love her any less.

When she shoved him against the wall at the top of the stairs, he was startled.

"Forget the past, Estrada. You're mine now." To seal her claim, she bit his neck.

"Jesus, woman."

She ran her tongue over the bite, then caught his mouth with hers, kissing him deeply, wanting more, wanting him to take her right there on the landing. As uninhibited as she'd become, Sensara still refused to have sex outside the flat.

He wondered why the sudden change but couldn't think.

Catching her hair in his fingers, he pulled gently, bending her back, so she could feel every inch of him hard against her belly.

"You're *all* I think about," she confessed. "I want you all the time." Unsnapping his jeans, she slipped her hand inside.

"I can help you with that," he said, and kissed her again. She was stroking him, increasing the rhythm. If she didn't slow down... He broke off the kiss. "Easy baby. No need to rush."

Grasping the top of his jeans in her fists, she wrenched them down to his thighs. "But I want you now," she breathed.

Lifting her long skirt, he ran his hand up the back of her thigh. "No panties? My, my, Sara. Did you plan this?"

Grinning, she nodded. "Surprised?"

"Amazed. But I don't have a condom. Do you?"

She shook her head. "It doesn't matter. You're mine and I want you now."

Aware of his past liaisons, she'd made him attend a clinic for testing and always insisted on protection even though he'd come back clean. "Are you sure? What about—?"

"Stop talking." Covering his mouth with hers, she kissed him again.

With both hands, he scooped her up. She gasped, then kissed his neck. Turning, he wedged her into the corner, the quickening rhythm of her hips urging him on. Clinging to him with her thighs, she moaned, heedless of the creaking wood that braced her back.

"I love you more than him," she said, through ragged breaths. "Promise me that—"

The door opened, silencing her request. Caught on the edge, Estrada froze, slowed his breath and stayed still, feeling the tantric wait surge through his body.

"Oh, excuse me," Nigel said. "I thought I heard something."

Sensara buried her face in Estrada's shoulder. For her sake, Estrada was grateful for the long coat that covered them.

"So glad you could come, Sandolino." Suave and astute, Nigel could allay the most awkward of situations.

Glancing over his shoulder, Estrada smiled. "Actually, sir,"—he took a breath—"we'll be another minute or two."

"Take all the time you need."

It took no time at all. Getting caught only heightened his desire. In the final second, he cried out, "I love you, Sara." She needed to hear it, was feeling insecure. In the midst of it, she'd said something curious. *I love you more than him.* Who did she fear? Michael or the killer?

Abashed in the aftermath, Sensara clung to his arm as they entered.

"Ah, The Divine Sensara," Michael said. "I'm honored that you've graced my humble abode with your presence at last."

Estrada watched as she took in the elegant silk draperies, burgundy leather couches, Michael's collection of imported hookahs, and the Persian carpets that ran rampant throughout the flat like so many opaline serpents. Like Byron, Michael had a penchant for the exotic.

As Estrada expected, Michael was not in bed as he should have been, considering the extent of his injuries, but lounging on a chaise the color of cognac. He looked alluring in black silk trousers and kimono, his honey-blond hair falling freely around his face. The mark of the weapon was fading from his hollow cheek and the sling gone. When he beckoned them in with a sweep of his hand, Estrada noticed that his long fingernails were painted black and decorated in scarlet tear drops. Obviously, the prince was being well tended.

"I feel like I should kiss his ring," Sensara whispered.

"He'd prefer you kiss something else," Estrada said.

She smacked him, and then clung to him as they crossed the room. He leaned down and hugged Michael, then settled in beside Sensara on a couch as soft as butter.

Nigel brought in a tea tray and set it on the table, along with biscuits and cheese. "Please, help yourself. I'm delighted you're both here. I can't wait to tell you what I've discovered about your wayward priest—Gabriel Grace."

"Do tell," Estrada said.

"Do you mind if I smoke?" Nigel asked Sensara, picking up a full pipe from the table beside his chair.

She shook her head—another unusual response.

"Right then." Nigel lit his pipe with a few puffs. Aromatic tobacco perfumed the air. "Where to begin? I suppose with his identity. The man's real name is not Gabriel Grace. It's Gerald Gardner."

"No!" Sensara said. Gerald Gardner, who'd written many texts on the craft, was to many the father of Wicca.

"I thought you'd like that. His mother's maiden name was Gardner and, as she never married, I suppose she thought it auspicious to name her child after her long-deceased mentor. She was a Gardnerian witch, you see. A high priestess no less. She must have felt some mystical connection to the man."

Estrada felt Sensara tense against him and knew she was wondering how much Nigel knew about witchcraft and Hollystone and such things. He was a man who left nothing to chance; who believed in the old Bacon adage that knowledge is power.

"Gabriel, or rather, Gerald, is an ordained Catholic priest, raised for the most part in a strictly religious home, which is no doubt where he found his calling. As a young child, however . . . Well, suffice to say, his childhood was tragic."

They waited as Nigel puffed on his pipe and collected his thoughts.

"Twenty odd years ago, there was a sensational case involving a coven of witches who exploited children in pornographic films."

"Wasn't that on the island?" Sensara said.

"That's correct."

"They were arrested and convicted."

"Yes. Gerald's mother was the coach and director. Gerald was a child star."

"My God!" Sensara was appalled. "Real Wiccans would never do something like that! That goes against everything the craft stands for."

Nigel's raised eyebrows only exacerbated things.

"Well, it's true. Wiccans do no harm, especially to children."

"So, damaged child, sexually abused by witches, grows up and takes his revenge?" Estrada said.

Nigel nodded. "It would appear so. When the Crown prosecuted, six of the children were put in foster care. Gerald, who was eight, ended up with a wealthy Catholic family in the valley. They tried their best to rehabilitate him. According to the evidence, he'd been starring in these films since he was four years old."

"*Christ*," Estrada said, feeling sudden compassion for the child who fathered the man. No wonder he was so fucked up about sex.

"The man is incredibly intelligent. He graduated with an Honors B.A. in philosophy and religion, and then was awarded a Master of Divinity. This is his second parish. The first, which was in northern Manitoba, made no complaints. On paper, Father Grace appears exemplary."

"Well, he's not. He nearly raped Maggie, and if he's the man who's been abducting these women . . ."

He felt Sensara snuggle in closer as her voice drifted off. "How did he ever get this far?"

"Serial killers are among the most intelligent of men: charismatic, organized, masters of illusion. It's how they avoid detection and continue to kill."

"So I've been told," Michael quipped.

It suddenly all made sense to Estrada, who'd been raised a Catholic himself. A young child cast as a porn star was not only tainted goods but wounded. That made him easy prey. Desperately needing love but not knowing how to get it, he'd become a victim of his own desire. He'd joined the priesthood to avoid sex, but still had the desire. Denied sex by his religion, he was forced to steal it, and seeing in all female witches the mother who'd abused him, he burned them with reason. He even disguised himself as Christ—the betrayed messiah—on a mission to right the injustices of the world.

Clive appeared from the kitchen and helped himself to a cup of tea. Why was *he* here? Was he now included in all family business? Michael was spending far too much time with him. He may not be the killer, but there was still something menacing about him.

After settling into a leather recliner and taking a sip of tea, Clive turned to Estrada. "So, *magician*, what are your thoughts on this revelation?" The insolent bastard had nerve calling him that. Worse still, how did he know? Had he been listening outside the cave that day?

"He thinks it's positively tragic so many innocent people have been hurt," Michael said. "Don't you, compadre?"

"Tragic, yes." Estrada's narrow eyes cast threats of their own.

Sensara leaned into his shoulder. "Do the police have any idea where Grace is now?"

"As far as I know, they've got nothing." Nigel puffed on his pipe. "The man seems to have vanished."

"But you were the last person to see him, weren't you, Estrada? You *did* tell the coppers about your little tête-à-tête in the cave?"

The sinister tone of Clive's question raised the hackles on Estrada's back. He'd been there, spying on him. What did he want? Blackmail? Revenge?

"Outside," Estrada growled. "Now."

"Hush little brother. Stop trying to steal the show," Michael said.

Sensara sat up. "What's he talking about? What cave?"

"My brother has some unresolved angst concerning Estrada, who had the audacity to throw him out of Crimson many miles from here and many days ago. Drop it, Clive."

Ready to spring, Estrada stood and gestured toward the doorway. "Let's go. Now."

Easing back into the leather chair like a spoiled child, Clive dipped a biscuit into his tea and slowly chewed.

"Boys." Nigel's voice rose in subtle warning.

Estrada walked toward the door, not knowing exactly what Clive had witnessed, but guessing from his taunts, it was far more than he wished revealed with Sensara in the room. He needed this to end. Now. If the kid wouldn't leave, he would.

"Estrada, please don't go. My brother's just being an ass—something he does remarkably well."

But Estrada had already grabbed Sensara by the hand and was hauling her out the door.

"Why are you so upset?" she asked, as they descended the stairs.

"Why do you think?"

"I don't know. That's why I'm asking. What was he talking about? Why do you hate him so much?"

Estrada paused at the bottom of the stairs and turned to her. "You know how you get feelings about people."

She nodded.

"Well, I've got a bad feeling about Clive. For a while, I suspected *he* was the killer. He's a creep, a stalker who arrived out of nowhere. No one knows anything about him, except—"

Slow clapping interrupted his tirade. Looking up, he saw Clive, standing on the landing, smirking down at him.

"That's rich. You thought *I* was the killer. So, let me get this straight. You've been thinking all this time, that *we* had sex? That I was the *best lover* you ever had?"

"Shut up," Estrada growled.

"Oh, didn't he tell you, priestess? Your man is involved in quite the sordid liaison with this killer. They've done wild and wicked things. It started the night he abducted you—"

Estrada mounted the stairs two at a time. When his fist connected with the kid's mouth, it silenced his accusations. Wrenching Clive up by the shoulders, he smashed him against the wall. Wheezing and struggling, panic flooded the kid's face.

Nigel opened the door just as Estrada flung Clive to the floor and raised his foot for the first kick. "What's going on here?" He lunged between them, leaned down, and grasped Clive's chin. The kid swooned, spit out blood and tooth.

"Nothing. Clive just—" The slamming of a door caught Estrada's attention and he glanced down. Sensara was gone. He bounced down the stairs and raced out into the driveway. Where was she? How could he ever explain? He didn't even understand it himself. When he felt her behind him, he was afraid to turn and face her.

"I don't know who you are," Sensara said. "Before it didn't matter. All the women, the men—" She was crying. He could hear it in her voice. "But he was going to *burn* me. Were you with him *that* night? Is that when you had *sex*? While I was in the hospital? And then you came to me and—"

"It wasn't like that. Clive knows nothing."

A cab appeared on the street and stopped. Sensara walked toward it.

"Don't go, Sara. Let me explain."

"There are some things that no explanation will ever make right." She closed the door of the cab.

Even though he knew this moment was inevitable, Estrada was not prepared for the feeling of loss that overwhelmed him as the cab drove away. Feeling abandoned, he stood on the sidewalk, paralyzed.

Maggie pulled out her ID to examine again. She couldn't believe she was now Kyra Vallely. It wasn't her power name, only a name that came to her after seeing an envelope addressed to Primrose's roommate, Kieran. "It means black-haired," Primrose had said. "Suits you."

Now, as Kyra Vallely, an eighteen-year-old Irish girl, she was perched on a bar stool in a busy Galway pub, listening to traditional music and drinking pints. Mere weeks ago, she'd been writing a *Macbeth* essay for senior English class, and now her own life was a maze of murder and intrigue. She'd been assaulted by her priest, escaped a kidnapper, flown alone to an island across the ocean, and was now drinking in an Irish pub with a witch who was becoming increasingly fey.

Having tried the Guinness at Tig Coili, the first pub on their crawl, and finding it a little too thick, the bartender suggested she switch to cider.

"At least it's made from apples," Primrose said, "and they are a magical fruit. I'm sure you've seen what happens when you slice an apple in half horizontally?"

Maggie had not.

"Why the seeds form a pentagram."

Maggie was now on her fifth or sixth pint. Really, she'd lost count. Primrose was back on the subject of apples and talking too quickly to comprehend. "Of course, the apple has been maligned in the anti-magic myths. It always contains poison or some such thing." She caught Maggie fumbling around in her bag after the ID and yelled: "Put that away. They'll be thinking you're daft. Don't you know better than to call attention to yourself?" This, coming from a woman whose shaved head was tattooed in Celtic symbols. "And don't you be getting pissed. We're here to do business. You can't be cracking your head open falling down the steps to the can."

Giggling, Maggie tucked the card away in her pocket. It was the first time she'd laughed in days. As Kyra, she felt a newfound freedom, her Canadian self craved but had never dared to seize. Tig Coili was a frequent haunt of traditional musicians and fans and so packed by ten, they had to squeeze in at the bar to watch the players. It was marvelous. Everyone who swooped in to grab a pint had something clever to say.

"The craic's always ninety in here," Primrose said.

"The *crack*?"

"Aye. The craic. C R A I C—the flirting, the conversation, the wisecracks, the chat. It's what we do here in Ireland. It's what we're famous for. You mean to say you're Irish and you've never heard that."

"No, but I like it. And I like being Irish." The music was as intoxicating as the brew. Double and triple fast melodies echoed in riveting trills that ran round and round in spirals. The secret of how the melody moved was shared only by the players, who had some ingenious tracking system known only to the initiated. To a novice, tunes were almost impossible to differentiate, but the players knew them by name, and there were hundreds, even thousands of tunes that had been handed down through centuries. One flick of an eyebrow and the whole lot of them would carry the tune off in a different direction, only to wind it back to its beginning some time later. Some tunes were thought to be gifts from the faeries...faeries that people still believed existed in their own kind of parallel world.

Most of this, she'd learned from the man sitting on the stool next to her at the bar. An aficionado, he traveled the island catching traditional music sessions. Unfortunately, he'd never heard of Padraig Vallely or Paddy Vale. Nor had the three players at Tig Coili. Only the flute player was Irish though, and he was young and fresh from Dublin. The other two were Dutchmen, a somber fiddler who never smiled, and a talented ginger-haired accordion player who carried the melody with flying fingers. The bartender thought he'd heard of a fella named Vallely once upon a time who played a decent fiddle, but he hadn't been around Galway in ages.

Having completed their business, the two women walked around the corner to Taaffe's, where Maggie cozied up to the fire to sip another cider.

"I'm off to chat with the lads," Primrose said. "That's your parting glass now. Make it last."

"Oh right. I thought you were all about freedom and suddenly you're my mother," replied Maggie, in a distinctly sloppy voice.

"Suit yourself but know this. We're heading off early tomorrow morning on a lengthy excursion and there'll be no puking down the back of my jacket while I'm driving."

"What? How could I—?"

Primrose turned and walked over to chat with the musicians, who'd taken a break from playing to enjoy a few pints. She'd no sooner left than a scruffy man with a rather large gold earring settled into the seat beside Maggie.

"Hello gorgeous. What's the craic?" His accent was as thick as Guinness.

Unsure how to respond, Maggie simply smiled.

"What's your name, gorgeous?"

"Kyra," she said, with drunken pride.

"Kyra. A raven-haired beauty and all alone. More's the pity." He patted her leg and winked.

"I'm not alone. I'm with Primrose. We're looking for my granddad. Do you know him?"

"I might. What's his name then?"

"Pad-dy Vale-ale-y. Plays fiddle." Tilting her head, she mimicked a bow stroke with her hands.

"Lost then, is he?"

As Maggie watched, his face wavered and slowly split in two.

"You look a might peeked, gorgeous. I'll just whisk you outside, shall I?"

"If there's whisking to be done, "I'll be doing it," Primrose said, and the man vanished into the crowd. "Come along, Miss Kyra."

The next thing Maggie knew, she was on her knees bent over the toilet at Taaffe's. Primrose stood behind her and held back her hair.

"Is this why you shaved your head?"

"No, it's not. You probably didn't notice, but I don't drink alcohol."

"Why not?"

"Ah well. You'll have the answer to that soon enough."

Maggie dug her tear-streaked face into her fey friend's leather back and tightened the grip around her waist. They were careening up the N17 on Primrose's motorbike as if it was midsummer and there were no speed limits. As slight as a willow stick and twice as pliant, Primrose was so slender, Maggie could slip her hands inside her opposite sleeves. Thank God. The weather had turned bitter cold, too cold for riding a motorbike, yet here they were, racing up the slick Irish tarmac in the late November dawn.

Primrose emanated heat like a micro furnace while Maggie wished for mittens and a parka, wished she could perform movie magic—the blink and it's done stuff. What was the point of being a witch if you still felt everything like everybody else and could do nothing about it?

One thing Maggie had learned about Primrose was that there was no stopping her. She was a woman in constant motion. Maggie still didn't understand where they were going or why. When she asked, Primrose answered with one of her usual cryptic questions. *You never really know where you're going till you get there, do you now?*

Maggie fought the urge to puke down the back of the woman's leather jacket—vaguely recalling a comment from the previous night—but knew there could be dire consequences. Still, it would serve Primrose right for letting her get drunk, encouraging her even. She was just a kid and Primrose had set her up. Who provides an underage kid with fake ID and then takes her on a pub crawl? Maggie's head was throbbing.

They whizzed by another sign, this one perched on the edge of the hedge bordering the N4, and then another, written in Gaelic, *Sligeach*—however that was said—and then suddenly Primrose veered left at the roundabout, and they raced down the narrow edge of Ballysadare Bay. Even the sea emitted a green sheen in Ireland. Perhaps it was the algae or some reflection from the lush fields surrounding them on all sides. Ireland was as green as its reputation, carpeted in verdant grasslands, dotted with cottages and cows, giant boulders and leafy shrubs.

The drizzle began as Primrose stopped the motorbike. They were parked in the middle of a farmer's field. Chubby calves, some sleekly white, others curly black or brown, blinked at them, then continued munching the wet salty grass.

"This way." Primrose cocked her head and darted along a dirt lane rutted by tractor tires. A huge cairn of gray rocks piled on top of a hill, caught Maggie's attention. She was about to ask about it when suddenly the world spun. Her stomach heaved and ejected what she prayed was the last of its contents. When she straightened up, Primrose thrust a small flask into her hand.

"Drink up. You'll be dehydrated," she ordered in her usual clipped tone, without a hint of sympathy.

"I'm never drinking again," Maggie stated. After draining the bottle, she wiped her mouth with her sleeve, and pointed up. "What's that rock pile? Tell me we're not hiking up there."

"That before you is Knocknarea. It's—"

"Wait. I know this. Yeats wrote about Knocknarea in the book Estrada gave me." She fished through her bag and produced the paperback. "His poem is called 'The Hosting of the Sidhe' and—"

"That's pronounced *shee*," Primrose said, "and do you know who the sidhe are?"

"Well, Yeats says: 'Away, come away; empty your heart of its mortal dream.' Obviously, they're immortal. Probably ghosts or the faeries Estrada wants to meet."

"Or both," Primrose said winking slyly. "Now *Cnoc na Riabh*—*cnoc* meaning hill and *riabh* meaning royalty—is so named because it holds Maeve's Cairn, or as we say in Irish, *Miosgán Meadhbha*."

"I wish I could speak Irish. It's beautiful."

"Aye. You can, and you will."

Maggie considered this. Was she just being optimistic? Or was Primrose a psychic like Sensara? "Who was Maeve?" she asked.

"Queen of all Connacht. And this rock pile, as you put it, is part of the passage tomb in which she was buried five thousand years ago—standing straight up, they say, sword in hand and armed for battle. We Celtic women are warriors."

Warriors. Am I a warrior too? Entranced, Maggie said nothing.

"Now, are you steady girl? We're going to climb to the top of this mound of stones, so you can see the land of your ancestors. It's time you got to know who you are and where you come from."

Maggie hiked up the steep worn path, grasping rocks to steady herself in the slick mud. Her haggard breaths revealed just how out of shape she'd become. A night of ciders hadn't helped either. She swallowed to relieve her parched throat, then slid backwards and braced her foot against a rock. Primrose produced the small flask again and passed it back. Maggie eyed it cautiously.

"Pure water," Primrose said.

Maggie shot her a questioning glance, but Primrose just laughed, her face glowing like the morning sun that hovered over the pasture. The water tasted rich and earthy, like it had come from a spring deep inside the earth. Maggie drank and drank, yet when she handed back the flask, the weight felt unchanged.

"Holy well," Primrose said by way of explanation.

Maggie shook her head warily, her thoughts drifting back to Yeats' faerie caution—never drink or eat their food. The consequence of such a blunder was the loss of one's senses and the ability to return home; at least until the faeries finished with you, and that could take seven human years. Was this really one of their haunts? What secrets were buried beneath five thousand years of rock and dirt? The erect skeleton of a warrior queen? The brittle bones of her own ancestors?

"During the Iron Age, Ireland was split into five kingdoms," explained Primrose, pointing as she spoke. "Ulster in the north, Leinster in the east, Munster in the south, and Connacht in the west, which is where we're standing. Mide was dead center at Tara and that was where the High King lived. We'll go there sometime, so." Primrose turned and continued climbing.

"Soon, I hope," Maggie said. She'd always liked history, but this was fascinating because it was *her* story. She wanted to see and hear it all.

Just over an hour later, they reached the top. Revived by holy water and pure oxygenated air, Maggie forgot about her headache and danced in circles, arms outstretched. There by the cairn on the top of the world, she felt the heart of the land beat within her blood. Rocks and cows dotted the green fields and, in the distance, stood a misty city by the sea.

"What's that place?" She had to shout as the strong wind on the hilltop caught their voices.

"Sligeach."

"Sly-go," Maggie repeated slowly.

"Aye. *Sligeach*—the place of the shells."

Shells. Seafood. Clam chowder. "Can we get something to eat there?"

"Aye sure. Tomorrow."

"Tomorrow? But I'm starving now."

Icy rain splattered Estrada's cheeks as he crossed the Old Alexandra Bridge on his Harley. He parked his bike in a stand of trees, stashed his helmet, and grabbed his pack. Then, after tucking everything beneath a tarp, he set off toward the cave. Beside him, the surging

Fraser River was peppered with raindrops from an ominous sky. It was early Friday night—a night he usually performed his show at Pegasus—and he shivered. Like Macbeth, his world had swung "out of joint."

Wending his way through the rock trail, he wondered how it had come to this. Confounded by his obsession, he imagined the killer, called to him, begged him to come, to take the risk. His only redemption was in finding the man and taking him down, even if it meant going down with him. He patted his leather boot, felt the hard, thin, shape of the knife, and picked up his pace. He'd not used a weapon in a very long time—had sworn once never to use one again. But that was then, and this was now. This man was a lunatic who kidnapped women and burned them—a psychopath who needed to be put out of his misery.

He made good time following the trail which, marked and broken by police, now led directly to the cave. Investigators, in search of evidence, had cordoned off the area with bright yellow tape and sifted methodically through Dylan's rubble. He didn't know what they'd found but suspected his DNA would turn up somewhere someday—preferably not in a courtroom. Rocks had been rolled or carried from the opening, and the cave, now clear of debris, looked remarkably like it had the first time he'd seen it.

The man's body had not been found. Like the wind, he'd slipped through a fissure to freedom.

Estrada crawled inside, lit four candles, and placed one in each cardinal direction. Then, he laid down on the earthen floor and conjured him—remembering the scent and feel of him, the moist fingers against his lips, and the ferocious details of their first baffling encounter. He could not identify the man by sight, but if ever he touched him again, even for a moment, he'd know.

Betrayed by his wayward body, he fought for control. What the hell was it? Pheromones? Karma? The charm? What drew him so intensely to this lunatic? He scowled at his own lack of restraint. What if the man came now and saw him like this, aroused and waiting? Would he be able to confront and capture him? Or would the man bemuse him yet again?

As the fire cast flickering shadows against the darkened walls, he pulled himself up to a seated position, slipped off his wet boots, and crossed his legs. Like the Buddha, he would meditate until he was no longer at the mercy of his demons.

But that too was short-lived. An undisciplined extrovert, he could neither stand seclusion nor control the chaos in his mind. Constantly drawn from observing his breath by howling wind and scraping branches, he began his own "wild imaginings." Had he, like Macbeth, succumbed to the spell cast by the witches. Witches who were no Weird Sisters but, ironically, healers from his own coven? He had neither murdered like Macbeth, nor intentionally harmed anyone, yet he'd caused suffering. Stricken by lust, his own hedonistic pleasure, he accepted that he was the sole creator of this tragedy. There really was no one else to blame.

As night dragged on, he slept fitfully, turning from back to side and back again, feeling every bump and dip in the pounded earth. Finally, needing to urinate, he opened his eyes to darkness and fished around in his coat pocket until he produced a lighter. Removing two candles from his pack, he lit them, then crawled on his knees to the opening in the rock and peered out into the screeching night.

Snow pelted helter-skelter in hard icy flakes and formed crystalline ridges sculpted by the wind. Still in his sock feet, he unzipped his fly and sent a steaming stream of piss arcing three feet from the door. The temperature had dropped to below freezing with the wind chill. Shivering, he returned to his pack and pulled out a fleece blanket. Unrolling it, he produced a mickey of his father's best friend, Mexican tequila. Just a few sips—that's all he needed.

As Breath into the Wind

Maggie was hunkered down inside a dolmen. Like all the megaliths at Carrowmore, it was erected from immense granite boulders dislodged by retreating glaciers after the last Ice Age. Thousands of years ago, some Neolithic tribe managed to move these boulders into position; six slabs in a circular formation covered by a seventh—a flat capstone that crowned them all. Knowing it had stood for millennia did nothing to stem the sensation of being crushed beneath it.

Naturally, this was Primrose's idea. This particular dolmen was one of the witch's favorites and one she frequented at propitious times. Tonight was a dark moon. A time for introspection, for peeling back daylight layers and exposing inner truth, and Maggie was tasked with spending the night alone in meditation. She sat on the rough earthen floor, wrapped in a brown woolen blanket, and gazed through the stone portal into the night sky. Thick stratus clouds threatened rain and obscured any chance of stargazing. At least if it rained, the capstone would provide some shelter from the elements, if not the elementals.

She wasn't scared. Not really. There was nothing to fear. No bands of drunken marauders looking to party, no bears or cougars like in the woods at Buntzen Lake. Besides, Primrose was nearby, herself in solitary contemplation, somewhere amidst the sixty odd monuments.

The Neolithic farmers came by boat with seeds, cattle, and pigs, Primrose said. Using stone tools, they cleared the forests and planted fields of barley. The megaliths were huge stone tombs that housed the cremated bones of their dead. Maggie felt like a tiny pinprick in the vastness of time, smaller than the ash on the sole of her shoe, this dust of her ancestors.

Surely, the tomb builders understood the spirit separated from the body after its decline. Perhaps that's why they built these megaliths and buried the ashes of their families and friends. Where did they think spirits went when they died? Maggie had never known anyone who'd died, but her father *could* die. Where would his spirit go? A month ago, she would have said heaven—that's what she'd been taught. But now she wasn't sure. She'd crossed an ocean running from a priest and that threw everything she'd ever believed into question.

She closed her eyes and imagined an indigo blue circle in the center of her forehead. Touching it gave her focus. With each breath her chest rose and fell. In the distance, a cow bellowed, forgotten in the darkness. Raindrops hit the rock with a light tap and the scent of wet earth teased her nostrils.

Soon there was nothing. No sound but the drumming of her own heart as it pumped blood through her body. In her mind, she visualized pulsing veins and arteries. In this body there was muscle, bone, breath, and flesh. Then suddenly, she was no longer in that body, but above it. Hovering under the granite capstone, tethered by a silver cord, Maggie stared at the girl who sat below as contemplative as a yogi.

Suddenly aware of her body again, she felt cold and cramped. She stretched out her legs, rubbed her hands together to generate heat, blew on her palms, and massaged her arms, legs, and feet. What time was it? How long had she hovered outside like that? Seconds? Hours? Her belly growled for food, but she had none. Primrose had laid down the rules. She must fast and stay awake throughout the night. She knew this was some kind of test, an initiation of sorts, and she was just stubborn enough to try and pass it.

The scent of savory grilled meat made her salivate. Maggie opened her eyes. People wandered in the grass beyond the curbstones encircling the dolmen. A family was cooking over a wood fire pit. She rubbed her eyes to dislodge the hallucination, but the images remained. Laughing children tossed berries into shells as they played an ancient carnival game. Then others came, carrying baskets and wearing a fabric of woven plants, berry red and leafy green, their long hair hanging jagged or plaited with vines. Two men played flutes, while others drummed, and soon the people were dancing. Nothing looked the same. The grassy meadows were no longer barren, but swaddled by trees, their branches quivering with songbirds. Wild roses perfumed the air and ripe juicy berries drooped low, begging to be plucked. Neolithic Ireland.

Maggie sprang from the dolmen and ran into their midst. She spied Primrose, near naked, with only a fragment tied across her hips. Dancing among them, her tattooed head waved with the music. Maggie caught her hand and joined in. As walls fell away, she forgot everything but the throbbing music and the heartbeat of the Mother Earth surging up her bare legs and through her body. Weaving between them, she laughed and touched their shadowy skin and felt more alive than she'd ever felt before.

If this was Faerie, seven years was too short a time. Given the chance, she'd stay forever.

When Maggie awoke, she and Primrose were cuddled up like sisters under the woolen blanket.

"Ah, you're back," the fey witch whispered.

"Wow. That was"—she searched for the words—"Did you . . .?"

"Aye, sure." Primrose sat up and stretched. "Look, the sun's rising over the valley. It's grand, yeah?"

"Yeah," agreed Maggie, struggling to stand in the cramped dolmen.

"You must be starved, girleen. Let's drive to Sligo and find a good fry-up. Then you can tell me about your night."

"Yum. Hash browns." A vision of Bastian flashed through her mind, drawing her back to the kitchen of the log house. "When we get there, I'd like to call my mom. It's weird, but I miss her. I want to know why she left this place. It seems like we never really talked about anything important, and I feel like I don't know her at all. Do you know what I mean?"

"Leaving something is a sure way of telling whether you still love it or have had your fill. I think that's why some folks get back and others never do."

Maggie had the feeling Primrose wasn't just talking about this world anymore.

"There's some that want to come back and can't. They get so enthralled they can't break free. To ease the pain, they try to forget everything that's come before. Then, after a while they forget who they are and where they belong."

When Primrose stepped out of the dolmen, Maggie followed. As they walked through the wet grass, she called back over her shoulder, "Maybe your ma was one of those. The question is: which one are you?"

Estrada awoke to the stench of charring salmon. He was nauseous. Refused to open his eyes. Repulsed by the rancid taste of his own breath, every cell in his body deranged, he laid still for several minutes, trying to will the hangover away. *Damn tequila.* He tried to remember how he'd ended up here.

On a hunch, he'd gone back to the cave hoping Grace would appear. But, he hadn't. At least, Maggie was safely on her way to Ireland. He could go back to sleep. No one would know. No one would care. He was almost there when the thought struck him. *Someone is cooking fish. It could be him.*

He bolted upright, got the spins and puked. His head pounded. It took several deep breaths to regain his equilibrium. When he did, he took the knife from his boot and crawled on his knees through the cramped tunnel toward the invading crack of light. Pushing back the bushes, he spied the outline of a man a few feet distant. Squatting over an open fire, he was busy cooking fish, and didn't glance up. *Was it him?*

Estrada pressed open the switchblade. It lacked the balance of his stage knives, but after years of hitting his mark, he surely wouldn't miss. Black toque and rain jacket, blue jeans and hiking boots. His hands were dark-skinned like his own, his long black hair pulled back in a ponytail. Pinching the knife end between his thumb and fingertips, Estrada considered.

"I sure hope you're not planning to wing that knife at me." As the man stood, Estrada noticed he was only slightly taller than Sensara, maybe five foot five. Way too short for the man, who stood eye to eye with him and must be at least six two. "That wouldn't be friendly. Especially not after I cooked you breakfast." His voice was husky for his size—like maybe he smoked even more than Michael—and when he smiled, he showed a mouthful of pale even teeth.

"Who are you?" Estrada closed the knife and slipped it in his pocket.

"I was about to ask you the same thing."

"I asked first."

"Okay. Okay." Judging by the condition of the coals, he'd been out there a while. He'd cut open the fish, gutted it, and was grilling it skin-side down on a cedar plank over the open fire. As horrible as he felt, Estrada's stomach growled. "Name's Josh," he said. He poured water into his cupped hand and sprinkled it over the fire. It sputtered as steam puffed into the air mixing with the smoke.

"Estrada."

"Well, Estrada, think you can eat some of this salmon? I figured since this is hangover day, you might be hungry."

Estrada surveyed the small glade. Everything was covered with a couple of inches of pristine snow.

"You can sit out here, but you'll end up with a cold wet ass. I was hoping to keep mine dry." Josh must have been in his early twenties, but when he smiled, he lit up like a kid.

Estrada nodded. "I could eat. Come in." The fish would fill his belly and maybe mask the taste of dead tequila.

Josh carefully picked up the cedar plank and followed him into the cave. He deposited it on the bench, then unzipped his jacket and made himself comfortable sitting with his back against the wall, short legs stretched out in front.

Josh gestured to the platter of steaming salmon. "Help yourself." Taking a pouch of tobacco and packet of papers from his pocket, he rolled a cigarette.

"How long have you been out there?" Estrada asked. Leaning over, he picked off a moist chunk of fish and slipped it into his mouth. Fresh and slightly charred, it tasted so savory he quickly ate another.

"Came up this morning at first light." He flicked his lighter and lit his smoke.

"You see anyone else around here?"

Settling back and smoking, he briefly considered the question. "Nah. No one. Your partner a no show?"

"Partner?"

"The guy you met here last week."

"You saw me—?" With sudden interest, Estrada perched on the stone bench.

"Yeah man."

"What did you see?"

Josh sniffed and exhaled a large mouthful of smoke. "Saw you arrive with hair like mine and leave looking like you'd been scalped." He grinned.

"Where were you?"

"Fishing downriver."

"Ah. Right." He remembered seeing some guys fishing.

"See I noticed that red car you drove up in. She's a real beauty." After butting out his smoke, he took a hunk of salmon and swallowed it. "Then yesterday, I was fishing again when you drove up on that Harley. Man, you got some fine wheels."

"The bike's mine, but the car belongs to a friend."

Josh drank from his canteen and offered it to Estrada. "Tequila leaves you dryer than sagebrush, eh?"

Estrada took a healthy swallow and passed it back.

"My old man used to drink that shit when he could get it," Josh said. "My brother and me were just kids, but we tried it a few times. Stole it from him. Fucks you up good." He smiled at the memory, and then sniffed it into a frown. "Shit killed them. I gave it up."

"Sorry man." How did a man react to a statement like that? "You stopped drinking. You're smart, smarter than me."

"Hell. Alcohol's always been a problem for us," Josh said gesturing between them. "I just learned my lesson early." Taking out his tobacco pouch, he rolled another smoke and lit it.

"Still smoke though."

"Don't have to worry about stunting my growth. I've always been a runt, and hey . . . Tobacco's sacred. I'm praying with this stuff. What tribe you from?"

"Tribe? Oh, right. My mother's Mayan," Estrada said, not that he knew much about his culture. His memories of the Yucatan were ephemeral. What he remembered most were bad times in L.A. and worse times in Canada.

"Mayan? No shit." Josh shook his head in disbelief. "Well, you're one heck of a long way from home, brother."

Estrada nodded. It was true. He hadn't been back to Mexico since he left with his parents and sisters, even though his grandmother still wrote to him every few months. Sometimes she even came to him in dreams. One day, he'd go back.

"So, why you so eager to kill yourself?" The question, asked so matter-of-factly, left Estrada speechless. Sensing his discomfort, Josh rambled off in a different direction. "You ever hear of the Stó:lō people?" Estrada shook his head. "Well, this is Stó:lō land. We've always fished this river. Hell, Stó:lō means river. I'm curious. What brings you to our river?"

"Private matter."

Josh nodded. "That's cool." He stood up. "Well, I just wanted to make sure you hadn't died in here. My brothers and I hole up here sometimes. We don't bring that shit with us, though. We bring our medicine." He pulled another pouch out of his jacket pocket, opened it, and handed Estrada a twisted stick of dried leaves.

Estrada stood, accepted the herb, and smelled it. "Sage. We use this too. Thank you."

"Okay, then."

"Do you really have to leave? I didn't mean to be rude. I just—"

Josh shook his head. "I'm in no hurry. Light her up."

Estrada used a candle to light the sage wand, and then offered the smoke to Josh, who gathered it in his hands and spread it over his eyes, hair, and body. When he was finished, he nodded to Estrada, who bathed his own body in the pungent smoke.

"Man, that's good. I feel better already."

"You need anything else? If not, I'm gonna leave you to eat the rest of this salmon." He grinned. "I've got other fish to fry."

"Hey man, thanks for everything."

"Word of advice? Lay off the booze. It just fucks you up."

"I know."

"Oh, and one more thing. There's a big old black bear spends every winter here. Maybe don't stay too long. After last night's snowfall he might come snuffling around looking for his bed."

Estrada grimaced.

"I don't know what kind of medicine you've been doing in here with these candles, but that old bear, he won't care one way or the other."

"You sure you didn't see anybody, Josh?"

He shook his head. "You know, I really hope you don't find this guy."

"Why's that?" Estrada asked.

"You were aiming to kill me, man, and you don't strike me as the killing type. Ask me, you should just go home and spend some time with your brothers. Leave this bastard to the elements." He gestured to the empty bottle of tequila lying on its side in the corner of the cave. "Hell. Look what it's done to you already." He sniffed and scraped a knuckle across his nose. "My father always said that when you take a man's life, you end up dragging his corpse around with you."

"True enough." Leaning over, Estrada grabbed his pack, took out his cell phone and turned it on. "Twenty messages."

"Always good to have friends, man."

Busy scrolling through texts, Estrada had stopped listening. His face, suddenly grave, caught Josh's attention.

"Bad news?"

"Yeah. It's from my friend, Dylan." Estrada read it aloud, not as much for Josh to hear, as to make sense of it himself:

"3 nights sensara dreams grace in ireland. maggie in danger."

"That sounds like some kind of friggin' code. Sensara dreams grace in Ireland?"

"Yeah. Sensara's my—" Estrada slipped the phone back in his pocket. "Sensara knows things. She's psychic." He took a deep breath. "This guy named Grace, kidnapped this girl, Maggie. We got her back, in fact, we found her just up the road from here. Her mother sent her to Ireland to stay with family. But now, it looks like Grace has gone after her. What I don't understand is why he'd go that far and how he got there so fast? Maggie just left last week. How could he know?"

"I know someone like Sensara. You know, dreamers don't always dream in *this* time. You know what I mean? Like this Grace might be there now, but she might also be dreaming the past or the future."

"Yeah, you're right. Sensara has dreams and premonitions all the time. They rarely come in sequence with this reality."

Josh nodded. "So, this girl might be in danger, but maybe not yet."

"The thing is Josh, I'm a big part of the reason this shit's happening, and my friend Dylan loves this girl."

"So, you're going to Ireland, eh man? The land of lucky charms?"

"Lucky charms." Estrada rubbed his three-day beard. "I wish I had one. Nothing seems to work for me lately."

"This Grace, he's not the same guy that—?"

"You are one astute son-of-a-bitch." Estrada rubbed his head. "I don't care about my hair, but this guy's crazy. When he kidnaps girls, he kills them. Burns them. We were lucky to get Maggie back alive."

"That's some bad shit, man." Josh fished around in the pocket of his jeans, then held out his fist to Estrada. "Take this. Keep it on you all the time, even when you're in the shower or sleeping or . . . Well, it *is* a lucky charm."

"What does it do?" Estrada held the tiny cedar carving in the palm of his hand. It was no bigger than an acorn and as smooth and round as a stone. He'd seen his share of talismans but never anything quite like it.

"I don't know, man, but it works. It'll keep you safe. Hey, who knows? It might even help grow back your hair."

Wedged in a thin tunnel above the cave, the man laid on his belly, cradling his chin in his hands. He was listening intently to the conversation. Though stiff from lying so long in such a cold, hard place, it had been worth it. After the magician passed out, he'd crawled down into the cave and lain beside him for hours, feeling the beat of his heart, but resisting the urge to caress and awaken him.

And now, this perfect man, this hero, was flying to Ireland to rescue a damsel *he'd* put in distress. Assured his plan was working perfectly, the man pictured Estrada, free and willing and thinking only of him. One day, they'd be together again, and there'd be no need for ropes or drugs. There'd only be love.

"Seems to me there was a fella name o' Paddy Vale who used to play with Finn O'Farrell. Older fella, crackerjack fiddler."

Maggie wondered just how much older that could be. Declan was definitely a pensioner himself. Clutching his pint affectionately with both hands, he ruminated, wiggling his nose occasionally and snuffling somberly. Recollecting the names and faces of the past took concentration as the stories of a thousand and one pub nights jigged and reeled through his mind.

Ensconced in a cozy snug, Maggie and Primrose sipped through a second pot of strong black tea. Primrose had discovered Declan on one of her many forays into the crowd. After canvassing the locals with her great elfin eyes, she'd venture out and return with some old-timer whose portly paunch was a testament to his extent of pub lore. Although a few of Sligo's older patrons had heard tales of the supposedly renowned fiddler, none could give the young women a firm answer as to his whereabouts. Declan, they hoped, would pay off for the price of a Guinness or three.

With his leathered face etched in a scowl, Declan reminded Maggie of an old cowboy. His boorish snuffling didn't give him quite the charm of Clint Eastwood or Sam Elliott, but he was a compelling character, mostly because he reminded her of her dad. Cowboys were her childhood heroes because of John. The two of them had cradled each other through hours of western melodrama in the log house. So much so, Maggie grew up dreaming of living on a ranch where herds of horses ran free through raging rivers, where cows might get branded but never slaughtered, where bad guys got their comeuppance, and good guys rode off into the sunset leaving the town behind them a safer, albeit lonelier, place.

Declan snorted, jarring her back from her reverie, and then set his pint squarely on the table. "Sure, I'm almost certain. I can see him in my mind's eye."

Now for the million-dollar question. "Any idea where we can find him?"

Fureys was the third pub they'd visited in Sligo featuring traditional Irish music and after a long uneventful day, Maggie was drained. Constant travel, at Primrose's frenetic pace, was taking its toll. Apart from the platter of scrambled eggs, smoked salmon, and brown bread she'd wolfed down for brunch, the day had been a bust and she just wanted it to end.

To make matters worse, she'd called home several times and couldn't reach her mother at the house, at work, or at the hospital where John still lay comatose, his condition unchanged according to the on-call nurse. Finally, after deciding that Shannon must have gone off somewhere to have a moment's peace, Maggie gave up, and set about explaining away the uneasy sensation now settled in her belly. An alcoholic binge, followed by fasting, a quick brunch, and several vats of black tea could wreak havoc on any digestive track. Shannon would say she was paying penance—a Catholic euphemism for hangover—and so far from home, where no amount of worrying would have any effect, she could accept that theory.

Declan was still ruminating on the question. "No, can't say that I do," he replied at last, and rubbed his stubbly chin. Then, just when Maggie had decided they'd be leaving empty-handed again, he proffered a clue. "Finn, though, Finn might know. He lives up the Donegal Road, up around Drumcliffe."

"Oh. Can we call Finn?" asked Maggie.

Declan pursed his lip and sniffed. "No, no phone. Finn doesn't believe in modern conveniences. Says stuff just ties a man down, stuff does."

Maggie glanced around the pub. Furey's was filling rapidly as a session was promised after ten. A flutist and banjo player, who'd already set up in the front booth by the window, chatted casually in the spot reserved for musicians. It was rumored, some famous trad player might show up later. Furey's was the haunt of Dervish, one of the biggest bands in Irish traditional music, and although they were out of town touring, plenty of friends and fans dropped by to sit in on sessions with the local players who frequented the pub. Someone was always popping in, according to Declan, who loved the music and the pints, but really came for the craic.

"How would you go about tracking this Finn down?" Primrose asked.

Maggie couldn't believe how different Ireland was from Canada. In Vancouver, everyone had a cell phone; sometimes everyone in the family had their own. In Ireland, although she'd seen plenty of people with cell phones, there were still old folks who lived in cottages way out in the middle of nowhere; cottages without phones or computers, or the myriad appliances Canadians took for granted. *Stuff just ties a man down.* She'd have to think on that. Maybe this Finn had a point. They had been traveling without technology for days and she hadn't missed a thing.

Declan drained his glass and set it down on the table with a flourish. "It seems to me Finn has a granddaughter who works at the tea shop at Drumcliffe Cemetery."

"There's a tea shop at a cemetery?" Maggie asked. *Of course there is.* Ireland was full of the dear departed and people anxious to track them down, just as she was doing—people who needed to be fortified with tea.

"Aye, sure. Drumcliffe is where the famous Willie Yeats is interred. Always draws a crowd. You should see this town in summer when his festival's raging. Folks come from all over the world just to see where himself is buried; as if seeing his grave might connect them somehow to his soul, which God bless us all"—crossing himself, he raised his eyes to the roof— "is with the Lord in heaven and not hovering over some stone cold slab by the sea."

"I wouldn't be so sure," Primrose whispered to Maggie with a quick wink, while Declan turned his attention to his empty glass and the keg of Guinness at the bar.

The remark gave Maggie goose bumps. But, Yeats' grave—that was something worth seeing, even if they couldn't find Finn's daughter at the teashop. She loved his poem about "The Stolen Child" who was seduced away by faeries who believed the human world was just too sad a place for the child to live: "a world more full of weeping than he can understand." Shocked, she realized her literature class had studied it only three weeks before, and yet it seemed as if months, or even years, had passed. She felt another shiver.

"Do you know how to get to Drumcliffe Cemetery?" she asked Primrose, who flashed her anime eyes at Declan.

"Ah, just drive straight up the Donegal Road and you'll find it sure," he repeated with a wink of his leathery eye. "Are you all right now? Would you like a pint? This conjuring up the past is a dry affair."

"No thank you, Declan," Maggie said. "I don't think I'll ever need a pint again. But have one on me."

Primrose winked, obviously pleased she'd learned her lesson.

"Say, can I ask you something?" Declan said to Primrose. "I've been admiring your artwork. What's the meaning of that?" He motioned to the symbols interwoven through the dark trees silhouetted on her head.

Primrose laughed, her sparkling brown eyes half-filling her pixie face. *But, hadn't her eyes been green that first day on Shop Street, green as grapes?* Maybe she wore colored contacts like some of the girls at school, or then again, maybe . . .

"Ah, you're after knowing my secrets, are you, my man? Well, they wouldn't be secrets long if I told them, would they?"

Maggie examined the tattoo with fresh interest. She hadn't noticed the tiny spirals and lightning bolts embedded in the dark tree branches or speculated at all about what any of it could mean. Gazing at her own tattoo, the rearing Celtic horse, she realized it too had meaning. It was a source of strength and power, its amber eyes shining like fire.

"Are you needing a place to sleep tonight, girls? The wife and I've a hideaway."

"Thanks anyway, Declan," Maggie replied quickly. "We're camping." Now, there was something that would never happen in Vancouver—not so innocently at any rate.

It was barely four miles to the village of Drumcliffe. All the while, Maggie could sense the dark hollow of the sea on her left, and off to her right the solid mass of a large mountain. In places, the highway was cinched still tighter by waist-high rock walls, and once, when a huge truck barreled by, she felt the wind pick them right up off the tarmac and for a fraction of a second, they were airborne. Gasping, she closed her eyes and imagined them bashing into the side of the mountain.

"Ben Bulben," Primrose said when they skidded to a stop in the gravel car park at Drumcliffe Cemetery. Maggie stared blankly. Her world was moving at light speed and sometimes she just couldn't keep up. "Ben means mountain," Primrose explained, gesturing toward it. "That one's Ben Bulben."

"Oh." Maggie took off her helmet and ran her fingers through her hair. "Yeats mentioned Ben Bulben in—"

"The book Estrada gave you."

"Yeah. There's a white square near the top that's said to be the door to Faerie. At night they ride out of there to kidnap babies and young brides."

"Well, it's a good thing you're not promised then," Primrose said, as they unpacked the gear from the motorcycle. "Or, maybe you are. Anyone special in your life? Anyone you love?"

"Not really," Maggie said. She thought of Dylan and felt a pang of guilt.

"Ah well, when you're in love, you don't think it, you feel it. Sometimes it creeps up on you, slow-like; other times, it hits you like a knife in the heart and takes your breath away. Either way, you'll know when it's got you. You'll want to scream with the divine agony of it."

"Sounds like you've been there."

"Once, long ago, before this land was free. 'Twas his blood helped make it so."

"You mean in a past life?" She'd read Ireland had been a free state since 1922. It took a civil war to make it happen.

"Past. Present. Love's eternal. Do you not listen to the radio?"

Maggie laughed.

"Don't fret, pet. One day someone will take *your* breath away." Primrose sighed, and then asked, "What about this Estrada? What's his story?"

"Estrada. Now there's a man to take your breath away. I don't really know him, but on looks alone, he could beat out Taylor Lautner as Sexiest Man Alive." Maggie tried to picture Estrada again the way she'd first seen him, tall and angular in his black robes, his inky hair falling in waves, but her daydream was interrupted by Primrose's cackle. "What? Why are you laughing?"

"I can think of a few contenders for that title that would leave young Taylor tramping in the dust."

"Oh, really. Like who?"

"Stuart Townsend, Aidan Turner, Jamie Dornan—"

"Never heard of them."

"Ah well, I suppose I'm partial to the local lads."

"Well, Estrada could beat any of them. He's just... He's beautiful. I had this dream about him once. I felt safe, like nothing could ever harm me. Of course, he's the high priest of Hollystone Coven and a magician, so—"

"Sounds like a real god. So you do have someone special."

"No. I mean, he's special, but he's not mine. He's with Sensara, the high priestess."

"Ah, I see. Priest and priestess. Good match then, are they?"

Maggie shrugged. Maybe it was just jealousy, but from what she'd seen, they had a complicated relationship. "He sure was all over her the night before I left. Too bad. I think he'd be perfect for you. He just shaved his head too. His hair was so long it hung almost to his elbows, and then it was gone. Buzzed off."

"Is that so? Well, perhaps I'll have a chance to meet this beautiful man one day and I can judge for myself."

Looking askance into the shadows, Maggie saw there was no campground. "We're spending another night in a cemetery, aren't we?"

"Ah, no one will mind."

I'll mind. Maggie turned on the flashlight and beamed the yellow light slowly around. A gigantic Celtic cross dominated the churchyard, but there were hundreds of other graves; some mere flattened slabs in the ground wedged between colossal intricately carved Victorian monuments. There was also a sweet old church with a high spire, and a tidy modern bungalow—the teashop, no doubt.

"How old is this place?"

"Ah, this stuff's young, relatively speaking, though you never know what's buried beneath the earth." Maggie glanced down. "Saint Columba built a monastery here in the sixth century, just before his exile. The cross is his handiwork." Elaborate carvings along the vertical base depicted triads of monks; the cross itself was fitted inside a circle. On the whole, it seemed more pagan than Christian.

"Why was he exiled?"

"Difference of opinion. His monks borrowed a manuscript, you see, and then copied it without permission. You know how the monks used to create illuminated scripts like in *The Book of Kells*? Have you heard of it?"

"I've seen pictures of it."

"Well, it was a book like that. Saint Finian—the owner of the book—sent his men after it, and a great battle ensued just up the road."

"Over plagiarism?"

"I suppose so."

"Who won?"

"Won?" Primrose shrugged. "No one ever wins. Three thousand men died over a book, and poor Saint Columba was so grieved he left Ireland, crossed the sea, and began his missionary work on Iona. This is a tragic land, overrun by ghosts."

"Ghosts."

"Do you not believe in such things?"

Maggie shook her head.

"Have you forgotten so soon our midnight soiree at Carrowmore?"

"Those weren't ghosts. Those were . . ." Shocked to realize that the whole fantastic episode had slipped her mind until the moment Primrose mentioned it, Maggie asked timidly, "What happened that night? Was I dreaming or hallucinating or—?"

"Ah, we'll talk more later. Let's get the tent up before the rain. Mind your feet. Don't stumble over any graves."

"Why? Will the ghosts come up and grab me?" Though spoken sarcastically, Maggie's trepidation trickled through.

"Mind your tongue and your feet, girleen. The old folks say if you stumble over a grave, you'll be dead by year's end."

"*Jesus*, Primrose. Have you forgotten why I was sent here?"

"Just mind, is all."

By the time the tent was pitched and sleeping bags set inside, Maggie had decided to forego her midnight stroll through the dark graveyard. Sulky and fretful, she crawled inside the tent beside Primrose.

"No adventure tonight?"

"Too tired," replied Maggie, yawning feebly to illustrate the extent of her exhaustion.

In the darkness of the tent, only the shape of Primrose's round head was visible—that and her small pointy ears. "Ah, are you scared?" she cackled.

"No."

"Ah, don't be scared, wee girl," Primrose teased. "I won't let any harm come to you."

"I'm not scared." Maggie lay stiffly, her face flushed with annoyance, until she could stand it no longer. Grabbing the flashlight, she crawled back out into the damp night. It irked her that this was another of Primrose's manipulations—the witch was a master at it—yet she felt compelled. "Fine. I'll go look for Yeats' grave. Maybe the faeries will fly down from Ben Bulben and spirit me away."

"Just mind your feet," Primrose sang.

At first, Maggie's ears rang with the silence. She stopped and listened, could distinguish the distant roaring of the sea against the rocks, the night wind rattling the tree branches, the odd bleat of a lonely sheep. Gazing up at the thin silver curl blinking its way through the black star-studded sky, she realized, although they were in different time zones, this moon was the very same moon that hung over Buntzen Lake. Feeling suddenly at peace, she cursed and praised Primrose, who always seemed to know what she needed.

She did her best to tiptoe around gravestones, but some name would pop from the grass and send her leaping for new ground or stumbling on uneven edges. She even tried to avoid stepping on the cracks. *Step on a crack and you break your mother's back.* There'd been days, as a child, when she went out of her way to step on cracks. Now Shannon's tragic courage filled her mind, and she made a mental note to be kinder to her mother once all this madness had run its course.

Picking her way through the grave markers, she read inscriptions, looking for Yeats, but also Vallely. Oddly enough, there seemed to be no one named Vallely here at all, though Primrose claimed it was an old Irish name. Maybe she'd never find her mother's people. Maybe she'd just go on traveling around the island with Primrose forever. No, she couldn't do that. She'd go mad, never quite knowing which thoughts were hers and which had been embedded.

Far around the back of the cemetery, shadowed by the church, the trees grew denser and the gravestones more obscure. Perhaps they'd started here in the old days and moved steadily westward toward the sea as time wore on.

Startled by a dark shape emerging from the woods, she tripped on the edge of a flat stone and dropped the flashlight. Quickly regaining her footing, she crouched to pick it up, then watched fearfully as the shape moved steadily forward. Perhaps a caretaker lived nearby, or a neighbor seeing them arrive on the motorbike had come to investigate. Should she make a run for it? Surrounded by tombstones, there was no free path. Did people carry guns in Ireland?

Standing perfectly still, she watched the eerie figure draw closer and closer. Then, flipping on the flashlight, she shone the beam of light directly in his eyes. If he intended to hurt her, perhaps she could blind him long enough to escape. Shivers of goose bumps rose on her flesh.

This was no stranger.

"Daddy," she breathed. "You can't be here." Still, the shape continued to glide slowly and steadily toward her, skirting the tops of graves, dissolving through weathered tombstones like a hazy mist. "You can't be—" she repeated, as the adrenaline surged through her legs, buckling her knees. Falling hard on her butt, she hit a cold granite slab with the edge of her hip and cursed as pain shot through her leg. Pushing herself back to her feet, she staggered and fought for balance.

Mere steps away now, Maggie could see him clearly—the soft puffiness of his ashen face, the corners of his mouth turned down in a frown. Wearing his best sable suit and the burgundy shirt she'd bought him last Christmas, he looked ready for mass, or as if—

"No Daddy." He stretched out his arms to draw her in and she took two steps toward him. "If you're here Daddy, it means . . . It means you're . . ." her whisper faded against the dreadful thumping of her own heart and she sobbed. "Does it hurt? Does it—?"

The mouth opened, and she froze as soft susurrations escaped the slowly pulsing lips. "He's coming," he said, with such anguish, the oxygen rushed from her lungs. "He's coming for *you*."

Gasping, she fought for breath against the rapid beating of her heart; slipping from her panicked state only as a sliver of night air passed through one nostril.

And then he was gone.

"Daddy," she gasped, "I'm sorry. I'm so sorry."

"What's happened?" Primrose was suddenly there with her hands on Maggie's shoulders. "Did you stumble?"

Had Primrose seen nothing? Heard nothing? How could she have missed it? John Taylor—standing, speaking, and looking as real as if he were alive. Except that he wasn't. He was dead. *And, I killed him. If I hadn't flirted with Father Grace, he'd never have kidnapped me, and my dad wouldn't have fallen down the stairs trying to find me.*

"Yeah, I stumbled—" Her words spun out with a keen edge but with them came ferocious tears. Wiping her cheeks, she looked down, and saw below, the name Burke etched in the stone beside her knee. "And, you're right as usual, Primrose. I probably will be dead within the year because that psycho priest—the one who kidnaps and burns witches—he's coming. He's coming for me. My daddy says."

Nothing mattered now. Even after Finn's granddaughter Siobhan, who had known the Vallelys all her life, gave them explicit directions to her grandparents' home, Maggie couldn't be stirred.

Descending from the Irish mist, John Taylor's ghost had snuffed her out as deftly as a candle.

I Am a Man Again

Michael was submerged in a sulk deeper than the ocean. "Do you have any idea how many times I called you, compadre? Why the hell didn't you pick up?"

"I'm sorry, man, I . . ." Estrada began, then paused. He could find no adequate explanation and a lie would not do, not for Michael. He knew exactly how many times Michael had called. He'd seen the messages. He'd even listened to some of them. They were all the same. A heartfelt plea to call, something he just couldn't do. Even now, he paced Michael's gothic tower, looking to pacify the demon lurking inside his head. "Are we alone?"

"Quite. Clive is filling in for me at Pegasus until I've recovered."

"Oh, that's sweet. *Club Manager Attacked in Alley: Baby Brother Usurps Throne.* That beating affected your brain, man. Can you *not* see what's going on?"

Michael lit a cigarette and leaned against the bar. Wearing nothing but a slouchy pair of black leggings, he looked semi-starved. His busted arm was braced by a black silk sling. "Perhaps you should enlighten me since things seem to be going so well for you."

"Don't pout, man." Estrada knelt in the window seat. Pressing his hands against the pane, he stared into the night and wondered if *he* was out there. Palms chilled, he held them against his cheeks and looked at the prints his hands left on the glass.

"Pouting is my prerogative. Now come and open the wine. I can't manage the bloody corkscrew yet."

Estrada obeyed. "Chateau Margaux 2004? What's the occasion?"

"Homecoming, of course."

He popped the cork. "We really should let this sit a while."

"It can sit in the glass." Michael was hunched over the coffee table crushing a pile of white powder with a razor blade. Estrada filled two tumblers with the fleshy Bordeaux and set them down at the other end.

"I see *that's* no problem for you."

"There are many things I've learned to do with one hand." Content with his work, Michael dipped in a silver coke spoon and snorted some in each nostril. "Come here, compadre," he said and, after refilling the spoon, held it out for Estrada. "It seems like eons since we've done this together."

"That's true." Estrada snorted.

"And again," Michael said, repeating the ritual.

The ensuing rush tinged the back of Estrada's brain.

"Feels good, yes?" Michael dipped the spoon and took another long snort himself.

Estrada sniffed and wiped his nose. "Yes, but the subject still stands. Your little bastard brother has done nothing but wreak havoc since he appeared."

Michael slouched on the chaise. "Wreaking havoc? That's your forte."

Estrada exhaled loudly, buzzed by the powder. "He stalked you."

"He was trying to get to know me."

"By peeking from behind parked cars? Why didn't he just introduce himself like any normal person would?"

"I'm sorry," Michael said, with a slight cough. "Normal?"

Sitting back in the window seat, Estrada grasped the tumbler and downed the contents. "Have you not noticed that every time something bad happens, Clive's lurking in the shadows? When Jade disappeared, when Sensara and I were abducted, and again when you were beaten? And, when we went to Yale, he disappeared, but he knew what happened and what was said."

"You don't think they're conspirators? Why would Clive . . .?" He sat for a moment pondering, and then concluded, "No, that's impossible. It's merely coincidence."

Estrada shrugged, then finished his wine. "You know as well as I do, there are no coincidences." Sitting the tumbler on the table, he refilled it to the brim.

Michael lit a cigarette. With a shrug, he blew a smoke ring and watched it fade. "I think you're taking this far too personally, compadre."

"And you're not?" Estrada swallowed another mouthful of wine. Michael was definitely defensive, and he wasn't sure why. "Did you hear what the little bastard said to Sensara?"

"Payback's a bitch."

"Payback? Clive tells my girlfriend that I had sex with a killer and that somehow equates to hitching home from the valley?" He swallowed the rest of the wine in one gulp and crashed the glass down so viciously on the window ledge, it broke. "This is why I didn't answer your calls. You've been fucking bromanced."

"Come now. If anyone's been bromanced—" Catching the blaze in Estrada's eye, he stopped and took a deep breath. "Look, compadre. We're both under pressure, but there should be no bad blood between us. Please, come here."

Ignoring the pass, Estrada scraped the broken glass into his hand and disappeared into the kitchen. Emerging with another glass, he filled it, flopped on the other couch, and put his feet up. The wine and cocaine were rollicking through his body.

Michael sighed and rolled his eyes. "Listen love, I know the kid can be an ass, but he's my baby brother. He's family. God, we've talked for hours since I've been laid up."

"Not about me, I trust."

"About family. He came here from England because he wanted to start a relationship. You know that he was still an infant when Nigel emigrated with me, and I told you about the Twyfford-Farringtons. Nigel tells me there's no family in Britain quite like them. Just think of anything derogatory you've ever heard about pompous heartless Brits and multiply it by a million."

"So?"

Michael downed his wine and finished off the bottle. He sauntered to the bar and picked up another bottle, then set it beside the corkscrew on the table. "So, Clive grew up with these people. The bloody Twyffs brainwashed him against us. Naturally, when he arrived, he was hesitant to make himself known. He wanted to see for himself, and then, when he did—apparently I'm the clone of my maniacal father—well, it made him a little crazy."

"Rage and madness, both great motives for murder."

Michael shook his head. "It's not like that. Clive believes that our father is culpable for our mother's death."

"Why?"

"I told you they were killed in a car crash." Estrada nodded. "Well, there's more to it. Apparently, they were returning from a Queen concert in London. After consuming copious amounts of alcohol and drugs, my father opted to drive home from Wembley in his Ferrari. He was so wasted, he crashed the car into an iron railing at 150 miles per hour. My mother was decapitated."

"*Jesus*. I'm sorry, man."

Michael shrugged. "I know it sounds horrible, but I don't remember either of my parents. I only know them from photos and tidbits I've heard from my grandmother. Nigel always downplayed the accident, but the Twyffs turned it into a family melodrama that starred my father as a drug-crazed murderer. Clive grew up with that shit." He sniffed. "Oh, and get this, my father's Ferrari was red."

"So?"

"Crimson?"

"So you both like fast red cars."

"Or, it's genetic. Don't tell anyone I said this, but sometimes I don't know why I do the things I do."

Estrada gazed out the window into the darkling night. "You're not alone there, amigo."

"Now, I know you don't trust Clive, but we all have our stuff."

As does every criminal in and out of prison, thought Estrada. Nodding, he opened an ornate box on the glass table, took out a joint, lit it, smoked some, and passed it to Michael. Then picking up the corkscrew, he opened the second bottle of wine. Michael might say it didn't bother him to speak of his parents' deaths, but Estrada knew better.

"Thank you, compadre. You know, I called you a dozen times over the last three days. I know you're mad at me because of Clive, but I need you to understand." He held the smoke in his lungs and then exhaled. "How I feel about him, and how I feel about you... They're two separate things."

Estrada accepted the joint and nodded. "I'm not mad at you. I never was."

"Then why did you disappear?"

"I had to go back to that cave. I thought he might... I needed to..." He finished the joint and stubbed it out. After blazing up another, he passed it to Michael.

"So, it's true what Clive said? You're involved—"

"Not like that. It's hard to explain." Estrada's head was swimming in the smoke. He perched in the corner and drew up one knee. "It's weird. An obsession."

"Obsession? God, I'm jealous."

"Don't be. You and me, we're... us. But this thing with him. It's like crawling through shadows. You know, I've never even seen his face. He wears a mask and the first time he kept me blindfolded and tied to the bed."

"Good God. How does he know your proclivities?"

Estrada shrugged and stared at the flickering candles on the mantle. "Exactly. How *does* he know?" He accepted the joint and inhaled deeply. "It must be the spell."

"Really? You people can do that?"

Estrada laughed. "Yeah, I suppose we can. The thing is though, even if I *could* break this spell, I don't know if I *should*. I mean, he's the killer—the man who burned Jade and grabbed Sensara and Maggie. Maybe this connection is meant to help me catch him."

"I'd like a crack at him myself." Michael lit a cigarette and leaned his head on the arm of the couch. "So, you think you're obsessed with him because—?"

"Because I have to know him to stop him."

"Know him intimately."

Estrada sighed. "Yeah."

"But that day in the cave, the day he shaved your head, why didn't you just pull out a gun? Hit him with a rock? Or bludgeon him?" He sniffed. "I like that word bludgeon."

Estrada grinned. "For one thing, he patted me down and, for another, how could I prove anything? I have no evidence. I'd end up doing time, and if there's anything I cannot do—"

"I understand, compadre." Setting his cigarette in the ashtray, Michael turned slyly. "So just how intimately do you know him?"

"Does it matter?"

"You know I like details."

"It's not just sex. If it was . . ." Estrada shook his head and then finished his glass of wine. "This man, this *killer* . . . He said he loves me."

"*Loves you?* Now I'm really jealous." Reaching across, he scratched the magician's stubbly cheek. "But, why wouldn't he love you?"

Estrada rolled his eyes. "There's more."

"Do tell."

"He said he had to shave my head to save my life." Estrada was still trying to solve that riddle.

"That's rather cryptic."

"Yeah. He said that my hair was my power."

"And was it?"

"I feel different. Not powerless. But different."

The room was suddenly silent. Michael lit another joint, took a couple of huge tokes, coughed, and passed it over. Stretching out on the soft leather couch, he laid his head in Estrada's lap. "Untie this sling please. I'm feeling fettered."

Estrada undid the knot and let the silk scarf fall to the floor.

"You know that, with or without your hair, I adore you, compadre."

"But *you* are no killer," Estrada said.

"There are those who would disagree . . . like the Empress."

"I assume you're referring to Sensara?"

Estrada pressed his palm on his friend's bare chest and felt the slow beating of his heart beneath his bare skin. He'd missed these moments.

Michael purred contentedly and placed his hand on top. "Have you two spoken at all?"

"No. We're done. And I'm afraid it will affect the coven. How can we lead ceremonies when she won't even talk to me? When we were just friends, before sex got in the way—"

"Oh, don't disparage sex, compadre. It wasn't sex that got in the way. Look at us."

Estrada played with Michael's fine hair and felt like himself again.

"Sex is rapture," continued Michael. "A gift from the gods. It wasn't sex that was the problem. It was her rules *about* sex; her enforced monogamy. The preposterous expectation that you would never desire to share this divine gift with anyone but her. I mean, why do the gods make us so hard so often if not to—"

Estrada started to laugh and couldn't stop. Perhaps it was the smoke, or perhaps it was this moment of freedom. Leaning over, he clutched Michael and laughed until tears ran down his face. Caught up in the craziness, Michael burst out laughing too. It felt so good to finally release some of the accumulated tension of the last few weeks. And Michael was absolutely right. Until Estrada looked through her eyes, he'd felt free to enjoy his body and the pleasure it gave him with anyone of his choosing at any time. *She'd* made it into something else with her rules. *She'd* made him feel guilty.

"It's the truth, amigo. And while we're being honest, I have to say, I never liked the tight-assed bitch. Never." He brushed a scattering of white dust off his nose with his fist. "Well, maybe there were a couple of nights at the club, when she wore that little leather thing with the laces—"

"Whoa. I'm trying to forget her."

"Easily done. I can arrange whatever you desire."

"Ah, but I can't, man. I've got to catch a plane in the morning."

Miffed, Michael sat up and reached for the wine. "Where the hell are you going now?"

"That's what I came to tell you. I know you dislike Sensara but you have to admit she's a credible psychic."

Michael nodded. "Go on."

"Well, she's been dreaming about that priest, Grace. She's convinced he's gone after Maggie. So, I'm going after him."

"But, didn't that girl go abroad?"

"Yeah. She's in Ireland."

"Ireland. And you're going there to—"

"Find him. Stop him."

"In the morning."

"Yeah, and I still have to pack and get some sleep."

"You piss me off," Michael said sternly. "We'll do another few lines and party all night. You can sleep on the plane."

"Man, I'm so wasted right now, I can barely sit up."

Michael rolled off the couch and settled on the floor. Reaching up he clutched Estrada's arm. "Come join me, compadre. Be comforted."

Estrada slipped off the couch and rolled onto his back. Clasping his hands behind his head, he closed his eyes, and sank into the thick Persian rug. "I drained a mickey of tequila the night before last and I'm still not right. If it hadn't been for this Stó:lō guy who showed up and cooked me some fish, I might not have made it home."

"You really must stop having adventures without me."

Estrada felt around in the pocket of his jeans and pulled out the charm Josh had given him. "He gave me this."

"A wooden bead with mysterious powers."

Estrada smiled. "He told me to stop drinking and go home to my brother. That would be you."

"Here. Here," Michael said, and propping his back against the base of the couch, he raised his glass. "A toast to our Indigenous brothers." After draining the glass, he set it down and lit another joint.

Estrada was lost in a spin.

"I'll tell you this, compadre. You are more of a brother to me than Clive ever will be, despite our blood ties. We share something more vital than blood."

"More vital than blood to a vampire?" Estrada pulled up one corner of his lip in a crooked grin.

"Yes, our lives. Everything that happens in our lives, and no one can ever change that—no smart-ass brother, no prudish priestess, not even this psycho killer. You understand? I take you as you are, and every way I can."

Sensing his closeness, Estrada opened his eyes. Michael was leaning over him and staring. "Are you trying to mesmerize me, my vampire friend? You look hungry."

"That I am, but I wear no fangs tonight." Taking a big puff on the joint, he leaned down and blew the smoke through Estrada's open mouth.

Closing his eyes, Estrada breathed it in. Then their lips touched. It was something they rarely did, and he savored the intricacies of Michael's long smoky kiss, his silken tongue, and fluttering fingertips that knew exactly where and how to touch. Heart pounding, he rode the wave, his body arcing with pleasure. Michael was a virtuoso, and within seconds he was near to bursting without ever having loosed his clothing.

"I feel like fucking you," Michael breathed in his ear. Leaning over, he kissed the magician's lips again, filling his mouth with more love than lust. "Nailing you to the floor with my—"

"*Jesus*," Estrada said. "If you do that, neither of us will ever leave."

"Exactly, compadre. I don't want you running off to Ireland to confront a killer who's mad for you." While Michael settled back against the couch, Estrada held his gaze, desperate to imprint in his mind, the face of a man he truly trusted. "I think I should come along."

"I'd love that, I really would—"

"But—"

"But, I'd rather you stayed here and kept watch on little brother. I still don't trust him."

Michael frowned and lit another cigarette.

"You don't have to worry about me, amigo. I can take care of myself. Besides, Maggie's staying with a friend of Sylvia's—a very powerful witch named Primrose. I'm sure if there's trouble . . . "

"Primrose. Good lord. I can see her now—an elderly matron puttering about in a rhubarb patch."

"With a feather in her hat and horn-rimmed glasses—"

"And a black cat in a tweed handbag. Well, at least I won't have to worry about you getting into any mischief without me while you're abroad, not with *Primrose* at least."

Michael poured them each another glass of wine. "I love to see you smile, compadre. Now, relax and sip your wine, and allow me to say *adiós* in my own way."

Cong was the kind of place a girl wished her long-lost grandparents lived—a village with the feel of Tolkien's Shire—before the invasion of the Nazgûl. According to the brochure at Sean Thornton's B&B—which Maggie had read thoroughly while ensconced in a hot bath away from the ever-perky Primrose—*Cung* was Irish for "the land between two waters." And, so it was: edged along the eastern shore of Lough—pronounced lock, not luff or loo—Corrib and Lough Mask. The landscape was fiercely green, and even in the November gloom, the village was hedged in rhododendrons and massive hot pink fuchsias. Seeing Ireland, Maggie understood why her mother chose the property at Hawk's Claw Lane. There was an uncanny similarity between the two verdant landscapes.

Cong was a quaint village, a living museum, still the picture of what it had been when a Hollywood film company invaded it in the early 1950s to film *The Quiet Man* with John Wayne and Maureen O'Hara. A fifty-year dalliance with tourism had kept it that way. The only signs of modernity were satellite dishes that clung to the steep shingled roofs of pastel bungalows, waiting each night for Hollywood's return. Even the nearby five-star hotel was ensconced in the eight-hundred-year-old Ashford Castle.

Maggie had watched the film once with her mother and couldn't fathom how it had won two Oscars. She hated it. Hated watching John Wayne—his character an ex-fighter—drag his poor bride for miles by the hair, kick her, throw her to the ground, and then haul her up, only to beat her down again. It was abuse, pure and simple, and yet the townsfolk cheered him on. Shannon advised her to take the film with a grain of salt.

How horrible it must have been for Shannon to watch the film, shot so near her childhood home, and not be able to say, *I've been there*, or *I know that place*. And why hadn't she directed Maggie here first, instead of sending her on a wild ride with Primrose?

Shannon herself had been beaten down, just as surely as John Wayne's bride. Too ashamed to speak the truth, she'd constructed a fraudulent life for them all. Maggie wished her mother was here now, wished they could walk up the front path together, meet and talk as one family, and make it right. She needed something to go right. She hadn't slept since her ghostly encounter at Drumcliffe Cemetery and was convinced her father had passed on. She was waiting to call Shannon until she met her grandparents, so hopefully, she could cheer her mother up with some good news.

"Aren't you coming with me?" Maggie felt guilty about taking her anger out on the only friend she had in this strange land. "Don't you want to meet them?"

Primrose leaned against her bike and shook her head. "Aye, sure. In good time."

"But—"

"I'll just take a wee walk. Go on now. Do it for your ma?"

The faerie-tale house was built of stone, its roof thatched with rushes. Big bay windows perched on either side of a scarlet door. With shaggy blinds hung halfway down its paned glass like sleepy lids, it appeared to gaze drowsily down the narrow lane. An enormous ivy clutched it from beneath and crept across the flagstones. Wrapped around the house, its leaves obscured one entire side of the attic. Smoke curled from the chimney like the square houses Maggie had drawn as a child. Wistfully, she thought, *I could have lived in this house. Perhaps still could. We could all be together again—one big family, except for—*

The door opened before she'd even knocked, and an old man stared down at her. He filled the doorway, as wide as he was tall. His forehead shone, as he was bald except for two strips of white hair that ran around the sides above his rosy ears. He had a creamy mustache, a large red nose, and a stern no nonsense manner, though his eyes shone like ripe chestnuts.

"Mr. Vallely?"

"Could be. Who's askin'?"

"Don't be grumpy now, Paddy." It was a woman's voice, as soft as kitten fur and just as soothing.

"My name is Maggie Taylor. Your daughter Shannon is my mother, and she asked me—"

"I've no daughter name o' Shannon," he shouted.

"Paddy!" chastised the woman. "Don't—"

Maggie strained to see her, but the colossal man blocked her view. If only *she* had answered.

"Wrong house. Sorry for your trouble," he said, closing the door so abruptly he almost caught her hand.

Stepping back chagrined, Maggie took a deep breath and banged on the scarlet door again. She could hear them arguing inside, but no one opened the door. Finally, she turned and walked away from the faerie-tale house, tears shining in her eyes. *Stupid old man—wouldn't even listen—stupid mean old man. No wonder my mother left.*

Maggie was slouching on the bike when Primrose returned. "Let's go. Wrong place."

"Are you sure?"

"Yes," she snapped.

There was no such thing as a faerie-tale ending.

No daybreak, no rising sun, no solace could end the unfathomable night that smothered Galway Bay in black and murky sheets. Water dripped from the end of Maggie's nose, mingling with teary snot. Swiping at it with the end of her soggy sleeve, she sat with her legs hung over the edge of the sidewalk and stared into the churning river below. Swelled with the rain, the River Corrib rushed to the sea in green brackish waves spiked with ivory caps. Glancing downriver, she saw the charging current catch in circling eddies beneath the triple arches of the gray rebel bridge.

Wet, cold, and inconsolable, Maggie mused how easy it would be to push off with her hands into that murky swell and allow the river to carry her downstream to the sea like Ophelia. What else was there? Her father was surely dead and her mother incommunicado. The grandfather she'd tried so hard to find had slammed the future in her face, and a psychotic priest was dogging her trail.

Where would she live? If she lived?

Fishing around in her pocket for the tiny blue bottle of peace-inducing frankincense, her fingers touched the pendulum Daphne had given her. She held the end of the silver chain between her right thumb and index finger and allowed the crystal to dangle in the air just above her left palm. After asking if it would speak to her and divulge its secrets, she waited. The crystal began to move instantly, caught up in her turbulence. Careening clockwise in huge round circles, it shouted *yes*.

Fearful, but needing to know the truth, she asked silently. *Is my father—* Then realizing that she now had two fathers, she clarified: *Is John Taylor dead?* Crystal whizzing, the circles continued, sweeping so violently, she had to raise her elbow to avoid a collision. *Yes.* John Taylor was dead. This bittersweet validation confirmed both the sad fact of his death and her ability to converse with spirits.

Excited by the emphatic voice of the crystal, she asked: *Will Father Grace find me and kill me?* The pendulum pivoted sharply as if to swing straight back and forth, then changed course and swung erratically in circles; finally, it ended up zigzagging in a crazy figure eight.

Startled by the sound of footsteps on the stone bridge, she caught the chaotic crystal in her left hand and closed her fist around it. Two figures in long hooded garments had just crossed and were rapidly approaching. In the wake of what she'd been experiencing lately, Maggie wondered if they were dead or alive, enemy or friend, or simply strangers en route to some Druidic ceremony. Galway had more than its share of pagan eccentrics. She swung her legs around just as a tall man pushed back the hood of his long black raincoat.

"Oh my God. Estrada!" Maggie ran to him, threw her arms around him, and clung.

"Hey, it's good to see you too."

"I can't believe you're here," Maggie sang, surprised at how the presence of someone from home brought instant comfort.

"Neither can I."

"Well, I'll leave you to it," Primrose said. "If you're of a mind to amble downtown later, I'll be working on Shop Street near Abbeygate."

"What?" Releasing Estrada, Maggie glanced at the witch.

Draped and hooded in a forest green cloak which dragged upon the stones in folds, Primrose stood serenely, her hands hidden beneath gaping sleeves. Clustered branches of appliquéd emerald and silver oak leaves meandered over the cloak like a shimmering forest. The tiny elfish face beneath the hood was painted bright green, except for the area around her eyes, which was etched in dark spirals to resemble the knots of a tree. Her ever-changing irises glowed with golden iridescence as she smiled.

"You look like a nature goddess."

"She's Danu, matriarch of the Irish gods," Estrada said.

Maggie turned and cocked her head, surprised by his knowledge.

"I asked," Estrada explained. "But you look like you've been crying."

"Ah, she's done now," Primrose said. "Aren't you, girleen? Just like this rain."

Maggie nodded. It was true. The sight of Estrada had yanked her from the depths of sorrow into another mood completely.

"They've just turned on the Christmas lights and the shops will be open late," Primrose said.

"But what are you going to do on Shop Street?"

"Sing and dance, so the folks fill my pockets with gold. Did you think I was independently wealthy or perhaps in league with a leprechaun?"

"Oh, show us," Maggie begged.

"Please," Estrada said. There was something different about him. He had a rugged edge and a growth of beard the same length as his cropped hair, but his voice was as smooth as velvet.

"Ah sure. Why not?" Primrose winked, then took a deep breath and sang, her clear high voice meandering triplets and trills like water over stones. It was a slow and sultry song, and she swayed in the evening breeze, as her hands told the story.

> *"I am the wind that blows across the sea*
> *I am the wave of the deep*
> *I am the roar of the ocean*
> *I am the stag of seven battles*
> *I am the hawk on the cliff*
> *I am a ray of sunlight*
> *I am the greenest of plants*
> *I am a wild boar*
> *I am a salmon in the river*
> *I am a lake on the plain*
> *I am the word of knowledge*
> *I am the point of a spear*
> *I am the lure beyond the ends of the earth*
> *I can shift my shape like a god."*

"I bet you can," Maggie said, and Estrada nodded in agreement. Then they both clapped, as Primrose folded her hands in Namaste and bowed to each of them. "Oh, can't we come with you?"

"I thought you'd want to catch up, like."

"Can't we do both?"

"Aye, sure. Why not? You can keep an eye on my cash box."

Maggie forgot her despair on Shop Street. The storm had indeed blown over and by the light of the waxing moon, Primrose captivated everyone with what she called her performance art. Posing like a statue on a small raised stage, she sang and danced in English and Irish, while people tossed euros into her willow basket. She was not the only performer. The Galway street swarmed with buskers, jugglers, step dancers, and other costumed characters in a bustling pagan carnival.

"You could do magic here," Maggie said to Estrada. "They'd love you. It's just like Oz."

He nodded. "They certainly have their share of wizards."

Afterwards, they went for a pint at Tig Coili. Perching against the bar in the traditional pub, they watched the musicians play beneath the wrought iron windows. A few people recognized Primrose and begged her to dance. So, she raised her skirts and tapped out a jig in her sleek red boots, while the room rocked to the beat of the large frame drum, they called the bodhrán. Estrada stood as still as a manikin; mesmerized, his dark eyes absorbing her every move.

"I knew it," shouted Maggie, nodding toward Primrose. "I knew you'd love her."

Embarrassed, he laughed. "She *is* extraordinary. I've never met anyone quite like her."

"Well, I've never met anyone quite like you. So you two are perfect together." She thought suddenly of Sensara and decided not to ask. Why threaten destiny? And she was right. By the time they left Tig Coili, Primrose and Estrada were strolling arm in arm, and Maggie felt suddenly lonely.

"I wonder how Dylan is."

"He told me that he's written to you a few times," Estrada said. "Don't you ever check your email?"

"He has?" Startled by the question, Maggie stopped in the street. "I haven't even thought about email for days. Do you think any Internet cafés are still open?"

Primrose glanced up at the stars and shook her head. "It's near midnight. But, we're almost home. I'm sure you can conjure up your email on Kieran's laptop, if he hasn't taken it with him to Dublin."

"Kieran?" Estrada raised his eyebrows.

"My flat mate. Carries on a lively cyber life from what I can tell."

Back at the flat, Primrose showed Maggie to the laptop in Kieran's bedroom, and turned to leave. "Can I sleep here tonight?" Maggie asked, gesturing to the cozy little bed.

The two girls exchanged wicked glances, and then Primrose replied in her usual clipped way, "Ah sure. Why not? Your man can always bed down on the floor."

Maggie laughed. "Yeah, sure."

"I think he wants a wee chat before you turn in though. I'll send him in, shall I?"

Estrada appeared in the doorway a few minutes later, knocked quietly, and stood looking awkwardly for a place to sit while Maggie did her best not to stare. Even jet-lagged, in a simple black T-shirt and jeans, he was delicious. Kieran's tiny room had no furniture save a thin chest of drawers and the small bed on which she was sitting with her legs crossed, the computer on her lap.

Finally, he took an envelope from his pocket and handed it to her. "Special delivery from your mom."

"Oh God," she said. "Sit." His hovering was making her nervous.

"Are you sure you want me to stay? Maybe you'd like to—"

"I don't want to read this alone."

He nodded and sat cross-legged at the farthest end of the bed, hands resting on his knees.

She ripped open the envelope, unfolded the letter, and began to read silently. "It's sad. Can I read it out loud? Sometimes it's easier if—"

"Go for it."

"*My Dearest Maggie,*" she began. "She's never called me that before." She swallowed, and then read on: *"I hope this letter finds you well and you've had no problem finding my parents—* No problem there, mom. We've only been to hell and back," she interjected sarcastically. His smile urged her on. *"I wish I could tell you this in person, but I can't leave right now. Maggie, your dear father has passed on. He died in his sleep on Saturday after a series of strokes. The doctor says it had nothing to do with his fall. He's been having strokes this past year, increasing in severity. Do not blame yourself. I tried to reach you Sunday but there was no answer. His body will be cremated on Tuesday. We'll have a service when everything is settled, and we're together.*

Maggie, I want to come home. Estrada has another letter I'd like you to give to my parents. I realize that moving to Ireland would mean leaving your school and friends, and if you say no, I'll understand. But it could mean a new life for us, a better life. I love you. I know I've never said that enough. Mom"

Maggie folded the letter and put it in her pocket, then sniffed and sighed. "Wow."

"Sorry about your dad."

"I already knew. I saw his ghost." She assumed that meeting disembodied spirits was an everyday occurrence for Estrada.

"That must've been scary."

"At the time, yeah." She took a deep breath. "He came to warn me about Grace. He said he's coming here, coming after me."

Estrada nodded. "Yeah, Sensara's been dreaming. We think that he's either here already or on his way. That's why I came. They think I can protect you."

"My very own champion. But you don't think you can?"

"I'll do whatever it takes. It's just that . . ." He shrugged. "It's complicated."

Maggie waited for him to elaborate until the silence grew too awkward. "I don't understand my mother. If she wants to come home, why doesn't she just get on a plane?"

"She's stressed and seeing her family again after so long could be difficult."

"You're telling me. My grandfather's an ogre."

"Sounds like your ma needs her folks but can't face them until she knows she has their blessing." Primrose was suddenly in the room, dressed in a long green T-shirt, her pale face scrubbed clean. She sat on the bed beside Maggie and rubbed her back. "Your father's at peace now and your mother deserves the same, as do you."

Maggie nodded, then remembered the look on Paddy Vallely's face. "But her father wants nothing to do with us."

Primrose squeezed her shoulder. "Ah sure, the old fiddler was just in shock. When daughters of daughters drop from the sky, it takes a while for some men to come around. Go back and talk to him, girleen. Make it right for your ma to come home. It's where she belongs."

"But—"

"I'll go get the tea and put a wee something in it, so you can sleep. Tomorrow we three will go to Cong, and you can make peace with your folks." She ruffled Maggie's hair, then hopped up and slipped from the room.

"Primrose is right," Estrada said. "If you have the chance to fix things with your family, you should take it."

Maggie eyed him curiously.

"I lost a father too. He disappeared when I was a kid."

"I'm sorry." Maggie felt closer to him after this surprising confession. "We were in a cemetery when I saw my dad's ghost—" She gasped. "Oh, it was the cemetery where Yeats is buried. I saw his grave, and I saw Ben Bulben, the mountain where Yeats said the faeries fly from, and we went to Carrowmore. That's an ancient megalithic tomb. And I saw—" Maggie stopped talking suddenly, unable to put her experience into words.

"Yeah? You saw?"

"I don't know exactly. Maybe I saw—"

"Herself saw the Tribes. The Gentry. But, that's a story for another day." Primrose handed them each a cup of sweet milky tea. "Drink up now, pet. We don't want to scare off Estrada his first night in Galway with talk of spirits. Besides, your man and I have things to do."

"Maybe we can go there and you can see them for yourself," Maggie said, remembering Estrada's desire to see faeries. Then she feigned a yawn. "I'm really tired, and I still have to check my email."

"We'll leave you to it then," Primrose said, taking Estrada's hand and leading him from the room.

"Tell Dylan to let the others know I arrived safely. Okay?" he shouted over his shoulder.

"Sure," Maggie said, and turned her attention to the laptop. There were several messages from Dylan, one from Damien, two from girls who wanted to know why she wasn't in school, and a recent one from Bastian. She opened it first. She wasn't quite ready to deal with her feelings for Dylan.

Hey Maggie. I hope you don't mind me emailing you. You said we could keep in touch. I heard about your father. So sorry. I will miss him too but not like you will. So, where are you? Is Ireland as green as they say? What's going on? Did you find your grandparents? Are you coming home soon? Write back. B.

Maggie hit reply and wrote.

Hey Bastian. I'm glad you wrote to me. I know you'll miss my dad. You were always so good to him. Ireland is beautiful. Estrada arrived today and has fallen instantly in love with Primrose—she's the woman I'm staying with here in Galway. Tomorrow we're all going to Cong. It's a village not far from here where my grandparents live in a real faerie-tale cottage covered in ivy. My grandfather's awful but my mother wants to move here, so who knows? Maybe I'll end up living there and you can visit sometime and see it for yourself. Take care. Maggie

She hit send, and then opened Dylan's last letter. He apologized for calling her a slut. "It's my own stuff," he said. He assumed she hadn't answered his emails because she was still angry. He was furious with himself because he hadn't stayed around the night Father Grace abducted her. "Maybe if I'd stayed none of this would have happened."

It was strange how time changed, but people stayed stuck in their memories. That night on the porch had been awful, but the night before she left had been worse because Dylan was right. She *had* conjured a spell and used him to get into the coven, and although she had feelings for him, she wasn't sure what they were. Still, she hoped they could have the slow kind of love Primrose talked about and she wanted to explore it.

As soft susurrations emanated from the other room, she stroked the pink stone heart Dylan had given her and imagined kissing him again as she had that night on the porch. He was sweet and strong, a nice guy who'd always be there and do anything for her. Not ready to give up that dream, she hit reply and wrote:

Hi Dylan. I've been traveling with Primrose. She took me to see the dolmens at Carrowmore. You would love it there. Estrada arrived today and says hello. Tomorrow we're all going back to Cong to talk to my grandparents. Dylan, you need to know that nothing is your fault. I kissed you that night because I wanted to. I am wearing your rose heart. Love Maggie

Full of Scorpions is my Mind

Primrose came out of the bathroom drying her hands with a towel. "I ran a hot bath for you, Sorcerer. Always feels good to wash off the travel dust before bedding down in a new land, don't you think?"

"Absolutely," Estrada said. There was something about Primrose he couldn't resist. Her eyes were slightly upturned, like Sensara's, but wide and deep and full of mischief he couldn't wait to explore. "But, I'm no sorcerer, just a lowly illusionist."

"Ah, go on with you," she said, tossing him the towel and an elfish smile that sent his blood racing.

He stood for a moment entranced as the force of her shot through his sinew. He felt young and potent and very much alive.

"Or, perhaps, it's a cold shower you're needing."

"No, a hot bath is perfect."

Primrose was even more perceptive than Sensara. It was an old claw tub and she'd lit candles around it, so a pale scented cloud rose just above the surface of the water. After stripping quickly, he slipped into the tepid pool, leaned back against the slanted iron, and waited. Surely, she was coming.

After a while, he slid down under the water and stayed submerged as long as he could hold his breath. Then pushing upward, he broke the surface and ran his hands over his stubbly face and head. Leaning over the tub, he grabbed his traveling case and retrieved a razor. Perhaps, she wasn't coming. Perhaps, she was just congenial, and he'd read her wrong. Or perhaps, she was waiting for him to finish his bath, in which case, he should get moving.

He propped up the tiny mirror, lathered his face, and shaved off his beard. Then, after soaping and rinsing, he climbed out of the tub, toweled off, and pulled the stopper.

It felt good to be naked, and he dreaded climbing back into his tight black jeans, but he hadn't brought any other clothes into the bathroom. Should he walk out wrapped in a towel, or was that too presumptuous? Miffed, he wondered why he was even concerned. Back home he would have sauntered out naked and fully armed. It was Primrose—she unnerved him.

A rusty brown robe, the same shade as her eyes, hung on a hook behind the door. He tried it on and was surprised to find it a perfect fit. It must belong to the roommate, Kieran. Examining the small bathroom, he saw signs of him everywhere. Not that it was any of his business if she had a male roommate, or even that it mattered. Except it did.

Glancing in the mirror, he was startled by his reflection. At twenty-eight, he looked like a tired old man. His hair, he realized, had done much to hide his true self. Perhaps, as the man who'd taken it claimed, it did contain his power. With his finger, he traced lines he'd never seen before. His cheeks were thin and hollow and dark shadows fell below his eyes that revealed more than jet lag. He brushed his teeth, and then finding a tube of green tea lotion in the corner, smoothed it over his hands and face, paying the wrinkles particular attention. The least he could do was smell good.

Quietly he opened the door. She'd lit candles in the living room and was sitting cross-legged on an old red leather sofa. As he entered, she gestured toward a bed of quilts she'd made up on the floor in the middle of a floral-patterned rug. "Lie down on your back, Sorcerer. Let go of the world."

Not knowing how to respond but appreciating an invitation similar to one he'd savored the previous night in a land across the sea, he smiled and laid down. A huge sigh escaped. It had been a long day where, for much of the time, he'd been trapped alone in his own anxious thoughts, and he hated being alone.

She knelt beside him and touched his smooth cheek. "Lovely. Do you work with a healer back home?"

The question startled him. He considered the word healer and finally said, "Sensara's a massage therapist and she does psychic healings."

"Ah, your woman."

"We're not together now." He wanted that made clear. "She—"

"No need," she said, shrugging it off. "It's just that, sometimes I can see things and sometimes I can help. If you're of a mind to let me."

"See things?"

"Aye. There's a great heaviness around your heart, and your third eye is near closed," she said, touching his forehead. "And, there's a heap of . . . chaos and debris. Aye, that's what it is. Here in the lower extremity." Her hands swept through the air as if she were conducting a symphony. "And here," she said, laying her palm across his stomach. "I fear your power has dwindled to almost nothing."

"So, I'm a write-off."

"Ah, not quite. You're still lovely." She stroked his cheek again. "You're just in no fit state to go off fighting dragons." When she placed one palm on his forehead and the other on his belly, he sighed and closed his eyes. "That's it now. Sigh it out. Then lie still and let me have my way with you. I'll take good care of you, mind." Her words came slow and breathy, and although he couldn't feel her hands against his flesh, heat emanated from her palms as they swept over his body.

"Ah, impotence is no problem, I see." With a giggle, she tossed a blanket over the erection that had popped through the robe. "I'll just put that away for now, shall I?"

He grinned, unashamed, and tried to flirt, but his tongue felt thick and heavy and words would not come. Soon he forgot what he was going to say, feeling only the focused heat of her hands. Images formed in his mind. Lover after lover appeared: some he remembered, while others were nameless and faceless; flesh and scents and pounding rhythms, beginning long ago when he was just a boy. And then, he felt the man's seductive lips and he grew so aroused he gasped.

"Let them fly, now. Don't grasp or cling." With her jarring voice, he pushed the man away, and slipped into Sensara, and then he was with Michael and felt infused by the familiarity of their love.

"Let them go. Let them fly," she repeated. "When so many are piled one on top of the other, the flavors mingle until you cannot savor any." The breeze from her hands swirled in the air above his pelvis, and he imagined her cutting the strings of past liaisons. For a moment, such a deep sense of loss overcame him, he fought to resurrect them. Michael. An ocean of disparate dreams, they sailed into the ethers.

"You're not alone, Sorcerer," she said, holding his hand tenderly, "and your memories will remain, just not the desperate anguished energy you've been carrying. Heaps upon heaps of bodies belong only to the grave." Feeling stripped and empty, awkward and alone, he reached out to clutch her.

"Easy, beautiful man. Lie back and breathe with me now." Taking each of his hands in hers, she pushed him down gently, so that the backs of his hands settled into the blanket, and she hovered over him.

Palm to palm, a vibrant current spiked through his hands and up his arms, warming his entire body. Her sweet breath grazed his forehead, and as he felt her inhale deeply and then release, a sense of calm swept through him. Joining her in synchronized breaths, that grew slower and slower until his heart barely beat, he sank into the floor.

"That's better. I've got you."

He felt her lift her hands and sweep them across his solar plexus.

"Now, I want you to create a cloud of swirling saffron dust right here above your navel."

Feeling the heat from her hands, he imagined a beautiful mist, the shade of a monk's robe, drifting just below his heart.

"This is your power center," she said, and spreading wide his robe, she laid her warm palms just below his ribs. "Together we're going to fill you with power. Now open your rib cage and let the cloud descend and spiral through your diaphragm. Let it grow and fill you, washing over all your bones and muscles and internal organs."

With the visions, he felt suddenly expanded, as if he'd been blown full of warm air.

"This power's yours. No one can take it from you, unless you give it freely."

Again, he felt the swirling sense of images being carved in the air above him.

Then suddenly her hot hands were on his breasts, her thumbs digging into his ribs. Feeling torn, he burst into tears.

"Ah, you'll be fine. Your sweet heart's been cloaked in darkness for a long, long time and it needs setting free."

"It burns." Tears escaped as he saw images too horrible to describe, and in the midst of it all, a great black demon rose up clutching knives in both its clawed hands, and its eyes were gold and lined in kohl, and they were his. "Stop. No more. The pain—"

"Aye, there's pain, but you cannot love like this, and I know you long for love. If you didn't, you'd feel no pain at all. The demon would consume you."

"Please," he begged, and cried so hard he choked.

"Sorcerer. Take control. Imagine the most beautiful green fields."

"I can't. It hurts. It's too much. I'm going to—"

"Open your eyes, Estrada. Look at me."

Slowly, he opened his riffling lids and stared into her eyes, and they were shimmering as deep and bright as a turquoise lagoon.

"There, now. Take the cool sea from my eyes—I'll do it with you—and spread it over the fire in your heart. It's an ocean wave, a cool blue blanket. That's right. It's putting out the flames and soothing the pain. The darkness is gone but your heart is still open, still able to love. Do you feel it?"

"Yes," he whispered, and held up his hands to touch her face, still unable to take his eyes from hers. "I love you."

She dried his tears with the sleeve of her shirt. "Ah sure, it's grand to love with an open heart. Now, close your eyes one more time."

Leaning over, she brushed her lips across each eyelid and angels filled his head, hovering in clouds with serene, androgynous faces and glimmering white wings lifted by the winds of heaven. As a small child, these were the images he loved most from his religion.

He remembered the candles, the cathedral, and the robed priest chanting in Latin and Spanish.

"We've one more thing to do, my beautiful man," she whispered, breaking his trance.

He felt her change position. Kneeling at the top of his head, she gazed down on him. "I'm going to help you open your third eye. When I do this, you'll see things—some things may frighten you even more than that demon you just saw, because you don't yet understand. But you must remember, Estrada, you're always in control of your own mind. These are not *my* visions and I'm not putting these images in your head. If it's too much and you really must stop, say the word and we will. Do you understand?"

"Yes," he said, feeling suddenly like he could trust her with his life.

Somewhere in the hollows of his mind, he recalled something a woman named Van Gelder had written about opening the third eye. Then he felt fingertips against his forehead and with it came the sensation of light beaming into his skull. Collecting at a small point in the center of his head, rays emanated outwards, as colors swirled through his mind. They formed shapes—a luminescent pentagram at first, and then the sides of the star formed arms and legs, like DaVinci's Vitruvian man, ancient and . . . "Beautiful," he whispered. Myriad shapes swirled together, and, in the center, he saw a passageway. They beckoned him down inside, but it was cold and dark and smelled of fecund earth and bone and ash and decay. "No, I can't. I can't." And, suddenly her hands were gone from his brow and he lay panting on the floor.

"Aye. It's not your time, not yet. But there now. You've seen what your man Yeats longed to see and never did."

"But I can't move or be alone. Will you sleep with me?"

"Aye, my beautiful man." She sunk beside him and covered them both with the blanket. With Primrose in his arms, her cheek brushing his breast and her palm on his open heart, he fell into a deep sleep, thinking of nothing but her.

It was a woman who opened the door of the faerie-tale house when Maggie knocked the next day; a tiny walnut-skinned woman, rounded about the shoulders and stooped over a hand-carved cane.

"Ah, at last," she said, as if she'd been waiting, "Come in. Come in." Popping her head outside the door, she glanced around as if she were expecting others. Seeing no one else, she stood back and smiled. "I'll just put the kettle on, shall I?"

Primrose had said that some things a girl had to do on her own and this was one of them. She'd taken Estrada for a ramble in the woods around Ashford Castle and promised to return with him later. But that did nothing for Maggie's anxiety. She hesitated, then stepped through the door and glanced around.

"Ah, you're safe enough, pet. Paddy's scooted off to Achill Island for a session. That man never could sit still."

"Do you know who I am?"

"Aye, sure. You're Margaret Mary." The syllables rolled slowly off her tongue. "That's me mam's name, bless her soul. But you go by Maggie, don't you? Ah, you're the spitting image of Shannon. She was just about your age when she left us. That's what threw your granddad into such a dither the other day. Poor man couldn't believe his eyes."

"So, you're really my grandmother?" It was almost unbelievable. "Can I call you Grandma?" Suddenly she wanted nothing more than to be the grandchild of this dear woman.

"Name's Moira," she said, opening wide her arms, "Moira Vallely. But I'd be blessed if you'd call me Gran. I've been waiting a long time to hear you speak it."

And for the very first time, Maggie hugged her gran.

"So, you know about me?"

"Come along, pet. We'll make tea, then sit by the fire, and I'll tell you what I know."

In the old-fashioned kitchen, Gran filled the teapot with tea leaves, just like Dylan's great-grandmother would have done.

When it was brewed, Maggie picked up the tray that held the teapot, strainer, cups, milk, sugar, spoons, and thick oat biscuits, and followed her gran into the front room.

"Set it down there," Gran said, pointing to the polished wood table in front of the hearth. It was worn and scarred with years of use. "Candlelight is so much warmer than those horrid electric light bulbs." And she shuffled about the room lighting candles.

"Yes, it's lovely. But I have to tell you something, Gran, and it's not good news."

"News rarely is but go on then. Tell me what brought you back again so soon after your grandfather's foul greeting."

"It's about my mother. She wants to come home. Here, to Ireland."

"Well, that's grand news."

"Yes, but—" Maggie stumbled, caught on the edge of all that had happened, and then it spilled out in a torrent. "You see, our priest kidnapped me. He didn't hurt me much, but while I was gone, my father got confused and fell down the stairs, and then he had a stroke, and well, he died a few days ago. So, my mother sent me here to find you because she was afraid that the priest would come after me again, and now she's all alone in Canada and wants to come home. Here. She thought I'd be safe here, but the thing is, Gran, I think he's here too. The priest, I mean. I think he followed me."

"Good lord, a priest who kidnaps young girls? What's this world coming to?"

"I know. I'm afraid he might find out where you live. I'm afraid he might try to kill us all."

"Why on Earth would he do that?"

"It's a long story and I really don't understand it, but it seems to have started because he hates witches. You remember in the old days when they burned witches?"

Her grandmother nodded.

"Well, Gabriel Grace—that's his name—he burns witches. At least, he burned a witch named Jade, and he probably would have burned me too, if Dylan and Estrada hadn't found me. I think he might try to kill me because I know him and what he's done."

"Jesus, Mary, and Joseph! No priest in his right mind would do that. He must be tormented so." Picking up the teapot, she poured two cups. "Come fix your tea, pet, and have a biscuit. It will make you feel better."

Maggie did as she was told, then huddled in one of the cozy armchairs by the fire and took a sip. The tea was milky sweet and immediately brought comfort.

Gran settled into the other armchair and balanced her teacup in her lap. "Now, tell me more about this priest."

"He used to help us. My father had a head injury and Father Grace was always around, taking him out for a drive in his car, or just sitting with him. I can't believe it, really. I mean, one minute I wanted to get away and thought I never would and then—" She sighed what words could not express.

"You poor dear. Death is a hard thing to fathom, especially for a young thing like yourself." Sipping her tea, she gazed lovingly at Maggie.

"But Gran, what if he *is* coming here? Shouldn't we do something?"

"Ah, you're safe enough in this house. Drink your tea, loveen."

Maggie looked at the door which she hadn't bothered to lock. She looked at the cane carved in Celtic spirals like the ones etched on Primrose's head, and then she looked again at her grandmother. Something very strange was going on. Either her grandmother didn't understand or—

"That Primrose. Isn't she grand?" Gran giggled, her eyes twinkling in the candle glow. "I brought that one into the world."

"What?"

"Held her in my hands and blessed her."

"I don't understand. You know Primrose?"

"Why, her mother Nuala and I were best friends our whole lives. Rory and Paddy played every weekend together in the pub. The Macaulay cottage is just across the field, you see. We're neighbors."

"Get out!" Maggie was flabbergasted. "Primrose? All this time, she knew? She knew you and where you lived and exactly who you were. Why did she drag me to all those pubs and off to sleep in cemeteries and prehistoric sites, if she knew exactly where you were?"

"How much fun would that have been?"

"I'll kill her."

Moira giggled. "Ah, go on. You had a grand time, and who knows, you may need her yet."

Maggie scowled. "You do know she's a witch."

"We don't use that word, dear. Dreadful connotations."

"We? You're not a witch, too, are you?"

Her gran grinned and sipped her tea.

This was too much. Was everyone in Ireland either magical or fey? "Why did you say that we're safe here?"

"Oh, the ivy tree, of course. Didn't you notice when you walked up the path?"

"You mean the tree that's wrapped around the house?"

"Aye. She'll not let anyone inside this house intent on doing harm. Then there's the mistletoe and holly."

"Really?"

"Aye, sure," Gran said.

Maggie giggled and then stifled a yawn.

"You look as if you need a nap, pet. I'm almost ready for one myself."

Maggie looked anxiously at the door.

"Primrose won't be along until supper time at least."

"How do you know that? Are you telepathic?" Maggie was beginning to believe anything was possible.

"You don't need to be a mind reader when you know someone. Come along. I'll show you your mother's old room. I've left everything just as it was when she left. I knew she'd come home one day. You can sleep there tonight." Smiling, she touched Maggie's cheek. "Then in the morning you must go see Colin Burke."

"Burke? Why do I know that name? Who is he? And what about my granddad? He doesn't want me here."

"Ah, don't fret. Himself won't be back for a day or two, and by then, it'll all be sorted. Come along now. I think you'll like Shannon's old room."

"But wait. Who's Colin Burke?"

"Our neighbor across the creek."

"So?" she shrugged.

"Why Colin's your father, pet. Did your mam not tell you?"

Estrada watched Primrose flip over a pale flat rock and retrieve a worn brass skeleton key. Fitting it in the lock on the top half of the bright red door, she gave one quick turn and with a clunk, it swung wide.

"Charming," he said. "Like a postcard cottage." The outside was whitewashed, the roof thatched in flaxen reeds, and the surrounding green fields fenced in stone.

"So I'm told. There's always someone after having it to film something or other." Reaching inside, she opened the latch to the bottom door. "In you come. Those clouds are about to explode."

Sure enough, as they stepped inside, rain pelted down.

The cottage itself was tiny—two small rooms, kitchen and sitting room, separated by a central stone hearth that heated both sides.

"Where's the bedroom?"

"Down boy. We sleep in the loft." Laughing, she shook her head. "I've never met a man so driven by desire. You've a healthy libido, Sorcerer."

Suddenly sensitive, Estrada shrugged. He busied himself by snooping around the cottage while Primrose lit an oil lamp and built a peat fire. The tiny windowpanes were edged in red, and another red leather sofa, quite like the one in her Galway flat, stood in front of the fireplace. Comfortably swathed with vibrant pillows and knitted throws, he thought how wonderful it would be to forget the hectic world and live in a bygone era.

Wandering into the kitchen, he skirted the wooden table and chairs, ducked around a large wooden dresser with shelves of vine-patterned dishes, and poked his head into the pantry. There seemed to be no sink or running water, no refrigerator or stove. Not even a bathroom.

"Is this your grandparents' cottage?"

"It was. The Macaulay family farmed this land for generations. If they knew the cash this cottage brings in now, just for having her picture taken, they'd be shocked."

He peeked at Primrose through the open hearth. The peat had flared and its oily scent filled the room with a homey feeling. Despite her tight leather jacket and tattooed head, she seemed a creature from another time.

"Primrose," he mused to himself.

"Aye?"

"I was just wondering about your name."

"I was born with hair the color of farmhouse butter, just like the flower. It means first rose, and I was their first and only child. So, there you have it."

She came around the corner then and wrapped her arms around him, as if she'd done it a million times. He held her to his chest and hugged her. When she drew away, he continued to hold her hands as they talked. He couldn't let her go.

"I can understand why you were an only child. Where could your parents go to be alone?"

"Are you kidding me, man? Have you any idea how many Catholic wives trudged around pregnant year after year, just spitting out babies in cottages like this? When you're wanting it, there's always a place to have it; even if it means cavorting in the hills, or being stealthy, like."

"Stealthy has its own appeal. We lived in a place like this too, in Mexico, when my parents were first married."

"And later?"

"Later, my father got rich and famous—"

"Ah, you're having me on." She hopped up on the kitchen table, slipped off her jacket, and unwound her vibrant scarf. In bright yellow leggings and red pointy boots, she looked elfish, but a tight sapphire sweater that fell off her shoulders and showed every ridge of her nipples, reminded him just how much of a woman she was.

"I'm not," he growled. He desperately wanted to touch one, to lower his mouth and close his lips around it, sweater and all.

Placing her finger beneath his chin, she tilted his face upward to meet her eyes, and he laughed, caught in his own lustful nature.

"It's true. My father was a movie star in Mexico. He shot a couple of big roles in Los Angeles, so we moved there, and then—"

"Then your troubles began."

Estrada nodded. "Yeah. He changed, and soon after that, he disappeared."

"I'm sorry, Sorcerer, but it seems you gained some good along with the bad."

"How's that?"

"Well, look at you. There's movie star written all over you. Of course, there's flaws too, and well, you saw some of that last night. But your past has made you strong; stronger than you know."

"I hope so." He watched as she fondled the scarf.

Then, winding it around both hands, she flipped it over his head and drew him in. "You've been aching to kiss me since we first met," she said, tilting her lips. "Standing here so close like, with your movie star charm, I wish you would."

He caught her tiny face in the palms of his hands and lightly brushed his lips against her cheek, and then softly across her lips. It was a fraction of what he wanted, but he was determined to wait—though he felt like pulling down her leggings and bending her over the kitchen table. A week ago, he would have and got away with it. In exorcizing those who'd come before, she'd made him feel vulnerable, virginal even. He kissed the top of her head where the three trees merged.

"You're a strange man. You're the size of an oak, yet you kiss me like I'm a porcelain doll. Tell me, Sorcerer, if I fell to my knees right now on this cold stone floor, would you turn my face away?"

"Oh, please don't. You know I couldn't, and I don't want it to be like that for us."

"Hmmm," she breathed, and he felt that somehow, he'd passed a test. "Will you help me brew the potion for tonight, then?" Leaving the scarf around his neck, she grasped his shoulders and jumped off the table. "If you can walk, mind."

"Eye of newt, and toe of frog, wool of bat, and tongue of dog," he chanted.

"Are you after brewing a hell broth?"

"You tell me. What's going to happen tonight?"

Dropping her head back suddenly, Primrose rolled her eyes so only the whites were visible. He'd never seen this before, and it scared him. Even when Sensara drew down the moon, she never looked possessed, not like this. Watching, he waited.

"Your man's close," she said at last.

"*Christ*. We have to get back to Maggie."

"He's not here for Maggie. He's here for you."

A noise at the open doorway broke the spell. They both jumped, and she was suddenly herself again. "Ah, it's just Angus Murphy wanting a bite in out of the rain." Taking a sheaf of dried clover from the countless bundles of herbs hanging from the oak beams above their heads, she held it out for the old merino sheep, who caught it between his tiny teeth and yanked.

"Wait," Estrada said, catching her hand. "How will it end?"

"That I cannot say. All I can do is stoke the peat and brew you a protective potion. I'm counting on you to know the right thing to do when the time comes. And Sorcerer, sometimes what you think is right and what needs to be done doesn't quite align. You must trust that whatever happens is fated."

He didn't like that and clutched her to his chest while Hecate's prophecy rattled through his brain. *Four souls pass over into light.* As his chin settled on the top of her head, he could feel her moist lips against his heart. Running his thumb along the tips of her ears, she tilted her head back, and he gazed into her amber eyes.

"I do love you, Primrose, and I haven't been able to say that to anyone in a very long time. Whatever happens you need to know that. And, you're right. I do want to make love to you. As you said, I am driven by lust, but it's more than that with you. If it never happened, it wouldn't matter."

"All that and a poet too." She smiled. "But you forget that I'm a woman with needs of my own, and as romantic as you sound, if it never happened, why, I'd toss you out with the wash water."

Picking her up in his arms, Estrada cradled her, opening his lips to her dancing tongue, as the late winter sun slipped through the open doorway.

Suddenly, breaking the kiss, she whispered, "Put me down, Sorcerer."

"What's wrong?" he asked, hoping it wasn't something he'd done.

"Your killer's close, so close I can smell him."

"What does he smell like?"

"Cinnamon."

Maggie looked through some of her mother's old books, then fell asleep listening to the patter of raindrops against the windowpane. She slept so soundly, she suspected Moira of spiking her tea with some sedative herb, as Primrose had done the night before. She didn't usually take afternoon naps. When she awoke, she went looking for Moira, and found her outside in the garden.

After the rain, the Vallely's back garden sparkled, as tiny raindrops adhered to the myriad leaves and reflected the pale rays of the late afternoon sun. Standing on the back step, she watched her gran glide through the garden greeting her plants and feeding her birds. No cane needed here. How had Shannon left this enchanted place? And how did she turn out so mean when Moira was so kind? Questions bubbled through her mind.

Finally, unable to restrain herself, Maggie blurted out, "What happened to my mother?"

"Ah, now that's a long story." Gran wandered back toward the door. "But it's yours, so you've a right to hear it. I'll put the kettle on."

The story revolved around a man named Frank Burke, who owned a large equestrian center just a couple of miles from the Vallely's home. Part of his two hundred acres, bordered the other side of the creek just beyond their garden. According to Moira, Shannon had worked for Frank Burke since she was a child, as a groom and stable hand.

"She had the knack, our Shannon. Could get a horse to do anything. Only had to ask."

"My mother hates horses."

"Ah, not then. Shannon adored horses, could talk to them and they talked back. She really loved them as much as she loved Colin."

Maggie touched her horse tattoo and thought about how many times she'd asked Shannon if she could go riding next door and been vehemently refused.

"Colin, my father?"

"Aye, loveen. Young Colin was his father's son, and when Shannon got in the family way, sure he'd have nothing to do with her. Broke her heart, poor lass." She stopped talking to sip her tea and gaze into the garden. "I knew right off—could feel the difference in her, the stirring of a new life. That was you."

Maggie smiled. How could she not? She felt like such a child with Gran.

"Here in Ireland, if a girl got pregnant, either she married, or her family raised the child. And I suppose a few babies were given away."

"What about abortion?"

"It's illegal unless the mother's life is at risk. Oh, some girls disappeared off to England and came back empty and the sadder for it. We didn't want our Shannon to do that. We're Catholic, you see. We don't accept it."

"You're Catholic *and* you're a witch?"

"Ah, things aren't always black and white. You've got to understand our history, what we've lived through in this country. Frank Burke is old money Protestant and insists his people are descended from William de Burgh, an Anglo-Norman knight who invaded Ireland in the Twelfth Century. His son, Richard de Burgh built Ashford Castle in 1228." She rolled her eyes. "Still lords *that* over us. Twelfth Century." Gran scoffed. "Why that's yesterday. *Our* people have been on this island for six thousand years, since the first ones sailed across the channel with their sheep and cows. Burke's no Lord over us. Ah, it makes me mad, it does. I need a cup of tea."

"I'll get it," Maggie said. "Just one minute. I want to hear the rest of this story."

"Thank you, pet."

As Moira sipped her tea, she relaxed into her comfy chair. Maggie found her gran the easiest person in the world to listen to, not just because she had a pleasant lilting voice, but because she knew that she spoke the truth—her truth—and she realized most of her life she'd been living a lie. Her true identity was all tied up in the history of this place and its people.

"Where were we? Aye, I remember now. Shannon was in the family way. Himself, Frank Burke—brute of a man he is still—insisted that she end it. Said he'd pay all costs. Well, poor Paddy wouldn't allow that. Murder, he said it was. So, a huge feud broke out, went on for years. Why, it's still going on."

"I hadn't noticed," Maggie said facetiously.

"Ah, you're just like your mother. She had the wit too. Bless her soul."

"So, what did she do?"

"Well, poor girl was in a spot. Couldn't kill her child and thank the Lord for that. Yet, she couldn't stay here and raise you either. Burke would have destroyed her, destroyed us all. Made it his life's mission at the very least."

"So, what did she do?"

"Took the payoff and despised herself for it. You see, when she refused to end it, Burke offered her money to disappear. Paid her passage to Canada aboard a freighter. Shipped her off with some of his horses; pretended she was going along to look after them. Of course, she didn't tell Paddy she was leaving. He would never have let her go."

"Really?"

"As God is my witness. Sent her off to his sister's home in Toronto. She was to get Shannon settled, that was all. But her son fell in love with Shannon and wanted to marry her. And, he loved you too, Maggie. Why you'd been born on the ship, just before they docked."

"I was born on a ship?"

"In a stall like a foal. But look at you now. You're strong, and you're wearing the mark of the horse on your arm. You've affinity with them, sure."

"And the man that loved us—who was that?"

"Ah," she sighed. "John Taylor was his name."

"No way! I can't believe it. Do you know what that means?"

"You tell me."

"It means that my father, at least the father I grew up with, is really my cousin."

"Very astute, just like your mother."

"She said we had no relatives."

"Well, I suppose that was true in a way. John and Shannon were disowned, thrown out of the Taylor home in Toronto. John turned Catholic for Shannon before he married her, and they were livid at that. Frank Burke sent Shannon money for her education and to help care for you but disparaged poor Paddy every chance he got. Made his life hell. I think that's why Paddy's never been able to settle. He's been wandering for years, just like one of the old bards."

"But you stayed."

"Ah, the Burkes don't bother me. I'm just a batty old woman what grows plants."

"Where's Frank Burke now?"

"Still lord of the manor. Just not as spry as he used to be. Colin runs things now, and they're not welcoming men, so don't go over there alone. You wait for Primrose."

"Yeah. What time is it? They've been gone for hours."

"Perhaps they've gone for a tramp in the hills. The sky's clearing tonight and she'll be brewing something special. Speaking of brewing, it must nearly be time for supper."

But supper came and went, and still Primrose and Estrada had not appeared. Moira grew sleepy again after eating and dozed off in her armchair, so Maggie stoked up the peat fire, blew out most of the remaining candles, and slipped out the red door.

Just as Gran had said, the moon was rising like a silver curl over the hill. She walked down the lane toward the highway and turned in the direction of the Burke's Horse Farm. Before her mother moved back home, Maggie had a score to settle with the bastards who'd wanted her dead before she'd even been born.

A Deed of Dreadful Note

When Primrose spoke, Estrada shivered. "Drink your brew. I mean it. I'll not have you out tonight without some sort of protection. Not when this devil has you in his sights."

"What about you? Aren't you having any?" Lying on his side in the damp grass, Estrada rested his head on his palm, entranced by the silvery moon reflected in her eyes.

"Your man has no quarrel with me. Now, drink up."

Taking the canteen from her hands, he unscrewed the cap and took a healthy swig. "Ugh. This tastes like shit. What is it? Dirt and weeds?"

"Must be the pinch of sheep dung you taste, courtesy of Angus Murphy. All the great poets drank it. Your man Yeats marveled at its capacity to connect a man with his muse."

"Sheep dung. I believe you."

"Good man. I'll not steer you wrong." She giggled. "Truth is, it's just herbs you taste. My gran had an affinity with all sentient beings and because of her kindness, they still share their spirit."

"Really? I know someone like that too," he said, thinking of Daphne. And for a moment, his thoughts drifted back to Hollystone and home, and Sensara who hated him, and Michael who loved him.

"There's hawthorn, hazel, and heather for protection," she explained, breaking his reverie, "and a little ginger root and thyme for courage—not that I don't think you have your own, but it never hurts to have more."

"Do I have to drink it all?"

"Do you want to live?"

Her tone, suddenly grave, frightened him, and sitting up he tilted his head back and guzzled every drop. When he wiped his mouth with the back of his hand, he shivered. "I feel weird. Did you spike it with something? Ecstasy, perhaps?"

"Ah, we've no need of that synthetic stuff here, not with all of this natural bounty," she said, looking widely at the surrounding countryside. "You see that solitary whitethorn tree?" She pointed to the thin tree in the center of the hill, its naked branches tilting upwards toward the moon.

"Yeah?"

"Well, she's never been cut for a reason. They say the whitethorn marks the door to the home of the Good People. The ones who've lived before and live still, beneath this faerie ráth.

"Seriously?"

"Oh, aye. So, if you're feeling anything peculiar, Sorcerer, it's magic."

Burke's Equestrian Center bustled with activity as everyone hurried to complete tasks in the early dusk. Though the moon was waxing, late November days grew shorter as nights grew longer, and that left little time for outdoor pursuits. Maggie peered inside, at the indoor ring, where children wearing their customary riding attire, trotted around on magnificent ponies; their tan breeches, tall riding boots, and black velveteen helmets, a trademark of their sport. By contrast, a couple of shabbily dressed stable hands hovered nearby on the alert to catch anything that might drop and soil the smooth earthen floor.

Out in the front paddock, two young women on stunning hunter jumpers ran the circuit, leaping bars and ditches at breakneck speed under the floodlights. Maggie stood watching as a group of kids returned from a trail ride with rosy cheeks and eyes stained with tired joy, stroked their horse's necks and handed them over reluctantly to waiting hands. Sighing, she thought how much she'd wanted this, craved it over the years.

Somewhere here was the scene of her conception—or misconception, depending on how you looked at it—and she was determined to find it, along with the man who'd spawned her and betrayed her mother. Having traded her goth look for a pair of cheap jeans, and a toque and rainproof jacket from Penney's, she was confident she fit in rather well. She'd even found a bright green shamrock scarf on Shannon's dresser and tied it around her neck for luck. She might not pass for a rich equestrian, but she made a decent stable hand.

Maggie had no idea what Colin Burke looked like but was convinced she'd know him when she saw him; after all, his genes flowed through her body. Several hands milled about—mostly girls in jeans and gumboots—cleaning stalls, spreading fresh bedding, and brushing and currying handsome horses. She tried to imagine her mother as one of them. Although on some level, Maggie understood Shannon's reluctance to let her daughter become a rider, she wished she'd had a crack at this life. Horses were the most beautiful animals in the world.

She stopped and stroked the nose of a sleek bay mare. "Hello beauty," she crooned to the mare.

"Her name is Epona," corrected a young boy, who looked to be around twelve years old. "Like the goddess."

"Oh?"

"Yes, Epona was a Celtic goddess who protected horses."

"Hello Epona. Are you a goddess?" The mare nickered and blew breath into her face.

"That means she likes you."

Maggie giggled. "Well, I like her too. Say, do you have any idea where Colin Burke might be?" The casual voice that slipped out covered the trepidation twisting her guts in circles.

"He's in the brood mares' barn, the green building down at the end there. He's checking on the pregnant mares. We're expecting a grand batch of foals, some real trophy winners. Premium stuff."

"I see." So, that's what horses were all about for Colin Burke. Trophies. "You work here then?"

The young boy rolled his eyes. "Work? Heavens no. I'm Christopher Burke. My grandfather owns this place," he said, gazing over his tiny empire.

Jolted by this news, Maggie produced a tight-lipped smile to hide the rage beneath. Of course, it made perfect sense. Colin gets Shannon pregnant, disposes of her, and then marries someone suitable, someone worthy of the name. This snobby arrogant boy, with his short brown hair and small squirrely eyes was her stepbrother—the heir apparent. Figured. Finally, after years of wanting siblings, she discovers a brother and he's a pretentious little jerk.

"Right," she said curtly, and made her way toward the barn.

Colin Burke stood next to a glossy chestnut mare with a white five-pointed star on her forehead.

Witch horse, thought Maggie.

He ran his hands over her swelling belly, appraising the growing foal. Poster boy for *Equine Entrepreneur,* dressed for a day of horsemanship in high brown leather boots, gloves, jodhpurs, an ivory turtleneck and brown leather blazer, the man obviously spent no time mucking about. Wouldn't want to get his hands dirty, when there were stable hands for that, and other things. It was hard to imagine this slender dark-haired man could really be her father. Exactly how many of his genes inhabited her body and soul?

Corridors of spacious box stalls lined three walls of the main floor and housed the mares. The whitewashed barn shone immaculately and felt like a luxury hotel. A heady scent of leather issued from the tack room, covering any possible odor of manure, while copious certificates and blue ribbons lined the walls of the adjacent office. Premium stuff. Through the open door, Maggie spied a near-empty bottle of Irish whiskey on the huge mahogany desk beside a large tumbler. So, Colin tippled.

An open hayloft, framed in heavy beams, hovered above two-thirds of the building, and was accessible by a central wooden staircase. Maggie stood for a moment inhaling the rich earthy fragrance of hay. It was a scent she'd always loved and now she wondered why. Had she ingested it somehow while in her mother's womb? Perhaps been conceived in this barn, in this very hayloft?

Engrossed in the examination of his expected commodity, Burke neglected to notice her.

"She's beautiful," Maggie said at last. "What's her name?"

"Macha," he said, without raising his eyes.

"Are you Colin Burke?" She needed to be sure.

At this, he shot an annoyed glance her way. "It's Mr. Burke. You should know that." When she didn't leave or respond, he straightened up and squinted, looking her over in much the same way he'd done the mare. Probably needed glasses and was too vain to admit it. "I don't recognize you. Who hired you? My wife?"

"No one hired me. I don't work for you."

"Well, in that case, you shouldn't be here. This barn is for brood mares. You must make an appointment for viewing—if you're interested in a purchase." He spoke the last phrase as if someone such as herself couldn't possibly be in that position.

"That's all it is to you, isn't it? Buying and selling. It's all about the money."

He stopped stroking the mare then, led her back into the stall and bolted the metal door. "I run a business and I certainly don't have to justify myself to you."

With a start, she saw herself reflected in his gold-flecked eyes.

With pursed pink lips, he glared. "Who are you? Do I know you?"

"Why? Do I look familiar?" Seeing more of herself in him with every passing second—something in the high cheekbones, the thin rigid nose—she shivered.

"Vaguely," he replied, shrugging. "You remind me of someone, but I can't—"

"Place her? Perhaps if my mother had been a horse, you'd remember her better."

His eyes shifted, mind spinning, as he attempted to recall his past liaisons. How many others had there been? Young girls seduced by his pompous charm and, she had to admit, good looks. Colin Burke was still a handsome man, despite the leathered skin that testified to years spent out of doors and graying streaks at his temples.

"Your mother? I don't—"

"Shannon Vallely."

"Shannon." He tested the name as if he was in court. "I don't recall anyone named Shannon."

"Give me a fucking break. Her parents live across the creek."

"Mind your tongue, young lady. We don't talk like that here."

"Right, I forgot Sir Posh. You know, I'm glad I didn't end up having you for a father. Your cousin John was kind and caring. You do recall John Taylor? He loved my mother, and he took care of us as best he could, at least until his accident. He wasn't some pretentious bastard."

"Leave now." As he marched toward her, green eyes flashing, she realized he could throttle her.

"Mr. Burke." The voice was insanely familiar, and it stopped Burke in his tracks. Sauntering casually through the open door, Father Grace appeared with his hands in his pockets, his stiff white collar still in place.

For a moment Maggie stood speechless, taking in this unbelievable occurrence. "You two know each other? How could you—?" It just wasn't possible. Not only had the priest found her, he'd infiltrated her life. How had he finagled his way into Burke's social circle so soon?

"This is the girl I mentioned to you, Mr. Burke. The one I've been trying to locate."

"I see," Burke said. "Well, I'll leave you to it then."

"Don't believe him," Maggie yelled. "Call the police. This man—"

"No need for that," Grace said. "I'll take care of this."

"Just be discrete," Burke replied, relieved to delegate his problems.

As Burke brushed by her on his way out of the barn, Maggie grabbed his arm. "Please. Call the police."

Shaking her off, he shut the door.

"Maggie. Relax. I'm not here to hurt you. I'm here to help you."

"Help me?" Facing him, she shook her fist. "How did you find me? How do you know Colin Burke?"

"John told me about Burke months ago in one of his more lucid moments. When I heard you'd gone to Ireland, I knew you'd find your way here eventually. Maggie, please. I have so many things

I want to tell you. There are things you need to understand." He motioned to a bench outside the tack room. "Give me a chance."

"A chance? Nothing you could possibly say... Well, there is one thing I'd like to know. Why would a priest—if you really are a priest—kill women?"

"I haven't killed anyone. And I *am* a priest. These things you're saying are just not true. Please, let me explain."

"Fine. Explain why you nearly raped me and why you kidnapped me and tied me to a bed and took those other women and burned them because they were witches."

"You've got it wrong."

As he moved toward her, she backed up into the horse barn. There was no way he'd ever get near her again.

"I'm sorry, Maggie. I know I scared you when I kissed you like that. That was wrong. I just wanted to show you how I felt about you, and then I lost control because... Well, even though I'm a priest and I've taken vows of celibacy, I'm in love with you."

"In love with me?" A sharp pain struck her gut.

"Yes. I never meant to hurt you. And I didn't burn any women. I was taken too that night. Drugged and tied up for days." His face was flushed and beaded with sweat. "That's when I realized... God, I've practiced this a million times. I need you to understand."

Dropping to his knees, he held out his hands. "Maggie, I've loved you since I first laid eyes on you. I've fought it, and it's nearly driven me mad. But I prayed and God gave me the answer. We can be together through eternity."

"What?" By now, she'd backed up as far as the central ladder that led into the loft and, as he reached out to touch her, she sprinted up it. "Don't come up here," she yelled, and grabbed a pitchfork. "I'll never be with you. I hate you!"

Startled by a loud crash, she jumped. A high-pitched whinny came from one of the mares, followed by stamping and other anxious sounds. Stepping away, Maggie edged around the loft and peered into the box stalls below, and to her left. She saw nothing out of place, but when she came back to the ladder and looked down again, dark smoke swirled skyward.

"Father. No!" She started climbing back down, but realized it was already too late. Flames twisted up the ladder fed by a heap of dry straw he'd scattered around the base of it. There was no way down and no sign of the priest. *Damn him.*

Below, the horses, locked in their stalls, neighed and paced with mounting fear as the threatening stench filled the barn.

"Fire! Help! I'm trapped." Adrenaline coursing through her veins, Maggie realized that the loft was one giant torch poised to ignite. The fire would claim her first, and then the floor would cave in. The horses would die. A barn full of pregnant mares. She could not let that happen.

After tying her scarf over her nose and mouth, she searched for an escape route. The smoke burned her eyes. Surely, someone would notice. It billowed in great clouds, filling the loft, devouring the oxygen, and drifting like a thick blanket into the mares' stalls. Kicking now, bashing boards and screaming, the mares panicked, as flames consumed the brittle hay and wooden beams.

Beams. Running both horizontally and vertically, they connected the loft with the main floor. If she could cross the diagonal beam before it burned through, she could reach a vertical beam, and then what? Shimmy down? Jump? Time was running out. The beams were already flecked with flame.

Maggie picked her way through the fire, and started across the nearest beam, one step at a time. *Don't look down.* It was a thirty-foot drop to the cement floor. If she fell—

I can do this. Must do this. I've walked the balance beam a million times before. Things began to thud and crash amidst the crackling wood as the horses pounded their bodies against the walls of their cells and shrieked. *I'm almost there—*

And then, she was careening through the air beside the fractured beam.

With a thud, Maggie hit the floor, her fall broken only by a cushion of straw in the stall below. One long gasp and then no breath. Panic, and then a voice, singing in her head. *Be calm. You've just knocked the wind out of your lungs. Relax, and breathe out through your mouth. This will pass. The air will come back in. Take small sips through your nose.*

But the painted mare thrashed, beating the wooden stall door with her hooves. There was no time. Crawling to her knees, still with no air entering her lungs, she used the wall to push herself up. She had to free the horses. And then, as a trickle of smoky air found its way through, the panic subsided.

Gasping and coughing, she edged her way along the wall toward the door. "Easy girl, I'm going to let you out." The mare's screaming lessened as Maggie touched her shoulder.

Keeping one hand on the horse's neck to steady her, she used her other to lift the latch and open the door. With a rush, the mare bolted and cantered in panicked circles. "I have to get the others." Running along the corridors, she hit the latches. Stall doors opened, as fiery beams crashed around her. Catching her foot on a busted beam, she careened across the corridor and crashed to the floor.

"*Christ!*" She'd scraped her knee and turned her right ankle. She tried to stand on it, but it could take no weight. Rising on the other foot, she saw the white pentagram on the dark face. The witch horse was there, breathing in her face, staring with wide eyes. Stepping up on a broken beam, Maggie swung her sore ankle over the horse's back and held on with both hands.

The mare cantered toward the main door, then standing on her hind legs, crashed against it with her front hooves. *"Jesus!"* Maggie yelled and sliding backwards, gripped her mane. Repeatedly, the witch horse battered the door. When the hinges gave way at last, it swung wide and out they flew like a herd of wild mustangs.

When the mare stopped running, Maggie hugged her damp neck and inhaled the heady scent. From the edge of her burning eyes, she saw her horse tattoo, scratched and burned and smudged with soot.

"What the hell did you do?"

Maggie looked down, into the bulging eyes of Colin Burke.

"Chew on this," Primrose said, tickling Estrada's nose with a sprig of peppermint. "It's sweet and calming, so."

"Where did you get this?" he asked, opening his mouth to accept the cool fresh leaves.

"Grows wild along the ditch there," she said, gesturing below. "My mam said every plant has a purpose."

"And a time for every purpose under heaven." They'd been lying side by side on their backs in her secret place, for hours it seemed, fingers touching in the soft wet grass. He'd forgotten everything else, intoxicated by the moment—the wet earth, the silhouetted trees in the distance, the shadows that crossed the bright curled moon, and her.

Snuggling close beside him, she put her hand on his heart. "It's good to see you let down, Sorcerer. I think your world is too much with you."

He laughed. "All that and she quotes Wordsworth too."

"We Irish girls go to school."

"How is it that I've known you for only a day and yet I feel as if I've known you forever?"

"Ah, there's a simple answer to that."

"Tell me."

"This brief walk we call life is but a fraction of eternity. Do you not believe in immortality, Sorcerer?"

"I want to. Especially now that I've met you."

"But you'll not believe it until you've seen it with your own eyes? Is that it?"

"It's hard to believe in something you can't see or touch."

"And you a magician and a witch," she scoffed.

"When I do magic, I know it's an illusion."

"And when your priestess draws down the moon and the goddess speaks through her, is that just an illusion too?"

Estrada shivered, remembering that night at Buntzen Lake and the horrible riddle Sensara had spoken in the voice of Hecate—one would be burned and four would die. He'd tried to put it out of his mind, hoping it would never happen. But John Taylor had died. And once he, himself, had merged with a raven and flown over a town called Hope, and there was no explaining that. And then there was the killer and feeling so enthralled by him.

"You're right," he said solemnly. "There's more to it than what we can see and feel."

"Aye. Faith. Of course, there are signs, and now that your inner eye is open and your heart's strong again, you'll see them and know them for what they are. Like this. What's this a sign of?" Leaning over, she brushed her lips against his.

He opened his mouth and kissed her for what seemed an eternity. Then shivering, he rolled on top of her. "Approaching orgasm?"

"Ah. You're still thinking with this." She pushed her pelvis against his. "What else? What's better than sex?" Shoving him over, she sat on top of him.

"Is that a trick question?" He gazed into her eyes. "Wait. Let me think . . . Love?"

Shifting, she sat on top of him. "Aye, love. Faith and love are like this," she said, crossing one finger over the other. "So whenever you doubt your faith, remember this." Leaning over, she held his hands against the moist grass and gave him a long sensual kiss. Falling down beside him, she stared into his soul. "You, my beautiful man, have much love still to come in this life—many brilliant lovers and much adventure and much hardship too."

Confused, he cocked his head. "What about you?" Content for the first time in his life, he hoped he might stay here with her forever.

"I can't read myself. Never could." Leaning over, she touched his lips with her finger, and then touched her finger to her own lips. "Now, tell me what you see."

He sat up and looked around. "I see the wet green grass on this hilltop shimmering like silver in the moonlight, and the silhouette of the whitethorn tree, and farther away, the shadows of the forest by the creek, and in the sky, clouds scudding across the moon."

"Light and shadow. Illusion, as the masters say. Do you see how none of it's real?"

"You're real," he said, touching her face.

"Aye, and so are *they*. As real as you or me, and full of life and love and delicious freedom."

He cocked his head. "Do you mean—?"

"The Good People, the Gentry, the Faeries, the Angels that fell from heaven. They've been called many names, but they've always been with us and the country people have always seen them and respected their ways."

"Can you see them?"

"Aye, sure. Them and all they've left behind. Their earthworks, like this ráth we're lying on, where they lived and buried the ashes and bones of their dead. Why they're my family, my tribe. They teach me. I walk and dance among them, and I love them so."

"This is really a faerie ráth?"

"Aye."

"Who are they exactly?"

"The Tuatha de Danann built these ráths thousands of years ago when they farmed this land. They were the tribes of the goddess Danu. The invading Milesians forced them underground but couldn't destroy them."

"Really," he breathed, entranced by her voice.

"Ah, there's another place I must take you. It's in a beautiful fertile valley along the River Boyne. Now, it's called Newgrange, but it's not new. It's housed the Irish people for millennia and is at the center of all our stories. The ráth itself is part of a Necropolis—a cluster of tombs where the tribes interred the ashes of their dead once a year at Winter Solstice. When the sun rises over the ridge of the valley, its light hits the roof box just above the entrance stone and creeps down the passageway. In the dead time, the sun illuminates the path to the inner chamber with the promise of new light and new life. Rebirth. Immortality."

"I know that story. It sounds like a beautiful place."

"Well, if you're still around in late December, I'll take you there. I had the luck this year of winning two tickets in the annual lottery. That's the only way in nowadays."

"It's a date. There's nothing I'd like more than to be with you when the sun rises at Newgrange on Winter Solstice. Well, maybe there's one thing—"

"Hush now. They're coming."

"Who's coming?"

"Listen. There's drums and music and— Look. There they are."

"I can't see anything."

Kneeling against his back, Primrose placed her left palm on his heart and her right palm across his forehead. "Close your eyes and breathe," she whispered in his ear. "Be still and go inside and find your own sweet heartbeat. I can feel it in my hand." Tapping her fingers lightly, she kept the rhythm until he found it himself. "Now open your eyes just a flutter, just enough to let in the light and look straight on into the night."

In the distance, pale shimmering shapes as silvery as moonlight, grew denser and more distinct as he watched. Some rode horses, while others walked beside cows and sheep. They were all ages, the men bearded, and the women's hair long and free. Barefoot or with skins wrapped round like boots, they wore clothing woven from the wild, and their bodies were tall and magnificent. Near the front of the procession were several pipers and other men beating skin drums. He could hear the music clearly, like the tunes in the pub only infinitely sweeter, and he longed to dance.

"They're incredible."

"Aye, and full of love. Once you know them, you can join the dance. But I must caution you, Sorcerer. The more time you spend with them, the more you become like them. More fey and less human."

"Really?"

"Oh aye. They're grand, sure, but if you're attached to your humanity."

"God, I can't believe this. I've always wanted to—"

Leaping suddenly to her feet, he thought she would take him to dance among them, but she gestured across the field and shouted, "Fire! That's the Burke's farm!"

Forgetting the faeries, Primrose yanked him by the arm, and they raced toward the billowing smoke and flames that streaked the sky scarlet beyond the trees. Primrose sprinted like a deer as they hurtled across country, leaping fences and ditches. He could barely keep up. Crossing the stream, he realized he could no longer hear the faerie music—only the crash of falling timbers amidst the cries of anxious people, as helplessly they watched the barn erupt in a surging wall of flame.

"Maggie," Primrose cried, rushing into the midst of the chaos.

He saw her then himself, standing among the horses.

"Are you alright?" Primrose asked. Maggie was weeping and clutching her arms across her chest. "Ah, you're burned, poor thing."

The fire trucks and ambulance arrived then, and Maggie fought them, refusing to go. "The horses. Are they all safe? And Father Grace? Where's Father Grace? Did they find him? They've got to find him."

"Grace? The priest was here?" Estrada asked, feeling suddenly guilty that he'd been sent here to protect her and when he was needed most, he'd been out cavorting in the hills with Primrose.

"He started it. He tried to kill me."

Estrada glanced at the slim man beside her who stood shaking his head. "No one else got out."

"I guess that's karma," Maggie said. "Father Grace burns witches and ends up dying in a fire."

Estrada gazed at the flickering candles in the Valley's living room and grimaced. He knew Maggie had been through hell but there had been far too much talk of fire. His skin still reeked of smoke.

"Ah, it's tragic," Moira said. "No one should die like that."

"Yeah. It's weird. I feel so sad for him," Maggie said. "I know he was a bad man but—"

"He was sexually abused as a child," Estrada said. "His mother belonged to a coven that used the kids to make pornographic films."

"Good Lord," Moira said. "That turns my stomach. No wonder the poor soul went insane."

"Yeah. People rarely get over things like that. Did he say anything before the fire started?" Estrada couldn't get Hecate's prophecy out of his mind—now two had died and Maggie had been burned.

"Yes, but—"

"Ah, it's fine. You don't need to say anything that makes you feel uncomfortable." Primrose put her arm around Maggie and gave her a squeeze. "There'll be time for talk tomorrow."

"No, I can say it. He kept apologizing for hurting me. He said that he was in love with me. He said God had shown him a way we could be together for eternity." She shivered.

"Murder-suicide. Pain will make a man do strange things," Estrada said, remembering once he'd been told something similar. He tried to comprehend the mind of the madman who claimed to love them both. "We'll probably never understand."

Moira looked at her watch. "Well, it's near midnight, but I'd like to give Shannon a call. She must come home. I've already called Paddy, Eamonn, and Michael, and they'll all be here by week's end."

"Did you have all boys, Gran?" Maggie asked.

"Two boys and three girls, but Shannon's the only girl that survived." She made the sign of the cross on her chest. "Bless their souls. Tell me, what time is it in Vancouver? I can never keep it straight."

"They're eight hours behind us, so it's around four p.m. But Gran, what about the feud?"

"Well, the way I see it, Colin Burke got duped by a priest who set his barn on fire and you saved his stock. The man owes you, and if he owes you, he owes us all. I doubt we'll have any nasty business from the Burkes now." Rising from her chair, she waved her hand. "Sleep well."

"Goodnight Gran." Maggie grimaced. "Damn. Thinking about the fire's making my arm hurt again."

"Let me have a look at that." Primrose unwrapped the gauze and turned up her nose. Needs a poultice of nettle and calendula. I've some at the cottage." She hopped up.

"You're not going *now*?" Estrada said, feeling his breath catch in his throat.

"Aye."

"But, it's after midnight."

"I'm not Cinderella."

"Well, you can't go alone." Estrada frowned. He couldn't handle the idea of Primrose wandering alone through the fields in the dark after what they'd just witnessed. "I'll come with you."

"Don't be daft. I've been running through these fields in the dead of night since I was wee. Did you forget? I've friends out there. And with Moira gone to bed, Maggie needs you here. Even if she doesn't know it." Primrose shook her head. "Ah, don't go all macho on me. Holy God. What have I got myself into?"

Estrada jumped up nervously, knowing he couldn't win. Still, his belly ached. "Please be careful, and hurry back. I'll be waiting for you."

The whole time Primrose was gone Estrada felt uneasy, assuming it was because they hadn't been apart since their initial meeting. Strange what could happen between people in a matter of hours.

Maggie browsed her grandparents' library, read some, and dozed on the couch, while he continued to pace closer and closer to the back door.

"I'm just going outside to look for Primrose."

"Okay, Lover Boy. Don't get taken by the faeries."

The moon shining overhead created a densely gray and shadowy world. There was no sign of Primrose. A faint rustle in the bushes broke the quiet. A long-eared owl cruised silently overhead, and then drawn by the same rustling sound, dove into the bushes beyond the hedge, and rose with a limp mouse in its beak. A line from *Macbeth* played through his mind. "*I heard the owl scream and the crickets cry.*"

He shivered, then realized he'd been holding his breath. It didn't take a scholar to know the owl was a harbinger of death. Of course, there'd been one death already this night. Grace was dead and the ordeal finally over. Still a faint film of sweat burst from his flesh. He felt raw.

Why is Primrose taking so long?

Crouching near the wooden bench outside the back door, his eyes adjusted to the darkness. Something was on the arm rail—something small and dark and curiously heart-shaped. Picking it up, he examined it, and then, just to be sure, gave it a quick lick. *Cinnamon heart.* Just like the one he'd found in his pocket that day on the highway.

Having never considered it before, he now thought it strange that Gabriel Grace had known about his love of cinnamon, and even stranger that he'd planned far enough ahead to have brought along the candy. Perhaps, he'd bought it that night at the shop. But, why was this one here now? Had he overlooked it when they arrived, so agitated by the fire? Surely, someone would have seen it? They'd all passed by the bench on their way into the house. Rolling it between his thumb and index finger, he passed it under his nose again and inhaled. What secrets did it hold? A tiny spiced heart, it seemed benign, and yet—

The man came for me, just as Primrose prophesied. He came here to this house.

Estrada found a flashlight inside the back porch and began to search. Another heart was on open ground about a foot from the bench, and a couple of feet beyond that, still another. *Damn.* Could Grace have somehow fled through another door in the barn and escaped the fire? When they left, his body had not been found.

Hackles up, Estrada followed the trail of candy hearts. Skirting the edge of the woods, it stopped at the back pasture. But he strode on, moving on impulse through the cold damp grass in the direction of the ráth where Primrose had shown him faeries just hours before.

Out in the open, a sudden wind caught at his eyes. He'd just wiped his face with the back of his hand, when he spotted a shadowy figure approaching from across the field. He assumed it was a male, but with a dark hoodie pulled down low, in the dim moonlight the features were indistinguishable. Estrada began to walk toward the figure, and then broke into a lope. *Was it him?* He had to know. A few feet distant, he halted and turned on the flashlight.

For several seconds, a pair of startled turquoise eyes caught in the golden beam, and then the man blinked, and lifted his hand to shield them.

"Bastian? What are you—?"

"Finally," he said, relief edging his voice. "Turn out the light, man. You're blinding me."

"What are you doing here?" Taken aback, Estrada realized the flashlight was the only weapon he had besides his own hands. Bastian was the last person he expected to see here, and he needed time to think.

"You've forgotten me. A week ago, you summoned me to our cave. You wanted me."

Estrada's mouth fell open. "You? It was you?" he asked, his voice rising in pitch. He stared incredulously.

"Now all you want is *her*." With his scarlet face and piercing blue eyes seeping tears, the man looked deranged. If he'd been in the barn, Maggie hadn't seen him. "I saw you here with her."

Bastian had come from the direction of Primrose's cottage. "Did you hurt her? What did you do? Tell me."

"Why would I hurt her? She's not like *them*." He shrugged. "I don't even hurt them anymore. I stopped because of you. I changed everything for you," Bastian said.

Had he stopped hurting women? He sounded sincere, and neither Sensara nor Maggie had been hurt after they were abducted. He'd even let Sensara go free that night. Estrada's gut discerned a tenderness in the man's soul that betrayed his villainy. But, after what he'd shared with him, dare he trust it? He had to know more. He had to know it all.

"I don't understand," Estrada said. Fragments from the night in the cave swirled through his mind as he tried to make sense of it all. *I burn them with reason. I cut your hair to save your life. I love you.*

God, was that really Bastian in the cave? In the cabin? Estrada almost laughed at the absurdity of it. The man had been right there, comforting Shannon with cups of tea and not one of them had been the least bit suspicious. Was it because of the spell? Had all of their intuitive senses been numbed? And then Estrada remembered his fascination with Bastian, the first time he opened the door. Perhaps, they'd all been so intent on finding Maggie, they'd ignored everything else.

"You should have told me," Estrada said, lowering the light. "All this time we thought it was Grace."

Bastian laughed feverishly. "Of course, you did." He fingered the emerald cross around his neck, and then ripped it off and flung it into the grass. "I made you believe."

Alarmed by his volatility, Estrada lowered his voice. He needed to keep the man calm. "Why Grace?"

"You don't know him, man. He's sick, and he was after Maggie. I saw what he did to her on the porch that night. I was there. I took him."

Estrada's brow furled. "You *took* him? Didn't he kidnap Maggie?"

"No man. I took her too." He flashed his eyes flirtatiously. "I knew you'd come for her. And I had to see you—"

"*Jesus.*" Estrada could barely breathe. Daphne had been right. Maggie was only bait. "And Sensara? Is that why you took her too?"

Bastian smiled. "You're a hero. I love that about you."

"And my hair? Why did you shave my head?"

"I told you man, to save your life. I was afraid I might hurt you. My goddamn mother had long black hair and—"

"Oh." Estrada nodded with sudden understanding. So, this was all about Bastian's mother.

"Some new *uncle* every couple of months and none of them gave a shit about me"—he rolled his eyes—"except the pedophiles. She'd get drunk and pass out and . . ." He glanced away, shamed by the memory. "She pretended she didn't know, but she did. I told her."

"I'm sorry." Stepping closer, Estrada smiled sadly.

"Don't pity me. I don't want your pity." Bastian spat in the grass. "I got her back. Burned the bitch in her bed. Unfortunately, she passed out and spoiled it, just like she spoiled every fucking thing she touched. She never knew it was me who flicked her cigarette off the ashtray."

"You wanted her to know—"

"Wouldn't you?" He rubbed at his eyes, looked as if he'd been crying for hours.

"But you kept doing it—"

"Until that night in the cabin when we . . ." Bastian's voice drifted off. "I can't stop thinking about you. I want to crawl inside your skin." He chewed at his bottom lip and moved closer.

The obsession went both ways. Perhaps it was because of the spell but seeing Bastian confess broke Estrada's heart. As crazy as it seemed, he understood his torment, and in that moment wanted only to comfort him. Bastian was, like so many others, an abused and orphaned child, and in this world of shadows, as Primrose said, there was no black and white, only shades of gray.

"Was your mother into Wicca?"

"No, she was into men. Kind of like me." He grinned shyly. "Gerry's mother, though, she was big into it."

"Gerry?"

"Gerry Gardner. He changed his name when he became a priest."

"Right. I heard about that," Estrada said, remembering the story Nigel had related. "Some coven on the island."

"Yeah. That's how we ended up in the same foster home—a couple of born-again Catholics down near Hope."

"So, you knew Grace before."

"Oh yeah, I knew him. *Intimately*."

His cheeks pulsed and Estrada sensed another bout of rage bubbling just under this tepid surface.

"Gerry was there when I arrived. He was the oldest and the strongest. At first, he just used to blame shit on us and threaten to beat us up. Then one afternoon, when they were out, he . . ." His voice drifted off again into images Estrada tried not to imagine. "Like I said, Gerry was sick. He taught us spells and ceremonies and he made us do things."

"Us?"

"Yeah. There were three of us . . . and him." Tears glazed his eyes. "I couldn't let a man like that near Maggie."

"I'm sorry," Estrada said softly. He wanted to hold him, hug him.

"Don't pity me." Bastian pushed back his hood and rubbed his hands roughly through his fair hair. "You wanted to know so I told you, but I don't want your pity."

"Tell me the rest." Years of neglect and abuse followed by years of torture. It was hard not to pity him.

"You'll judge me."

"I want to understand you." Estrada dropped to one knee and leaned closer. "What happened to Gerry after that?"

"We all went our separate ways two years later except for him. They kept *him*. He was their golden boy." Bastian squatted in the grass and gazed at Estrada with sad eyes. "When I saw him at the hospital where I worked, I couldn't believe he'd had the balls to become a priest. He didn't know me." Bastian crouched silently for several seconds deep in thought. "Christ, that's when it started."

"What started?"

Grasping the back of his skull, Bastian cried out. "My head hurts."

"Sit down, man." Estrada gestured to the remnants of an old stone wall. "It's probably just pressure. Tension."

Collapsing on the stones, Bastian dropped his head in his hands and moaned.

"Is that when you started to hurt the women? When you saw Gerry again at the hospital?"

Bastian nodded his head as tears slipped down his cheeks. "It makes the pain go away."

Estrada drew close enough to hold him, then flinched and steadied himself. The butt end of a hunting knife protruded from a leather sheath at the top of Bastian's right boot.

"He triggers you, man. There are people who can help you through this."

"Yeah, right. Help me right into lockup."

Of course, he was right. The best Bastian could expect was a long stretch in a psychiatric hospital once the cops heard this story.

"But there are people who care about you. Maggie, and her mother . . . and *me*."

"You only care about that woman," Bastian said.

"Listen man. If I didn't care, I wouldn't be out here in the friggin' dead of night, freezing my friggin' ass off, talking to you. I'd have kicked your friggin' head in by now."

That provoked a smile. "I saw you out here kissing—"

"So, we kissed." Estrada shrugged. "Relax man. I just met her." In his periphery, Estrada spied a slight figure crossing the field about thirty paces to Bastian's left. Primrose. He needed to end this ragged conversation before she could reach them. Of course, he *could* kick Bastian's head in. He was quick and skilled, a street fighter, who knew his way around knives. But Bastian had been victimized enough and there was still that bond.

"It's weird," Estrada went on, a plan formulating in his mind. "The first time I saw you—when you opened the Taylor's door, I saw your turquoise eyes and I was so attracted, Sensara got jealous." He smiled seductively and Bastian grinned shyly. "You *are* the best lover I ever had. No one has ever made me feel like that."

"I know."

"You must feel this." Estrada gestured to the invisible bond between them.

Staring wide-eyed, Bastian nodded. "It's agony being apart."

Kneeling before him, Estrada touched the hand above the boot. "I think there might be a way through this for us, now I know you. Now I understand, I think we could—"

"Be together?" Incredulous, Bastian shivered, his voice wispy.

Edging closer, Estrada brushed his cheek with his other hand. "There's no one here to stop us. We can do anything we want."

Bastian jerked backward and stood up, wrenching away from Estrada. "I don't believe you. You'll turn me in, and they'll lock me up. I've worked in those places. I wouldn't survive."

"Don't think like that." Estrada stood and took off his leather jacket, while Bastian stared. Tossing it aside, he unbuttoned his shirt and tugged it free of his jeans. "Trust me, man." He held out his hand. "Come here. Kiss me like you did that first time. I dream about that kiss."

Primrose was now mere steps away. Somehow, Estrada had to get that knife.

"Come to me, Bastian," he said, staring into those turquoise eyes.

Entranced, the man moved toward him. "I want you. You know I do." Reaching out, he grasped Estrada's shoulder. "But I know you, magician. You're all tricks."

And then, as Primrose slipped into the shadows between them, time slowed to an unearthly crawl. Bastian was still clutching Estrada's shoulder, as the back of Primrose's leather jacket brushed his bare chest. Gazing down, Estrada saw the violet trees that encircled the top of her head, heard the low thunk of the knife as it pierced her heart, felt her shudder and pitch forward with a low gasp and slowly collapse. Catching her in his arms, Estrada stared at the wooden handle protruding just below her rib cage, blood oozing with every heartbeat.

"No!" Screaming, Estrada swept her up in his arms. Then, laying her down gently in the grass, he began to pull the knife slowly from her broken body.

"Don't. Leave it in. Press on it."

Estrada stared up at Bastian's horrified face. "Yeah, you'd like that."

"You gotta trust me. Never pull out a knife. It'll hemorrhage."

Eyes so clouded, Estrada could barely see, he extracted the knife and flung it, then swiped at his tears with the back of his bloody hand. Blood everywhere. Her blood. Gushing from the wound. Estrada's ears were ringing.

"Why Primrose? Why did you step between us?"

Primrose didn't answer. Couldn't answer. The blood. He had to stop the blood. Ripping off his shirt, Estrada balled it up and pressed it against the wound. Blood dripped from her lips, as her eyes rolled back in her head. "Don't die on me," Estrada murmured, but even as the words left his lips, he knew . . . And a pain cut through his chest so sharp it took his breath away.

"I'm so sorry. I didn't know she was there. I didn't mean to kill her."

"No, you meant to kill *me*, you crazy motherfucker." Glancing up, he saw Bastian standing over them as pale and still as a ghost. Yowling, Estrada picked up the bloody knife and hefted its weight in his hand. The veins in his wrists stood out like ropes as his hackles flared.

Bastian's eyes grew wide and he turned, but Estrada sprang up, leaping, flung his left arm around Bastian's shoulders and threw him to the ground. Wedging his body between his thighs, Estrada caught Bastian's face beneath his forearm, and played the razor-sharp blade across his throat. Blood beads erupted through the pale skin.

"Do it." Bastian's voice was insistent. "Please." He was crying. Wanted to die.

For a moment, Estrada pressed deeper. Blood spurted. And then, an echo sang from somewhere in his brain. *When you take a man's life, you end up dragging his corpse around with you.*

Tossing the knife aside, Estrada yanked Bastian to his feet, and shoved him hard. Staring at Primrose, lying in the blood-soaked grass, he muttered, "No more corpses. No more demons." She had only just healed him and he couldn't dishonor her memory. Wouldn't kill another man. She wouldn't want him to.

"Sorcerer, hold me," Primrose whispered.

Hearing her plea, Estrada knelt beside her. Leaning over, he stroked her cheek and kissed her sweet lips, his face and hands slick with her blood. "I love you, Primrose. Please don't leave me."

Off somewhere in the darkness, Estrada heard a muffled cry and the obscure thump of flesh hitting rock, and then silence. Instinctively, he looked. Bastian's crumpled body lay several feet away in the long grass by the edge of the stone wall. "Karma," Estrada muttered, and felt relieved. That, at least, would keep the madman quiet until the police came and took him away. Now, if he could just get Primrose to a hospital.

Gathering her in his arms, he lifted her head and shoulders and was just about to rise when—

"Look," she wheezed, entranced by something behind him. "Look. They've come for me." Her voice was raspy, her lungs filling. "Ah, I love them so. I've been waiting for them my whole life."

Turning, Estrada saw them. *Faeries.* Hundreds of them, a great host of luminous beings, pale and silvery in the moonlight, tall and beautiful, and madly glorious.

"But *I've* been waiting for *you*. Please, don't leave me now."

When Estrada didn't return, Maggie tied gauze around her burns and limped outside. Alarmed by voices in the distance, she forgot the pain in her ankle and raced through the field. She stopped dead when she saw them. *Faeries.* Just as they'd been at Carrowmore, standing together, one luminous shadow like a sparkling cloud of alien mist, and Primrose among them, dressed in a fine woven gown.

Maggie staggered forward, then tripped and gaped at the carnage beneath her feet. One man laid face down by the stone wall to her left. And Primrose, blood everywhere and staring wide-eyed, and Estrada sprawled over her, half-naked, with his face buried in her neck.

When her legs gave way, Maggie fell to the ground. Reaching out, she touched the slowly pulsing vein beneath Estrada's jaw.

Primrose was gone—her wide green eyes staring straight ahead. But he was still alive.

"Estrada?" she whispered and shoved him gently. Then hugging them both, she wept.

He raised his grieving eyes for a moment, and then passed out.

"Estrada." Maggie prodded and shook him, trying to wake him. But it was no use. Turning him on his back, she laid her ear against his bare breast. He had a faint but steady heartbeat and no obvious wounds, though he was covered in blood. Shock.

She crawled across the field on hands and knees and tried to push over the body of the other man, but it was caught in the stones, wedged sideways. Then, with only half his face visible, she recognized him. *Bastian?* It wasn't possible. Yet, taking in the bloody scrape across his cheek and the vacant blue eye, she knew it was. It looked as if he'd only fallen against the rocks, yet there was no pulse. And then she saw the blood pooling beneath his neck and the handle of a knife wedged beneath.

"Bastian! I don't understand."

Tears Shall Drown the Wind

Maggie was still weeping. Had been for hours, alternating between vicious storms where grief poured out in torrents and dry silent rage when she wished she were dead. "What's wrong with him, Gran? Why won't he wake up?"

Primrose was gone, her bloody body taken to the morgue. And Bastian. Poor Bastian. What was *he* doing in that field? She just could not accept that he'd stabbed Primrose with a knife and tried to run off, as the police suspected. Estrada was still unconscious.

"He's off with them," Gran said. "I saw it once before, a long time ago, when I was still a young woman. My friend, Kathleen—it happened the night before her wedding."

"A bride," Maggie murmured. She clutched the tattered copy of *The Celtic Twilight* Estrada had given her as if it were a talisman.

"Aye, but she came back within the week. Poor girl couldn't remember a thing that happened but knew where she'd been. 'I've been off with the Good People,' she said." Gran rubbed Maggie's back. "They take the ones who are most filled with love—children, brides, and lovers."

"Primrose took him. I saw her standing with them, shining like an angel. He looked up at me and he was so sad, and then— Oh God, what are we going to do?"

She looked around Primrose's cottage. Estrada was laid out on the kitchen table like a corpse. After he'd been photographed by police and examined by the doctor, they'd allowed Maggie and her grandmother to wash and dress him. They'd put a pillow beneath his head and covered him with a blanket. "Shouldn't he be in the hospital? When my dad was like this, they kept him in intensive care. He needed treatment and—"

"Oh Maggie, the doctor said he was fine right here for the moment. His heart, his breathing, everything's perfect."

"Everything's *not* perfect. What was he? Some kind of faerie doctor?"

"Ah, pet. Your friend is having a good long sleep. You know, the old folks said people sometimes stayed like this for weeks or even years."

"Years? Oh Gran, he can't stay like this for years." Another frantic burst of tears overtook her and settled at length into pathetic sobs. "This is all my fault. I wanted to be in the coven. Bastian worked for us. Father Grace was our priest. My father died looking for me. Estrada came here to protect me, and Primrose—"

"Maggie. Stop. You cannot take this all on yourself."

"I'll never forgive myself."

"But you must. Don't you see? If you never forgive yourself, they'll have died for nothing." Gran opened her arms and hugged Maggie to her breast. "Oh dear, what are we going to do? It's almost suppertime and the boys are about to land on my doorstep. I have so much to do."

"I know. Dylan and Sylvia are coming too. You go. I'll stay here with him."

"Please don't fret, pet. The one thing I know for sure is that Estrada is not alone."

"Come," laughed Primrose, taking his hand. "Come, dance, Sorcerer."

And he ran behind her into their midst and grasped the proffered hand of a beautiful blond man, while she clutched the other, and they danced the circle dance, hundreds of them, jigging round and round to the beat of the bodhrán, barefoot in the grass, snaking in and out with the whistling flutes, and then all raising their arms and rushing to meet in the center, as the energy coursed through the air like lightning and sizzled through his soul.

Wrenching him away into the murmuring trees, a mist rose around them, and she danced as she had that day on Shop Street, her hands and eyes telling a story of fierce enduring love. Then fetching a doeskin bag from the crook of the tree, she squeezed sweet mulled wine into his mouth and laughing he swallowed, feeling like Dionysus, the lord of his own oak grove. Taking his face between her tiny hands, she kissed him on the mouth and his head filled with the sound of harps as he envisioned a host of angels. She stripped away the woven cloth around his waist, stopping all thoughts but one. Then holding back his hands with her own, she fell to her knees, and when she took him in her warm mouth, he gasped with the sudden pleasure of it all, arching his back against the tree as if it were the first time he'd ever felt such a thing.

When he gazed down again, expecting to see her tattooed skull beneath his belly, his breath caught to see the blond man in her place, his hands clenching his hips and his eyes wild with desire. Losing control, he reached down to catch the long soft hair in his fingertips, but it was her small pointed ears he felt, and he laughed. Then catching her by the arms, he lifted her with long silken kisses, and sinking to the earth together, he filled her, while harps filled his head.

This was joy as he'd never known it. Hours later, it seemed, when he could hold back no longer, he cried out and burst inside her. Then together they laid on their backs in the damp grass, counting the stars that filled the blue velvet sky, until she laughed and said, "Come. Come, dance, Sorcerer."

And he followed her into their midst, and they circled through again and again.

As the sound of bagpipes filled the small stone church, Maggie felt a pain in her chest so intense she could barely breathe. She was sure her heart was breaking in two. Sobbing, she leaned against the wooden pew and watched Dylan march up the aisle in Highland regalia with "Amazing Grace" flying from his breath and fingers.

His eyes were glazed with tears. At the front of the church he stopped and took a seat beside Dr. Black. The way he held his pipes in his lap with his head bowed, Maggie knew he was sobbing too.

Gran and the professor had strewn the wooden coffin with greenery from the surrounding countryside. They'd even brought herbs and dried primroses and scattered them. The lights were out, and the entire church lit only by candles. Hundreds of flames flickered off the priest's adornments as he wafted incense through the air. Then joining with the others, Maggie chanted, "Hail Mary, full of grace, the Lord is with thee; blessed art thou among women." And she thought of Primrose dancing on Shop Street in her shimmering green gown—the goddess Danu, pagan mother of the tribes—and for the first time in days, she smiled through her tears with the realization. Primrose had joined her ancestors in becoming fully fey.

"Are you flying back to Vancouver with Dr. Black tomorrow, Dylan?" Seated on the stone steps under the northern archway of the old Augustinian abbey, though rain pelted down around them in the dusk, Maggie felt oddly tranquil.

"No. I'll stay with Estrada a while longer; at least, until his mate arrives."

"His mate?"

"Michael Stryker. I've never met the man, but I've heard stories. He's legendary. Sensara loathes him. She called him though. Told him what happened."

"But she's not coming herself."

"No. She's broke in two. Loves him, you know, but hearing that he'd fallen for Primrose so soon after . . ." Dylan's voice drifted off, and she wondered if he was also broken in two. "But, that's just Estrada's way. Everyone loves him and he loves them back. He's a free spirit. Never been any different. That's why it's so hard to see him stuck like this."

"My gran says he's just away with the faeries and he'll come back."

"Well, if she's right, he'll not be suffering. That's something he's always wanted, and if you believe the stories, Faerie is just one wild party."

"He'd like that." Thinking back suddenly to Samhain and that night at Buntzen Lake, Maggie whispered, "Dylan, do you remember Hecate's prophecy?"

"How could I not?"

"Don't you think it's weird how it all came true?"

"You know where that word comes from, don't you?"

She shook her head.

"*Wyrd* is an Old English word that means having the power to control fate or destiny."

"But who had the power?"

"We did. We set this in motion when we spun that charm."

"So, nothing could stop it? Four people were destined to die?" She was mortified they were all connected to her—Bastian, Father Grace, Primrose, even her own father.

Dylan shrugged. "Seems so."

She glanced at the marks on her hands. "I got burned like she said, and if Estrada's with the faeries, he's the one who gained his heart's desire."

"And Jeremy Jones was deceived by lust."

"Oh, I forgot that part. What happened?"

"He went out with a stranger who asked questions about us. I suppose it was that fella who looked after your dad, Bastian Stone, the one who . . ." His voice drifted off.

"Really?" Maggie was shocked to hear this news. She still couldn't believe that Bastian had done all those terrible things.

"Sensara banished Jones from the coven."

"That's harsh."

"That's the rules. Wicca is no game as I tried to tell you."

"Oh Dylan, do you think it's over?"

"Honestly? I don't know. The killer's dead, so perhaps the charm is complete. Still, there's Estrada to consider. At least the police understand what happened and they're not charging him with anything. They know he was a victim in all of this."

"I'm just so sorry—"

"Why are you sorry? We're the ones who spun that charm. Daphne may have inspired it, but it took the combined power of us all to manifest it. You just got caught in the ripples."

Maggie wanted desperately to lean her head against his warm shoulder, close her eyes, and wish it all away. "Dylan, do you think that you and I could ever—"

"Once Michael comes, I'm going to Tarbert to visit my granddad," he said, cutting her off. "That's just across the water." Standing, he pointed northeast. "If you promise not to spin anymore love spells."

"Oh Dylan. I promise. I am so over that. Love spells, I mean. Look," she said, parting her hair, "I'm even growing my natural color back in."

He cleared his throat. "We could pick up a box of magic from the chemist and I could help you with that," Dylan said, tousling her hair. Then clutching her cheek in his hand, he leaned in and kissed her on the mouth, gently at first, and then with an intensity that sent small fires bursting through her soul.

"I've missed you, Maggie Taylor, and I'm pleased to finally meet the real you."

"This business with Sandolino upsets me. I know how you feel about him, Michael, and it saddens me, but even more than that, I'm disgusted—"

Michael glanced at his grandfather, noting the stern downward tipping eyes set so closely to the fiercely pointed nose and thin closed lips curled to one side. Looking away, he glanced at Clive who slouched smugly across the table. People were scrambling, preparing the club for a hectic Friday night, and Michael hoped they wouldn't hear what he knew was surely coming next. Nervously, he stared at his watch. It was just after six.

Primrose. What a surprise she'd been. Her body would have been sent for cremation by now, her final mass completed. Michael lit a cigarette knowing better than to interrupt Nigel with any sort of emotional reaction when he was in such a state. He'd returned to work two days ago, only to be razed by Sensara's cold morning announcement: *The killer is dead. Estrada caught him, but something happened. He's in a coma.*

Unable to do anything about that, now there was this.

"I'm disgusted that a man would come into our club and target someone. That a man would follow Sandolino abroad, attempt to kill him, and slaughter an innocent woman in the process. That any man would set another man up in such a heinous way—" He threw back a shot of Scotch whiskey, sniffed and sat back in his chair. "It's abhorrent."

"I agree. It's bloody evil," Clive said. "And it's appalling that the coppers weren't able to apprehend this psycho before it came to this. Perhaps, if Estrada had listened to me—"

Michael took a drag of his cigarette and lifted his lip in a stream of smoke. *Oh, to be a vampire.*

"I'm pleased that you boys have had the opportunity to get to know each other. It's never good when brothers are split apart." He chased his shot with half a glass of beer. "At any rate, I think it's admirable Clive took it upon himself to seek you out, Michael—to come here on his own initiative and ingratiate himself into our little family."

Michael caught a flicker in Nigel's eye and responded with one slow nod of acknowledgment. There were subtleties he'd picked up over the years, nuances, shifts in tone and body language that others might not notice. Settling back in his chair, he sucked back a shot of Scotch himself and listened.

"Michael has his vices." Nigel was speaking to Clive now as if no one else was in the room. "There's no doubt about it. He has a reputation a lesser man might envy but he would never hurt someone maliciously. He would never, for example, target someone, or set someone up to be beaten. Like his father, Michael has a wild heart, but it's a good kind heart. That's why I love him and can tell him so."

"Thank you, Nigel. I love you too. You've been a better father to me than any man could have been."

"Oh please," Clive whined. "You know what goes on here."

"Well, that's the strange thing. You see, I had surveillance cameras installed in the back alley after that business with Sandolino. Of course, Michael's been off work for some time, so I can't comment on his activities, but we've been watching *you*, Clive."

Shifting uncomfortably in his chair, Clive looked at his watch.

"I didn't want to believe what I saw, but there it was in black and white."

"I don't know what you're referring to."

"No? Let's watch," Nigel said, raising his hand. "Roll it."

Instantly, one of the white screens behind the bar lit up and an image of the back alley appeared. Clive walked into the shot. He handed a wad of bills to an addict who often crashed in the alley. The man stashed the money in his pocket, put on a pair of gloves, and took the tire iron that Clive offered.

"You paid a *junkie* to beat the living hell out of me?" Michael yelled.

The next scene showed Michael coming around the corner of the alley and the junkie smashing his face with the tire iron before he could raise his arms to defend himself.

Michael turned to his brother. "*What the fuck, Clive.* What did I ever do to you?"

"You were born," Clive said, pushing back his chair.

"Oh no," Nigel said, signaling his boys. "Our meeting isn't over." From behind the bar, the Sentries stepped forward. Flanking Clive, they put a hand on each shoulder and pushed him down hard in the chair, then remained standing on either side of him.

"I also know you've been dealing drugs out of the club, Clive, and trying to cast the blame on Michael. Would you care to see *that* footage too?"

"I had to. I needed—"

"Money. Yes, I know that too. I'd hoped your motive for beating Michael was something romantic, like jealousy, but this was all about money, wasn't it? You wanted the club."

"You're a doctor. Why do you need the club?" Michael was incredulous. How had he been so wrong?

"You're *not* a doctor, though, are you Clive? My old friend at Cambridge told me that you—"

"Flunked out, yes. That parsimonious arse wouldn't give me one penny beyond tuition. I had to 'understand the value of money' by working my way through uni. Meanwhile, my big brother got everything handed to him on a silver spoon, including the shit he crammed up his nose."

"So, you *are* jealous." Michael had snorted enough cocaine with Nigel over the years to know that condemnation would get him nowhere.

"Waiting bloody tables for nights on end? Oh, *fuck you all*. Why should I explain anything?"

Nigel swallowed another shot of Scotch and slammed the glass down hard on the table. "I'm sorry to hear how difficult your life has been, Clive. Knowing Bernard as I do, I can sympathize with you. But it didn't give you the right to come here and lie to us, to have Michael beaten, and God knows what else." He rubbed his palms together and took a deep breath. "Why didn't you just ask?"

"You mean you would have given me money?"

"I would have considered a loan and a paid position in the club. You are my grandson."

"Would you still—?"

Nigel shook his head. "No. I am willing to give you something though. Not cash, but a free ticket back to London."

"But I want to stay here."

"That's impossible. You have no backing, no sponsor, no job, and no funds," Nigel said.

"And, I'll have you charged with assault," Michael said. "You'll do time."

"You know, I've always loved happy endings," Nigel said. "I'm a romantic myself in that way." He walked around the corner of the bar and picked up a wad of paper. "I'm sending you both on the same plane to Heathrow. Perhaps ten hours in the air will give you boys time to sort things out."

Nigel handed two tickets to Michael. "This is the quickest way to get you to Ireland, Michael. Your ticket is open-ended, and there's a ticket here for Sandolino. Please go and stay with him as long as it takes. Then, bring him home when he's well enough to travel. I can't imagine what he's going through."

He set a third ticket on the table. "Clive, your ticket is one way."

"Come," laughed Primrose, taking Estrada's hand. "Come. I must show you something."

"But the dance—"

"The dance goes on forever. This is something you must see now."

He walked beside her through the verdant fields until they came to a cottage. "This place looks familiar," Estrada said, and stared at the thatched roof, the whitewashed walls, the bright red double door.

"It should, my beautiful man. It's my cottage. Do you not remember the day we came here, and I brewed you a potion?"

He shook his head. "Who cares what happened before when we can dance and make love today?"

"Ah, you've gone right Zen on me, just as I feared." She hung over the bottom door and looked inside. Refusing to let her go, Estrada stood behind her and rocked her in his arms. "Look here and tell me what you see."

"That's weird," Estrada cocked his head. "That looks like me sleeping on the red couch. And that's—" Narrowing his eyes, he searched for memories. "That's Michael. He looks so sad."

"He misses you, Sorcerer. Your man needs you back."

Estrada looked at her curiously.

"It's time. You've got to go back now, before you forget him completely. That's what happens."

"But I don't want to—"

"Ah, just look at him. It's killing him to see you like this. He's been this way for days. Doesn't eat, doesn't sleep, doesn't bathe. Just sits there despairing and holding you, weeping and waiting for you to wake up. Your man loves you."

"But I love *you*," Estrada said, and taking her in his arms, he kissed her mouth. "I want to stay here with you."

"I know you do. But you see, Sorcerer, you still have a body to return to, and return to it you must. Do you see that crockery jar on the mantle there?"

He nodded.

"All that's left of me is in that jar. Just ashes, dust, and bone."

"No," he said, running his hands over her breasts. "You're perfect."

"Aye, but only in *this* world." Taking his hands in hers, she kissed them and held them to her cheeks. "Now, I have a humongous favor to ask you, and I need you to promise, and I need you to remember."

"Anything. You know I'll do anything for you."

"I know. You've a heart as wide as the heavens and twice as pure." She kissed his bare chest, and turned his cheek to face the door. "Do you see that envelope there, beside that jar of my bones?"

He nodded again.

"Well, inside are two tickets to the Winter Solstice festivities at Newgrange. You remember me telling you about it?"

"Not really." He shook his head.

"Well, you will. It's where the Tuatha de Danann interred the bones of their dead each year. It's where my ancestors are buried. And, here's the thing, Sorcerer. I need you to take my ashes there, in secret like, and scatter them inside the tomb on solstice morning. Can you promise to do that for me?"

"But how?" Spreading his arms, he watched them melt through the wall of the cottage.

"In that body right there."

"But that would mean—"

"Now listen to me. Soon, they'll be carting it off to the hospital. You're fortunate they've waited this long. And your man there can't take much more. Himself loves you so much, he'll soon be needing the hospital too. And then there's Maggie, and all the others so sick with grief they can't go on with their lives until you've come home. And then there's your promise. Now the moon is full tonight and that means December is upon us. You know that I'll always love you, Sorcerer, but it's time that we two parted."

"But how can I leave you and never see you again?"

"Ah, you've a mind like a sieve. It's fortunate you're a beauty," Primrose said, slapping his cheek playfully. "I am the wind," she began in her melodic way, "and the waves of the sea, and the sunlight's rays and the greenery. You see me all around you. I am the hawk in the air and the salmon in the stream, and I will be with you always, in all your dreams even beyond the ends of the Earth." Reaching up on her toes, she kissed his forehead. "Now you must close your eyes, and if you remember nothing else from this moment on, remember this. Whenever you're out walking in the natural world, you'll find me in the very air you breathe and in the essence of all sentient beings—"

Sweeping her up in his arms, Estrada stopped her words with a deep lingering kiss.

"I see you're after having something more substantial, Sorcerer."

"Time, Primrose. We haven't had enough time."

"It's not the time you have; it's what you make of it. Live and love, my beautiful man. It's what you were meant to do." She kissed him again. "And if you're ever in need of help, call on me and I'll come. You've a faerie in your pocket now and nothing to fear."

When she touched his heart, a sense of peace enveloped him. Like petrified stone, there was energy in his limbs, though they refused to move. His eyes were shut, their slight depressions heaped with sand. His lips sealed tight. He couldn't swallow. Had to piss.

"Drink," he thought, and sound emerged from the back of his throat. But, when the fluid trickled in, he shuddered and spat out the vile burning liquid. "*Fuck*," he growled, and coughed.

"Sorry compadre, I've only got whiskey. But you . . . you're back."

A body fell on him. Warm face against his breast, cool hands gripping his bare shoulders, lips brushing his neck.

"Up," Estrada said. He needed to move, to stand, to walk.

"Of course."

Rubbing brought a rush of blood to his eyelids and he opened them and focused on the face before him. Michael—his eyes streaked red, sunken and furrowed in deep purple half-moons, his wan hollow cheeks, his greasy hair hanging lank against his shoulders.

"You look like shit, man."

"And you, compadre, 'walk in beauty like the night'" Smiling, Michael touched his cheek. "I thought I'd lost you. Be forewarned: if you ever do that again, I'll fucking kill you. Ah, I should have—"

"Nailed me to the floor?"

Michael laughed so hard he broke down coughing. "Thank God you haven't lost your memory."

"I wish I had." Estrada glanced at the mantelpiece, shuddered and burst, unable to contain the grief that flooded his soul. "Primrose. She stepped in front of the knife. He was going to kill me and she . . ." He rubbed his wet face with his hands. "You would have loved her, amigo."

"She's a part of you, and so I do."

"And Bastian. He had us all fooled. Did they catch him?"

"He's dead, man."

"What? How?"

"He tripped. Fell on a knife."

Jesus." Remembering that muffled cry, Estrada's eyes glazed over. Whatever bond the two men had shared was severed, but still, he'd hoped for a different end to their eerie liaison. Sure, Bastian had tried to kill him, but he too was a victim, of his mother and her lovers, and the priest. It was amazing, really, that he'd come as far as he had, helping John Taylor and others like him. Perhaps for Bastian, death was better than prison or the psych ward. He would finally be free of his demons.

"It's over now, compadre."

Michael's melancholy smile lit up the small dark cottage, and for the moment that was enough. The rest was too much to digest.

"Help me up. I have to piss."

Michael wedged his thin shoulder beneath his armpit and lifted him. Feeling suddenly chilled, Estrada glanced down. "I'm naked."

Michael shrugged. "It's only us."

Epilogue

In the predawn darkness of December 21st, Maggie and Dylan, sat cross-legged on a tarp outside of Newgrange Neolithic tomb, and listened to their guide describe the phenomenon they were about to witness. Gazing through the crowd, Maggie saw Estrada and his best friend, Michael Stryker, huddled together beneath a tree. She was thrilled the four of them could experience this together. Thrilled that when the people at Brú na Bóinne read their story in the newspaper, they'd called and offered two more tickets.

"This beautiful fertile valley, that we call the Boyne, has housed the Irish people for millennia. This tomb itself is part of a Necropolis, a cluster of tombs, where the farmers interred the ashes of their dead, once a year at this time. When the sun rises over the ridge of the valley, its rays hit the roof box just above the entrance stone, creep down the passageway, and illuminate the inner chamber."

"The stone is carved with the same triple spirals Primrose had tattooed on her head," Maggie whispered.

"Aye, the symbols of the mother. If you look at these three spirals together, the two at the top and one below, what do you see?" Dylan asked.

"A woman's body?"

"Aye. We're born from the mother and to the mother we return. The truth is always written in the stones."

"Winter Solstice is a time of resurrection. In the darkest days of winter, the sun brings a promise of light," said the guide.

"I can't believe all these people are into this," Maggie said.

The grassy lawn in front of the immense circular tomb was crowded with people, all eager to experience what their ancestors had witnessed long ago. The top of the huge kidney-shaped mound was grassed over, but the side façade sparkled with white quartz. The entire mound was encircled in gray curbstones, ninety-seven in all, decorated in spirals, chevrons, and other geometric shapes. Television cameras were set up to record the phenomenon and broadcast it to the world. This was magic.

Estrada stood beside Michael just inside the dark inner chamber of the tomb. As he ran his hands along the spirals, the sun rose, and a shaft of light filtered down the long rectangular passageway. The cruciform chamber had three recesses. The one on the left housed a huge solid granite basin. This was where the priests had placed the cremated ashes of the dead along with grave goods. As the chamber filled with light, the spectators gazed up at the intricate corbelled roof high above them.

Slipping his hand into his pocket, Estrada retrieved the vile and pushed off the cork with his thumb. Then, running his hand beneath the back of Michael's coat, he scattered what remained of her ashes on the floor of the inner chamber.

You're home now Primrose, where you belong.

Just past Michael's shoulder, Estrada suddenly saw her. Pressed up against the wall, she glimmered like the stars, her shape shifting as her corporeal form melded between earth and air. Smiling, he put his arm around Michael's neck and touched the frittered edges of her faerie form. Wavering like the air on a hot sultry day, her aura blossomed and joined the sun in filling the entire chamber.

In the blink of an eye, she'd filled his heart with ecstasy. The kind that could never be found in a pill but was born of true magic. The magic of love. Recognizing what he'd been searching for as long as he could remember—the attainment of his heart's desire—he realized he could neither hold nor keep her, for she belonged to the Otherworld. She always had. And his grief lifted in her joy.

As he placed the empty vial back inside his pocket, Estrada's fingers brushed against the charm Josh had given him in the cave.

For a moment, he twirled it between his fingertips, and then he slipped it into Michael's pocket. Josh had given him far more than a round cedar bead that morning, and now it was time to pass it on.

Series Characters

The Witches of Hollystone Coven

Sensara Narado: High Priestess. Psychic counsellor. Sensara created the coven and enforces the rules. Sensara is the mother of Lucy, Estrada's daughter.

Sandolino Estrada: High Priest. Estrada is a free-spirited bisexual magician who performs at Club Pegasus in Vancouver when he's not performing at other venues, or off solving crimes.

Dylan McBride: a Canadian archaeology student, raised by his grandfather in Tarbert, Scotland, Dylan travels the world playing bagpipes with the university pipe band.

Daphne Sky: a landscaper gardener and Earth mother

Raine Carrera: a journalist for an alternative press who recently joined the coven. Raine and Daphne are partners.

Dr. Sylvia Black: a Welsh university professor who teaches, lectures, and publishes books on Celtic Studies. When Dylan arrived from Scotland, Sylvia adopted him and introduced him to the witches of Hollystone Coven.

Supporting Characters

Nigel Stryker: a dapper British gangster and owner of Club Pegasus in Vancouver, Canada. Nigel is Michael's grandfather.

Michael Stryker aka Mandragora: hedonistic manager of Club Pegasus, Michael is Estrada's best friend and lover. He believes himself to be the reincarnation of Lord Byron and likes to play vampire.

Sorcha O'Hallorhan: a feisty Irish archaeologist who assists Estrada in *To Sleep with Stones*. Sorcha time-travels with Cernunnos to Iron Age Ireland in *To Kill a King* and falls in love with Ruairí Mac Nia. In *To Dance with Destiny*, Sorcha reunites with her ex-girlfriend, Franya Rousseau in Lullymore, Ireland and solves a mystery of her own.

Franya Rousseau: Sorcha's ex. A corporate attorney living at Sullivan Stables in Lullymore, Co. Kildare, Ireland

Declan Doyle: a horse enthusiast from Cork who manages Sullivan Stables

Ruairí Mac Nia: the "bog man" who is destined to become King of Tuath Croghan and then ritually murdered. His story forms the bones of *To Kill a King* but his story echoes in *To Dance with Destiny*.

Conall Ceol: a sensitive, talented Druid warrior-bard. Conall is Ruairí's best friend in *To Kill a King*, and escapes through the wormhole with Estrada and Sorcha at the end of the story.

Cernunnos: the ancient Celtic Horned God. Estrada first conjures Cernunnos in *To Sleep with Stones*; after that, Cernunnos makes several appearances.

Máire Manus McBride: (pronounced Moy-ra) a young healer who catches Dylan's eye and then captures his heart.

Magus Dubh: the tattooed half-fey dwarf who is proprietor of The Blue Door, an antiquities shop in Glasgow

Leopold Blosch: chef and owner of Ecos, a vegetarian bistro near Robson Street in Vancouver. Estrada meets Blosch in *To Render a Raven* and again in *To Dance with Destiny*.

Dell: head of the sentinels (the security team at Club Pegasus)

Don Diego: father of the vampires, Diego can transform into a thunderbird that resembles a pterosaur

Zion: a vampire from Africa

Eliseo: a vampire from Peru, the first vampire Diego makes to replace his drowned son

Primrose: an Irish fey witch Estrada falls in love with in *To Charm a Killer*

Acknowledgements

Thank you, family, friends, and readers for your continuing support.

The characters in this novel are fictitious; however, most settings in British Columbia and Ireland are real places I've explored. I take artistic liberty, but in every case attempt to be gracious. With this in mind, I'd like to acknowledge the following:

Brú na Bóinne for allowing us to experience the magic of our Neolithic past via Newgrange and Tara; The Quays and Tig Cóilí Pub in Galway; Carrowmore Megalithic Cemetery where Maggie meets the Good People; Drumcliffe Cemetery in Sligo where WB Yeats is buried; Fureys in Sligo where the craic was ninety; the quaint village of Cong in Mayo; Shop Street in Galway where Primrose reveals her talent for performance art; and finally, the folks at Boghill Center in Clare who taught me to play and sing Irish traditional music.

Ireland, its people and places touched and changed me in ways I can't explain, but as this beautiful land became a part of me, it became a part of my story, and I'm most grateful for that. I must acknowledge too, the ancient Druid bard, Amergin, for the mystical poem that inspires Primrose and haunts me still.

A huge thank you to Yasaman Mohandesi, for creating unique covers for the Tattoo Editions of this series. Each tattoo belongs to a character in the series. You'll recognize Maggie's Celtic horse on the cover of this book. See Yasaman's work on Instagram @ ym_blackrose_art.

Many people have touched *To Charm a Killer* over its life: Tara, Judi, Lynne, Shane, Joanna, Kyleigh, and of course, you, my readers.

I'm most grateful to two great authors. William Shakespeare for his magnificent play *Macbeth* (1606), whose themes and threads interweave this story, and whose phrases are chapter titles. And, W.B. Yeats for *The Celtic Twilight* (1893). Like Yeats, Estrada and I long to see faeries.

Finally, to Estrada and Michael. You've been whispering in my ear for years now. Thank you, lads. Without you, there would be no stories.

About the Author

W. L. Hawkin writes the kind of books she loves to read from her home in the Pacific Northwest. Because she's a genre-blender, you might find crime, mystery, romance, suspense, fantasy, adventure, and even time travel, interwoven in her stories.

If you like "myth, magic, and mayhem" her Hollystone Mysteries feature a coven of West Coast witches who solve murders using ritual magic and a little help from the gods. The books—*To Charm a Killer, To Sleep with Stones, To Render a Raven, To Kill a King,* and *To Dance with Destiny*—follow Estrada, a free-spirited, bisexual magician and coven high priest as he endeavors to save his family and friends while sorting through his own personal issues.

Her standalone novel, *Lure: Jesse & Hawk* (2022) won a National Indie Excellence Award, a Gold Reader's Choice award from *Connections E-magazine,* a Crowned Heart Review from *InD'tale Magazine,* and placed as a finalist in The UK Wishing Shelf Book Awards. Lure is a small-town romantic suspense story set on a Chippewa Reservation in the American Midwest near the fictional town of Lure River.

As an intuitive writer, Wendy captures what she sees and hears on the page, and allows her muses to guide her through the creative process. In an upcoming book, *Writing with your Muse: a Guide to Creative Inspiration,* she explains her writing process and offers tips and techniques to help writers get their words on the page.

Wendy needs to feel the energy of the land so, although she's an introvert, in each book her characters go on a journey where she's traveled herself.

If you don't find her at Blue Haven Press, she's out wandering the woods or beaches of Vancouver Island with her beautiful yellow dog.

If you enjoyed this book, please take a moment to leave a few words with your favorite retailer. Thank you.

Are you curious to know more about Lure River, Hollystone Coven, and W. L. Hawkin's latest news? Come by Blue Haven Press, subscribe to Wendy's seasonal newsletter, and follow her on social media.

facebook.com/wlhawkin

instagram.com/w.l.hawkin

goodreads.com/author/show/16142078.W_L_Hawkin

linkedin.com/in/wendy-hawkin-4321b2215/

bookbub.com/profile/w-l-hawkin

youtube.com/@wlhawkin/videos

http://bluehavenpress.com

Praise for To Sleep with Stones

"Hawkin's tight and well-paced writing and knowledge of Celtic myths, combined with multi-layered characters, lush language, and plot twists and turns, draw the reader in. The hallmark of this novel is the author's seamless interweaving of myth and reality. She appeals to our intellect, and our desire for vicarious adventure."

—Gail M. Murray, Ottawa Review of Books

"The whole narrative plays out like an HBO show waiting to be developed, combining elements of LGBTQ+ and adult storytelling into a complex character study . . ."

—Anthony Avina, Readers Entertainment Magazine

"A fascinating book brimming with tension . . . briskly-paced, immersive adventure . . . gorgeous prose, dialogues that sparkle. The author makes a world of fantasy feel real to readers, thanks to the imaginative world-building and the realistic characters, and while this is the second entry in a series, it reads like a standalone novel."

—The Serial Reader

"Highly literary, occasionally surreal, and grounded by characters clipped, matter-of-fact voice, *To Sleep with Stones* is a dark murder mystery that readers will have trouble leaving behind. The buzz for this novel is deafening."

—John Kerry, The Reviewer

Manufactured by Amazon.ca
Bolton, ON